Barley

by Jack Charles

COPYRIGHT

Book designed by www.joi.agency
Original cover image Mirrorpix

ISBN 978-1-917393-11-9

Paperback published by Northside House Limited.
www.northsidehouse.com

For Jane, who taught me the alphabet.

For Melissa, who gave me shelter.

And for Nemah, who turned these pages first.

We pick our friends not only because they are kind and enjoyable company, but also, perhaps more importantly, because they understand us for who we think we are.

Alain de Botton

Barley Sugar

LEWIS

London, 2004

The boys' toilets stank of endeavour.

Another lit match hit the urinal troth and extinguished in the piss and spit. A third, flicked from across the room, fell short, smouldered, and then died on the tiles.

Perched on the edge of a sink, Lewis Coles listened and tried to separate real sound from the school playground outside. 'Hurry up!' he said, slipping the matchbox back into his blazer and checking his watch; it wasn't time yet. He hopped down quietly and pushed open one of the cubicle doors.

Sammy Butler looked over his shoulder. He was facing the wrong way, kneeling on the toilet seat, both arms stretched up behind the cistern. He coughed, squinting. 'I can't get the fucking tape off,' he said, craning his chin so Lewis could relieve him of his cigarette.

'Why did you even hide it there?'

'In case they did another one of them bag searches,' Sammy said, his focus back on his hands. 'I see it in a film; a bloke had a pistol stashed behind one of these things.'

Lewis nodded. 'What did you do with the other stuff?'

'It's in my bag,' Sammy answered, finally managing to pull free a screwdriver bound up in brown parcel tape. He rocked backwards, steadied himself, and then clambered down, grinning. 'How long we got?'

Lewis offered him back the cigarette. 'A couple of minutes,' he said. 'It's *definitely* a flat-head, yeah?'

'Course,' Sammy said, accepting the fag end and blowing smoke. He inhaled hard, rushing, draining the fog to the filter before squashing it out between a big pair of felt-tip tits drawn on the cubicle wall. Lewis was already rifling through the bag for the hats and gloves. 'They're underneath my football kit,' Sammy told him, lifting his shirt and tucking the tool into the waistband of his trousers. Its weight was lopsided, the black handle curious against his stomach, the sharp end digging into the top of his leg. He pushed it lower and then pogoed on the spot. He was shorter than Lewis, stockier, the remnants of a black eye dirtying a fair headed face already too cynical for a boy of fifteen. 'Oi, if I slip, this screwdriver is going straight into my nuts.'

'If I was you, I'd keep hold of it while we're running then,' Lewis advised, retying the laces in his trainers. He handed Sammy a baseball cap with a pair of plastic gloves bunched up inside it, and then examined his own. The hat was fine, but the gloves ... 'They're massive,' he said, licking his fingers to peel them apart. 'And there's no left and right.'

Sammy laughed. 'I got them out of one of them dispensers at Texaco.' Lewis stared at him, baffled. 'If you don't want them, I got some football socks in my bag you can use.'

'*Socks...?*'

Sammy forced the peak of his hat down as low as it would go, and then set about manoeuvring one of his sweaty palms into one of the oversized gloves. 'Yeah,' he said. 'My uncle told me whenever he breaks into a house, if he ain't got gloves, he goes straight for the sock drawer.'

'Fuck off bruv! I ain't wearing your smelly socks on my hands,' Lewis said, smiling. He walked over to the mirror and crammed his cap over his canerows. He rechecked his watch…'*Shhhh!*' he said, suddenly switched on.

Sammy froze.

There were footfalls marching along the corridor outside.

Lewis crept over to the main door and cocked an ear. 'That's *him*,' he said, his voice instantly becoming a whisper. Holding a finger over his lips he beckoned Sammy towards him. Sammy squatted down and returned a nod: they were going through with it.

The off beats banged. The footsteps, making the door seem thin, resonated almost on top of them. They crouched together, poised. Lewis could feel Sammy nudging him, wriggling the screwdriver out from his trousers, expecting the door to come swinging inwards.

Within a few feet of their noses, without so much as slowing, the footsteps passed.

Noiselessly, Lewis pressed his cheek to the wood and let himself exhale, 'I *told* you,' he mouthed, and then gradually cracked open the door.

In position, ready to run, adrenaline drugging their guts and holding their nerve, Lewis Coles and Sammy Butler peeked out into the hall and waited for the signal.

Alistair Cassels – head of the English department and

aspiring author – once described the leathery slap his well-heeled shoes made in an empty school corridor as a *Gestapo rhythm*. As was his habit, he took his first tour of the school's lower corridor exactly twenty minutes inside the lunch hour. And, just as Lewis had observed on the three previous Fridays, he showed no interest in invading the toilets. It would be a waste of his time; it was too early. Most of the kids were still busy finding their friends after lessons and piling into the cafeteria for chips; and as for the seasoned smokers, the ones who couldn't wait, if they had any nous whatsoever, they had long learnt to hedge their bets and stick to the playing fields.

So he strode on, tall, an impersonation of the old School-Master he himself had studied under, his too-clever eyes raking beneath a widow's peak of flecked hair and the walls returning the sound of his soles. He'd had to work hard as a younger man to impress authority into that stride; an avid speed-walker, he'd hidden a tendency to misuse his hips. Nonetheless, the timing was now impeccable, his left arm a pendulum, the wedding band on his closed fist swinging back and forth heavy with hard feelings. He still wore it though, out of spite; lest he forget the fickle nature of the beast.

The divorce was yet to be clarified; *oh* he'd sign, be glad to, but once his book was finished. Until then, her and her *girlfriend* would have to hold their bloody horses. For years she had stunted *his* progress, so why should he pat her on the backside and speed things up? No, he would make her wait and suffer like he'd had to, the rumour mill slowly grinding his good name into dust.

The story went that Mrs Cassels, herself a tutor at the school, had begun an affair with one of the music teachers, Misses Istas, and now they had run away together. True or false, when the new term started, Alistair had been the only one of the three present in the assembly hall. The whispers flourished; sniggers and dropped gazes eventually working their way out of the faculty lounge and into the waiting mouths of the parents. Inevitably, it goes in one end and out of the other, gets trodden into the playground, where should it fester for long enough someone will always bring it in on their shoes. And of course it *would* have to be the Butler boy, wouldn't it? Loud and at the top of his voice, and to the delight of a cackling classroom, after having his mobile phone confiscated, Butler had accused him of *'turning his wife lesbian.'* Cassels had snapped; the incident resulting in him being given a fortnight's paid absence and the first disciplinary of his career, a further indignity. It had been a whole month since then, and as yet he still hadn't given the boy back his possessions – because the little victories are victories all the same.

So here he was, proceeding, all business and stiff maintenance, a mere slither to the anxious eyes stalking him from the toilet doorway. Onwards he went, learned and highbrow, but with no iota that he was almost exactly where they wanted him. He turned in the direction of the staffroom and halted, the fabric of his jacket just visible in the mouth of the passage. Along the same narrow hallway, out of sight to Lewis and Sammy, was the school nurse's office.

'What is it *this* time, Campbell?' Cassels said. As always

his speech was satirical.

Ezra Campbell was sat on a chair with a bucket balanced on his lap; he didn't look up. 'I don't feel well, sir. It's my stomach.' He lowered his face into the bucket, a wide Caribbean grin reflected in the disinfectant at the bottom.

'If you're about to be sick, then this isn't the place to do it. Have they not informed your mother?'

Ezra nodded.

Cassels scrutinized the barber-patterns shaved into the back of the boy's hair, 'And...?'

Ezra groaned, the acoustics making him more convincing. 'I think she's coming to pick me up.'

No reply...

His head hidden, Ezra waited until he felt Cassels pass him and heard the click of the staffroom door. He raised his eyes steadily, placing the bucket down between his feet. With one last look to double check he was alone; he jumped up, lunged to the end of the passage, stuck his arm out from behind the wall, and gave the signal.

That was their cue.

On their toes, like greyhounds, Lewis and Sammy bolted from the toilets and were at speed in seconds. They ran – *run* – ran, trainers yelping on the hardwood, baggy plastic sheaths flapping and rattling over their knifed fingers. Sprinting, they made it the length of the hall, crashed through a set of double doors, and took the first set of stairs two at a time. Up – *on* – up, three floors, higher, the screwdriver clutched in Sammy's shifting fist poking into his leg and urging him faster. More doors, more halls, these ones cut in half by winter sunlight searing through the skywards windows. Faster – *further* – faster, until they skidded and stopped outside the empty classroom. Panting, thief drums beating behind his ears, Lewis clawed for the knob, twisted it, and they burst inside.

Every detail had been planned perfectly. Cassels' lunch duty routine was waterproof: after taking ten to herd the canteen lines into twos, he made a quick sweep of the playground and then came back on himself via the lower corridor. From there Lewis had timed him: once he'd disappeared into the staffroom, it usually took four minutes for him to re-emerge with a coffee cup. Then, unless he got cornered by Miss Weatley at the school reception, he stalked straight back outside to his perch on the top of the concrete steps, where he conducted order until the bell. That gave them four – maybe five – minutes, to get in, get it, and get out.

They slalomed between the desks, chair legs budging and bending over backwards in front of the white board to let them through. The stock cupboard at the back of the room gaped easily. Lewis rolled the television trolley out of his way and ducked his head beneath the hanging coats. Sammy handed him the screwdriver and stood back; copies of Harper Lee's, *To Kill a Mockingbird*, tumbling out and covering the floor.

There it was, Cassels' trove: a wooden footlocker with a brass padlock rocking on its buckle. Lewis hunkered down and set about the hinges, the screwdriver working in dogged little jerks.

'Are they coming off?'

'Easily,' Lewis answered. The first screw fell out and tinkled somewhere in the dark. He moved on to the second. Originally, the idea had been to unscrew the hinges on the locker door, open it up backwards, take what they needed, and then fasten them back again so Cassels would never know. Not now though, there wasn't enough time.

The second screw came away.

'You're taking too long,' Sammy said, watching the classroom door.

'It's these fucking gloves,' Lewis snapped. He turned the screw and the hinge sagged.

'Now, just pull it.'

'What?'

'Squeeze your fingers into the gap and yank it,' Sammy said.

Lewis tried to force his fingertips under the box-top to pry it open, but his gloves lost purchase. The wood snapped back into place. Animated, Sammy loomed over his shoulder and added his grip next to Lewis's. They pulled together; the wood splintered and gave. The second hinge popped off as the lid flipped open and hung on the padlock.

Sammy smacked Lewis on the back triumphantly, 'It looks like a fucking corner shop.'

The box was a hoard, items Cassels had painstakingly taken the time to discover and confiscate from their rightful owners: dozens of silver and gold cigarette packets; mobile phones, magazines, sweets, lipsticks, chewing gum, lighters, and even a can of hair spray. Sammy and Lewis rooted through, grabbing anything of worth and cramming it into any crevice in their uniforms.

'C'mon, I've got it,' Lewis said, fishing the Motorola from underneath a makeup bag and palming it off to Sammy. He shot up off of his haunches and checked the time, 'Shit!'

Sammy stuffed one more pack of Sovereigns into his sock, slammed the lid of the box closed, and scarpered behind Lewis. He rallied his way across the classroom and dashed out into the hall, 'What have you got *that* for?' he called, spotting the makeup bag in Lewis's hand as he barged into the stairwell.

'It's Sophie's,' Lewis shouted without looking back.

They flew down the staircase skipping most of the steps and littering the landings. Out of necessity they'd taken a different route: these stairs – the ones nearest Cassels' classroom – were at the far end of the school; true they would get them down quicker, but they'd also spit them out on the wrong side of the staffroom. It was too late. The double doors at the bottom shook their hands like reluctant friends, banged open, bounced off the rubber doorstops on the skirting and winged back into place.

Ezra was on his feet, head poking out from behind the wall. He hadn't expected to see them coming from that direction; he waved a frantic arm, urging the tempo. Behind him, the staffroom door clicked and a coffee mug, the words, *Teachers Breath*, printed on its side slowly developing. Fuck it...Ezra clutched his stomach and kicked the bucket. There was a slosh as the disinfectant flooded the passageway, spreading back towards the staffroom. He braced an arm against the wall, hunched, and began retching over the puddle.

Cassels backed up checking his shoes, 'I told you to go to the toilets, Campbell. Nobody wants to clean up after you.'

Ezra spluttered, 'I tried to sir, but I can't walk properly –'

Holding their hats down, Lewis and Sammy shot past in full view.

'NO RUNNING!' Cassels bellowed, his attention immediately drawn. Spilling coffee, he stepped over the mess and ushered Ezra back into his seat. 'Use the *bucket*, boy…' And with that he swivelled and set off.

On the final straight, heads down, Lewis and Sammy could hear the glorious noise and freedom of the outside. They veered around the last corner making more squash sounds, running, desperate to cross the border and disappear.

'STOP!' Cassels' voice travelled along the walls and beat them to the exit. Tracking them with coffee dowsing his cuff, Cassels had paced into the main corridor just in time to catch a glimpse of two baseball caps hightailing out of the building. Blowing, out of sight, Lewis and Sammy tore off their hats and gloves and stuffed them deep down inside one of the litter bins. 'Stay *exactly* where you are.' Cassels quickened, fully expecting to find the two leggy teenagers waiting for him when he rounded the corner.

Instead he found fresh air, a pair of slowly closing doors, and a lone plastic glove pirouetting in the draft.

The sky was pencilled in, dark thumb smudge clouds rubbing out the sun and gobbing into the breeze. They were too warm to feel cold. For a distance of uncountable seconds, Lewis and Sammy walked into the mass of the playground on trespassers heels, every instinct pinching their arses. It was hard to move slowly. They separated and eased through the crowd, two gluttonous mouths stretched in sinful grin, bouncing weightlessly on their achievements.

In slow motion, they could finally feel real. They'd done it, taken a step *(leap)* in the right direction. After all, this was school, as much a place for thieves as anybody else. It was education, for all and for small, righties and lefties; they all came here and ran these halls or others like them ...*Olly, Olly, Olly, tits in a trolley, balls tied up with string.* They all learned somewhere; Artists and Brasses, Bankers, Wankers, and Plod. Little boys and girls taught to make papier-mâché masks out of old newspaper and thick glue, and then how to wear them over their faces. It was a factory, year after year churning out porcelain dolls in traditional costume. It was where they sent you; made you; conditioned and drilled you for citizenship. A dress rehearsal for the big wide world, designed to weed out the wrong 'uns from the straight goers. They even got you out of bed early and made you raise your hand before you spoke. All good practice for buying into their 9-5 premise.

Free and dangerous, Lewis and Sammy moved, magnificent, feeling watched but brand new. They edged into the fray of the football match going on in the centre of the playground, sucking in air and kicking out at the sodden tennis ball as if they'd been there all along. They took opposite sides: Sammy shoving his way onto the winning team, Lewis – makeup bag wedged under his arm inside his blazer – skating on the fringe, half an eye on Cassels.

On the periphery, omnipotent atop the steps, Cassels took a long look. Steam rising, he swallowed a mouthful of coffee, his pupils scanning the student body for discrepancies. It was hard to tell: there were no hats and too many trainers. He peered over the rim of his mug, his better judgment starting to stick to the Butler boy. He watched him, apparently playing football; as per usual the boy's mouth was working harder than the rest of him. It wasn't just that though, or the far too proud of himself posture the little shit was sporting. It was the fact that he hadn't once taken his hands out of his pockets – not once. It was unnatural, almost awkward.

Cassels took a final sip of coffee, lifted his gaze, and then discreetly spilled the rest of his drink away. There was no point standing *here*; whatever the bastard had been up to, he'd been up to it at the opposite end of the school. Collected, cup in hand, he turned on his heel and went back inside.

Lewis and Sammy exchanged a look, the story of success tagged all over their faces. They shouldered through the crowd towards each other, the game rushing on around them, surface water flicking up from the ball and clearing the air. They were riding the high, snorting the fabulous narcotic of winning and grinning about it. Right now, *they* were the ones: the takers, old kings in youthful trim. In seconds they'd become the leaders of parliament; the future rulers of the underworld and lords in the house of commoners. They were immense. They'd reached out and seized what they wanted, turning this awful bloody place into a hunters' paradise. They were now authentic, different from every other body out here. The rest were a bunch of talk-and-hopers; cowards; goodies who crossed their fingers behind their backs when they told a lie. Fuck 'em ... all of 'em. What had they ever done besides what they were told? If *they* wanted to swallow balls and rules that was up to them but some people wanted to live. They wanted to thrive, and maybe, once in a while, some people even wanted to throw a punch back instead of getting hit. And sometimes, *special* people – Lewis and Sammy included – dared to whip their winkles out, stand up flush against the tree of life, and piss in the faces of the tiny little mites crawling about between the bark.

'Did you see him clocking you?'

'I was trying not to look,' Sammy said, grinning. He bumped his fist into Lewis's. 'Was he pissed?'

Lewis shrugged. 'He will be when he walks into his classroom.'

'Good!' Sammy pulled a packet of twenty out of his pocket, opened it, and began indiscriminately offering singles out to all friends and ponces – they swarmed.

'Got the phone?'

Sammy tapped his breast pocket lightly, 'Soon as I see him, I'm gonna get that Paul kid who lives on my block to hold it for me.'

'Good idea,' Lewis remarked, ignoring the rabble and bending his neck to get a look over at the netball courts. 'Saying that, I need to get rid of this bag.'

Sammy jolted him playfully. 'You better take these, then.' he said, conjuring a pack of half-eaten chewing gums from somewhere. 'And don't forget to use some of that lipstick before you kiss her arse.'

Lewis snorted. 'Dick 'ed!'

The boys all laughed.

'Oi, Lou..?' Sammy tossed a box of Benson & Hedges at him. 'Give these to Vicki for me.'

Halfway along the hall, Cassels stopped. In sharp focus he peered down between his shoes. A cigarette lighter – white with a grotesque green marijuana leaf decorating its side – lay dormant on the parquet floor. He nudged it with his foot, as if to check it were dead before he crouched to pick it up. With one finger, one thumb, he rotated it slowly in front of his face, nostrils flaring, his intuition slowly beginning to roast. There it was, the very same little horseshoe burn in the plastic: as odd and noticeable now as it had been the first time he'd found it two days ago. He could also, quite clearly, recall exactly what he had done with it.

He straightened up, knees clicking. Inside his mind the cogs turned, racking the evidence. He lifted his head hastily and started moving, beating a harsh path back towards his classroom.

The baggy chain-link fence around the netball court rippled. Hinges screeching, Lewis slid the clunky bolt out of its hole and pushed the gate open. The playing-field beyond cut up into a thousand tiny diamonds. The air out here was vanilla musk.

Peacocking, he walked across the faded line-markings, the pink in his cheeks a decoy. Twittering giggles: the small flock of girls became a choir of lip-gloss and ponytails. They shuffled their pack, gabbling, and eventually presented him with the pretty girl he'd come looking for. Encouraged, Sophie tottered forward, the pleats of her skirt hovering over the goose-bumps on her knees.

'I've got a present for you,' Lewis said, matching her shine and raising her a smile.

'What is it?'

'If you close your eyes and hold out your hands, you'll find out,' he said, keeping his arm tucked inside his blazer. She looked at him suspiciously, the eyeliner at the corners of her eyes drawn up into exotic little points.

'It better not be anything nasty, Lewis.'

'It ain't, I swear.'

'If you –'

'I won't, I promise.'

'Okay,' she agreed hesitantly. 'But if you *even* – I swear I won't never forgive you, Lewis.'

Performing for the audience behind her, Lewis swished open his school blazer and placed the makeup bag on her hands. She laughed excitedly, wary at first, gradually opening her eyes.

'How did you get *this?*'

'Don't be so inner,' he told her, his eyes hazel and mysterious. 'Just try and keep it out of sight.'

'Are you going to get into trouble for it?'

Lewis shrugged.

Sophie's gaze skipped away from his face, 'Thank you,' she said, leaning forward to hug him. He slipped an arm around her puffy jacket and breathed in the secret scent of warm washing powder – a loud titter rose from the spectators.

Lewis whispered something into Sophie's ear and then let go. 'Oi, Vicki...?' he called, gesturing to one of the troop, 'Sammy told me to give you these...'

The reply was snappy: 'Why?'

'To say sorry for the other day,' Lewis lied. 'And because he wants you to come on Sunday.'

Showing a large set of teeth, Vicki broke rank and started towards him. 'So why couldn't he tell me himself?'

'*Fear*,' Lewis said, teasing. 'You might try and fly-kick him again.'

'As if,' she said, snatching the fag box out of his hand ungratefully. 'Anyway,' she added, staring over at the playground. 'From where I'm standing, it looks like he's got more important things to be worrying about.'

'Get your *fucking* hands off me!' Sammy yapped, dragging his body weight and wrenching his arm away.

Cassels whirled in a half circle, livid, seeing everything

and nothing of the boys jostling around him. 'Turn out your pockets,' he ordered, making a grab for something shiny in somebody else's hand, 'c'mon, each and every one of you.' Nobody moved. He spun to face off with Sammy again, 'As for you, Butler,' he said, managing his tone back to suede. 'You can take yourself straight to the headmaster's office. How dare you –'

'Who do you think you're grabbing?' Sammy demanded, standing his ground. 'Don't ever touch me again, you *mug*.'

Cassels sized him up, a patronising little flinch capturing each side of his mouth. 'Do yourself a favour and stop showing off, Samuel.' The onlookers murmured. 'Nobody's intimidated by you, *or* your oversized mouth.' Sammy stared at him, his pupils strategizing. Cassels took a step forward. 'The headmaster's office ... *now*,' he said, reaching out and prodding him in the chest. 'I'm not going to tell you again –'

From point blank range, without warning, screwing his features up into a tight, snarled little arsehole, Sammy spat; the muscles in his neck violently projecting the fluid.

The glob of saliva coated the teachers eyelash.

The reaction stuttered and then took off, reverberating around the playground in shits and giggles. At first Cassels didn't appear to be able to comprehend what had happened; he stood there, upended, frowning down his nose as if to take offence were beneath him.

Already a legend, Sammy didn't wait to see what was coming. A head full of vertigo, he turned towards the building and stole a march on him. Sniggers rioting behind his back, Cassels pulled a crumpled, used tissue from inside his sleeve and dabbed his face. He rounded on those closest to him, desperate to hold on to his composure.

'You have until the end of the lunch hour to hand in anything Butler's given you.' he said, wiping his cheek dry. 'Beyond that, anybody seen with anything they shouldn't have will be treated as equally culpable.'

The boys stared back at him stupidly. Never, in all his years of service, had he wanted so brutally to teach someone an actual lesson. To seize one of the gibbering little puppets by the throat and squeeze until his smirk turned blue. It was a mockery – a shambles of authority. Gone were the days of respect, when a cane or birch was allowed to ingrain society's expectations into the seat of a schoolboy's grey trousers. And *this* was the result; the teacher had become a jester, nothing more than a fool to be jeered and hooted at by a band of moronic delinquents. To tolerate and endure, that was the job now; to stand beside a white board and watch them get away with it, going as slowly as they could, slithering through the education system on their bellies, until one fine day they plopped out of the other end and onto the streets of a once great nation, completely and utterly *useless*.

Cassels redirected his gaze, the desire to strike breaking in malevolent waves across his bow. He pinned down his rage and went after the Butler boy, gaining on him, breathing down his neck, so close his toes were scraping the back of Sammy's heels.

'Who the hell do you think you are?' Cassels hissed, the enthusiasm of each syllable spraying Sammy's ear. 'You're out on your ear this time, Butler. I'll see that they have your hide for what you just did to me.'

Sammy smirked, strutting on and ignoring him, his shoulders emphasising the point: as far as he was concerned he'd won. Cassels wouldn't touch him again, not now; the scuffle it would provoke was more than the prick's job was worth.

'You *really* think you're something, don't you?' Cassels scoffed, holding onto his own wrist to keep from reaching out and snatching a fist of the boy's hair. He pursued him up the concrete steps, wrestling the urge to lash out, imagining the severe sound of a wooden ruler splintering across sore knuckles. 'Give it time. It's a lot harder for stupid little boys to impress people on the other side of that gate. Let's see if you're still convinced you're the big man in ten years' time, after you've been feeding on scraps for the last decade.'

Sammy swung the door back, winked at him, and then disappeared inside.

Abruptly, Cassels stopped himself. He hadn't followed: not because the want to hound the boy out of sight and trip him up in the empty hall had suddenly gone, but because he'd seen something, a glimpse. It had been slight, perhaps unintentional, but from the very top of the steps, before going into the building, Butler had looked a little too long for notoriety over at the netball courts. By compassing, drawing a baleful line of sight in the general direction, Cassels could join the dots. It was elementary: Lewis Coles was penned in, watching the plight of his friend with his fingertips looped through the holes in the fence, already as good as caught.

DEBORAH

The wheels of the baby's buggy skewed on the pavement and jutted sideways, halting its progress. The teenaged mother, one of her ex-boyfriend's jackets hanging off her shoulders, wrestled the thing straight and got it moving again.

She flashed a humourless little grin at the woman watching her through the coffee shop window. The woman with the magazine lifestyle; the one with the dark and lovely curls who'd casually popped out on her lunch break looking like a glossy copy of Naomi Campbell. One of *those* women – *them* women; the ones who no doubt owned a home, drove a car, and had no idea what it felt like to struggle home on the bus with a buggy and a wrist full of carrier bags, or to have to cut up a towel when she'd run out of tampons.

The pushchair hitched again – one step forward and two steps back – it was like trying to get around in a pair of those Fisher Price skates which clipped on over your shoes. This time the wailing started; her son's dummy flying up in the air and rolling underneath the wheels. Bending down, she scrambled around to find it whilst trying to keep her benefit book from falling out of her pocket.

The lady inside the coffee shop returned to her book. No longer interested in what she had been reading, she gave up and dog-eared the page; Chapter 12 *fantasy lives, how to reimagine yourself happy*.

From the outside, through the looking glass, the view of Deborah Coles had been distorted. Her life no longer existed; she'd been widowed from it. This version of her – the one who wore a pristine trouser suit and had worked as an estate agent for the past four years – was still practically a stranger.

Whether or not things happened for a reason, they happened anyway. Five years ago – on the morning of the 1st of March 1999 – Deborah had heard her husband for the last time. Eyes closed, she had lay still, one hand in the cold beneath the pillow, listening to him stumbling into his work jeans at the end of the bed. The door handle clicked. The toilet flushed. Then came the tinkering from the kitchen; first the cutlery drawer, then the draining board. She could picture him, a shadow, flattening down his hair while he waited for the kettle to boil. They were only sounds, false memories, tiny noises played on instruments she'd heard a thousand times before and then never again. It was all quiet. The rising steam covered the purr of the fridge and the tacky kiss that the seal around the door made when the milk was put away – she'd wondered if he'd noticed Lewis's crayon picture stuck between the magnets. And then, after a few seconds, came the happy sound of a cup and spoon waltzing together at dawn.

But there was no more after that. She could pretend that she'd pulled on her nightgown and stalked out into the hallway to kiss him goodbye. Or that she'd waited – like she sometimes did – until he was just about to leave before she'd call him back to bed in a husky whisper, rolling around naked and laughing at him as he tried to tread back out of his jeans, belt buckle jangling around his boots. But those things were wishes and sometime regrets. The truth was, the last time Deborah had ever seen her husband, her eyes had been closed.

Call it what you like; so far, the best Deborah had managed to come up with was *Fate* – that or something else as close to bad luck. To attribute it to God would be to cheapen it; to try and give it some divine relevance by choosing to believe in old chestnuts about him picking his brightest flowers first. No, for her, Fate was cleaner, and somehow more deserving of faith. Charlie hadn't died because God had needed another angel for company in heaven; her little boy needed his father more. Charlie had died because he had been in the wrong place at the wrong time. He had died because Fate was senseless and unfair, but easier to understand and accept than fairy tales. And because Fate was better, better than asking deaf questions and getting mute answers, and better than spending her forever nights angry and arguing with a God she wanted so desperately to believe in.

There were no miracles, not anymore. When the rug had been pulled out from beneath her feet – the rug she and Charlie had made; the one they had changed their son's nappies and warmed their feet on: the two bedroom flat they had skinted themselves and exercised their right to buy from Wandsworth borough council; by no means perfect but good enough for people who were happy just to be happy. When she'd stood on the verge of losing *that*, pressing her palms together and speaking to the ceiling, it had been Charlie's mum and dad who had saved her from the flood. It had been them who had lifted her up and kept her feet out of the water. And it had been them who, for more than a year, had taken over the mortgage payments and given her enough time to get Lewis settled into secondary school and work her way back to work.

So here she was, thirty seven years old, a refugee from her first life and an immigrant in her next. She'd dragged herself here, a reluctant partygoer, whose sole occupation since she'd fallen pregnant at twenty one had been as a full time mother. In what now felt like a single moon, she had emerged from the loved world of scabbed knees, playgroups, and afternoon cartoons, to arrive in an adult universe she hadn't recognised: a working utopia of calorie counting, yoga mats, and lunch breaks in coffee shops. She was now one of *those* women: head of a single parent family bringing up a teenage son all by herself; one of the ones repairing themselves, gradually rebuilding now that the days were getting longer. The ones who'd had no choice but to start again, piece by piece, pretending that the world had never stopped, not even for a minute, not even in those loose, warped few seconds after the telephone rang and the voice on the other end asked if you wouldn't mind confirming your name before they could inform you there had been an accident...

Deborah peered down at the author's photograph on the rear dust jacket of her book, *Move On without Forgetting*, was both the title and mantra, and its author, Jillian Tully, a grey lady posed in a woollen roll neck, appeared to have every confidence in it.

'I was half expecting you might have finished that book of yours, the amount of time I was stood in that queue.' Mara Collins' lively voice made Deborah jump. She smiled, woken up. 'I was there for so bloody long staring at all the stuff, I couldn't resist,' Mara said, setting down a tray with two cups and saucers and a triangle of carrot cake on it. 'Will you have half with me?'

Deborah scooped up a dollop of soft topping with her finger and popped it into her mouth, 'I wouldn't *dream* of it,' she said sarcastically, 'I'm watching my weight.'

'Me too,' Mara said, rolling her eyes, 'and it's *growing* well.' They both laughed at the sheer cheapness of the joke. Wrapping her long hair around one side of her neck, Mara sat down, leaned forward in her chair, and then, blowing, attempted to take a sip without using her hands. 'What?' she giggled, looking up at the expression on Deborah's face, 'I don't want to burn my fingers; I've got typing to do this afternoon.'

'I'm surprised you're not more worried about your lips.'

By her own reckoning, Mara's bold red lips were her best and most defining asset. 'Good point,' she said, pulling back, 'I'd better look after the old blow-jobbers, they're the only reason Adam keeps me around.' She picked up a napkin and blotted her mouth. 'I'm serious – maybe not for you, because you've got boobs and a bum – but for girls like me, they're our best weapons. That's why we get two sets: one set for sleeping with....' She glanced down at her lap and then brought her eyes up, pouting, '...and another set to keep-him-with.'

About to take a sip Deborah was forced to return her cup to its saucer. 'Did you make that up yourself?' she asked, cracking up again.

Mara shook her head. 'I stole it out of a dirty valentine card somebody sent me.'

'It's good.'

'I thought so too.' Mara chuckled, grinning and sticking a fork into their cake. 'So c'mon,' she said, chewing sinfully, 'now I've got you smiling, you can tell me about you and James.'

Deborah sighed, uneasy, 'There isn't a *me* and James.'

Mara looked disappointed. 'What do you mean; I thought he took you out for lunch?'

Deborah frowned. 'I wouldn't say he took me out; we bumped into each other in the sandwich shop and shared a table.'

'Did *he* pay?'

'Yes,' Deborah conceded.

'Well then, he took you out, hun.' Mara hesitated a moment, her fork in mid-flight. 'What's the matter, haven't you heard from him?'

Deborah was hiding her smile well, 'I have, actually,' she said. 'He wants me to meet him for dinner on Saturday –' Mara issued an excited, cake-muffled little squeak. 'But...' Deborah tried and then decided to wait for Mara to run out of breath. 'But ... I'm not sure whether or not I should go...'

Mara eyed her, unimpressed. 'You're going,' she said, asserting herself. 'You are, hun, it's time.' Deborah looked at her, taken aback. 'Why wouldn't you? I can already tell that you like him. And from what I've seen of him walking past the office window, he seems nice. Not being funny or nothing, but climbing back on the horse might do you some good.'

Deborah thought about it, and then said: 'I might not be ready though, Mar. I feel bad. And what am I supposed to say to Lewis?'

'Lewis doesn't need to know,' Mara said, putting her fork down. 'You can cross that bridge when, and *if*, you come to it. But for now, you need to concentrate on yourself, Debs.' She watched her friend swallow a thin mouthful of cappuccino. 'Listen to me – and I'm only saying this because you need to hear it: the past is a big part of your life, hun, but it doesn't have to be your *whole* life. You're not just a widow and a mother. You're a good looking, thirty-seven-year-old lady, with a wonderful teenage son, who's almost grown up. What you've both been through is awful, I know – and I know I haven't experienced it so maybe I don't understand – but you can't let it go on making you feel guilty about wanting to live. You mustn't, babe. Otherwise you'll completely disappear underneath it.' Mara breathed. She reached across the table and turned Deborah's book over so the title was staring her in the face. 'Read what it says, hun: move on *without* forgetting.'

'Are you sure that's necessary?' Deborah asked, pinning

the telephone to her ear with her shoulder so she could multitask. She peeled the post-it note off of her computer monitor – the cerise pink rectangle mounted on the black screen absurdly reminding her of a liquorice all-sort. It read: the school phoned 1:45pm, call them back A.S.A ... the P had been lost somewhere in the squiggle. 'I finish work at five, maybe I could –'

'Unfortunately,' Pam Weatley interrupted, her bitter-sweet voice warbling through the pepper pot holes in the receiver, 'this is not something which can be resolved over the phone. The Headmaster will need to discuss it with you in person, from what I understand, Mrs Coles, at some point the police may become involved.'

'*The police...?*' Deborah said, shocked. 'What's happened?'

'I'm afraid I don't know the specifics...'

Deborah waited, expecting more but only getting the pitch quiet of a false smile on the other end. 'Lewis *is* okay, though?'

'Oh, yes, it's nothing like that,' Weatley scoffed a little, 'he's just got himself into some hot water. I'm sure it can all be sorted out easily enough.'

Deborah rubbed her temple in tired frustration. 'I'll be there as soon as I can.'

After half an hour of hushed discussion, Cassels swept out of the headmaster's office and pointed the boys inside. He didn't speak, just stood there holding the door, close enough for his presence to brush against their sleeves.

'Take a seat,' Mr Lynch said. The Headmaster's orderly tone masked the sound of the door closing behind them. There were two chairs in front of the desk. Lewis looked around before he sat down, fully expecting Cassels to have followed them in, he hadn't. 'Right,' he started, having to wait for Lewis to take up his seat beside Sammy. He stood patiently, arms folded, an understated man without much of a chin and a silver Ictus fish pinned onto his lapel; he would have looked as much at home behind a pulpit as he did his desk. He tried again: 'Right, let me start by telling the both of you how seriously I'm taking the information given to me this afternoon –' He broke off again, eyes studious. 'I would appreciate it if you would look at me when I'm talking to you ...'

Lewis and Sammy peered up from under their eyebrows.

'Thank you,' Lynch said. Satisfied, he eased himself down into his own chair, crossed one knee over the other, and tilted his head back. The headmaster liked to talk with his eyes closed. It was only a matter of time; once he found his flow, the lids would come down for the duration of the lecture. 'As hard as I find what Mr Cassels has told me to fathom, somehow it doesn't surprise me. What I find harder to believe, is that either of you could have entered into this escapade thinking that what you were doing was anything less than criminal. Therefore, my initial reaction was to treat it as such – in no uncertain terms, breaking into a teacher's private locker and taking, not only *his* things, but things which belong to your fellow students, is nothing short of *theft*. It has only been at Mr Cassels's insistence that you be given a chance to rectify the situation, that I am yet to inform the police.' He interlocked his fingers over his stomach. 'So, here's where we are: if Mr Cassels has both his wallet and car keys returned to him immediately, the matter doesn't have to go any further.'

Lewis and Sammy stared at each other.

Lynch startled them both by sitting up in his chair and opening his eyes. 'Under the circumstances, I feel that he's being more than reasonable,' he said, focusing solely on Sammy. 'You really should thank your stars that you have such an understanding teacher.'

He was looking at Sammy, because Sammy had the most to lose. Thanks to an idiot letting off a fire extinguisher, he'd already had his collar felt. In the summer, at gone midnight, Sammy had been stopped by a patrol car making his way home, his clothes covered in dried fire foam and his rucksack jingling. After refusing to give the names of the older lads involved, he'd found himself stood up in Balham Youth Court, accused of breaking into the local youth club and emptying the arcade machines of their coin trays. The district judge had handed him a six month suspended sentence, along with an assurance that, should he find himself in any more trouble this side of Christmas, the court would have no alternative other than to send him to a youth offenders facility. As the headmaster of the school he attended, Lynch had been informed of the situation by Sammy's probation officer. There had been a sit down meeting at the start of term, but what Sammy didn't know, was that as head of year ten, Cassels had also been made aware.

'But we ain't got his wallet or his keys,' Sammy protested. 'What you on about?'

Lynch blinked. 'Well, what have you done with them?'

'Nothing,' Sammy said. 'We never had them.'

Mr Lynch shifted his eyes sideways to implicate Lewis, who just shrugged and shook his head. 'Fair enough,' he said, 'but I expected you both to have a little more respect for yourselves. Do you actually expect me to believe you had nothing to do with this? If you think making this harder than it has to be is going to get you any more street cred out there...' he pointed to the window which overlooked the playground, '...let me be the bearer of the bad news: several of the students who were found in possession of items taken from Mr Cassels's classroom have already told us that they got them from you.' He hoisted Sophie's makeup bag up from his desktop and let it hang there like a dead rabbit to be observed. 'Samuel, are you going to deny that you gave this to –'

'*I* had that,' Lewis blurted out proudly. 'I returned it to its rightful owner.'

Confusing himself, Mr Lynch leant back in his chair and consulted his notes. Slowly he lowered the bag, his mind churning over the information he'd been given and perhaps taken down wrong. 'So it was *you* who spat at Mr Cassels?'

'Nah, that was me,' Sammy said unapologetically.

Lynch glanced up and then went back to his piece of paper. 'And it was you, Samuel, who had the mobile telephone?' When he heard no objection, he put a line through something.

He wasn't asking questions now, merely confirming the details he had were correct. 'And the makeup bag was Lewis's,' he mumbled to himself, crossing something out and jotting a word next to it. 'What about the cigarettes and so forth?' To that there was no reply; Lewis and Sammy gaped at one another, brows furrowed. Lynch peered around his piece of paper, the light from the window showing all of his working out. 'Let me get this straight,' he said, clearing his throat. 'You are admitting to taking the phone and the makeup bag, but apparently, you know nothing about the cigarettes, the wallet, or the car keys. Is that what you're saying to me?'

'We ain't saying we took anything,' Lewis said, kissing his teeth. 'Only that I *had* a makeup bag, which I gave to somebody else. And that *he*,' he gestured towards Sammy, 'had a mobile, which belongs to *him*. And none of us … had, or *have* …any keys or wallet.'

Lynch exhaled, his palms open on his desktop, contemplating what he had in front of him. 'Is that your final word?' He gave them longer than they needed to change their minds. 'And that goes for you as well?' he asked, probing Sammy one last time before getting to his feet.

'We didn't take his wallet,' Sammy muttered, resolute, his thumb picking at his fingernails.

'Well then, you've given me no choice. We'll let the police deal with it…' Lynch paused, waiting for a reaction. When none came, he stepped out and closed the door behind him.

'He's chattin' shit, trying to set us up,' Lewis said. He was pacing back and forth from his chair to the window, already feeling trapped, as if there was no room left to manoeuvre.

'It's *me*,' Sammy corrected, spinning the miniature globe on the edge of Lynch's desk. 'It's me who he's trying to fuck over.'

Lewis parted the Venetian blind with his fingers. 'Same thing,' he said, expecting to see a disco of blue lights flashing through the school gates at any minute.

Sammy purposely didn't turn around. He moved across the room to the bookcase in the corner. 'I'm going no comment all the way,' he announced, absently fumbling with the objects on the shelves. 'That's what I did last time.'

Lewis didn't respond.

Sammy's voice suddenly found its usual key. 'Oi, look at this...' Lewis tore his attention away from the window. Sammy had hold of a silver picture frame. Inside, captured in still life, were Mr Lynch and his wife smiling hand in hand on a hillside. 'State of it,' he said, grinning. 'She's all nipple and no tit. No wonder he loves his job so much, it's got to be better than staying in bed with that...'

Voices outside the door cut short the half-hearted laughter. Sammy put the picture back in its place and sprang back to his seat beside Lewis.

'In my opinion,' Pam Weatley was saying, 'they should be marched straight down to the station. That would teach them to –'

Mr Lynch cut her off as politely as he could: 'Pam, if

you wouldn't mind, do you think you could rattle off a letter explaining everything to the parents? They'll need it in writing.'

'Of course,' Pam said eagerly.

'Much appreciated,' Lynch replied. The boys watched the door handle dip slightly under the pressure of his hand.

'*Right...*' Lynch said, enunciating the T. 'I've just spoken with the local police Sargent, and he's advised – seeing as, at this point, Mr Cassels is reluctant to press charges and all he wants are his things back – that it would be wise to give you some time, so that you can seriously think about the situation before it goes any further.' He'd come back different, swollen, like a committee leader chairing a community meeting. 'We think,' he continued, drifting back behind his desk but not sitting down, 'that with it already being Friday afternoon, the best thing to do is to suspend you both until Tuesday morning. That way, you should have sufficient time over the weekend to reconsider the stance which you are taking on this.' He clapped his hands together, clasped them for a second, and then opened his palms as if releasing a butterfly. 'Boys, I strongly suggest that you mull it over properly. Because on your return there will be police officers present to interview you.'

Lewis and Sammy gazed at him with clenched faces. Lynch let his words hang in the air for almost half a minute before he finally sat down. 'Also,' he said, 'you will both need to be accompanied by an appropriate adult or guardian. Lewis, I believe your mother is on her way now so I will speak with her when she gets here. Samuel, as yet, we haven't been able to get hold of anyone at your home –'

'The phone's been cut off,' Sammy snapped.

'Oh, right...' Lynch said, giving it a second. 'Well, I've already made sure that there will be a letter you can take home which will explain everything to your folks...' Lynch was about to say something else but a sharp rap on the office door broke his train of thought.

Uninvited, Pam Weatley poked her turtle shell glasses in. 'I'm sorry to interrupt, Headmaster.' She spoke over the boy's heads. 'I thought you'd like to know that Mrs Coles has just arrived.'

Ignoring a prod from Sammy, Lewis blew out his cheeks and let his head rock back on his shoulders.

Barley Sugar

FRANCIS

Council estates are bilingual, they speak in tongues. It's a primitive, wonderfully coloured language born of the mentality seeping through the bricks and mortar. They're places with rules of their own; open prisons, lawless beneath the surface, cut off from the new world only by low fences, grasslands, and imaginary boarders. These are scaffolded forests. Institutions whose residents *(inmates)* look first left and then right once they step over their thresholds and onto the communal landings. Elbows rest over balcony railings and bullshit about great escapes fly high. This is where the children can ignore the no ball games signs whilst they break apart the kitchen appliances dumped on the corner. These communes are quarries of freedom, walled prairies where kids have the liberty to throw stones and then scatter in packs when the slow-moving, dinosaur-eyed, police patrols circle. These places are abandoned fairy-tale castles with boarded up windows; storybook towers where little girls can wait out their prince charming drunk on council pop, earwigging as their baby brothers are brought up on the fantastic tales of their forefathers daring-do.

By four o' clock in the afternoon it was almost dark. Inside his burgundy '69 Daimler, Francis Coles turned on to the estate and slowed down to a roll, searching for a parking space in one of the fjords between the tower-blocks. The vehicle looked almost self-conscious; the other cars, squashed together on the pavement, side by side like idiot bouncers, glaring at the chrome headlamps.

Francis reversed in beside a white transit van and switched off his engine. He sat for a moment pushing the Brylcreem out of his hair. The duck's arse was gone, alongside the Rock 'n' roll; at 66 his hair was parted on the side, the decades having dyed it the colour of coin. He smiled, reminiscing, the crows-feet beside his eyes picking apart the things his daughter-in-law had told him on the phone. What was he supposed to tell her? Debs, it ain't you, love. No fifteen-year-old boy listens to his mother - and why would they? Young minds are supposed to believe they're ten feet tall and destined to live forever.

He stepped out of the car, fastening his double-breasted coat across his chest, and then started towards the block.

The black bin liners below the rubbish shoot had been ripped open and scavenged by foxes; a line of litter curled around the corner and onto the grass in a tin can rats-tail. The entry door was wedged open. Without need of the intercom, Francis walked inside and pressed the button to call the lift. Somewhere a baby wailed...and then the cables inside the shaft began to groan.

'*He's lying*,' Lewis repeated.

'Oh, for God's sake, Lewis.'

She was beginning to get sick of the sound of her own voice. She'd been on at him since they'd got home, in spats, to and fro, her leaving the room and him then thinking it was safe to switch on the TV.

Deborah turned the television off, for the umpteenth time, and then stood staring at her son. In truth she was more worried than angry; seeing him there, slouched into the sofa cushions wearing his school uniform, he still looked so young – too young. 'Do you want to end up in prison, Lewis, is that it?' Lewis let his head fall into his hands: she was back to that again. 'They're talking about the police, Lewis … the *police*. Believe me, you don't want to go down that road –'

Lewis let out a groan of frustration, 'How many more times do I need to say it? We *didn't* take his wallet, mum. He's talking shit'

'Lewis, language! I don't see why he would lie.' She shrugged. '*Why* would he do that?'

'Because he's a dick 'ed,' Lewis said. 'And he hates Sammy.'

'Oh, so it's *Sammy* who's the victim here, is it? Tell me, Lewis, why is it that any time you're in any kind of trouble, it's always him who's right there beside you?'

'What's that got to do with anything?' Lewis raised his head and looked at her. 'Why do you always want to blame Sammy? I knew what I was doing.' He screwed up his face. 'I did it because I wanted to … and I'm glad I done it. It ain't that deep, mum. All we did was get Sammy's phone back and give some girl her makeup. How were we supposed to know our teacher would lie to try get us nicked?'

'Lewis, has it ever occurred to you, that maybe – just *maybe* – your poor, hard-done-by little friend Sammy might've taken that wallet? Have you even stopped to think, just for a second, that maybe he kept it for himself? And that maybe it's not that Mr Cassels has got a vendetta against him, but that he has simply had his things stolen.' Lewis didn't answer. 'That boy is bad news, Lewis. You're not stupid; I've told you before, those sorts of people only go *one* way.'

'What you on about? Lewis said. 'Last time I checked, *we* were those sorts of people.'

'Is that what you think?' Deborah asked, annoyed. 'Is that who you think you are? That boy's mother can barely keep a set of teeth in her head, let alone bring up children.' She paused, offended. 'This has been going on since you were little. Do you have any idea how many times I've had to listen to that woman banging on about the trouble Sammy's older brothers were in? Telling me how unfair it was that the police kept raiding her house looking for them, time after time, and then locking them up? Don't you *dare* compare yourself to him; that's not who you are. And it's definitely not how you grew up; me and your dad did our utmost to give you a good life. And even if you like to pretend otherwise, we taught you right from wrong.'

'Yeah, but as if dad didn't get into trouble when he was young – I *know* that he did, you told me.'

'He didn't just go around taking things which didn't belong to him for the sake of it, Lewis.'

'Neither did we.'

Deborah shook her head, disappointed. 'You can't possibly have any idea how hard your father had to fight *not* to have that life. He didn't want it for himself; therefore, he certainly wouldn't want it for his son, would he?'

Silence…

The quiet wasn't broken until the letterbox flapped and Deborah walked out into the hallway. A few seconds later Lewis heard the front door open and the low sound of his grandfather's voice. He sat up a little straighter.

'If I was you,' Francis said, following Deborah into the living room, 'I'd try and keep the noise down a bit; I could hear every word you were saying the moment the lift opened.'

'She's not listening to me,' Lewis remonstrated. 'And I'm trying to tell her the truth.'

'If that's the case,' Francis said, smiling, 'then you should have even less reason to be shouting.'

'Sorry to drag you over here,' Deborah said. 'But he's not interested in anything I've got to say. I thought you might be able to have a word with him...?' Each time she was this close to her father-in-law it was the same: she could never get over how much he moved like Charlie – or rather, how much Charlie had moved like him. '...at the end of the day, you've got more experience being a boy then I do.'

Francis laughed, gently squeezing her hand. 'Fair enough,' he said. He looked at them both, one after the other. 'So who wants to fill me in on what's happened?'

'Lewis is a big boy,' Deborah said, 'he can explain himself. But I *will* offer you a cup of tea.'

'Cheers.' Francis took off his coat and laid it over the arm of the sofa. Lewis watched his mother until she'd disappeared into the kitchen. 'So c'mon then,' Francis said, looking his grandson in the eye. 'What you done?'

The kitchen was small enough for Francis to cross it in two strides. He ran the tap over his tea mug and then left it to stand in the sink. 'I've sent him to his room so he can chuck a few things in a bag,' he said. 'If it's okay with you, I'll let him tag along with me for the weekend; give you two a little break from each other.'

The gas hob on top of the cooker was hissing out a yellow and blue flame beneath the rice pot, the steam rising up and haloing around the spotlights in the ceiling. Deborah glanced up at him from the chopping board. 'Are you sure?'

'Yeah, it's no skin off my nose,' Francis said. 'It won't do him any good sitting around in here and stewing until Tuesday, will it? He can keep me company. I'm driving up north to see an old friend of mine to hopefully sort something out for a pair of old timepieces we've been hanging onto. Whatever happens, it'll give me and Lewis a chance to spend some proper time together.'

'What day will you be coming back?'

'Monday; I'll drop him off in the evening.'

All of a sudden, all at once, the nasty, nauseous, selfish thought of being able to go out for dinner with James tomorrow night was dangling in front of her. She waved it away, fanning the air with a dishcloth. She looked the other way, choosing to concentrate on the red pepper she'd been slicing. 'Did he say anything to you about what happened today?'

'Only what he told you,' Francis said. 'That the teacher is twisting things so he can stitch up Lewis's pal.'

'And you believe him?' Deborah asked.

'Stranger things have happened.'

Deborah looked doubtful. 'That Sammy kid is a wrong'un,' she said. 'He's forever dragging Lewis into something.'

'Maybe so,' Francis said, 'but you'll be wasting your breath prattling on about it. He won't hear you, not yet, not at his age.' He glistened at her. 'Boys are as stubborn as *girls*.'

'I'm doing the best I can,' she said, suddenly defensive. 'I want to bring him up to be more than a –'

'And you've done *brilliant*,' Francis told her. He reached out and touched the top of her arm. 'But you can't make peoples mistakes for them, love. All you can do is stand by their side while they make their own.' He found her eyes. 'And if you can do that, in my experience, the people who are meant to straighten out usually do.'

As the crow flies, there were only a few miles between the flat and Lewis's grandparent's house. The big wide world, as far as Francis was concerned, had been a stone's throw from his backyard in Wandsworth.

He'd owned the house – a three floor, brick built, Victorian home opposite Putney Common – since the early sixties, before times had changed. By modern standards, he never would've been able to steal enough to afford it – let alone to pay for it outright as he had. Nowadays, urchins with the stench of the local brewery in their skin had long been priced out. This was merchant banker country; the green banks of the River Thames had been exclusively confiscated for the well-to-do. The place was respectable; a cracked and tilted paving slab, unearthed by the tree roots of an evenly spaced oak, was as crooked as it got.

The dark had won its daily battle. The Daimler's headlamps flashed across the twiggy hedges and onto the drive. Francis turned in and parked. Before Lewis could fully open his door, a deep, baritone dog bark reverberated from somewhere inside the house. Seconds later two enormous paws thudded against the inside of the front door and rattled the lion-head doorknocker on the outside. The curtain covering the downstairs window twitched, *'Tudor, quiet!'* Behind the glass, Lewis's grandmother peered out, beamed, and then instantly disappeared in a swish of pleated fabric.

Lewis paced around to the boot of the car, lifted his holdall out, slung it over his shoulder, and slammed the lid.

'Who's that, then…?' His grandmother asked, letting go of the dog's collar so he could bound outside.

'Tudor!' Lewis greeted the huge bullmastiff as it barged into his legs, panting. He patted its great head and then stepped back to try and save his jeans from a string of slobber.

'He's missed you,' his grandmother said. She was standing inside the golden rectangle of light where the front door had been. Francis smiled at her over the roof of the car; it was good to see her happy again.

Connie Coles had always been a pleasure to look at; even now, into her sixties, thanks to colour foils and hairdressers, she had all but kept her auburn fall. She was old-fashioned and rosy-cheeked, her corduroy trousers giving the fresh air impression of a lady who liked to labour in the garden.

'Hello, my love,' she cooed, opening her arms to her grandson. The dog bounced in a circle and then ran around to the other side of the car to find his master.

'Alright Gran,' Lewis said, abiding by her rule: It had to be, *Gran* or *Granny*, as opposed to, *Nan* or *Nanny* – which is what most of Lewis's friends called their grandmothers. It was one of the few things she insisted upon. To Connie, to become a grandmother meant that a woman had endured enough life to have mothered and raised two families. It was a title earned and to be proud of – work a woman needed to have soft hands for.

'*My God,*' she said, taking him in her arms and kissing his cheek, 'You're getting taller by the day; you're almost as tall as you father.' She gave him another kiss, let go, and then tapped him on the bottom. 'And from what I'm hearing, you've inherited his sense of mischief.'

Lewis grinned cheekily and then squeezed past her to get inside.

For Lewis, with its wide hall and wooden stairs, the house had the same airy sense of memory as a local museum, everything old and with meaning. When his dad was alive they came here often. He could remember climbing up to the landing as a child and then bumping his way down the stairs on a cushion, arms out, his father waiting to catch him at the bottom. Staying here felt stranger now that his dad had passed. His old bedroom on the top floor, overlooking the cricket green, was crowded with junk and boxes of vintage football programmes. To Lewis, the room had taken on a grand significance. It was probably unwarranted – even before he'd died his old man hadn't set foot in there for years. But alone, Lewis couldn't help but imagine him here as a youngster – maybe dreaming, or maybe leaning on the window sill to smoke.

'Remember,' Connie whispered, 'he's only *fifteen*; you don't need to tell him everything about everything.' Holding both of her hands, Francis nodded and then kissed her on the forehead.

The Daimler had been fogging up the driveway for five minutes already, billowing hot morning breath against the early chill. Lewis rubbed the back of his hand across the inside of his window and took another look at the blurry figures having their quiet moment on the doorstep. He yawned, stretching to check if the vent on the dashboard was getting any warmer.

Eventually, his grandfather walked around to the boot of the car, double checked it was closed, and then climbed in to the driver's side. 'Make sure you get the edges,' he said cheerfully, handing Lewis a grubby cloth so he'd wipe the condensation off his side of the windscreen. His grandmother waited patiently, arms folded over her nightgown. Francis wound down his window and reversed alongside the front door. 'I'll give you a bell from the road,' he said, tilting his head out and saying the rest in silence.

The car turned out of the drive. Connie watched until it

was out of sight and then, calling for Tudor, she went back inside the house, her face tired and full of ghosts.

The roads were as quiet as they ever got south of the river. It was early doors, amber still reflecting in orbs on the bonnet as the car passed beneath the long-necked street lamps. Lewis rested his head back and gazed lazily at the misty sections of residential London flickering past the windows.

'No point in hanging about,' Francis said, nudging Lewis with his elbow. 'We might as well get a head start on the football traffic.'

Wanting to look like he understood why they'd had to leave so early, Lewis smiled. 'What's the name of the place we're going, again?'

'Durham,' Francis answered. The weather report crackled low in the background; Francis leaned forward and peered up at the wispy swirls of cloud over the rooftops. 'It's way up north,' he said, 'near where Newcastle play.'

Lewis nodded, having only a rough idea of the geography. 'Who are they playing today?'

'They're at home to Portsmouth,' Francis said. 'It's a three o' clock kick off. It won't affect us though; we're only going up as far as York today. I need to drop in on an old mate first thing tomorrow. We'll head on after that.'

As with any other thing Lewis's grandfather did, there was no rush. That was why they were setting out on Saturday to reach an appointment he had on the Monday morning. He liked to drive slow and travel in his own time. This way they could take it easy, stop halfway overnight, bump into his pal in York, and then do the final stretch of the journey fresh. They'd be in Durham with plenty of time to spare. They could find somewhere to stay, get themselves a slap up meal and then bed down for the night, ready for whatever it was that he had to do on Monday.

'There're a few big games on this afternoon,' Francis added, slowing the car down to a crawl. 'You'll have to mess about with the tuner and find us one to listen to on the radio.' He glared out at the yellow speed-camera mounted on the pavement and didn't touch the pedal until they were well clear of the white ladder lines painted on the road. He shook his head.

'You know, I actually feel sorry for you lot nowadays. It's all bloody cameras and internets; you're being watched all the time.' Lewis raised his eyebrows in appreciation. 'In our day we had way more freedom, they just used to let us get on with it. Even if you were only halfway clever you could get away with a few things.'

'Like what?'

'Well,' Francis said, slowing down for a red light. 'We used to swim in the river for one thing.' Lewis looked left out of his window; beyond the drop from the pavement he could see the grimy waters of the Thames rushing beneath Putney Bridge. 'I can remember one summer, a little bit further up our way, a young lad named Ernie Croft got caught in the current and some bloke who was working on one of the pleasure boats had to jump in to save his life. After that, they sent a man to our school to tell us all about the dangers of the undertow and we all had to promise our mothers that we wouldn't go anywhere near the water anymore. Not that it mattered, by the next summer we were all back, diving in head-first from the mooring posts.' He smiled. 'The point is, there weren't any cameras around to tell anybody any different, was there?'

The lights changed and the Daimler turned and rolled onto the bridge. Lewis was all ears, woken up, the grey daylight suddenly lifting the veil off of his imagination, and for a second, letting him see what his grandfather was talking about. It was there black and white, a picture, a piece of a city on film: kids lining up and leaping from the mouldy wooden stumps on the water's edge, happy just to land in the splash. It was a land without electronic bus timetables; the town his grandfather spoke of was an antique, a lost world, a temporarily preserved daydream buried only in the minds of those who had been there when the bombs dropped. Those people who had lived before the future was certain; back when, for the free-wheeling thinkers, the streets may well have still been paved with gold.

Francis pointed out Bishops Park on the other side of the river. 'Funnily enough, the first time I ever got nicked was in there.'

Lewis looked at him, 'How old were you?'

'Ten or eleven, I think,' Francis said, smiling. 'Well, to be fair we didn't really get arrested; they just took us down to the station and made our dads come and collect us.'

'What did you do?'

'Nothing,' Francis answered. 'It was my mate Winston's fault.' He chuckled. 'If you think *your* mum gives you grief about your pals, that's sod-all compared to how my old dear used to get on me for knocking about with him.' He flicked the indicator and changed lane. 'You see, in those days, things weren't like how they are now; no one batted an eyelid when your mum and dad got together and had you, but back then it was more or less unheard of for someone to have a black mother and a white father - or vice versa, for that matter. My old girl couldn't get her head round it; she used to say people mixing went against nature. She used to call Winston the little *half-caste* boy, making him sound sinister. It never made any sense to me though, he was the best boy I knew...the best friend I ever had.'

'*Half-caste!*' Lewis snickered. 'No one's ever called me that.'

Francis nodded. 'Like I said, this was a long time ago. People are small-minded at the best of times, but it's good to hear we've evolved a little bit.' He reached over and clicked the radio off. 'Anyway, as you know, my old man had the barber shop on the Trinity Road, and Henry McDaniels – that was Winston's father – used to come in there sometimes. Now, this was a tough man, a merchant seaman who'd sailed all over the world. The story goes that one day old Henry finds himself in the Caribbean somewhere hauling rum and sugar. When he gets on land, he sees these young ladies selling fruit on the side of the road and within a day and a night the soppy sod has fallen arse over tit in love with one of them. Winston showed me a photograph of her once, she was a pretty woman; she had one of those brilliant smiles which put little dimples in her cheeks. It weren't hard to see where Henry was going with it; and sure enough, by the time his ship set sail for home, he was having to leave her behind in the family way.'

Lewis had to think… 'Pregnant?'

Francis nodded, watching the road. 'Believe me,' he said, 'it's *easily* done.'

Lewis laughed. 'So what happened? Did he go back?'

'He did, but not for a couple years. Winston was about two when Henry finally went back for him.'

'He went and got him?' Lewis asked, surprised.

That's the remarkable bit,' Francis said. 'By then I reckon he must've fallen in and out of love at least twice. Apparently he'd forgotten all about the bird, just not about his boy. He couldn't let it go. The idea of his son growing up without him on the other side of the world was too much for him. He was a good man – nobody thought that he would actually do it but he *did*. The next time his ship docked in that part of the world … he stole him.'

Lewis's face contorted, 'How?'

'Don't know,' Francis said. 'Winston was too young to remember. He must have had help from some of the blokes on the ship or something because he hid him on board and smuggled him home.'

'What about the woman?'

Francis shrugged. 'All I know is that Winston never saw her again. He only had that photo.'

'Argh, that's shit,' Lewis said.

'It got worse than that,' Francis said. 'A few years later

when the war broke out, like a lot of blokes, Henry went off to fight and never made it home. He died at Dunkirk.' Lewis's eyes widened in recognition; he'd seen that in a film. 'I was lucky, my old man came back without a scratch, but a lot of lads weren't so fortunate. By the time me and Winston had become friends, he was living with his grandmother over on Armoury Way and having a hard time of it.'

There was a lull as the car joined the motorway, the windscreen wipers beginning their hypnotic strokes to fend off the drizzle. Lewis slipped further down into the crumpled leather seat. The bold white letters on the road signs passed overhead: THE NORTH.

'So what did he do then?' Lewis asked.

Francis looked at him. 'Who, Wince?'

'Yeah, what did he do that day in the park to get you lot in trouble?'

WINSTON

London, 1947

Despite his slap-coloured cheeks, the fat man from the cobblers could run after all.

He ploughed on, chasing, his shopkeeper's apron cutting into his stomach like a cheese wire. The boy was pulling away in front of him, small and plucky, ducking his head and weaving through the crowds on the riverbank. You had to give it to him: the half-breed had the front of bleedin' Brighton. Nice as pie he'd been to begin with, swanning into the shop and asking about boot laces. Then, the moment he had turned his back on him, quick as ninepence, the kid had hung out one of his tree swingers and helped himself to a pair of resoled shoes from the counter top. He was fast an 'all; the thieving little sod was sprinting like he was Jessie *fucking* Owens.

Up ahead, a pair of polished shoes on over his hands, young Winston McDaniels dodged past a woman in a white dress and vanished into the congregation. He was eleven years old and running for his life.

It was boat race day, a spectacle; Oxford versus Cambridge, their annual punt along the Thames. Either side of the river was packed: students spilling out of the clubhouse on one side, families picnicking on the other. Promanding the length of Bishop's Park, quiet couples and dog walkers broke stride to try and catch a glimpse of the row teams.

A little way downstream, enjoying the mild weather with their sleeves rolled up, two-ten-year old boys, one with black hair and one with blonde, were keeping an eager ear out for the starting pistol.

'Do you reckon it sounds the same as a real gun?' the blonde boy said, dragging a stick along the iron railings at the water's edge.

Francis shrugged, the sun catching on his blue eyes. He was on the other side of the railings, clutching onto the bars and shuffling sideways across the few inches of concrete which overhung the river.

Micky Meehan gave it some more thought. A wiry kid with a big mouth and a chipped tooth. 'It can't do,' he said, smoothing down his thick yellow hair, 'not if it ain't got any bullets in it.'

Francis let his weight fall backwards, until his arms were holding him diagonally over the drop. He tipped his head back and looked at the boats on the far side of the river from upside down. They were like long canoes, the rowers sitting inside, oars held straight up in the air. 'We'll find out soon,' he said, pulling himself in and climbing back over the railing. 'It's starting in a minute.'

The movement of the boats on the water stirred the crowd. People began to murmur, leaving their blankets and benches, leading their parties by the hand so they could gather a little closer to the action. The Muffin Man, determined to flog his wares, picked his way through the herd, his tray balancing on his head.

'Let's walk up that way,' Francis said, pointing out a cluster of tilted trees leaning over the river bank. A Candy floss stall stood not twenty feet away, the silver bowl spinning its pink thread under the tuition of an old man in a straw boater hat.

'Oi,' Micky said, tugging his friend's shirt to make sure he'd spotted it. He held up the stick he'd just been playing the railing with. 'How much Candy floss do you think I'll get, if I sneak up and shove this into his bowl?'

But before Francis could answer – BANG – the starting pistol went off and the race was underway. The sound had cracked the earth open, suddenly, powerful enough to wake the heavens and evoke chaos on the grass. Beneath the whoops and cheers of encouragement, sheltered below a ceiling of uproar, Francis and Micky shared two ten-year-old smiles.

With the stolen shoes pinned to his chest, Winston barrelled through the crowds like a small rugby player, his free arm bumping and brushing people out of his way. He didn't look behind him, nor did he notice the rowing teams powering alongside him on the river, their tall oars shaving the shine off of the water. He kept going, he had to. The fat cobbler was still back there, chasing, tears in his eyes and the coppery two-penny taste of loss bloody at the back of his throat. His cries of 'THIEF!' were getting louder, turning heads.

Winston thought briefly about jumping into the water,

about dying by trying to swim to the other side. Somewhere, a high-pitched policeman's whistle lanced his ears and thrust his feet forward. His legs felt wooden, frightened shocks darting upwards from his ankles to his knees. The whistle blew again, cutting through the crowd, piercing his ears and pinwheeling his balance.

Thick-set and strong-boned, Winston veered onto the grass at speed. A hand reached out and grabbed a handful of his V-neck jumper – it tightened momentarily around his throat, and then it sprang loose – only slowing him for a second. He stumbled, his feet sliding out underneath him, losing grip and then righting themselves on the uneven surface.

A foot, dangling from a picnic blanket on the grass, hooked his ankle, and down he went, head over heels. In a split second, the world tumbled and rolled over in a green and blue smudge. Winston pulled himself up, one arm clawing, his legs driving at the earth. At least if the shopkeeper caught him now, he thought – readying himself for a boot in the back – Fatso would more than likely be too puffed out to put much leather behind the walloping.

But no blow came, no clip round the ear, just a continuous string section of screams coming from the race goers. Finding his feet, Winston hurdled a sandwich basket, foot printed another set of sheets, and cantered towards the clear patch of grass ahead of him. Winston glanced over his shoulder. There was no policeman, not that he could see anyway, only the pale faces of the family he'd just trodden on. The cobbler had slowed to a trot and fallen behind, his eyes tiny black curses.

There were fewer people, less arms and legs. The further

down the river he got there were fewer heads, fewer mouths and whistles. Folks had their noses poked towards the water, clapping and cheering at the athletes. Heart drumming, Winston looked ahead of him and saw a cluster of trees next to a candy floss stall. He headed for cover, barging through a huddle of mothers and disappearing behind their dresses.

The policeman's whistle blew again, louder now, carrying on the breeze. This time, when Winston looked back through the forest of fabric, he spotted him – a large uniform with shiny buttons hurrying along the bank, causing a commotion. Head bobbing, beating a quick path for the trees, Winston saw two boys watching him. They were hidden, tucked in behind one of the trunks, one dark-haired and the other blonde. He knew one of them, his face anyway, it was Marge Meehan's little brother, Micky: every lad in Wandsworth had heard of their family – everybody's mother, or grandmother, had told them at least once to stay away from those kids.

'Hide these!' Winston panted. Holding on to the tree-trunk to slow himself down, he skidded in front of the two boys. 'That copper's after me. Hide 'em!' He was speaking to the boy he knew as Micky, his desperate eyes checking to see how close the policeman was. Micky stared at him, face furrowed into an aggressive snarl. But before he could open his mouth to tell Winston to 'fuck off' – for no good reason, the dark-haired boy reached out and took the shoes. Winston nodded his appreciation, and then took off, the sound of Micky asking his friend, 'What the fuck did you do that for?' loud in his ears.

'I thought you knew him,' Francis said, tucking the shoes behind the tree and wiping his blackened fingers against the bark. 'He was looking at you like he knew who you were.'

Micky pushed him flat against the tree as the policeman ran past. 'I do, sort of: he's that coloured kid what lives on Armoury Way. I think his name's Winston or –' The whistle bleated, piercing the conversation. '–Toby Everett told me that he chinned a kid two years above for calling him a chimp.' Micky finished, and then added, 'Toby reckons he's tough.'

Winston looked back one last time, and then ran head-first into the Muffin Man – the tray went skywards, muffins hitting the ground like stodgy little fists in the dirt. Dizzy and spinning, Winston only made it another few steps and then the old boy selling the candy floss helped him on his way down.

The tackle was honest, a good citizen doing his bit. With a huff of sweet smelling hot air, the old boy landed on top of Winston, his straw hat rolling away across the grass. 'Stay put now, there's a good lad,' he said, flagging an arm for the policeman. 'You mustn't run away from the law, son. It only serves to land you in more trouble.' Winston bucked beneath him, flailing his fists. Blinking, the old boy caught one on the end of his nose. He started to say something else – and then Winston's foot came up between his legs and split his sack. The squeal came after the slap: he swung a hand and cuffed Winston hard across the chops, before rolling over and cupping his jewels.

Scrambling up in a rapid panic, Winston was gone,

heading for the bushes at the far end of the park. There was a final, feeble toot of the whistle, and then, stumbling over the candy floss man, the policeman ran out of steam.

A full minute later, whilst Winston was swinging a trembling leg over the fence and making his escape, the fat cobbler caught up with the chase, only to discover that the fox had run away from the hounds. Bent double with his hands on his knees, pissing out of his pores, he lumbered, took a step backwards, and put his foot through a straw boater hat which someone had left lying on the grass.

'What a getaway!' Micky said. 'Did you see him boot that geezer in the knackers?'

Francis laughed. 'Toby wasn't wrong, was he? That was the scrap of a lifetime.' He stared at the patch of dirt where the scuffle had just taken place. The candy floss man, taking a deep breath, had only just managed to stagger back to his feet.

Behind him, the cobbler pleaded his misfortune and the policeman took notes. The onlookers, most of whom hadn't the foggiest about what had even happened, one by one, began to lose interest and return to the race. All except one: a teenage girl in a yellow dress with a ribbon in her hair. She was standing, pointing, a stick of candy floss in one hand and an accusation in the other.

'Whatever he pinched, he gave it to those two boys,' she said, her voice shrill and hopeful. The policeman turned slowly. Micky and Francis went stiff, their backs against the tree, the girl and her mother scowling at them in disgust. 'Over by the bushes,' the girl clarified, 'that brown boy gave them whatever he took. They're his friends.'

'Is that so?' the policeman inquired, speaking to the girl but fixing on Micky and Francis. 'And what was it that you saw the boy give to 'em?'

'I'm not sure; it looked like shoes or something.'

Francis slipped his hands into his pockets.

'Right, stay there,' the policeman warned, marching over towards the tree. Using his heel, Micky quickly tried to tuck the stolen shoes further out of sight. 'What is it you've got there?'

'Nothing,' Francis shrugged, 'I don't know what she's talking about. We just came to see the race.' The policeman nipped his ear, hard enough that the knuckles on his thumb and forefinger turned white. 'Argh!' Francis screamed, bending under the pain.

'Get off him,' Micky shouted – just as the cobbler arrived and seized a tuft of his hair. 'Piss off!' Micky said, jerking his head loose, 'we ain't done nothing ...we don't even know that kid.'

'Behind the tree,' the girl said. She was almost hopping on the spot, her face splitting in wide excitement. 'Whatever they've got, it's behind the tree. I saw them put it there.'

Taking Micky with him, the cobbler searched around for a second and then came up with a shoe. 'Thieving toe-rags!' he bellowed, whacking Micky across the back of the legs. 'I'll have their guts for bloody garters...'

'Who was the boy who gave 'em to you?' the policeman asked, squeezing Francis's ear.

'Don't know,' Francis yelped, 'we've never seen him before.'

Micky lifted a leg to avoid another smack. The cobbler glared at him through his tight, piggy eyes. 'Give me your friend's name, or so help me God, I'll *beat* it out of you.'

Swinging from the cobbler's grip, Micky looked first at Francis and then back at the fat man who had hold of him. 'Up yours!'

'My old man taught us better than that,' Micky declared. He was sitting, cross-legged, on the gravel behind the church, separating a tangle of rubber bands and sorting them into piles.

It had been almost a week since the day of the boat race, much of which Micky and Francis had spent retelling the details of their capture and interrogation to the other boys at school. In truth it had been short-lived; they'd pleaded their innocence for less than an hour before their fathers arrived to take them home, Micky's dad buying them a quarter of sweets to share for keeping their mouths shut.

'One thing I'll never be is a grass,' Francis said. He pulled a handful of wooden clothes pegs out of his pocket and then set himself down, shifting in the gravel to get comfortable.

'Same 'ere,' Micky said, agreeing without looking up.

Francis set about his job; snapping a pile of wooden clothes-pegs in half and collecting the little metal springs to use as ammunition. They were alone – unless you counted Beryl; she was wrapped in a piece of sack cloth and stashed in the bushes behind them. Beryl had been named in honour of the old lady whose table leg she'd been fashioned from; sawn down to size, magnificent mahogany with a carved spiral running the length of her barrel, she was the best peg-gun they'd ever made. It had taken 20 minutes of loving care for Micky to polish her up, so to leave her out in the open and risk losing her if the vicar came around the corner didn't bear thinking about.

Peg-guns are simple contraptions, whipped up in a jiffy. A mischievous lad takes a good length of whichever wood he can lay his hands on, fixes a peg to one end and strong nail to the other. The coil-springs are then harvested from a handful of remaining clothes pegs – pinched from his mother's laundry – and threaded onto elastic bands. The idea is: the ammo is looped around the nail at one end of the gun and stretched back along the length of the barrel, where the coil spring is held in place by the teeth of the affixed peg. So, when that lad is ready, he presses down on the trigger, the jaws open, and the rubber band is catapulted towards whatever it's been pointed at. Genius.

'Are you playing red?' Francis asked, peering up at the huge stained-glass window on the back of the church.

'Yeah,' Micky said. He slid Beryl out of the bush and unravelled her from her swaddling.

'I think I'm going for blue,' Francis mused, considering the coloured glass. Set into the stonework and framed by a layered arch, the window dominated the entire rear wall of the building. It depicted a biblical scene: two shepherds receiving gifts from a cloaked messenger, flanked by cherubs.

Micky glanced at him, working things out. 'Go for it,' he said. 'But there's more blue to hit.'

'That's the idea, it makes it easier.'

Micky pulled a face, and then shrugged. 'I'm having the first turn then.'

The object of the game was simple: fire at the window and take out as much of your designated colour as possible, the winner was the one who broke the most glass. Like a hunter tracking a stag, Micky dropped to one knee and extended Beryl from his shoulder. He squinted, crunching a leg in the gravel and waiting for his arm to stop shaking. Francis squatted silently beside him, focusing on the window. It was good form and sportsmanship to call out where one was aiming before he fired –

'The cape on the shepherd's back,' Micky hissed, taking a deep breath and holding it. He pressed down ... the peg opened ... the rubber band snapped ... and the metal coil sprang forward. Unbalanced – like an out-of-control trapeze artist from a flea circus – it chinked the glass and disappeared.

'You missed,' said Francis.

'No way,' Micky replied, 'I can see the mark from here.'

Francis stood up and walked over to examine the window. 'That's not on his cape.'

'It don't matter, I still get a point. I hit him.' Micky handed Beryl to Francis. 'Let's see you do better.'

Francis smiled, 'Okay, watch this!' With Beryl over his shoulder, he strutted back to the firing line, stopping and bending over at the pile of ammunition.

'Remember the black band's mine,' Micky said. 'I've already called dibs on it.'

Francis nodded, loading Beryl with what looked like the best rubber band besides the black one. He preferred a standing stance – he braced the gun, one eye closed, looking down the length of wood. Just as he'd made up his mind on aiming for a particularly ambitious patch of blue glass, and was about to call it out... he heard footsteps moving in the gravel on the other side of the church. Micky had already begun backing away towards the bushes, his feet making tiny scrunches. Francis dropped down into a squat and followed him, waddling on his haunches.

The undergrowth swallowed them pretty well, the spiny branches nicking their scalps and picking at the cotton on their backs. Crouching, an achy pull in the back of his ankles, Francis carefully laid Beryl down between them and waited. Micky looked at him, silently resting his hand on the gun: his message was clear, he had no scruples about shooting at a man of the cloth.

Small stones flew up and into view, as a pair of feet rounded the corner and stopped.

'It's that kid from the boat race,' Francis whispered, gawking through the leaves. 'What's he doing here?'

'Don't know,' Micky said. 'But he wants to watch he don't get shot.' He grabbed Beryl and started to shimmy his way out of the bush. 'What you playing at?' he called, sticking the gun out ahead of him. 'We thought you was the bloody vicar.'

Winston didn't speak until both Micky and Francis had bustled from their hiding place. 'I've been looking for you,' he said, smiling. 'Them girls by the shops told me you'd be here – I think one of them was your sister.'

'What do you know about my sister?' Micky said, snarling, the bridge of his nose a tiger-wrinkle. 'And why were you talking to her?'

Winston shrugged.

'What did you want with us?' Francis asked, stalking forwards. From up close, Winston was even bigger, his chubby face suddenly looking very large compared to Francis's clenched fists.

Without budging, Winton watched them; even with a peg-gun pointed at him and the prospect of a scrap two on one, not a single shingle shifted around his feet. 'I came to say thank you,' he said, feeling daft as soon as the words were out. 'For not grassing – Toby Everett said that when they asked you who I was, you told them you didn't know.'

'We got nicked,' Micky spat, doing his best to sound begrudging.

'Did they give you a hiding?'

'Not really,' Francis said. 'Nothing we couldn't shake off, anyway.'

Winston tossed his eyebrows, 'I would of got one; they would've beaten me black and blue if I hadn't of got away.'

Micky sniggered, 'What good would that do them? You're already black.'

'So people say,' Winston said, unashamed. 'but I'm actually half 'n half.'

Unsure about where to poke next, Micky stared at him.

Francis smiled; it was easy to admire this kid. 'So why was you stealing shoes, anyway?'

Winston beheld his shoes as if it was obvious. 'I needed them,' he said.

Francis and Micky both peered down at the tatty, worn shoes covering his feet.

'What's the matter with your old man?' Micky said. 'Why can't he get you none?'

'He's dead.' Winston puffed out his chest. 'The Krauts killed him.'

Micky turned up his lip, '*Your* dad ain't English...'

'He is,' Winston said proudly. 'He's from just down the road. It's my mother what was foreign. But I haven't even seen her since I was a baby. I live with my Nan.'

Micky lowered Beryl, now just interested. 'Why doesn't she get you some, then?'

"Because she don't like looking after me,' Winston said, amused. 'She won't treat me to a new pair until these are making holes in my socks.'

'Why?'

Winston shrugged, smiling. 'She thinks I ain't pure,' he said. "She reckons I'm mud-coloured because I was a mistake.' He laughed, hearing himself say it.

Micky and Francis joined him, giggling.

'Blimey, sounds like a new pair of trotters are the least of your worries,' Francis said, offering Winston his hand. Winston shook it. 'You already know who that is,' Francis said, tilting towards Micky, 'my name's Francis.'

'Pleased to meet you both,' Winston said. Micky nodded his acquaintance.

'Give him a go on Beryl,' Francis suggested.

A little reluctantly, Micky demonstrated how she worked and then handed Beryl over. 'Be careful with her,' he said, 'she's new. We were just testing her out on the window.'

'Don't go for blue or red,' Francis instructed, standing back. Winston fired.

There was an unremarkable chink as the peg spring found its mark on the glass. Nothing shattered, nothing broke. Winston tried to look impressed. He gave Beryl the respect of a further examination, and then passed her back to Micky. 'If you want to take it out, we'd probably do better with a grenade,' he said. Micky and Francis watched him. He plodded over to the bushes and then along the hedge-line, searching. 'Got one!' he announced, dusting off his knees. He came back, brandishing a rock. Gradually, he lumbered into a run, pretending to pull the pin out of his imaginary grenade with his gritted teeth. 'TAKE COVER!' he shouted, giving the order right before he hurled it in a high loop.

For a split second it appeared he might have overdone it, like the rock might clear the church roof... but then, at the last moment, it arched below the guttering and crashed through the stained-glass, taking an entire cherub with it.

The catastrophe was breath-taking; a cacophony of forbidden music, delightful to the three impressionable young children listening through their open mouths. They stood awestruck as shards of coloured glass fell from the heavens in hundreds and thousands, stabbing into the earth.

The long noise was like a blast from the top end of an organ – it went on, unrelenting, until the entire top section of the window had disintegrated and become what now looked like a few jagged teeth clinging onto a stony gum.

Francis, Micky and Winston, burst into excited laughter and ran. They skipped through the church yard in hysterics, their feet slinging up stones and reprimanding the holy ground. Micky leaped onto Winston's back and hitched a ride, whooping as they rounded the corner.

'Least you know you can count on us to keep our mouths shut,' Francis said, slinging an arm around Winston's shoulder once Micky had fallen off.

'Oi,' Micky jumped ahead and rounded on the others. 'Let's make a vow,' he said, holding his hand out flat in front of him. 'Stronger than blood-brothers ... let's swear right now, that no matter what happens, we will never ever tell on each other.'

'I'm in,' Francis said, and slapped his palm down on top of Micky's. They stopped moving, eyes on Winston. 'Well?'

Winston regarded the pair of them, back and forth, his thick hand squeezing both of theirs, 'I swear to God,' he said, and then grinned.

TEDDY BOYS

2004

For the first time since ... well, she couldn't remember when ... Deborah Coles took a shower with the door open. Liberated, toes curling into the bathroom mat, she peeled the shower cap off her head and checked her hair was still dry. The plughole gurgled. Naked, hopping on the balls of her feet, she made it across the hall and into her bedroom in three moves.

Prince – *could you be the most beautiful girl in the world* – was playing low on the radio. The double bed was covered with clothes, dresses – and a pair of black, can't-go-wrong heels that she'd already definitely decided on. Deborah glanced at the clock on the bedside table; it was only lunchtime, Saturday afternoon, she had hours before she needed to leave. But still, that didn't stop the butterflies in her tummy from bumping into one another.

The full-length mirrored doors on the wardrobe, returned her to herself in full living colour. She stared, a childlike expression of exploration furrowing her brow. What the reflection showed was a pretty lady in her thirties, still fairly trim, whose body showed only the natural scars of motherhood. She bounced up and down on the spot, cupping her buttocks, thumbs crossing her stretch marks. *Tiger stripes*...she thought, reminiscing on the pet name Charlie had used when soothing her skin. Her diet wasn't working

– not well enough. She pinched at the layer of chub beneath her bellybutton; the idea that someone – James – might potentially see her naked, was suddenly overwhelming.

That probably won't happen, Deborah thought, focusing on the dainty strip of hair she had left between her legs. *So why did you bother with that, then?* She asked herself, knowing full well what the answer was. She smiled; because a good ten of the twenty minutes she'd just idled in the shower, had been spent deliberating on whether or not to shave it all off. Call it old-fashioned, but a grown woman, one who'd once upon a time given birth, shaving her bits bald to give it a fresh, pre-pubescent appeal, somehow didn't feel right... even if it did look tidy.

The song on the radio had changed; Mariah Carey was now croaking out, *after tonight*.

The funny things you remember, Deborah thought, catching eyes with one of the picture frames on top of the dresser behind her. Her younger self was watching her from inside a shabby-chic window, sun-drunk with arms thrown ecstatically around Charlie's neck. It had been taken before Lewis was born, on holiday in Crete – literally a lifetime ago. Looking at it now, Deborah couldn't be sure that the girl in that picture would even recognise the naked mother standing and staring at her. Or worse, understand what she was doing. She must have looked at that photograph almost every day for sixteen odd years, but only now did it make her uncomfortable. Only now could she see the haunted, we-never-thought-this-could-happen-to-us expression on the faces; it was the same gullible, happy-go-lucky expressions you saw in those carefully selected photographs the families of missing girls offer to the press. Only now, in this naked instant, did she realise that the people in the picture were dead – her as well, a ghost. Without even knowing it, she too had become a memory of a memory.

The radio rolled another one.

Deborah turned, unhooked her kaftan from the back of the bedroom door, draped it over her, and then sat down on the edge of the bed. Absently, she picked up the underwear set she had bought herself yesterday and popped the tags. She passed it through her hands, black and lacy, and then held it up so the light from the window could sift through it. It now reminded her of a veil – funeral wear, to be worn as a memorial to her deceased former self, the girl who, once upon a time, had lived and loved and not had to pluck up the courage just to try on a dress.

'Until death do us part,' she said aloud, remembering what she'd read about moments like these. The book was still open, spread-eagled on the bedside table, as wide as a pair of promiscuous legs, Deborah's wedding band resting on the text. She'd completed the exercise: last night, for the first time since she'd been married, she removed her ring before bed. The book, *Move on Without Forgetting*, had a whole chapter devoted to the drawbacks of a widow continually wearing her ring. It could become a burden, a reminder of the lost life you were still living. Removing it – when you felt ready – was in itself a ritual. It was not only a statement of intent and a catalyst for pushing on with your own life, but also the beginning of a whole new healing process. *Until death do us part*, that was the vow, those were the rules; they were age-old and black and white, gospel.

Deborah sat there, feeling a little bit like a teenage girl about to *do it* for the first time, stomach equal parts excitement and fear. She didn't know what she thought, or what she wanted, only that she needed to at least go out with him to find out how she felt. Trying not to think about it, she examined the green dress on the top of the clothes pile, and wondered. When the telephone rang in the hallway, it came as a relief. She knew before she stood up that it would be Mara. She rushed, looking straight ahead and gliding out of the room, this time avoiding all eye contact with herself.

The motorway services rumbled on in the background: the unremitting murmur of arcade machines and people in transit, bleating and going in circles, anti-clockwise like the drying watermarks on the food court tables.

'What happened to Winston, then?' Lewis asked, speaking through a mouthful of chips, 'did he ever manage to get himself a new pair of shoes?' He leaned forward and excavated another piece of breaded chicken from the red and white KFC bucket he and his grandfather were sharing.

Watching him, Francis chuckled at the youthful attention to detail. 'If I remember rightly, I think Micky wound up swiping a pair from his older brother and giving them to him.' Lewis nodded, satisfied with stuffing his face; for the moment at least, the concept of having to go without was seemingly lost on a generation. 'Mind you,' Francis said, 'it didn't stay like that forever. By the time we was your age, we were a dandy little lot: young Teds in the making.'

Lewis sniggered, peering up from his chicken leg. 'Teds... what are Teds?'

'Teddy Boys,' Francis clarified. 'In the fifties, that's all anyone wanted to be. They were the teenage tearaways of the day – a bit like you lot in them hooded tracksuits, except with a lot more style.' Francis smiled, taking a swig of Pepsi and wincing at the taste. 'The older lot, the chaps who had jobs or could earn themselves a few bob, were well turned out. They used to wear the old drape jackets with the velvet lapels – nice and smart – with their hair slicked back on the sides and combed up in a quiff, like Elvis.'

Lewis tipped his head in recognition, even though he was only half certain of what Elvis actually looked like. For some reason, his mind was only showing him a vision of John Travolta wearing a leather jacket and singing in that film that his mum liked, *Grease*.

'The first time I ever encountered them up close, I was about thirteen or fourteen,' Francis reminisced. 'Micky's older brother, Marge – they called him that 'cause he used to do his hair with margarine when he'd run out of Brylcreem – turned up at our school with a few of his pals. He was a good five or six years older than us; he'd been expelled before we even started. They all had sideburns down to 'ere,' Francis ran a finger across his cheek to make a razor line. 'I can remember him walking past me and Winston; he didn't say anything to us, just marched straight towards the building.

'What had happened was, the day before, our geography teacher had lobbed a chalk eraser at Micky. It hit him square in the mouth and busted his jaw. To be honest,' Francis said, 'he probably deserved it ... either way, Micky's mum sent Marge down to the school to sort it out. I remember the PE teacher standing in front of the doors, trying to puff out his chest, but Marge just shoved him out of the way and kept going.' Lewis had stopped eating; rapt, he watched his grandfather, his eyes flickering like an old roll of film. 'You can imagine what we were all doing in the playground,' Francis said, twinkling. 'But it didn't even take five minutes. Marge came strutting back out as if he'd just popped by to drop off a letter of complaint or something. He wasn't even rushing. He walked over to the gate, gave me and Winston a little nod, and then disappeared onto the street to go about his business.'

'What had he done though?' Lewis said.

'Well, once we'd seen them up the road,' Francis said, 'we looked back up at the classroom window. The blinds were rolled all the way up and our geography teacher was standing there trying to hold his cheek together, blood pissing out all over his shirt ... then he fainted.' Francis paused, waiting, allowing the story room to breathe. 'Later on we found out what had happened: Marge had basically bowled straight into the classroom, dragged the geezer up from his desk, and then striped him all the way down one side of his face with a cut throat razor. He didn't say a word.'

Amazed, Lewis spat out a little giggle, more shocked than amused.

Francis picked at the last few chips in the bottom of the bucket. 'Naturally, after we saw that, we were all sold,' he said. 'From then on, every single kid I knew wanted to be a Teddy Boy.'

Refuelled and back on the road, the Daimler drove on into a watercolour, the bristled tree lines beside the motorway carving up the meadows and painting in the sky with the dirty water from the brush pot. To look at the countryside, the world suddenly didn't feel so modern.

'I reckon I'd have made a decent Ted,' Lewis said, pretending to pop his collar.

'They were good times to be alive,' Francis said. He was enjoying himself, sticking to the inside lane, talking with one hand and holding the wheel with the other. 'We used to pinch motors so we could drive to dancehalls and pick up girls. Rock n' roll was new. There were no nightclubs; if people wanted to dance they had to go to one of the big ballrooms and listen to a live band. '

'Did you dance?' Lewis asked, surprised. His face parted into a piss-taker's grin.

Francis cracked a smile of his own. 'Not really,' he said, 'we mainly stood around smoking cigarettes and waiting for it to kick off. Most nights ended in a tear up; what used to happen was gangs of Teds from other parts of London would travel over to a different manor looking for a ruck. Remember, this wasn't long after the war; people were a little bit more desensitised to violence. The majority went tooled up with something or other – there were a lot of knives about.' Francis shook his head, recalling something. 'I had a friend, Davey Thompson, who used to get his girlfriend to sew razor blades into the lapels of his jackets so no one could grab on to him while he was fighting.'

'Did you carry a knife?'

'Not often,' Francis said. 'I've never really been one for knives if I could help it –' He broke off, watching the road so he could overtake a lorry, passing and then pulling back into the slow lane. 'In my experience,' he said, being honest rather than boastful, 'blokes who take to stabbing people ain't never much good with their knuckles. I could always hold my hands up, so I never really had much use for one.' He made sure to meet Lewis's eyes before he continued. 'Take it from me: if you've got a problem with another lad and the option is there to have a knuckle with him and leave it there, do so. You'll find yourself in a lot less trouble that way. It's much easier than you think to do someone a mischief with one of them things – it takes more skill to core an apple properly than it does to kill someone once you start sticking things into 'em.' He raised his finger to underline his point. 'There are a lot of blokes doing life for killing someone without meaning to.'

Listening, Lewis looked at his grandfather – a wise old owl, the lines on his face seeming to validate the advice. It was weird; Lewis could see his father in there – a twinkle in his eye – a double, hidden somewhere inside those features. And the voice, steady and deep with perfect elocution, the working class pallet effortlessly dropping the T's and abandoning good grammar. It was hard to imagine that there was ever a time before this; that this man could ever have been a boy, and then a teenager. It was absurd that he was once out of control, young and in a hurry, stupid and reckless, unknowing, going full speed ahead in a stolen car too drunk to use the pedals or even find the break.

'Besides,' Francis added, 'back then they were still hanging people for murders. Just imagine what a Toby you'd feel if they swung you from a rope for killing someone by accident.' He snorted, mocking.

'No way!' Lewis exclaimed, getting an image of a man being dragged through a village and strung up on wooden gallows. 'Were you alive when they executed people?'

Francis nodded. 'Oh yeah,' he said, severely. 'If you got found guilty and the old judge reached for his black hat before he passed your sentence, that was your lot mate.' He cleared his throat dramatically, straightened up in his seat and poked out his nose. 'In committing this heinous crime,' he said, adopting the well-spoken accent of a judge, 'you have left me no choice. You shall be hung by the neck until you be dead.'

Lewis tittered, adding to the performance by wrapping his hands around his throat and pretending to choke.

'They had a death cell down the road from us, at Wandsworth nick,' Francis said. He flashed his attention at the road and then back again. 'I don't suppose you've ever heard of a fella called Derek Bentley, have you?'

'No, who is he?'

'He was a lad they hung there for shooting a copper,' Francis said. 'It's a famous case because he was innocent; I believe, years later, they may have made a film about it. It happened in 1953 though; I remember because I'd just turned sixteen.'

Lewis frowned, 'And what, he didn't do it?'

'Nah, some younger kid who was with him did it, but they dropped him for it because he was older,' Francis thought about it for a second. 'I'm sure he was about nineteen. They got caught breaking into a warehouse and tried to hide on the roof, but when the police climbed up to bring 'em down, this youngster pulls out a gun and starts firing. God only knows why – the little twit probably wasn't trying to hit anyone, but he did, and the boy Bentley got strung up for it.'

'Didn't they do anything to the younger one?'

'He done a bit of bird and came out, I think,' Francis answered. 'It was a huge injustice. It's one of the reasons they got rid of the hanging in the end. On the day, people were outside the prison protesting and all that. We all went up there to join in – we didn't know him or nothing, but we lived local and he was only a couple of years older than we were at the time.' He indicated and overtook another lorry, this one with a foreign football scarf flapping from its window. 'It's funny,' Francis said, thoughtful, reliving the events of that day, 'the Government went through with it because they wanted it to be a deterrent for all the other young scallywags,' he tipped Lewis a smile, 'but as *you* know only too well, teenage boys are idiots.' Lewis laughed, fully accepting the charge. 'It's like nothing seems to stick between the ears. Me, Micky and Winston were all there going on about how unfair it was and how we couldn't think of anything worse than ending up like the poor bastard. But once they'd hung him and the bloke came out with the notice and pinned it to the gates, we were straight off for something to eat in the café. By that afternoon we'd forgotten all about it; and, as soon as it got dark, we were straight out and back to our nonsense.

Barley Sugar

MICKY

1953

The sash window dropped a few inches lower, wheels squealing against the runners. Francis stopped, stock-statue-still, petrified somebody would wake up. He waited, heartbeat scattering through his chest and all the way to his ends. 'Shhhh, you clumsy bastard!' he mouthed – more of a mime than a whisper.

Winston's broad head and shoulders disappeared over the downstairs windowsill – one of his trailing feet taking an ornamental ballerina with him into the flowerbed outside. He scrambled to his feet, trampling the shrubs, and poked his arms back through the gap below the window frame so he could receive the goods. Francis stayed where he was, cautious, his muted breath showing in a frozen plume.

It was gone midnight and pitch dark, the half-moon hiding above Wimbledon Common only illuminating the first few feet of floor inside the drawing room window. Beyond that it was a blackout, an unfamiliar catalogue of errors – tables, chairs, and china trinkets which might as well have been alarm bells – waiting to give him away the second he put a foot wrong. He took a single, lonely step towards the window, the wooden box which surrounded the record player he was holding pushing splinters through his woollen gloves. The cold air blowing in from outside cleaned his brow; January was already a good couple of coats colder than Christmas had been, but still, now he was sweating, he wondered why the fuck he was wearing this jacket, the turned up collar irritating his neck.

Typically, this escapade had been Micky's idea – the hanging earlier in the day doing nothing much to dampen his spirits. And why would it? It wasn't as if such a misfortune would, or could ever befall *him* or his kin. 'Oi, I'm saying it now so we can all agree,' he'd said, walking away from the prison sandwiched between Francis and Winston – three teenage Teddy Boys all in a row – still a whole head shorter than the others, but as always, twice as loud. 'If they've ever got *me* in there with a rope around *my* neck, one of you two has got to come in and get me –' He held two fingers up in the shape of a pistol so they were all clear. 'And I'll do the same if it's the other way round, yeah?' And that had been that, a dandelion and burdock solution to the worst case scenario: simple as science. 'So if I can pinch us a motor, are we still on for that bit of work tonight?' That had been his next question, followed by him shooting off shortly afterwards, and then returning come nightfall behind the wheel of a green Morris Minor van with framed wooden panelling on its rear end.

'That's the one,' he'd said, when, a couple of hours later they'd pulled up on Wimbledon Parkside, 'rich pickings!' The house – *this* house – was set back from the road by a short driveway behind large barbed gates. 'As long as we can get the gates open, it's perfect.' Francis and Winston had then watched from the car as Micky had jumped out, crept across the road by himself, and then silently unhooked the latch on the gate, all the time flashing his torch towards the huge automobile sleeping soundly on the drive. Silently, the gates had opened like a pair of giant moth's wings. The torch had gone out … then Micky had scampered back across the road and waited to see if an upstairs light had come on. 'That's an omen,' he said, getting back into the Morris without closing the door. 'Who's going in, then?' he'd asked, facing two blank expressions. 'We'll flip a coin. It's only a two-man job; one of us needs to stay with the car and keep watch – and needs to move it down the road a bit, otherwise if a copper turns up it will give the whole game away.'

And as luck would have it, Micky Meehan had won the toss.

Francis took another step and handed the record player to Winston. Together, they managed to shimmy the thing over the window ledge, Francis having to lift the frame a little, forcing the steel runners to play their rousing high note once again. Winston – at the moment only a set of dim features and a pair of gloved hands – put the box down beneath his feet and beckoned for the rest. Half turning, about to reach out and lift the bag they'd just filled with whatever was shiny, Francis paused – ears open to the darkness beyond his nose.

There was movement upstairs, minuscule, the creak and peek of a door handle bending just enough to free the latch. Francis looked at Winston, then back into the cavernous space he was standing in. A floorboard yawned as if the roof may cave in. He made the decision, on impulse, frothy blood rushing up from his loins and thumping in his temples. He grabbed a hold of the bulging potato-sack, swung it up over his thigh, and shoved it under the window. It clattered and banged, drooping over the windowsill, half in and half out – they might as well have stuffed a brass band into the sack for all the chance they had of getting it out without making any noise. Winston dragged it, two fisted, until it came away and he staggered, balancing the bulk on his lap. Francis followed it head-first, bumping the window up with his lower-back as he wriggled out crawling on his hands until his legs fell free.

From down on the soil, Francis and Winston both looked up at the house: there were no lights on, by all appearances it was still dead to the world.

'Where the fuck is Micky?' Francis hissed, lifting his head to look at the road. He was supposed to be there, ready, pulled up just beyond the gates with the motor running and the doors open. 'I can't see him!'

Directly above their heads, like a distress signal sent up to mark their position, one of the bedroom lights came on.

'Shit!' Winston was rubbernecking, trying to spot any sign of Morris. 'What's the little prick fucking doing?'

'We can't stay here with all this,' Francis said, trying to move with the record player on his hands and knees. 'We'll have to go on foot.'

Another bedroom light flicked on … then another: the entire top floor of the house was now burning orange. 'WHO'S DOWN THERE?' the voice was male, calling out from some unseen vantage point. It came again, 'WHAT DO YOU THINK YOU'RE DOING?'

Francis and Winston slithered across the lawn, crawling, grovelling and pleading not to be seen. The potato-sack clanged mercilessly beside them. Francis let go of the record player so he could move faster. 'Just leave it all behind,' he spat. 'We're as good as fucked anyway.'

Over their escaping shoulders, inside the hallway of the house, a light suddenly shone a semi-circle of decorated light through the patterned glass in the front door. It flooded the grass around them …

More cries…

And then … as if struck by a lightning bolt heaven-sent by a God of thunder – headlights, wipers, and horn all working at once – the huge car dozing in the driveway erupted and roared into life.

The passenger side door flew open, Micky sprawling across both front seats to hold it. 'Why you rolling around down there like a couple of poofs?' he shouted over the engine. 'Hop in!'

Francis scrabbled towards the car, yanked open the back door and then launched himself in. Winston leapt up, tossed the sack in on top of him, and then bundled on to the back seat, stolen silverware filling up the foot-wells. Micky slammed his foot down on the accelerator and the car jerked backwards, screeching in reverse, the passenger door flapping open like a broken wing as it bumped backwards out of the drive and onto the road. The gearbox crunched, Micky on the edge of his seat palming the too-big steering-wheel, Francis and Winston bouncing around in the back. The vehicle bucked forwards, revving, and then powered away – its lawful owner left on his arse calling out after it.

'We thought you'd pissed off and left us,' Francis snapped, struggling to shift Winston's weight.

Micky glanced at the pile of limbs tussling about in the rear-view mirror. 'Don't be stupid.'

'Why the fuck didn't you tell us what you was doing?'

Micky sneered, 'What did you want me to do, come and knock on the door?' Winston found something metal on the floor and flung it at him. Micky ducked. 'What's the matter with you two tarts?' he said, grinning over his seat. 'Ain't you seen what we're driving: this is a bloody Roller!'

The big Rolls Royce was motoring – *the spirit of ecstasy* – the winged goddess above the grill being rammed bare-breasted into the wind. Micky wrestled with the weight of the bonnet to keep her centred, eyes bulging, the bottomless stream of tarmac gulping under the front wheels. He looked deranged, transfixed by the sleepy drunk tunnels of light shining on the empty road. His quiff had collapsed; it was now a strung out string of greasy curls hanging down over his forehead, turned upside down by his dip beneath the dashboard to rub the wires together. The pedals vibrated, adrenaline needles pricking the skin between his toes and administering their dose.

Micky polished the inside of the windscreen, 'Stop breathing so hard, I can hardly see where I'm going.'

Francis and Winston were flopped on the backseat, sweat gluing their clothes to their backs. Winston was muttering something about his jeans being covered in mud – Micky laughed at his own joke, but Francis wasn't listening.

Pawing at the leather, he sat forward and stuck his head between the two front seats to get his bearings. He strained, trying to map out the darkness beyond the glare of the headlights. Up ahead the trees were thinning out and the street lamps starting again, the damp mist blowing off the common giving them a steamy glow. He recognised where they were: if they continued straight, Tibbett's corner would be coming up in front of them. The quickest way home from there was to go right on the roundabout and down West Hill – the only problem being, if they chanced going that way, at the bottom they would have to pass Wandsworth police station. And the way Francis saw it, people who could afford solid silver milk jugs and tea-strainers would almost certainly have a telephone ... and even if they didn't, one of their neighbours would. Either way, the police had more than likely already been made aware that there was a Rolls Royce, rattling with stolen goods and burglars, rolling around somewhere near here.

'Don't worry, *Winifred*,' Micky was saying, a loony, toad-like grin wrapping his mouth, 'with all the lolly we're about to make off this little lot, you'll be able to get yourself some new clobber. Smart stuff, like what Marge and them wear –'

'What way are you going?' Francis demanded, hitting Micky's arm to get his attention. 'The second the law see us in *this*, we've had it.'

Micky didn't respond; he just glinted, as if Francis was making a fuss about nothing. His fingers flexed on the steering-wheel, in their element, in his mind's eye he was starring in a chase scene from a James Cagney flick and playing the part to perfection. *Micky Meehan*, already fully grown at sixteen with more bollocks than sense. By the look on his face, you would think they were doing nothing more serious than trolleying down a dusty hillside in an old apple crate with pram wheels on the sides.

Micky had no choice; it was either slow down for the roundabout, or wind up crash-landed on the island. He eased off, treading on the breaks several times and losing the back end in a fishtail. Francis and Winston rocked forwards, holding on to whatever was handy to keep their balance, swaying under the sudden change of speed. They steadied, wobbled, and were then pinned by gravity and chucked against the back seat as Micky unexpectedly stamped on the accelerator again.

The whole car veered.

'Copper!' Micky shouted, heaving the wheel, left hand down. The Rolls made a rubbery turn, leaning all of its weight onto one side – every single piece of precious metal – inside the sack and out – clanged against the doors. It swerved and then straightened up ... moaning ... like a great whale adjusting its course. Francis lifted his head and just caught a glimpse of some red tail lights before they bent out of view on the roundabout.

'They're coming,' Francis said, peering out the back. The other car had gone full circle around the roundabout and was now following them.

'It's a good fucking job I can smell the bastards, ain't it?' Micky said. 'My nose was bred for it.' Foot landed hard on the pedal, he squinted at his mirror laughing, 'Sod 'em, anyway, they'll never catch us in this.'

Winston popped up beside Francis and watched out of the back window in silence. For half a minute, the beady little headlights of the car behind were on them, finding them out and identifying their faces. The speedometer was at full tilt. Micky let out a howl of excitement and pounded on the wheel, willing the beast to carry them to safety. The Roller bellowed back, the pride of British engineering, each warhorse beneath the bonnet railing the cry for one final charge. A cemetery shot past on their left hand side ... then a factory – ghostly pale – the letters K.L.G standing out on the wall. When Francis looked again, their pursuers were running out of steam; the headlights were reducing, shrinking away, pulling back and becoming UFOs. A second later they were just blinkers on the horizon ...and then, they slipped off the edge of the earth and were gone.

'I told you,' Micky jeered, loosening the valve on his concentration, 'they had no chance.' He seized the moment and pogoed on the breaks, this time stronger armed, holding her steady and turning off the road, into an unlit parking area. Francis and Winston clung on and stayed upright. Gravel popped and crunched under the tyres, the Rolls skidding in a crest and coming to a juddering stop. The three of them ducked down, Micky yanking at the wires underneath the steering-wheel.

Instantly, the engine died alongside the lights.

Hidden in automotive luxury, Francis, Micky and Winston, waited, gobs closed. The fog was thicker here, the open expanse of playing fields allowing it to form a curtain.

Micky had done well to even spot this place; the entrance was no more than a missing section of the fence. From what they could see, it was a Rugby club; two small brick buildings, one which faced the playing fields, and another outbuilding with barn doors, which probably housed some equipment. There was a car parked outside, big and black – and on their second peek, they noticed a dim light on in one of the clubhouse windows.

The shed smelt musky – old mud and rusty flagpoles. A single strand of virgin silk, easily broken, hung in a bow from the corner of a spidery window, glistening and feeling every gust like a long licked finger.

Connie Whitaker now had a wet dress – the stack of tackle pads Oliver had first laid her down on had been holding mouldy water. They'd moved, together, Oliver taking her weight on his arms until her backside had found a new groove in a net of rugby balls. She felt another tug on her ponytail; the ribbon in her hair was tangled on something. She wriggled, trying to slow the kissing. The surface shifted beneath them, turning her head, him pressing harder, his tongue circulating the taste of beer.

She was dressed for a party, sweet sixteen, peppermint frills kicking out above the ankle. But tonight wasn't like last time; it was cold for one thing, perhaps that's why he hadn't bothered with her buttons. She was disappointed; there was no soft mouthing on her neck, no tingles starting to ring into beats down below, or the excited, bare feeling of lying there with no top on while he looked at her. It was chilly and dark. He'd given up on her chest, left it inside her dress and contented himself – squeezing hard enough to leave marks – with just a few cloth-covered handfuls. He just wanted to rub between her legs, his thick pink palm working at the front of her knickers, toiling endlessly, snatching at the hairs and hurting her.

She wriggled again, wondering what Trudy was doing. Trudy, whose idea *this* as well as *that* had been; Trudy, whose brother played on the same team and who had introduced Connie to Oliver a month ago; and Trudy, who tonight had arranged for her father to pick them both up an hour later than everybody else so they could stay behind and help Mrs Harris clean up the party. Trudy Marchbank, who Connie's real best friend, Marcia had told her not to knock about with.

Connie flinched. She closed her legs tight on his hand and nudged him. 'Let me,' she said, her voice chattering. It was uncomfortable like this, heavy; what with him being two years older and drunk. He gazed at her stupidly while she freed her hair and rolled out from under him. He flopped over onto his back, almost going over and having to slap the floor to stay on the mountain. She smiled without looking at him. He grunted, unable to see her, and sucked his stomach in so she could slide her hand down the front of his trousers. *It* was there straight away, stiff and nervous, raising the elastic of his underpants. She took it in her hand. Oliver breathed, tucking his face away and sucking in the perfume on the nape of her neck. She liked the sound of him there, shivering while she examined him, his thingamajig standing to attention. Her tingles started, pinging up her arm in numb hardness each time his foreskin ran over the bump of his helmet. He ground his hips to prompt her, keeping it going, lifting, the mucky fumbling under her skirt forgotten for the time being. He groaned, muffled, pretend. It doesn't take long, Trudy had told her. The throbbing had already started, a low pulse coming to the sweaty gaps between her fingers. It was beating on its own, as if it were his heart or something. Her wrist ached, persevering, his piece alive inside the swallows of her grip. She moved faster, restricted by fabric, until he gasped – out through his nose, in through his mouth. And then the warmth came, pumping in sticky hiccups, a thick mixture of her hand and him.

She stopped, him holding her still without looking, panting, embarrassed by the way he was writhing. Speechless, she let go, slipping her hand out politely.

Unsure of what girls were supposed to say, Connie turned away from him, staring up at the moonlit frost in their dark place to give him some privacy. He was fidgeting with himself behind her – when the sound of car tyres crunching in the gravel outside startled her. 'I'd better go,' she said, keeping her back to him, listening. 'That's probably Trudy's dad.'

Francis exhaled – a sigh of relief – his breath fogging up the car's rear window. 'It ain't a copper,' he whispered.

The three of them watched, a porthole evaporating on the glass, as the headlights which they could've sworn had been following them, slowed down, made the same turn into the car park, but then trundled harmlessly to a stop outside the clubhouse, the bespectacled driver not paying them a blind bit of notice.

'So much for your bleedin' breeding,' Winston mocked, flicking Micky's ear over the seat. 'Your sense of smell is shit, mate.'

'Fuck off!' Micky slapped Winston's hand away. 'I weren't wrong about it tailing us though, was I? What's he doing coming here for?'

'By the look of it,' Francis replied, 'he's picking someone up –'

Waving her goodbyes at the clubhouse door, a teenage girl in a party frock skipped over to the driver side window, bent over, and started speaking to him. 'She shouldn't be long; she's just helping carry some of the rubbish bags.' She stood back to look around, and then cupped her hand to the side of her mouth and called out, 'CONNIE...?'

There was a chinking of beer bottles – and then, from somewhere behind the small outbuilding, a second girl appeared into the glamour of the headlights. 'Sorry,' she cooed, dusting off her palms and getting into the back of the car beside her friend. From the shadows, the shape of a stocky lad stuck out a hand and bid them a fond farewell. The car reversed, chugging, its little pipe puffing out grandfatherly smoke as it turned about face and pulled away – those headlights finally leaving them alone with the moon.

'Thank fuck for that,' Francis said, sitting up straight.

Head lolling back on the driver's seat, Micky sniggered.

Winston kept his eyes on the figure in the shadows. Once the other car had left, the lad had hitched up his trousers and scraped a lazy path back towards the clubhouse. He'd struck a match, the tiny ball of fire floating in front of his face, glowing under his nose just long enough to light his cigarette and expose his features for a second. 'Oi,' Winston hushed, 'ain't that, Oliver Harris?'

Francis and Micky both twisted around in silence.

In Wandsworth, the name Harris had blood on it. During the summer, a local lad – Davey Thompson – had been worked over at the fairground by a gang of Teds from Kingston. Oliver Harris had kicked him while he was down, and then smashed a broken bottle into Davey's face so many times that he'd ground the bottles neck down to a nub. It had taken eighty-eight stitches to put what was left of the left side of Davey's face back together again, the scars branching out from his eye like tributary roads on a map.

'If it is, he don't look like I remember,' Francis said. The one and only time Francis had seen Oliver Harris, he'd had a ducks arse haircut and a drape on; the smoker in the shadows had a dry flop of fringe and was wearing some sort of mummies-boy blazer with a club crest sewn on the breast pocket. 'That bloke looks like a college boy.'

'Nah ... it's him,' Winston said. 'He's just dressed up for his rugby club. I recognise his face.'

The figure outside wasn't much more than a silhouette holding a smouldering orb.

Convinced, Micky sneered. 'Fucking ponce! He looks like his mother cuts the crusts of his sandwiches...' He eyed Francis and Winston over the seat, '...Shall we jump out and do him?'

'Are you joking?' Francis said.

Micky stared at him, blank. 'Why not? He's asking for it, standing there all by himself.'

Francis shook his head in disbelief, 'What are you on about?' he said, pinching his temples. 'We've got all *this* wrapped round us, Micky –' He shuffled his feet to disrupt some of the cutlery which was washing around under the back seat. 'We just saw that there're other people inside. For fuck's sake, don't draw any more attention to us – or are you trying to get us caught?'

Micky looked sideways, Winston agreed with Francis. 'Alright, alright ... if it means that much, you can both keep your bloody bras on,' he said, and then dipped his head beneath the steering-wheel to find the wires again, 'but I'm telling Marge that we saw him.'

Barley Sugar

CONNIE

'Of course I know him,' Francis's father said; speaking the way he always did, lathering the ears rather than spitting in them. He stopped what he was doing, looking at his son in the mirror, his straight razor balanced expertly over his fingers. 'The question is: why do you?'

Francis kept his head tilted forward, scrutinizing the tufts of snipped hair on the floor around the barber's chair. 'I don't,' he answered. 'Mick's going to meet him this afternoon at a pub and he wants me to go with him.' The wireless tapped on in the background, keeping perfect time. Francis glanced out of the shop window.

His father smirked, waiting for his son's attention, watching him through his calm, non-fussed blue eyes – eyes which by their own admission could handle a lady way better than they ever could hold their drink. 'What is it that he's trying to get rid of?'

Francis smiled. 'How did you know?'

'Because, the only reason anyone goes to see Arthur Cox, is if they're trying to shift something they ain't supposed to have.' The blade started again, deftly scraping the bum fluff from the back of Francis's neck. Outside, the fresh morning continued to twirl the red and white barbers' pole. 'You know why they call him, *How's-ya-father-Arthur*, don't you?' Francis shook his head without moving. 'Because he likes to talk other men's wives into bed, give 'em one, and then pinch their jewellery off the dresser on his way out.'

Francis snorted. 'God's honest,' his father said, 'Now you tell me what type of man would do that? He's a lowlife, France; a *Tupney-Apney* thief. I wouldn't trust him as far as I could throw him. You tell young Micky that he'd do well to keep him at arm's length.'

The shop door squeaked behind them.

Francis's father glanced in the mirror, and then back down at his son, 'Remember what I said: *arm's length*,' he clipped Francis on the top of his ear with the flat edge of the razor, winked, and then turned to greet his next customer.

Encased in the same neat brown suit he'd been wearing the last time Micky had seen him, How's-ya-father-Arthur-Cox was sat at the table farthest from the pub door, studying the racing form and circling horses.

The Marquis Arms had the grotty atmosphere of chesty laughter; its few grey-faced punters keeping their distance, knocking back short glasses and giving long stares to the boys who'd turned up at their doorstep. West London might as well have been the other side of the world; no sooner had they crossed the line and gone inside, their rock 'n' roller hairstyles immediately felt out of fashion.

'Wotcha, Lads!' Arthur shouted. He was on his feet and waving them over, his pencil moustache dancing above his top lip. 'No need to be shy, c'mon in.' Used to being the odd one out, Winston went first and shook his hand. 'Sit down … sit down,' Arthur said, fussing, greeting them all one at a time. He looked at Francis. 'Tipple...?'

'No thanks,' Francis answered, sitting down beside Winston. 'Cheers, though.'

'Good for you,' Arthur sang, grinning. 'You show your sense: business should always be a sober affair.' He had already moved on; eyeing the duffle-bag in Micky's hand. 'Did you bring it all?' Micky nodded at him, taking in the scene before taking his seat. 'Right then...' Arthur said, lowering himself into his own chair, his voice becoming a promise. 'Harry's upstairs – now I've spoken to him already, so he knows that you're coming – but he's a very busy man so we've got to give it a few minutes before we can go up.' His eyes shifted around the table, going from Winston to Francis, and then pausing on Micky. 'Best thing is for me to have a quick look at what you've got, just so we know we ain't wasting his time, yeah?' Arthur reached under the table, took hold of one of the bag handles, and then stopped where he was, head turning towards the door.

There was singing outside.

It rang bells, ominous and unseen, throaty, like a battle cry cresting a verge full of hope and anger. 'Scots, wha hae wi Wallace bled...Scots, wham Bruce has aften led...welcome tae yer gory bed...or tae victory...' The pub doors gave way and for a moment the street, marching in the January cold, was visible again – and then they swung and slammed shut on the backs of two men.

'A Scotsman and an Irishman walk intae a pub,' one of them cawed in a guttural Glaswegian accent, 'and all the wee Englishmen inside try nae tae shit theyselves!' He wiped his feet, laughing – a thin man, slightly more than thirty, his features wired craggily around wild, black eyes. He strode towards the bar in a well-made suit, humming, his dark, slathered hair ploughed straight back from his forehead. The man who was with him – unmistakably the Irishman in the joke – looked rural: a big ginger head sitting atop a roll neck jumper.

The boys looked on, drinks for the two men appearing on the bar before they'd been summoned. Arthur had hunkered down, head low, as if he were a stray dog wanting to sip from a puddle without being seen. Instinctively, his back had gone up – one of his legs working underneath the table to sweep Micky's bag further out of sight. And then, he was spotted.

The Scotsman called across the room: 'Arthur! What the fuck are yer doing here?' He poked his big Irish friend in the chest, 'Roy, dae yer remember *How's-yer-father-Arthur?*' The Irishman glanced away without acknowledgment. 'I hope yer nae doing anything backward tae those wee boys, Arthur...' He settled his eyes on Micky, 'Listen laddie, if he touches yer between the legs before he pays yer, yer just come and tell me.' He showed his teeth, a loud cackle peeling the lining off his lungs.

Sniggers and coughs.

Micky frowned at Francis and Winston; apparently, Arthur wasn't going to say a dickiebird about it. The Scotsman gave it a sip, and then he turned away better amused by the barmaid.

'Who's that?' Micky asked, his tongue a lump in his cheek.

Arthur didn't answer right away – he stood up, sheepish,

and beckoned the boys to follow. He led them, Micky carrying his own bag, first toward the gents and then eventually through a side door which opened onto a dingy stairwell. The Scotsman paid no attention to them leaving, but only once the door had closed behind them did Arthur speak: 'That there is Bertie Crogan,' he whispered with warning. 'And the Irishman is Roy Easter. They're not worth the time for likes of you and me. Thank God, it's heavies like them who ensure there are still gentlemen at the top of our trade.' He flashed his eyebrows, gathering in the three disappointed expressions which were following him up the stairs. 'Some fights you can't win, boys. If you want to live a long life and marry a virgin, you'll have to learn to swallow your medicine and wipe your mouth.' His moustache curled. 'Trust me, your mothers will sleep all the easier if you can keep men like those on your right side.'

Upstairs, the wooden hill gave to a narrow hall. There were doors – bedrooms – on both sides and another case of stairs winding up to the third floor at the far end. Francis, Micky and Winston went in single file behind Arthur, the cracks in the doors revealing sparse rooms, mirrors, and elaborately dressed single beds with brass knobs. A toilet flushed somewhere ahead of them – a lock rattled – and out of a bathroom flounced a buxom lady in a silk robe. Her hair was in curlers, bleached blonde. She came towards them, the bulk of her breasts teetering loosely beneath her gown. She stopped to let Arthur squeeze past, tipping a cheeky smile at the three sets of teenage eyes groping at her.

'Could one of you lot be a darlin' and ask him to turn the

pipes on?' she said, pointing at the dimples her nipples were making in her gown. 'I'm bloomin' freezing!'

Micky grinned and elbowed Winston in the ribs.

'I'll see what I can do,' Arthur said, calling over his shoulder from the end of the hall.

The third floor was less a knocking shop, more a dusty warehouse. The smaller attic rooms up here were filled with boxes, merchandise, stockpiles which didn't allow much daylight to intrude through the tiny windows. The temperature had dropped. Micky was walking in the middle, the silver sound of the precious metals in his bag gently rocking at his knees.

They found the man they'd come to see, Harry Guest, in a poky little space under the rafters. He was sat behind an old writing desk, fat, wearing round glasses and a neck scarf – a pig in a blanket.

'These are the boys I told you about, Harry,' Arthur announced. 'They've brought along some trinkets so you can have a gander.'

Harry raised his head, his squint pupils considering the faces in front of him, lingering on Micky's bag. 'And who did you tell me they was?'

'This here is Micky Meehan's boy,' Arthur told him, touching Micky on the shoulder. 'Micky *junior*,' he added, grinning. 'And these are his two good friends.'

Disregarding the others, Harry looked directly at Micky, 'And these two *good* friends of yours,' he said, 'are they your proper pals? What I mean to say is, was they in it with you?'

'Yeah,' Micky answered.

'Where?'

'A house in Wimbledon.'

Harry nodded slowly, still only looking at Micky. 'What is it then, silver?'

'Yeah,' Micky said.

Harry sucked in a deep breath and pulled a face, 'Shame!' he said regretfully. 'I'll have a butcher's at it of course – out of good will for your father – but before I do, I will say, the price of silver ain't what it was, Micky.' In the background, Francis and Winston shared an expression. Harry cleared away some paperwork on the desk, 'Nonetheless,' he said, 'stick it up on here and I'll see if I can help you out with it.'

Micky obliged, setting the bag down on the desk and then standing back.

Harry took his time, plucking each piece out individually, checking the hallmark, and then giving it a rub with the end of his scarf. Each time, he glanced up as if he'd found a flaw, gave a little tut, and then put the thing to one side. Arthur didn't say a word; the boys watching, exchanging their opinions soundlessly with one another behind his back.

'Well...' Harry strained, setting the last piece, an engraved silver hip flask down on the edge of the desk. 'I have to say, it's not the best quality. It's mostly tat, I'm afraid.' He sighed, picking something up and putting it back down in one move. 'Some of it's even plated. But listen, what I can do – and only because I go back with your old man mind you – is give you one price for the job-lot.' He scratched his head. 'What do you say we call it...'

Harry broke off before he could finish; Bertie Crogan was

standing in the doorway.

'I thought this was supposed tae be a respectable daisy house Harry, a place for men. Not some dingy hole where fat penny pinchers fuck wi wee boys.' His voice barked off the walls. He pushed Winston and Francis out the way and strode into the room. Arthur dropped his eyes. 'Fuck off wi 'em Arthur, I wannae speak tae Harry,' He walked his fingers along the edge of the desk, stopping at the hip flask. He picked it up –

'That's mine!' Micky said, standing his ground.

'This is Micky Meehan's boy,' Harry said, attempting an introduction. 'These bits are all his; I was just about to see if we could help him out with a fair price.'

Bertie's eyes hadn't loosened for Micky's since the boy had dared open his mouth. He smiled, 'Give yer daddy my regards, won't yer?' he said, slipping the hip flask into his jacket pocket. 'What are yer giving me that look for, laddie? Didnae 'e ever tell yer aboot paying yer taxes?' Micky glared at him, gamely. Bertie's hand continued, sweeping in careful whisper underneath his jacket, around to the small of his back where gripped and unhinged, ever so gently, a large hunting knife from the waistband of his trousers – wooden handled, for skinning deer. He held it up, not threatening, just close enough for the cold light of day to wet the blade and leave a watermark across Micky's face. 'A valuable lesson,' he said, mocking, 'lose yer tongue or mind yer manners, boy.'

For a brief moment, until he saw the blade, Winston was thinking about it...

Bertie looked at him, mirthless enthusiasm knotted up between his eyes. 'If yer think this is big blackie, yer should see the size of my cock!' There was stiff pause – and then Bertie laughed. 'I'm only joking lads,' he roared, slipping the knife back into his trousers like it meant nothing, 'no need to stand there and mess yourselves, just be on yer way.'

Francis checked over his shoulder – the Irishman was leaning against the wall in the hallway. 'Not until we get our money,' Francis said.

Bertie started to turn towards him –

'Let me just sort 'em out what I owe 'em, and then they can get on their way,' Harry piped up, rushing, leaning over his desk and stuffing a fistful of notes and coin into Micky's hand.

'We ain't agreed a price,' Francis said.

'Well, it's that or nothing,' Harry said, flatly, imploring him to take it.

Francis stared at him.

The silence stuck a moment, and then fell wide open.

The lady in the skimpy gown popped her head around the door, already speaking before she got there: 'Harry, it's bloody brass monkeys down there. Can you turn on the flippin–' She rang off, losing most of her pennies and all of her sense at the sight of Bertie standing in front of her.

'Rosie!' he sang, sounding surprised to see her. 'I didnae think you'd be working. Have yer had all of stitches out already?' She gaped at him, horrified, her robe slacking open and showing her breasts. Cheeks budding, she backed up and then scurried away down the landing. 'This time, let's hope yer lovely landlord here has done as he was told tae, eh.' Bertie called out after her –

'Sod it! Let's just go,' Micky said, using the distraction to pocket the money. He turned on his heel to leave, span, and then tripped over his own feet and tumbled head-first into Bertie. He staggered, seizing handfuls of Crogan's clothes in order to keep himself up.

Bertie stamped on his foot and shoved him towards the door, 'Fuck off yer shaan gadgie bastard,' he lashed out, sending Micky reeling past the Irishman and into the hallway. He whipped round on Francis and Winston. 'You as well,' he screamed, 'before I cut off one of yer wee pricks.'

As soon as they'd hit the pavement and put some slabs between themselves and the pub, Micky burst out laughing. 'Fuck me,' he said, 'did you two see the fropney's on that bird?' He slowed down. 'I'm telling you now; if we'd made a bit more off all that stuff I would've been half tempted to bid her for a little snuggle.'

'What you on about?' Francis said, annoyed. 'We got *fucking* robbed.'

Micky slapped him on the back, 'Are you sure about that, son?' he said, a cocky grin chasing his eyes up the sides of his face. 'The only thing we had of any worth was that hip flask.'

'Exactly,' Francis said, 'and we let that Scottish prick take it off us.'

Micky stopped walking. 'Did we...?' he said, pulling the hip flask out of his inside pocket and holding it aloft.

'How the fuck did you –'

'When I tripped up,' Micky answered, victorious. 'I dipped

the soppy cunt's pocket for it.'

Winston cheered, grabbed him around the legs, and then scooped him up and over his shoulder as if they'd just won the F.A cup. 'I fucking love you sometimes, Meehan! You're out of your bleedin' mind!'

'Yeah, well,' Micky said, upside down and laughing, 'we can't go around letting people take the piss out of us can we? Otherwise, we might as well snip our bollocks now and start cutting out handkerchiefs for a living.'

Sooner or later, a Friday night rolls around.

Connie Whitaker was dancing – a slip of auburn hair following her as she twirled, the sunray pleats in her skirt kicking out above the ankle and making shadows over the polished wooden floor. Around her, shoulder to shoulder, boppers wearing their old man's jackets were going up and under with their girlfriends, swinging to the hoots and horns. The dancehall was huge, two tiers of brass bannisters and balconies rising to a fabric-coated ceiling above the big band on stage. The crooner tapped his toe while he warbled about finding the one that he loved, his velvet tones going straight over the heads of the lads loitering at the side of the stage.

The song ended to a round of applause. Connie and her friend – her *real* best friend, Marcia Blake – clapped their hands, laughing. Watching them, Oliver Harris glanced over, his square face and busted nose easier at a distance. Lip-sticking to her smile, Connie waved back civilly and then turned away.

As the band struck up the next one – their version of *Rocket '88'*– the lead singer shifting in his shoes and pointing out at the curly girlies on the dance-floor – a few miles away in Wandsworth, the back doors of Marge Meehan's black Vauxhall Velox slammed shut, the engine fired, and two whitewall tyres rolled off the curb.

The party was in Davey Thompson's honour, so it was only right that his green Bedford removals van be at the head of the convoy. Marge was second, Francis, Micky and Winston, joining in with the big boys, crammed together on his back seat, their new drape jackets creased at the elbows. Following on behind them, there were another two car loads of Marge's pals; a good turnout considering the call to arms hadn't come until late last night.

Unlike his younger brother, Marge's driving was unrushed, laidback, the prospect of violence coming effortlessly to him. He was a premonition, Micky in some more years; older, taller, and wider, his dirty blonde hair modelled into a perfect duck's arse at the back. 'All set, Chappies?' he inquired, passing his cigarette to Clarky on the passenger seat – a big bruiser with a kiss curl hanging over his forehead – and then directing his eyes into the back.

Micky stopped fidgeting with the bicycle chain he was holding on his lap, and answered: 'Ready to rock n' roll!'

Winston and Francis both nodded.

The cigarette came over the seat and then Marge went back to driving. Francis took it, puffed, and then passed it along. He watched the darkened world outside the window, aware for the first time of the knuckle duster in his trouser pocket – of its cold weight against his thigh. It was raining, shaving cuts appearing on the glass as Marge and Clarky rabbited, Micky chinked his chain, and the car wove its way towards Kingston.

When Marge pulled in to the dusty car park behind the train station, Davey Thompson was leaning against the side of his van waiting, pink scars troubling his face.

'Jesus-fucking-Ada,' Winston remarked, seeing the damage up close, 'they properly carved him up!'

Marge scoffed, teasing. 'Why don't you go over and see if he'd like to borrow some of that boot polish you use,' he said, 'that'll cover 'em up for him.'

Winston rolled his eyes, 'Piss off!'

'Yeah, piss off *Margery*,' Micky jumped in for his friend, 'otherwise I'll tell 'em about your –' He ducked, his elder brother making a playful grab to mess up his hair.

They all got out and stood, preening themselves in the wing mirrors, milling around until the other cars had parked up and their people had joined them. On the other side of the road the dancehall was lit up, sparkling, wearing a pearl necklace of white bulbs above her entrance. The idea was that they would trickle in in groups, four or five at a time, keeping their heads down, staying separated until everyone was inside and they could mob up. Davey and Marge were going in last.

Micky, Francis and Winston, went together along with Clarky and his kiss curl. They strutted, four in a line, Micky's chain looped around his waist and hidden under his jacket. They took in a deep breath of winter and held it, until the doors had opened up and they could feel the foyer carpet beneath their brothel creepers.

'I recognise that boy,' Marcia said dancing. She pointed her nose up at the brass railing a few feet above the dance floor. 'He lives round the corner from my nan's, that's Micky Meehan.'

Connie glanced over, 'What one?'

'The little one standing next to that coloured boy.' Marcia clarified, pointing. 'When I was little, he chased me all the way down his street with a bumble bee in a jam jar. He's nice though, funny.'

Connie's eyes trained in hopelessly on the tall Teddy Boy who was tailored into his drape, leaning on the bannister beside him. 'Do you know the other lads that he's with?'

Marcia widened her smile. 'Not yet,' she said, and then waved.

A tier above, Winston nudged Micky with his elbow. 'Oi! Why is that girl waving at us?'

Micky knocked back a swig from his hip flask. 'What girl?' he said, perusing the crowd below.

'That whisky's turning you fucking blind, mate,' Winton said. 'She's got her bleedin' hand up in the air – the one with the black hair and big tits.'

'Gotcha,' Micky said squinting. 'Yeah, I know her. She's from round our way somewhere. Our old dears grew up together.' He waved back. 'Shall we go down and say hello?'

Behind them, the doors swung open and another group of Wandsworth boys came through and blended in. Without waiting for a reply, Micky set off down the stairs and out onto the dance floor, Winston and Francis sticking to his heel, Clarky staying put and leaving them to it.

'Hello there!' Marcia sang the second Micky got within earshot. 'I haven't seen you in ages. How are you? And what are you doing *here*?'

Micky accepted her embrace, rocking slightly. 'Same as you,' he said, grinning. 'We came out for a little knees-up; my brother will be in here any minute.' He took another drink and then offered up the hip flask. 'Do any of you two girls fancy a nip?'

Marcia shook her head, 'Are you not going to introduce your friends?'

Shy, Connie glimpsed sideways at Francis – he was beautiful, electric blue. She smiled and looked away. She felt something birth and then all of a sudden die, remembering Oliver would be somewhere in the background, watching.

Led by the arm, Francis drifted, his mouth showing her half a smile. 'I spy Harris,' Winston whispered in his ear. Francis followed direction: on the far side of the stage, across the dance floor, Oliver Harris was a face amongst many who were glaring over at them. Behind him he could hear Micky giving the girls their names...

'That's Winston,' he was saying, 'And the handsome one your friend was just wetting herself over, that's my mate Francis.' He laughed. 'They're both good boys, they might even make good husbands, you never know...'

Francis turned and smiled at her, properly this time, trying to pretend he hadn't noticed her before, that he hadn't wanted to reach out and stroke the fallen ringlet of red hair away from her brow so that he could see her whole face. Nameless to him, Connie reciprocated, her lips a scarlet bow. She could hear herself inside her own head, explaining it to Oliver if he came over, *they're friends of Marcia's, I was only saying hello, being polite* –

'Oi!' Oliver's shout stepped over the music. He started across the wood towards them, promenading, wide shoulders underlining his jaw. He had back-up, bodies on either side of him. 'Those girls ain't up for grabs,' he warned – blowing smoke, doing Bogart. 'Fuck off and leave them alone.'

The band continued to strum, but in two blinks the dance floor had shed a skin. From up on the stage it must have looked like the river had burst its banks, every Tom, Dick and Harry, taking his girl by the hand and skating to the side lines. Another wave of Wandsworth boys entered through the main doors and into the rush.

'What's it to you?' Micky said, reacting, too drunk to care whether Marge and the others had made it inside yet, 'or was you hoping we'd ask *you* to dance instead?' He grinned, cocky, unable to contain himself, 'come to think of it, I heard a rumour that this place was likely to be full of poofs.'

'Just ignore him,' Marcia advised, 'he thinks he's Connie's

boyfriend –'

The lanky lad strutting next to Oliver glared at Micky. 'You mouthy little *cunt*,' he spat. 'You got a fucking front ain't cha: coming in with that *spook* and then gobbin' off?' He directed his attention to Winston, '*Blackie!* Maybe no one didn't tell you on the banana boat, but *our* women don't go in for monkeys.' Francis had worked out who this was immediately; Marge had mentioned him in the car: his name was Riley Baker. He was a few years older, Marge had said that the two of them had been to Borstal together when they were younger and that Baker was a *tool merchant* – if it was Harris who'd made that mess of Davey's face, then it was Riley Baker who'd handed him the broken bottle.

'*Your* women,' Winston mocked. 'Who the fuck are *you?*'

Riley Baker hitched, taken aback. '*Who am I?*' he said, his voice a lean husk. 'I'll show ya who the fuck I am. You sure you wanna know?'

Winston took off his jacket and handed it backwards. 'C'mon then, show me.'

Francis slipped his hand into his pocket and pushed his fingers through the holes in the knuckle duster. He looked over his shoulder – it was Marcia who'd taken Winston's jacket. Clarky and the rest of the Wandsworth boys were coming through the crowd without Davey, Marge was in front. A brief rift and the girls were gone – lost – enveloped by the advancing troops.

Oliver took hold of Riley's sleeve and slowed him down. Riley halted, leering at Marge as he came forward and stood beside Winston. He nodded his head in recognition, 'Since when have you been keeping a pet coon, Meehan?'

Marge laughed. 'This one 'ere is the least of your worries, mate,' he said, placing his hand on Winston's back. 'Somebody else has got a much bigger bone to pick with you than him.'

'Oh, yeah?'

'*Yeah*,' Marge answered. He slid his eyes over to Oliver, 'you an' all.'

Casually, Riley flicked the blade out of the handle he'd been holding hidden the whole time. 'And who might that be then?' he asked; the dark, jail-bird rings around his eyes whirling.

Micky whipped the chain off from around his waist and let it hang lose.

'You know full well who, Baker, you scrawny piece of shit,' Marge said. He was staring past Riley and his blade, through him, into the faces of the opposition. 'He'll be along any minute to jog your memories.'

Micky exchanged a look with Francis behind his brother's back – two men who were backing the same dog. The band trailed off, the lead singer calling for calm on the microphone. There was a wail of feedback from the amplifier and then it went dead. The trenches were dug in, fifteen feet apart, a sole scratched no-man's-land of parquet floor. Every onlooker was now a murmur, an excited heartbeat somewhere in the background. The energy was palpable, building from the back in sways; two packs of Teddy Boys flicking fags and picking up glasses, waiting for the whistle before kick-off.

'Stand your ground,' Marge ordered, hissing at the boys

around him. 'Let them come to us.'

Opposite, Riley Baker and the rest of his friends were concentrating on what was stood in front of them, gamely facing forward, unafraid. Only Marge knew what was about to happen – was aware that Davey Thompson had looped around the entire dancehall unseen, had crept up behind them and become one of their number. He moved, head down, a lead beater clenched in his right fist. Nobody saw him, not until he swung from the hip and caught Oliver flush on the side of head above the ear.

The sound was a dense thud. He dropped, his scalp splitting and blowing claret bubbles under his hair. His arms thrashed for balance on the way down, knocking the knife clean out of Riley's hand – it fell hard, skidding on the varnished surface and disappearing underfoot. The reaction was on delay; a high-pitch scream coming from somewhere beyond the bannisters.

All the rest was panic and gasps.

Davey spun and hit someone else before three or four lads jumped on him. Marge steamed in, Winston right beside him. Micky, hot drunk and swinging, whipped his chain across the oncoming traffic, splitting lips and yellowing eyes. Like a newborn bull, Oliver struggled to his feet, bandy, and let someone drag him back out of harm's way. Apprehension abandoned, Francis and Clarky waded in, long right-handers dressed up with dusters connecting on anything's skull. This was war, a carnivorous blood-lust, teeth out, every man desperate to reel someone in and feed off him, to pummel a fist into his face for rank or reputation, because God forbid come morning you were the only soldier without a story to tell.

True to his grade, Riley brawled forward – a badger in a dog fight – his stringy blows tying together and landing against the top of Winston's head. Winston covered, elbows together, paws tucked in front of his face. He rolled with the punches, advancing, never a backwards step. A sharp slap licked him across the ribs – someone flogging him in the guts with an extended belt. He kept coming, wearing it, having to slip punches to get in and get close. Riley back-pedalled to try and find range. Then, peering through his guard, Winston found a thin slither of chin. He snapped in an uppercut and felt the crack of bone on his knuckles. Riley went instantly, legs folding, eyes white and sightless. He fell unconscious, unable to brace himself against the floor – and then his likeness vanished beneath a swarm of winkle pickers.

And now the Kingston Boys were running, scampering shoes, both the battle and the war already won. They fled, violent swears and taunts chasing them out of the fire exits and on to the street – Oliver in the lead, pissing claret all over the pavement as he went.

Opposite the dancehall, Oliver and some others had barricaded themselves inside the all night café. The windows went in, the glass making art-house pictures of people's faces. There was no lull, plates and cups were flying out of the break in the glass and shattering on the concrete. A dining table covered the distance and crashed into somebody's shins. Harris was in the doorway, swinging a chair to keep people back, a blood-soaked dishcloth tied around his head. Marge and Davey were leading the charge, lunging into sporadic attacks whenever the kitchen debris wasn't flying.

Marcia and Connie ran outside and into the road to see what was going on. The streets were heaving – the dancehall bringing up its dinner and spilling it in lumps into the gutter.

Out of the black and blue, Micky's reddened face appeared. 'Come with me,' he said, letting go of his chain and taking the girls by the hand, his whole voice singing the one important sentence. They went with him, Marcia dragging Connie away, their skirts billowing in the pandemonium.

There was a final charge, Oliver and his firm retreating under the pressure, swinging out blindly at the invaders. Francis and Winston went in, Clarky, Marge and Davey sticking with them all the way. They clambered over tables, the Kingston lot falling back inside the café, overrun. Francis felt somebody grab hold of him, his knuckle duster falling free as he scrambled to regain his footing, lashing out wildly at nothing. Winston's spattered white shirt was now a few feet to his left, he could see him holding onto a table top and stamping down on somebody who was cowering underneath it. Oliver Harris was trying to escape through a serving hatch on the back wall. Francis went after him, snatching up a thick plastic menu as he hurdled another table. He caught him by the collar, pulled him back, and steered the hard edge into his face. He punched it again and again, frenzied, catching him on the bridge of the nose and painting the tiles red.

'Get in the fucking motor!' Marge shouted, his voice traveling away, dwindling.

The police bells were ringing.

Underneath Winston's wing, Francis scrambled out of the fray and onto the pavement just in time to see a chrome bumper mount the curb. The back door sprung open, Clarky's kiss curl staring at them from the passenger seat, Micky behind the wheel. Marge ran around to the other side and jumped in. Francis and Winston ducked their heads and dived in, the door slamming closed behind them before they realised they were sitting on top of a pair of petticoats. Micky pulled away, the girls squealing in the back.

'What the fuck are they doing in 'ere?' Marge demanded, wanting to know who he was sitting on top of.

'I couldn't leave 'em could I?...' Micky said, in fits. 'Marcia's local; Harris would have had her pointing out our front door to the old bill.'

The car sped up, the bundle of bodies in the back having to rough and tumble until the girls were on top. Clarky and Micky were in hysterics, watching over their shoulders as five people tried to fit into a space made for two. Marcia was lifted up and balanced on Winston's lap, showing her knickers, her skirt puffed up around her waist. Connie hovered over Francis, every one of her muscles trying not to put down her whole weight. She stayed quiet while Marge complained, his cheek almost pressed against the glass of the rear window in his own car. While everybody was shouting over one another and telling their tales, Francis reached out and touched Connie's hand. It was trembling, upon a stranger's knee but not out of place. She held fast, not budging, the ruffles of fabric on her thighs quivering. They had privacy in the midst of chaos. Their fingers entwined. They each steadied one another making a silent promise.

Barley Sugar

JAMES

2004

They had seen twilight in the afternoon, full dark by five.

The radio fuzzed, the first of the full-time football results crackling in through the tinny speakers hidden inside the Daimler's doors. Francis had opted to come off the motorway and take a more scenic route towards the outskirts of York. It was pointless in this light; God's own country, Yorkshire, had been reduced to a navy green silhouette in bare season on the side of the lane – only a sprawl of shadow and twiggy hedge occasionally being disturbed by some headlamps.

'*Shrewsbury Town, three...*' the sports reporter said, '*York City, one...*' Lewis groaned and turned the volume lower. Normally he wouldn't care, but seeing as where they were it seemed to have relevance. He had been doing it for the past hour, listening out for the lower leagues to see how the teams from the towns they'd passed had been getting on.

The road sloped. A church steeple stuck up on the horizon, more of a presence than a vision, a giant led pencil scrawling scripture on the black. Stone faces loomed out of the bushes at the roadside – one mossy cottage and then another – before the first traffic light they'd seen in hours burned red underneath an overhang of trees up ahead.

Francis, who refused to wear glasses for driving, squinted perilously as the beams of an oncoming car shot towards them and blew past. 'My eyes have had it, I think,' he said.

'Shall we make a little stop?'

Lewis yawned and nodded, involuntarily stretching his arms behind his head. It was crazy to think that his grandfather had ever been young, that he had ever been unsure and as unknowing in the world as Lewis felt now. More stupid was that he and Lewis's grandmother hadn't just been born together, that they had actually had to go out to a place and meet by chance. 'Connie's grandma ain't she?'

Francis smiled but didn't look, 'I wouldn't be telling you if it weren't, would I?'

'You've been with her ever since you were sixteen?' It was both a question and a remark; Lewis couldn't help it, the thought of being with one girl from his next birthday until he was as old as the man next to him was –

'What's the face about?' Francis said. He hadn't taken his eyes off the road; he could just feel the expression his grandson was pulling. He reached across, dug his fingers in to Lewis's thigh just above the kneecap, and squeezed playfully, 'Cheeky little shit!'

'Argh!' Lewis yelped, laughing. 'I'm just saying, that's a *long* time man!'

Francis resumed his casual driving stance, elbow rested. 'It is, but not if you measure it by forever.' He couldn't keep a straight face; *he* didn't even know what that meant, but it sounded the part. 'The best piece of advice my mother ever gave me with regards to women was this: know when your bloody bread is buttered, son.' Lewis's giggles subsided a little. 'Falling in love is like anything else in life, mate,' Francis preached. 'There're only two ways you can get it:

right or wrong. So if you ain't doing one you can only be doing the other.' He looked his grandson in the eye, smiling. 'In other words, when it's *right* – whether it be your first or your last – there's fuck all you can do about it, it's *right*.

'It's *male bonding!*' James Parker said, airily. His voice reverberated around the bowl of his wine glass, the last swig of claret slopping over the rim and into his mouth. It was eight thirty and their first bottle was already empty. 'The only thing my grandfather ever talked to me about – other than schooling – was skiing.'

'Can you ski?' Deborah asked a little too quickly.

'Yes,' he said, 'but I haven't in years. It's a family passion, not one of my own.'

And so this was *it*, getting to know someone, the phrase floating at the front of Deborah's mind dressed up in inverted commas. These were them, the *modern mating rituals*. People did this, usually in restaurants, the man on one side, woman – a cosmopolitan with good shoes and an expensive handbag – on the other. American television had labelled it *'Dating'*: two adult humans separated by a starched tablecloth – both barely chewing whilst washing down white lies.

James looked at her for a long time, the alcohol bedding in slowly – a man of her age, wearing a pastel shirt with a horse embroidered on the pocket. He was ordinarily handsome, with an oval face, rose cheeks, and a middle-class line through his brow. It was strange to see him out of a suit; every time Deborah had ever seen him before, namely passing the estate agency window, he'd been dressed for the office. She thought he looked better like this. She liked listening to him talk, his voice was different.

'So,' James said, allowing the subject to waver, 'What about your son? How is he getting on at school?'

'Okay,' Deborah fibbed. 'I mean, that's not to say he doesn't have his moments of mischief.'

'Well, he wouldn't be a teenage boy without them, would he?' James said. 'It's what separates us from you *girls*...' he paused intentionally, tipping his eyes. '...that is, apart from the obvious I mean.' Deborah laughed, allowing him to flirt. 'So do you have any idea what you'd like him to do once he leaves school?'

'Be happy,' Deborah answered. 'As long as he's happy, I don't mind.' She'd spoken before she was aware of her response, of whether she was even telling the truth or not. 'He likes old things,' she added, 'His grandfather buys and sells things sometimes, I think he might enjoy doing something like that.'

'Antiquities?'

Deborah nodded.

'We should introduce him to my mother,' James said, 'She's got two houses full of the stuff. Honestly, she's obsessed. Given the chance, she could host that road-show on the BBC.' With that, he burst out laughing – the way people do when they've made fun of themselves – and then his arm shot up in the air to summon a waiter. 'Do you fancy another?'

Deborah had taken hold of the empty wine bottle and shaken it. Without provocation, she was making an insinuating action – at least to the drunken male mind she was; it was shameless, aimed directly at the male idea that a woman wanting alcohol is a woman wanting sex. She wasn't sure she knew what she was doing, but she was doing it anyway. The table lamp between them seemed to ignite, polishing James's brown eyes so as to imagine them as mahogany. Deborah smiled, not innocent, provocative, as if to say *another two glasses James and you've won.* For just a second Deborah felt as if it were a test, as if she might have been under cross-examination and the question was leading. She looked at him, reading the dopey rouge in his eye, and then said: 'Okay! But before I can drink anymore, I need a wee!'

James chuckled pleasantly. When the waiter arrived at his side, only as a gliding bow tie, he said: 'Excusez-moi.' His language easing into perfect French. 'Qu'en est-il pour toilettes des dames?'

Obedient, the waiter gestured. 'A travers les portes sur la gauche et suivez le couloir,' he glanced at Deborah who was still holding the empty bottle, 'Avez-vous besoin de plus vin, monsieur?'

'Oui,' James replied. 'Juste deux verres, merci!' He turned to face Deborah. 'It's through the doors and along the corridor,' he told her, his lopsided finger showing her the direction. 'I played it safe and order us two glasses instead of another whole bottle. I don't know about you, but *I'm* feeling a little touched.'

The waiter walked away.

Deborah stood up and unhooked her handbag, swooning slightly. 'Good idea,' she said, her smile intoxicated. 'And thank you!' She turned to leave and then stopped. 'By the way, your French is absolutely impressive.'

James grinned. 'Not pretentious?' She shook her head – it was an overshot, drunken movement, her straightened hair flicking across her cheeks. 'Shall I order us some food when he comes back with the drinks, then?'

'Okay,' Deborah said, fixing on the path she was going to take amongst the tables, 'Provided I can find my way back, that is.'

'Don't say that, I'll look pretty stupid sitting here alone with two starters and my fingers crossed behind my back. What would you like?'

'I'll trust your judgment,' Deborah said, 'I'll eat anything except snails.'

'Done!' he said, and then showed a moment's vulnerability. 'As long as you don't think I'm showing off…?'

She pretended to look puzzled, 'Are you?'

'Ridiculous as it sounds,' he said, beaming, 'I think I was – I think I *am!*'

Unable to keep her lips straight, Deborah shot him with a glare of mock scorn, giggled, and then tottered off in search of the toilets. *And why not?* she thought. Too aware that he would be watching, she walked away, the sudden change in altitude turning the whole restaurant into a giddy chandelier.

The femme toilette was all brass taps and fleur-de-lis. An older lady, washing her hands at one of the gilded basins, raised a small smile in reflection. Deborah smiled back at her, and then blew out her cheeks pleasantly; the universal silent for 'that last glass of wine has gone straight to my head.' After towelling off her hands, the lady picked up the white wedding rock she'd placed beside the sink, slipped it back onto her finger, and then left.

Deborah pretended not to notice. She closed the cubicle door, sat down and relaxed, her new knickers taught between her shoes. Alcohol stirred behind her eyes, she tittered and delved into her handbag. She found her mobile phone, a fountain of urine tinkling underneath her – the screen lit up …unlock … phonebook …calling … Mara.

The voice which answered was wanton and breathless, distracted.

'Can you talk?' Deborah asked, her tongue too heavy for a proper whisper.

'Yep…yes, I can,' Mara panted. Deborah heard a moment's rustling on the other end, shushed tones, and then Mara came back: 'So, how's it all going?'

'I'm in the toilets!' Deborah confessed as if it were the Queen's secret.

'Sounds like you're getting enough to drink though, which is good,' Mara said. 'Are you getting on well together?'

'Yeah we are. It's nice. I really enjoy his company.' Deborah's revelation surprised her more than Mara. 'It's a bit scary though; I'm not sure I know what I'm doing.' The flow from between her thighs had stopped. Deborah paused and then said: 'Am I being silly?'

'If it's silly for a woman to be taken out for dinner plied with wine, then romance is dead and we should both shoot ourselves,' Mara replied, giggling. 'What is it you're worried about love? Have you forgotten where *it* goes?' There was more laughter, and then Mara made a sudden wet gasp in pleasure, as if taken by surprise.

Deborah sat still, listening, her thoughts now dusty red and room temperature. 'He can speak French!' she revealed suddenly, out of context. 'He told me he lived there for two years after he'd finished his law degree.'

'That's good.' Mara said, husky, her mouth smothered. 'Lovely. Let's hope for your sake that he learned what else French tongues are famous for...' she broke off and exhaled, hot breath blowing into the mouthpiece. There was a male groan, and then the picture formed clear in Deborah's mind: Mara was speaking to her from the cushions of her sofa, naked, her legs crabbed open and Adam's face pressed into her crotch. She had the phone in one hand, the other gripping a fistful of his hair and trying to hold him at bay, so she could finish the conversation which had so rudely interrupted them. Deborah could remember Mara telling her once that she liked that when he went down on her; she got off on it, not allowing him to eat everything all at once. Holding him off and only giving herself little thrills so she could tease him by cooling down the sensation time and time again, building her orgasm up enough times before she would finally agree that he could make her come.

'He's going to ask me to go home with him,' Deborah said, returning, concerning herself with herself, 'I can tell already that he wants me to.'

More pause noise and then Mara said: 'You're overthinking

it, hun. It's simple; if he asks and you want to go with him, go, and if you don't, don't.'

'So I *am* being silly?'

'*Yes!*' Mara wined. 'Now get off the toilet and go and live your life, and only call me again if it's something serious – I'm a busy girl.'

'Okay,' Deborah said. 'I'll give you a ring in the morning or something.' To that Mara didn't reply. Deborah listened to the kerfuffle on the other end of the line for a second more and then hung up, the blue haze from her telephone lighting her smile.

Lewis was dreaming...

He was ten years old and the building didn't look like a hospital – it had revolving doors. His grandfather, impossibly tall, was walking next to him, his leather coat creaking at the elbows. There were lift lights and mirrors – chrome upper – and then a corridor, medical, a weak blue vein with a rubber floor. Flatfooted, it ran ahead into an L shape, leaving open doors – cells – in rows which gave glimpses of whole families crammed into tiny, disinfected spaces for feeding grapes and reading newspapers. They passed somebody, unseen, and then rounded the corner into a second sparse tunnel only lit by a neon drinks machine. An empty trolley-bed moved at a distance and Lewis could hear his mother wailing; she was crumbling somewhere into pieces, falling onto his grandmother's chest.

Once they stopped everything went to brick. The only thing which mattered was the closed door facing them, its blind drawn down over the small rectangle window in its belly. In the bright black Lewis could see soft, barley sugar light escaping the gaps around the edges. He gaped up at his grandfather, his terrified question lifeless. There was no point in reply because the boy knew: his daddy was in there and his daddy was gone. Somehow something had beaten the life from him. It had managed to defeat a man who just by sleeping close by could bay nightmares. All at once, standing in abandon, the little boy pined to hear his father's broken-nosed snores coming from across the landing to protect him in his doze. Now there was nothing, no lullaby, no rest. All sound had been replaced by the constant breathing of fear. His throat had taken hold of itself and was squeezing and squeezing so his tongue ached. Heavy, leaden heartbeats were banging beneath the whirling spin of the saltwater. His drowning eyes stung, and the taste of horrified vomit was bringing itself up from deep down low between his legs.

Lewis crept forward, a little man in a school jumper, his grandfather now only a presence. The door gave for him without a handle. The sick feeling bobbed to the surface again, broke apart, and then came floating back on the waves. He didn't want to look, not if there was blood. He didn't want to have to pull back a sheet and see a staring face; to be made to believe that his dad could've died that way, afraid and hidden like a small child in the small hours. The baby room rang desperately quiet. The reading light above the bed was on like a shrunken orange moon. Lewis felt his bladder soften; he hesitated, and then allowed the warmth to run down his front. He saw his father's feet first, pale and bare, dressed for the beach. The man was on his back, big, the sheet rolled down so it could wrap his middle. He didn't look dead – not forever. Not like he couldn't sit and say something – or that one day soon his whole voice would disappear like dreaming and his only son would completely forget any sound that he ever made. Lewis tried; he reached out wanting to touch him, to feel the animal hairs on his chest, to pat his face. He could no longer move. His school shoes were wedged on soundless tiles and caught in time. He went again, arm straining, his youthful skin cold and stretched, his small fingers making giant shadows across the lain body. And then he froze, holding back from nature, tips hovering …

For a moment longer he wanted to stay as he was, as a boy.

Lewis awoke, stiff. He lay still, waiting for conscious thought, the dead image of his dream hung over behind his eyelids. The bed was damp, sweaty, the round neck of his T-shirt clinging to his throat. For a horrified second he was convinced that he might've lost all control and pissed himself; it was only after he'd grabbed at the dry cotton on the front of his boxer shorts that he dared to open his eyes and swallow. His mouth was clotted. He peeled his clammy head off the pillow, his braids beginning to fray.

The Travelodge developed as a dark room around him – two single beds, a teas-maid kettle, and a television set mounted to the wall. The only light, strip-bulb blue was coming from the en-suite bathroom in the corner. Now

Lewis remembered: the drive, the fat man at the reception who'd checked them into their room, the shower he'd taken before crashing out on the bed and even the Bible he'd found in the dressing table drawer which his grandfather had told him was there in case –

'I thought you were out for the count,' Francis said. He opened the bathroom door, the light spreading in an open book shape until it touched the far wall. Lewis shrugged and looked at him: a naked man with wet skin and a white towel nip tucked around his waist, the many years of good living pushing his stomach out in front of him. Francis crossed the room and switched on the television. He turned the volume low, flicked through the channels to find Match of the Day, and sat down on the foot of the other bed.

Lewis stared at the screen in silence, not really watching, wanting to but choosing not to mention his dream. The TV hue, pitch-green, flickered against his grandfather's chest and shoulders and illuminated his scars – it had been years since Lewis had seen them. There were three in all: a jagged stripe on his upper arm, a flat chunk which appeared to have been shaved off the ball of his shoulder, and the largest of the three, which was a deep laceration on his upper back. His arm and back had healed into raised folds of lighter coloured flesh, but the missing piece on his shoulder, that one had become wrinkled and shiny, like a bad burn beyond years of skin grafts. Since he was a boy Lewis had been fascinated by them. And over the years he'd been told all sorts of fantastic stories about how his grandfather might have happened by such gruesome decorations – Lions, Tigers, Bears – but he'd never had the truth.

'I forgot you even had those scars,' Lewis said.

Still watching the screen Francis's hand instinctively covered his shoulder. 'They never did fade as much as the doctors said they would,' he said. 'Not that I should grumble, they were my prize for winning over your grandmother.' He glanced back at Lewis, the television glossing his face. 'That as well as a little bit of payback from Oliver Harris for the state I made of him that night at the dancehall.'

'*He* did those?'

Francis nodded, 'He did a hatchet job on me, him and that Riley Baker I told you about.' Lewis gaped at him, aggrieved over the top of a yawn – and there it was, mystery solved; no bones about it, his grandfather telling it that way he told everything, without prestige.

'What do you mean a hatchet job?'

Francis motioned with a flat hand, 'I was lucky. They jumped out of a car on me and chopped me a couple of times with a little hand axe.'

'An *axe*,' Lewis said, surprised; in his mind, Oliver Harris didn't have it in him.

'It was only small, about the size of a Tomahawk,' Francis said. 'But as you can see, he weren't shy of swinging it about. Mind you,' he went on, 'I've got to give him his due, he bided his time well: not long after that dust up in Kingston, me and Micky got sentenced to our first bit of Borstal. And at the same time, because he was that bit older, Harris got called up and had to do his two years national service in the army. He didn't catch up to me and get even until '55, after I got out.' Francis turned away to rearrange his towel. 'I don't know how he knew when I was coming home, but he did. He got me on the first night.'

OLIVER

1955

Francis emerged from Rochester Borstal with nothing but a
pile of grubby, finger-marked letters bound in elastic and the
navy blue drape jacket he'd worn to his court appearance.
He was eighteen and uncured; almost two years of shit food
and wank rags hadn't changed much but the hairs on his
chin. Micky's dad had been right: *you can go blind in there
if you ain't careful.*

Oliver Harris wiped his soiled, rugby players' hands against
his jeans. 'I don't know why *you're* snivelling,' he said. 'I'm
the one who's been made a fool of; you don't look any more
of a cunt than I do.' Connie stayed as she was, cowering,
sat on the bench with her head in her hands, the dollop of
mud Oliver had just rubbed into her hair dripping down
her neck and falling in filthy strings on the shoulders of her
cardigan. 'If you ask me, I've done your little lover-boy a
fucking favour,' he added, speaking slowly, labouring spite
into each syllable. 'Least this way, when the prick gets
out of stir he might be able to see you for what you are:
a dirty, two-timing, fat, carrot-top, slag!' he eye-balled her,
wanting a response, pupils glassy grey like the puddles on
the footpath. 'Just tell me one thing: if he's so wonderful,

how comes you're here?' He pretended to check the time. 'It's getting on; surely he should be out by now, shouldn't he?' Connie looked up at him, wondering how he knew. He turned up his lip. 'You ain't the only one who's got friends inside,' he said.

'I came because I thought it was the right thing to do,' Connie answered, choking back her tears. 'After everything you said in your letters – after what you asked – I thought the decent thing would be to see you face to face and talk…' she swallowed, losing control of her voice. 'I didn't think you'd treat me like *this*. I didn't think you'd act as if you never knew me.'

'Too fucking right I know you,' Oliver said, his grin setting a vulgar groove into his face. He made two of his fingers into a crude display. 'I know you better than he does; I know you inside and out. You'd do well to remember that.'

Connie's head shook, revolted. As much as she wanted to close her eyes and not see him standing where he was, she refused to shy away from his grimy fingernails. She blinked at him, full of holes, then and there hating him, not for what he'd said, for what she had allowed him to do. He'd soiled her, before today, before the mudslinging; he'd dirtied her by exploring her with his fingers – his wide, flat rugby players' hands had been on her and she'd wanted them there, she'd enjoyed them. And now he was taunting her for it, scolding her, hurting her for feeling anything for him. He was calling her names, *dirty*, tiddling his fingers and thumb in an off-handed, disgusting little wave goodbye.

'Did you tell him?' Oliver suddenly demanded, the thought

occurring to him.

'Tell him what?'

He scrutinized her. 'What I said in those fucking letters – what I fucking asked you,' he said, paranoid. 'Did you show him? Did you send them to him?'

'No!' Connie said, offended. 'They were private, why would I do that?'

Oliver's grin wilted. 'Were you writing him the whole time?'

'Yes, but I didn't mention you at all.'

'You better fucking not have,' Oliver warned. He turned away, his temper boiling. He swung back, going towards her and then stopping himself by holding back his fists. 'I swear to you, Connie, you ain't taking the fucking piss out of me. And neither is he. I promise you – mark my fucking words – the next time I see him, I'll make sure he ain't laughing.' He came in close, his mouth moist and gritted, 'And if I find out you've shown anyone what I wrote –'

'I haven't,' Connie squeaked, tearily. 'Please! I don't want you to fight over me. I don't want anyone to fight.'

'Don't flatter yourself,' he said, still close enough to slap her if he wanted to. Instead he spat, the foamy white spray dotting her shoes. 'I owe him one. I ain't forgotten what happened and neither has Riley, so you can tell him from me – *and* that spade mate of his – that we'll definitely be seeing 'em.'

'What are we walking for?' Micky slurred. He overbalanced,

one foot in front of the other, stumbling down the curb but managing to stay standing. He splayed his palms as if to beg the question of the group. 'These hands can work wonders,' he said, 'It won't take me five minutes to nab us a motor. We can go home in style.'

Tucked beneath Davey Thomson's arm, Suzanne Rose, a friend of Marcia's who'd tagged along for the night, shot him a glance and piped up. 'I'd rather have the blisters than get in one of *your* dodgy cars.'

'Ark at Suzie!' Micky teased. 'Since when was you so picky about what cars you climbed into the back of? What was it you used to say: the two best things in life both fit into your bra?'

'No I never!' she remonstrated, 'You fucking liar!' Micky laughed. She cut her eyes at him, a snub-nosed girl in a tight sweater, and then pulled Davey closer. 'Don't pay any attention to him, he's drunk.' With reputations being what they were, nowadays, Davey's scars seemed to be working in his favour. Following the faint whiff of sex, he'd left Marge and the rest of his pals in the dancehall and decided to walk her home. When she'd finished talking, he turned, winked, and mouthed something to Micky behind her back.

Taking the hint, Micky changed course to query Francis. 'What about you France? What do you say I find us a jam jar?'

It was midnight, and for Francis, for now, his first Friday of freedom only smelt of perfume. 1955 still sounded different, like live, drunk music. It was one of life's little handshakes; there'd been no trouble, the Streatham Locarno had simply spun and sung to birdsong, girls dancing, the perfect picture from one of the liquor flavoured lipstick dreams he'd been sleeping on ever since he'd been away.

'I'm fine where I am,' Francis replied, walking on sea legs, Winston was beside him, the pair of them concentrated on Connie and Marcia who were ten feet in front. 'It ain't worth risking getting nicked on my first night out. Besides, it's a good night for it, the moon's out.'

'The fucking *moon*,' Micky burst into another fit of bottled laughter. 'God knows what they did to you in there. Me, I came out as good as gold, my same old self. But *you* Francis, I'm starting to think they turned you, mate.'

'A little less talking and a little more walking, if you please, Meehan.' Marcia's voice sailed over her shoulder.

'Oh, not you an' all; what is it with these birds tonight?' Micky remarked. 'If I was *you* young lady, I'd give it a little less lip and a little more hip – or else I'll set Winston on you.' She looked back and smiled. Micky nudged Winston sideways. 'What about you Wince, are you enjoying this stroll?'

'I would be if I didn't have you in my ear hole,' Winston answered shoving his friend away.

Behind, Suzanne let out a shrill giggle between kisses; Davey had just bundled her into a shop doorway and begun warming his hands under her jumper.

'Suit yourselves, then,' Micky said, 'but don't say I didn't warn you: by the time you get these girls home, the only thing they'll be letting you rub will be their smelly feet.' He laughed at himself along with everyone else. 'The ruddy *moon*,' he mocked, 'our first night out in nearly two years and we're walking so you lot can look at the moon.'

Before Micky had even finished, Winston broke into song: *'Blue moon...you saw me standing alone ... without a dream in my heart...'* – Francis joined in at the top of his voice – *'Without a love of my own...'* Winston, who had now filled out to the width of a small shire horse, placed his heavy arm on his friend's shoulder and they serenaded the stars together. Micky ran and leaped onto Winston's back and howled along with them. *'Blue moon ... you know just what I was there for, you heard me saying a prayer for, someone I could really care for...'* Connie and Marcia, laughing, turned and started to walk backwards so they could watch; the three friends – three boys and men – reunited in unspoiled, legless, chaotic harmony. *'Blue moooooooon...'*

Inebriated, the hike from Streatham High Road towards Wandsworth felt like a short hop in good company. They ambled, a rabble, three sheets to the wind, singing songs and stamping their feet, the street lights doing little but showing the sky's spittle up against the glorious dark.

Connie and Marcia were ahead; out of ear shot, arm in arm, a pair of skirts, their heels clipping in tandem.

'I like that he's got colour in him,' Marcia said. She looked back; Winston was busy play-fighting with Francis and trying to shake Micky off his back. 'With his hair parted like that, he looks like one of those American singers.'

Connie smiled. 'It sounds to me like you've got a bit of a

crush on him.'

'I think so,' Marcia said, beaming. 'I don't really know him though.'

Connie squeezed her arm. 'All I can really tell you is that I know Francis thinks a lot of him. The three of them have been best friends since they were little.'

Marcia wrinkled her nose, 'I just worry a little bit about what people might say,' she said. 'I'm not sure my dad would like it either.'

Connie thought about it. 'Francis told me once that Winston lives with his nan because his dad died in the war; your dad mightn't care so much if he knew that.' Her eyes were bright, attentive. 'Family is one thing, but everyone else can bloody well mind their own!' she said. 'I think if the two of you like each other then there's no harm in it.'

The time had guzzled itself, spinning in that way it does once the drinks are in and the wits are out. To the half-cut eye, Tooting Bec Common was just a black expanse beyond the railings on their right. By the time they'd reached the tube station, the black gates criss-crossed over its sleeping mouth, most of the conversation had been replaced by meaningless gestures.

Micky had had enough. 'Sod this,' he said, recognising where he was, 'I ain't walking anymore.' He was looking around purposefully, selecting a direction to go exploring.

'Where the fuck is he going?' Davey shouted up from the back. Micky was jogging away, his silhouette tap-dancing before being swallowed by one of the side streets. A milk bottle was kicked and broke somewhere out of sight.

Winston shrugged, 'Fuck knows!'

Connie turned around and looked at Francis, 'What's Micky doing?'

'Probably pissing on his shoes,' Francis answered. 'He'll be back in a minute.'

Then, after a long lull, they all heard it: an engine, large and loud, an aroused creature grumbling in a cave. It backfired, the sound of fun to a gun dog. It came around the corner on two wheels; a red, double-decker bus, blowing coal-coloured smoke with Micky Meehan at the helm in a conductor's cap. He stepped on the brake, his head poking out of the cab window, 'All aboard!'

'C'mon, chop chop!' Micky ordered, waiting for Davey and Suzanne to catch up and climb on the back. 'Where are you two going, Fulham?'

Suzanne wafted exhaust fumes away from her face. 'We are, if you think you can make it that far.'

'We'll make it,' Micky said, positive. The bus rolled forwards. 'I'm going to have to stick to main drag though,' he added, hands tentatively orbiting the huge steering-wheel. 'I nearly tip it on that corner?'

The bus couldn't pick up much speed. It chugged, trundling first along Trinity Road, passing the prison, and then straight on until they were across Wandsworth Bridge and into Fulham. 'If you see anyone walking, tell me,' Micky called to his passengers, 'I'll stop and pick them up.' Micky checked his mirrors, laughed at the others larking about on the seats and poles, running up and down to the top deck and kissing in closed off cuddles. They saw no one and heard nothing but the constant complaining of the machine. It cranked and banged until finally a series of small explosions broke the bus's back at Parsons Green. It gurgled, jolting, smoke hissing from both ends, and then to everyone's disappointment, came to a close in the gutter, its big black tyres squashed grumpily against the curb.

'No wonder nobody bothered locking it up,' Micky cackled, 'it don't fucking work. It makes sense now why the keys were in it.'

From Parsons Green, with the smoke clearing over their shoulders, the group disbanded and went in separate directions. Micky, keeping the conductor's cap on his head, followed Winston and Marcia back across Wandsworth Bridge; Davey, winging it in hope, stuck with Suzanne and pushed on into Fulham, and alone, Francis and Connie turned towards Putney.

'Winston really loves you, doesn't he?' Connie said. Light rain had drawn the earthy scent up from the cracks in the pavement and watered the leafy oak canopy which covered the very top of Putney Hill. They had almost reached Southfields – the heath behind them and the spirited shape of the church steeple at the crest of Beaumont Road large as they cut through the lane and headed onward to Connie's parents' house. She had made no mention of Oliver or of what had happened at the park; not because she didn't want to, but because she didn't want to turn Francis's head and spoil the mood. For now, she just wanted him here with her, the two of them together, safe and away from the threat of other people.

'He's never had much else apart from me and Micky,' Francis said. 'We've looked out for him a lot – not that he needs looking after or anything, but you know what I mean.' He smiled.

'More like he's looking out for *you*,' she said, tittering. 'I was watching him; he doesn't let you out of his sight. A couple of times tonight, I thought he was going to thump one of the other lads for coming too close. It's like he's your minder.'

Francis laughed. 'I think he just feels guilty,' he said, 'because we kept his name out of it and were put away and he wasn't. It's his way of showing that he's willing to stick his neck out for us too.' Connie nodded sympathetically, allowing him to lead her by the hand across the road. In that moment she felt utterly guided, sheltered, as if right here, right now, was exactly where she was supposed to be; walking and talking beside this boy, holding onto him because everything he said to her sounded honest. 'I thought we was doing him a favour,' Francis continued, 'but sometimes I think he would've preferred to have been in there with us.'

Connie stopped and looked at him, 'Either way,' she said, 'I bet he's glad to have you home.' She lifted his hand to her mouth and kissed it, her lips cushioning themselves on the damp skin. 'I know I am.' She took a step back, shy warmth flooding her face. Francis admired her; the girl he'd met – an imagining, emerald-eyed and red-headed – who not twenty four hours ago had only been a fragrance sprayed on the bottom of a letter, but was now a young woman wearing everyday of her eighteen years exquisitely well in front of him.

He stooped forward and kissed her.

With breathless affection in their ears, blessed and falling in lustful sin, they christened holy ground together. The church stood in the dark, graceful, with love writhing out of sight against its rear wall. Inside their heated cuddle, Francis's mouth hot with rum, Connie devoted herself entirely. He moved through her, pushing into his place, the zip of his trousers teething hairs on its way to his ankles. They heaved together, coupling, rocking as one for the matter of minutes. She opened herself with wide, closed eyes to the boisterous pains and soft pleasure. He replied in kind, answering her murmur with a three worded whisper, listening as her velvet lining beat out a close rhythm for him to follow. She held on, arms clinging to his neck and a leg cradling his hip, hoarding all of their adolescence until his knees went weak and he sank away to fall further in love.

The brandy bottle slipped, fell, and rolled over in the foot-well of Riley Baker's Ford. The car had been parked for over an hour, unmoved, so the thing just lolled there, empty, a glass heart drowning its sorrows between Oliver's shoes.

'Ain't it about time we buggered off?' Riley croaked. He was flopped back in the driver's seat, head tilted, hair flattened against the window. 'I don't reckon she's coming home.'

Oliver didn't move; only his eyes slipped sideways.

'She's probably stopping at one of her friend's houses. We'll come back another night.' Riley clicked his lighter – a bright flame popped out of the golden square under his thumb and then vanished. He struck it again, this time the light lingering, showing up the pockmarks in his face. 'How do you know for certain that she even went out?' he asked peering out of the window. Oliver had made him pull up and park on Beaumont Road, directly opposite the low flight of concrete steps which descended the grassy slope and allowed access to Whitlock Drive. From where they were they could just see Connie's house. It stood, lights off and quiet, squashed into the middle of a short terrace of grey brick council homes at the bottom of the slope. 'For all we know she could be tucked up under her blanket and we're sitting out here for nothing.'

'I want to talk to her,' Oliver said, his voice had become a slow, determined drawl. 'I ain't fucking moving until she comes home.' He hoisted himself up and gaped at her bedroom window. It was a colourless eye in a stone face: she wasn't home. His mind was slurring in gurgles, the brandy's yammering now spinning his brain in his head like a fallen conker inside its spiked shell. Fuck knows how long he'd been here, waiting, like some sort of cunt, all the while she was out getting her jollies with her pretty boy. The grasp of who she was with – who he knew she was with – started another nauseous death roll in his guts. The anger curdled with the brandy and beer, speaking to him in barked ravings and sloppy lectures about what she had done – what she was *doing*: making a fucking mug out of him, for starters. Making him wait; making him write her letter after letter, word after word, saying it over and over again until now it meant nothing. Now it meant that *Francis* should have her, that he should be the one to creep into her bedroom, to snatch up her nightie and fuck her with the lights off while she groaned in his ear and her parents were asleep in the next room. Oliver blinked at the net curtains, the thoughts impossible to shake. His mouth was dry. He swallowed, jealousy slipping backwards down his throat and grabbing onto his tongue with both hands.

Riley looked at him, looked away, and then clicked his lighter again.

'Time to say goodnight,' Connie said, sounding something like her mother. She smiled. 'My mum will go spare if I get her out of bed to let me in and she sees you standing on her doorstep.'

Francis watched her lips. 'Fair enough,' he said, slowing, 'we'd better call it a night here then.' Connie stopped walking and buried her face into his neck, he smelled like Brylcreem. 'I'll come and see you Monday,' he said, letting his arm straighten until her hand broke away. She nodded and arranged her hair, took a few steps, and then turned and blew him a playful kiss. He stayed where he was, eyes going with her until she was just a shape in the dim, then he rounded on himself and started back the way they'd come.

Up ahead a lighter flame sparked, burned a moment, and then died inside a navy blue Ford which was parked on the side of the road.

Quiet, Riley flipped the lid of his lighter closed. He was peering out of the windscreen, squinting, seeing past the dew beads on the glass and studying the girl coming towards them. Stirring, his eyes shifted further back and focused on the male silhouette walking away in the other direction. 'Ain't that her?' he said.

Oliver snapped out of his stupor, head jerking, sight flared. There she was – *Connie* – there on the stair, a little whore with heels on. Fixated, he watched her tiptoeing her way home, sneaking, minding her step and looking straight ahead, her cheeks all pink and her dink stinking of kink-sweat. He lost it; the booze soup in his stomach now rhyming in singsong. He missed her, just like he had in all those letters they'd written. *So how do you know when you love a girl?* – One of the Army boys had asked – *when you'd rather throttle her than see her with someone else.*

The car door creaked open and Oliver was out, unsteady on his feet. The noise got her attention and she stopped. Unbuttoned to the navel, he crossed the road in a spluttered echo waving his arms and talking at her. From inside the car Riley eyed the house. When nobody immediately showed at the front door, he turned his attention back to the road to search for Connie's companion. On the steps, her hands tangled with his, Connie pushed Oliver back and tried to wriggle away. She broke free, descending a few steps closer to her house before he gripped her by the shoulders and forced her to listen.

'Fucking listen to me,' he growled, grabbing her wrists so she couldn't flail her arms. He blocked her with his whole body, hanging on, his shoes scraping the wet stone and mud. From his vantage point, it looked to Riley as if the two of them were dancing a violent tango. The incoherent protests were growing louder. There were still no lights on in the house. Connie had started ascending the stairs, backing up. Oliver followed her, frustration seething out of his mouth in drunken barks. He snatched at her face, digging his fingers into her cheeks. She ceased struggling, frightened, her head unable to move. Then, just as Riley was certain his friend was about to send her bandy-legged onto the grass, he spotted the front door to Connie's house swinging open.

Connie's father, bare footed and shirtless, came over the threshold, 'What on earth is going on out here?' he said. Oliver unhanded Connie and whirled around to try and pinpoint the sound. Mr Whitaker looked past the boy to his daughter, 'Connie, go inside.' Oliver stumbled stupidly up one of the steps. Her dad was carrying something; something heavy and black and instantly recognisable. He never raised it; just let it be seen as he moved towards the bottom of the steps to collect his daughter. He glared at the boy, checking Connie's face as she passed him on her way to the house. Obedient, Oliver muttered a single, mushed sentence, turned, and then staggered up the steps and out of sight.

Connie waited on the doorstep, Oliver's voice drawling at somebody else in the darkness. Before whoever's car he had come in fired up, and before her father ushered her into the hall and closed the front door, she made out just three words of what he was saying: 'Go after loverboy.'

Connie's father stared at her, bemused. '*Francis*,' she said again, making no sense. 'My God, they're going after *Francis*.' There were no headlights. The first Francis knew was the sound of tyres slashing through the puddles on the road and the yank of the handbrake locking the car's wheels into a skid. Riley's Ford cut the curb behind him, the passenger side door flung wide and hanging open. Francis whirled around, backpedalling. By the time he'd realised what was happening, Oliver Harris already had the ground beneath his feet and was barrelling towards him.

Connie tripped over the doormat, prized open the front door, and sprang out of the house without waiting for her father's permission. She stopped halfway up the concrete steps, kicked off her heels, and then started to run.

Eyes darting, working double-time to weigh the situation, Francis sidestepped off of the pavement and skated out a few feet into the road. Oliver came after him, his shirt open and his cufflinks lost, the loose sleeves swallowing his fists like the unhinged jaws on a pair of feeding snakes. The car's engine was still running. Francis stole a glance over at the driver –

Riley clicked his lighter. 'No one to back you up this time, is there Coles?'

Francis rounded a parked car and shook off his jacket. Oliver chased him, circling around and back into the road with his fists up. 'You smarmy *cunt*,' he spat, glaring. And then he came blundering towards him, swinging, cuffs peeled back to the elbows, his thick forearms in front of his face. He hurled a right hander, a left, and then caught Francis around the ear with another right. Francis's head bucked. The shot was hard, splaying his trailing leg. Francis stuck a stiff jab into Oliver's mouth, drawing blood and rocking him backwards. The two parted, all the time Francis checking over his shoulder to see where Riley was.

They scraped out another circle, the rain covered tarmac becoming a rink. Oliver stepped in, slurring wild accusations and launching into a rugby tackle. Francis swung and missed, the body weight landing in his ribs and draining his lungs. A deep, metallic prang gonged as Francis's head hit the car bonnet behind him, his spine bowing backwards, Oliver's feet scrounging for grip and driving him down. The punches he expected to land didn't, Oliver's head was ducked, his thick fingers gouging at Francis's face, fish hooking his cheeks. A sudden grip of pain clenched onto Francis's his chest: Oliver was biting him.

Francis fought back, thrashing wildly, smashing his knuckles against the rage writhing on top of him. He felt his head shake; Riley had hold of his hair and was banging his head on the bonnet to stop him fighting. Riley hit him, the blow closing one of his eyes and dripping blood into the other. The voices were purrs now, little vicious compared to the engine roaring beneath his back. In smeared vision, Francis saw Oliver's likeness as his head came level with his own. He pressed his forehead into Oliver's nose, long continuous pressure, dizzying him. Oliver pushed back, the two of them tied in a tangle, their heads locked together like stags in a rut. Francis managed to raise his knee and give himself some room; using everything he had left, he threw a string of uppercuts, aiming for his own chin and hoping for Oliver's. They rolled and tumbled off the side of the bonnet in a struggle, Francis letting his hands go, pummelling Oliver's face and head as they dropped onto the wet road beside the wheels.

Francis knew it was coming and it did: Riley came around the car and drove the damp sole of his shoe into his chin and sent him sideways. Free, he scampered shakily to his feet and staggered into a run – Oliver down, Riley somewhere behind him. For a brief moment he saw the houses on the street, a lit window, a twitching curtain, and then a foot clipped his heel and down he went.

Connie's father called out after her.

She kept going, the bottoms of her bare feet in concrete shock. She could hear raised voices – *Oliver's* – and see tail lights flaring somewhere in the road. The scene bobbed in and out of focus, her head jerking as she ran, Oliver's white shirt a blotch moving from side to side against the dark. She heard the bang of boot-lid, and then Riley's scorched orders, 'fucking chop him, Ollie! Go on!' The car's boot-lid banged shut and she saw his narrow figure moving quickly to hand something to Oliver. There was more disjointed shouting – a light came on in one of the houses – and then Oliver's blood-stained face disappeared behind his shoulders and he lumbered towards the heap lying at the side of the road.

Connie screamed.

A high note of panic ringing in his ear, Francis rolled onto his elbow and attempted to get up. He flopped back down, everything underneath him useless, his vision slanting out of one eye. The entire foreground above him was Oliver Harris; he was back on his feet and brandishing a weapon – a hand axe – leaning over him and shouting, threatening, a spray of blooded mucus gushing from the red smear which used to be his nose and mouth –

Oliver swung.

There was no timing in it, an instant, and then the axe-head struck Francis's arm and burst a gash in the flesh, the weight of the dull blade tucking shirt fabric into the wound. The limb went limp. Instinctively, Francis burrowed his head into his chest, desperately trying to scramble to his knees but only managing to ball up and roll into the gutter. The fear was numb, his body now nowhere. He didn't feel the second blow shave his shoulder, only the rush of air and the lax flow of blood spreading across his neck. A piece of him was missing. He twisted, doing nothing, placing himself only half up and half down the curb. Oliver bayed and swung again. This time Francis was aware of the thump, and of the heavy metal which had buried itself into the top of his back, so deep that he could feel it wriggle and slide as Oliver wrenched it loose and tossed it away. With no life in his lungs, waning, Francis howled. The rest was mute, the wailing scream falling unconscious under his tongue.

The road was deaf, the car engine gone and Connie crying. She was close; Francis could feel her sobs in his ear and her hair on his lips. There was a male voice, soft and assured and giving counsel. He wanted to sit up, to see who had him – but when he tried, the faces in the sky were only paint strokes.

Barley Sugar

Barley Sugar

PARIS

2004

Lewis rolled onto his back and opened his eyes. Plain as day, the Travelodge ceiling slotted into view like the blank sheet of paper at the start of a slide show. The room was exactly how he remembered it, only now the teas-maid kettle was issuing a subdued little hiss and the broken, red digits below the dead television screen were flashing the time at 8:09.

Standing in front of the window, sipping tea, his grandfather was already up and dressed. He spoke without turning around: 'Sleep well?'

Lewis croaked in reply, getting up and hobbling towards the bathroom with a hand cupped over the slit in the front of his boxer shorts. He was across the tiles and going before the door had swung shut behind him. Seat up, he stood for a whole minute waiting for a break in the clouds so his head could clear, the warm flow of urine splashing back off of the pan and sprinkling his knees. When he'd finished, he spat a foamy mouthful of morning breath into the yellow flush, and then stepped back into one of the watery, size ten footprints his grandfather had left next to the tub. There were still scented suds crackling over the plughole. Wavy, he pulled back the shower curtain and fiddled with the dial on the shower, the spray submarining everything. He tested the water with his hand, and then peeled off his underwear and stuck his face under the rush. Only then, with the cobwebs beginning to wash away and his ear drums temporarily deaf, did he start to remember the story his grandfather had been telling him before the sleep had taken over and stolen dreams from it.

'You cut off his *thumbs?*' Lewis asked, grinning in disbelief. He spiked one of the sausages on his plate and held it up on the end of his fork, 'seriously?'

Francis regarded the charred stub of meat his grandson was using as a prop and nodded. Trying to hide his smile, looking down, he instantly became a little boy admitting to something he shouldn't be proud of. 'I only managed one in the end though,' he said, 'the one from his right hand.'

'How did you do it?'

'With great difficulty,' Francis said, deliberately keeping his voice down. 'My arm still hadn't fully healed. I was wearing a sling.' He checked over his shoulder to make sure that the two Yorkshire lasses who served in the tea room weren't listening, and then said: 'I took it off with a pair of garden sheers.'

Lewis thought about it, 'Hedge trimmers?'

Francis finally finished spreading the piece of toast he'd been buttering and took a bite. 'Yep,' he said, somewhat regrettably. 'A set of old-fashioned, rusted ones with wooden handles.'

'What did it feel like?' Lewis said. 'Was there a lot of blood?' He was all eyes and ears, glancing down at the half demolished English breakfast on his plate, moving the food around to reveal the hand-painted windmill scene on the china. 'Was it hard to get through the bone?' As he asked the last, Lewis dipped the wet nub of sausage he had left on his fork into some baked beans and sank his teeth into the reality of what he was saying.

Francis sat forward, elbows on the table, his forehead creased in reply. 'I remember Winston offering to do it because I was having grief with my shoulder,' he said. 'But it was one of those things I had to do myself – I said I would, so I did. It wouldn't have meant anything otherwise.' His face flattened. 'It was quick,' he said, taking his time to slice through a rasher of bacon. 'I can only really remember the sound it made when it dropped onto the grass; it was light, like when you drop food on the carpet.'

Lewis had stopped chewing. 'Where were you?'

Francis paused, as if the memory was moving too fast for him. 'Richmond Park,' he answered, 'not too far from the gate at Robin Hood. It was nearest place that was quiet. And that was open at night.'

'Did *you* take him there?'

Francis gauged his grandson's pupils. 'Listen,' he said, 'I'm only telling you this because it happened and you asked. It's not for other peoples' ears; it's just for you to keep under your hat.' Lewis nodded, his scalp tingling the way it did whenever his grandfather's tone graduated to teacher. Francis swallowed another mouthful of tea before he went on: 'Your Grandmother knew where he lived, so once I was back on my feet I had her point it out and a couple of nights later we wrapped him up on his way home. Winston jumped out and knocked him arse backwards, Micky chucked a towel over his head, and the three of us bundled him into a car. At the time, after what he'd done to me, I didn't think anything of it. I just picked up the sheers and pruned him.' Lewis put down his knife and fork and took a drink. 'It made a lot of mess, and a lot of noise. The plan was to do both hands, but in all honesty one was enough for me. I left it at that.'

'Why his thumbs though?' Lewis whispered, mulling it over. 'How comes you didn't just stab him or chop him like he did to you?'

Amused, Francis gave him a small, clean smile. 'Because,' he said, 'I didn't fancy having a corpse to carry.' He leaned back in his chair, away from his grandson's hunkered down, immature view of the world. 'And,' he added, 'he was a rugby player.'

Lewis still looked confused. 'So?'

'So,' Francis said, 'try catching a ball without a thumb – try doing much of anything for that matter.'

'Yeah, but he tried to *kill* you,' Lewis said, a little disappointed.

'Did he?' Francis queried. 'Think about it; I was laid out in the road and he chose to chop me in the arm and the shoulder blade. To me at least, those are not targets for trying to kill someone. To me, those are places to swing an axe at if you want *other people* to think you're trying to kill someone.' He waited, watching for the naivety to fade from his grandsons' face. 'Personally, I've always believed in an eye for and eye.'

'Meaning what?' Lewis asked, inquisitive.

Francis chuckled, losing interest. 'Meaning, that I've always thought that what I did to him was a little worse than what he did to me.' He reached into his inside pocket, withdrew his mobile phone, and then slid it across the table. 'Now, all that aside – while I remember – make sure you give your mother a ring when you've finished eating. She's probably worried she hasn't heard from us.'

The leather underbelly of Deborah's handbag made a low, guttural rumble against the back-ash work surface in James Parker's kitchen. Inside, set to vibrate, her mobile phone was flashing.

Her eyes were already open, strange surroundings and body heat in the bed having seized the day an hour ago. She had forgotten how to share a bed, how uncomfortable it was. For the majority of the dark she had been uneasy, dozing on and off, slipping in and out of rest until eventually she'd given up. She had just lay there monitoring her breathing, desperately trying not to move, watching the daylight subtly grow in confidence through the blind until it had uncloaked the ceiling and chased away the illusion of the night before. Things were no clearer; she still couldn't remember how to wake up with someone.

His leg was so close she could feel the hairs on his thigh raising her skin. She studied the bedroom looking for clues. The John Grisham titles on the shelf offered nothing but legal sounding names. They were all straight and proper in their place, the lamp beside the bed still upright, undisturbed by overly excited limbs writhing in the midst of passion – on the contrary, James had reached over and switched off the light via the easy to reach little button on the wire. There were no suggestive wine spills on the carpet, no sweaty palm prints on the wall, and her dress hadn't been torn off of her and left in a provocative crumple on the floor. The only piece of evidence that anything had happened, or that she had even stayed over, was tied in a knot and scrunched up inside a ball of tissue paper on James' bedside table.

The sex had felt unrehearsed. The condom hadn't helped; that warm, unsure smell of latex reminding them that they really didn't know each other at all. She hadn't climaxed but she didn't mind, not that she hadn't expected to, it was just that thinking about it now she thought she had probably been battling with herself too much, concentrating too hard. He had felt nice though, mild, moving on her in more of an overly expressed cuddle than a quick, first time fuck.

'The best way to see Paris is from my bed.' That had been James's joke – and Deborah had laughed when she'd seen the framed picture of the skyline above the bed. From where she was now, if she tilted her head all the way back on the pillow, she could see the Eiffel Tower in black and white, made to look like an old Polaroid from a fashion magazine. She grinned inward, because it dawned on her, right there in that early light that she had never had any desire to see Paris. It was funny, she could remember reading somewhere that rather than it being the eyes, it was in fact the things people hung on their wall which were the gateway to their soul.

The buzzing in the kitchen stopped, and then started again.

For a moment Deborah thought she might stay put. Then she sat up, flicked back the duvet, and surfaced without causing a ripple. She floated across the bedroom on her tiptoes, making her legs look longer and covering her breasts with an arm. With all her weight on one foot, she looked back at James: he was still asleep, his hair sticking up from the pillow in brown tufts. He moved, stretching out an arm and holding on hopefully to the mound of fabric that she'd just left behind. That made her smile.

She touched the door handle, turning it like a burglar in mittens and then stepping out into the hall. The kitchen was straight ahead, a mass of stylised cupboards and mod cons – open plan living for the flat-pack cosmopolitan.

The phone buzzed. She took it out of her bag and stared at it as if it could see through her, as if she were X-ray thin. She answered, suddenly naked, her voice instinctively pretending for her. 'Hello!'

Despite the name in lights – *Grandad* – it was Lewis who was speaking: 'Mum? Were you sleeping? I tried to ring a minute ago.' His voice was joyful, blustering, fresh air blowing into the mouth piece.

'Sorry, love,' she said, whispering but trying not to. 'I was having a lay-in; trying to take advantage of the peace and quiet.' She tittered, shifting the weight of her lie. 'How is it? Are you enjoying yourself?'

'Yeah, it's good,' Lewis said. 'We've just had breakfast. Now we're on our way to see one of Grandad's pals before we get back on the road.'

He sounded like his father. Deborah squeezed herself, her free hand a comfort. 'Where are you now, then?' she asked, hearing the background.

'In York,' Lewis answered, before the line went quiet – muffled voices and rustling. 'Listen, Mum,' Lewis came back, 'I've got to go; we're trying to find this shop. Shall I pass you to Grandad?'

'No, no, don't worry; it sounds like you're both busy. I'd better let you get on.' Deborah covered her mouth.

'Okay,' Lewis said, only half listening. 'I love you. I'll speak to you later.' And with that he was gone.

As if it were a dirty secret, Deborah buried her phone back in her bag. She seesawed, up and down, going sickeningly low, a single tear on her cheek. Behind her the French doors, or whatever they were called, were letting in just enough of the pale outdoors to make it feel colder than it was. She had goose-bumps. In through her nose and out though her mouth, she inhaled ... exhaled, refusing to do this *here*. It wasn't fair, not on her and not on him, whatever had happened – whatever *this* was – it hadn't been done out of malice. It hadn't been wrong, just difficult. She reached out and fumbled a glass from the draining board, then filled it with water. She swallowed, the taste of stale wine and dry spit helping to wash the lump down her throat –

'Deborah?' The friendly inquiry sailed out of the bedroom on a still breeze. 'What are you up to?'

Deborah jumped as if she'd been caught in the act. There was a beat of silence. 'I was just putting the kettle on,' she said, regaining herself. She opened the cupboard and clinked some of the cups together. 'Do you take sugar?'

For a moment Deborah was sure James was going to show himself in the doorway; he didn't. 'I do indeed,' he called back. 'Two. But you should have said, *I* would've got up and made it.'

'It's fine,' she said, 'don't be silly. Stay where you are.'

Deborah seesawed again, this time upwards. She walked into the bedroom, a mug in each hand, having to force confidence into the fact that she was topless. A smile rose gently and all on its own. She was pleased to see him. Now that he was awake, sitting up and watching her with the intelligent dumbness bagged up underneath his eyes, she could remember why she had gone to bed with him – why she was here.

'When I first woke up, I thought you might've done a runner,' he said, holding out his hands to take her tidings.

'Careful, it's hot,' she said, laughing at him and his picture of Paris. She climbed in to *her* side of *his* bed and then kissed him on the cheek under the Eiffel Tower.

Later that morning they made love again. It was better;

Deborah ventured on top, placing herself as low as she could and rocking, watching as he made breathless catches at her nipples with his mouth. That time she came.

AVRAM ABRAHAM

2004

Lewis put his finger inside the brass bell-top to stop it tinkling.

'That's a Victorian servants' bell,' the old boy said. He hadn't lifted his head, just spoken, all the time studying the timepiece on his desk. Avram Abraham – and that was the way he'd introduced himself, formally, taking Lewis's young hand in an oiled palm – didn't look, at least to Lewis, like the kind of company his Grandfather would've kept. The bloke was an odd ball; he had that supple, cigarette-stained, balding squint which kids are warned not to take sweets from. When he spoke it was in rambles, old-fashioned and lippy, little balls of bright white spit caught in the corners of his mouth. Lewis put the bell back. 'Are you fond of cats, son?' Avram asked, still not looking, somehow intuitively knowing Lewis would be perusing the china felines on the next shelf. 'Those ones aren't worth much; I just keep them there to keep me company.'

Francis had his back to them, amusing himself with the war memorabilia inside the glass cabinets on the far wall. Lewis looked at him for help. None came and Avram went on: 'I love cats,' he said. 'I've got three real ones at home: *Olly, Dolly, and Molly.*' He scoffed. 'I have to say, I feel like a right prick standing outside in the garden and calling them in for their dinner.' He grinned and stood up, one eye twitching.

Lewis smiled politely, unable not to watch the little man's oversized shoes as they shuffled towards a giant stack of books standing in the dust. How the fuck he knew where to find anything was supernatural in itself. The shop was pandemonium; as quiet as a crypt but in chaos. The place was brimming, every shelf and most of the crooked square footage was overwhelmed by dusted junk, row after row of jumble sale rubbish and antiquities all thrown in together and trying to sell their story. And there were volumes, leather bound and broken, stacked everywhere. There was no cash till; Avram conducted business from the desk drawer, sat in his wingback armchair. Next to him, askew on four wooden stilts, was a huge, empty bamboo birdcage fashioned in the shape of a manor house. There were swords and bayonets mounted on the ceiling beams, and the World War Two helmets, railway signs, statues, telephones, ink pots, instruments, and thimbles were all beyond number. Plus there was *much more upstairs*, the handwritten sign beside the staircase said so.

'Francis,' Avram muttered, stepping slowly back behind his desk and turning chunks in the book he'd selected. 'If this turns out to be what I think it might be, then this might turn out to be an interesting afternoon.' Drowning in his corduroy jacket, he found his page and waited for Francis to join him. 'Abraham Louis Breguet,' he announced, pointing at the portrait on the page. 'Pronounced, *Bree-Gay* – I always remember him because we share a name; his first, my last.' He stared at Francis, then intensely down at the gold pocket watch on the desktop. 'He was a watchmaker; very much sought after. But,' he said, glancing up, 'I'm expecting that you probably already knew that.'

Francis smiled at him. 'That's all I *do* know.'

Lewis had stopped browsing now and was stood listening. Avram clocked him watching. 'And, would I be correct in imagining that this rare and valuable item of gentleman's finery just happened, one fine day, to fall into your lap?' It was a suggestion, his yellowed teeth showing. 'Shall we say, for now, that it may have been an act of God?'

'Whatever clears your conscience,' Francis said.

Avram sniggered into a cough. He broke eye-contact and said: do you know what happened to me the other day, lad?' Lewis gazed back at him, bemused. 'I knocked on a neighbours' door to borrow a cup of sugar and she refused me. She said that foreigners were responsible for all the murders and wrongs in the world.' He bunched up his nose. 'I said, I think you may have me confused with a German.' Lewis didn't know what to say, he just frowned. 'Do you do your history at school?' Avram asked him, studious. Lewis nodded. 'Good. Well there's an old chalkboard somewhere over there,' he said, pointing towards what looked like the frame of a four poster bed. 'Upstairs – don't ask me where mind you – is a beautiful teachers' cane which goes with it. If you can go up there and find it for me, I'll give you one of those Swiss Army knives in the cabinet as a reward.'

Lewis caught his grandfather's wink and did as he was told, ducking his head to avoid the cobwebs on the stairs.

'You don't mind do you?' Avram said, once Lewis was gone. 'You can never be too careful; I wouldn't want the boy to hear too much.'

A needle in a haystack, Lewis paced over the few bare boards of unoccupied loft space trying not to break anything. Within a minute he'd given up, the multi-stories of clutter too wide and eclectic to find anything as simple as a stick. More interested in seeing what was being said, he stopped looking and scuffed his way back to the top of the stairs. Despite the lowered tone, Avram's voice echoed in the hollows like a cough in a bottle. Lewis leaned over and peered through the break in the banister.

'It was made around seventeen eighty nine in Geneva,' Avram was saying. 'Breguet was living there at the time.' He turned the pocket watch over in his palm – bright gold – handling it in two fingers, as if it were an injured butterfly. 'Or, I should say, that's when *they* were made. There're two; a pair. This little beauty has a twin.' He paused, reading the reaction. 'But you knew that as well, didn't you?'

There was a creak as Francis sat down on the edge of the desk. 'The other one isn't mine to sell,' he whispered. 'I'm on my way to see about it. Hopefully, if all is well, we should be back with it some time Monday afternoon.'

'And you want me to make inquiries on the pair?' Avram confirmed, his hand groping around in the confusion of his desktop; he found it, a magnifying lens, hidden behind a cluster of dried fruit jars and biscuits. He held it up to his good eye. 'What of the other one's condition?'

'I'd imagine it'll be in a similar order to this one,' Francis told him. 'At least it was the last time that *I* saw it.'

'Astounding,' Avram muttered, examining with wonder the complexities of the cog mechanism. He ghosted a fingertip around the watch face. 'The inscription is Hebrew. It says: where *you* bleed, *I* will feel.' His eye watery, he rested the watch down on a piece of cloth he'd laid out for it. He picked up his book, flicked through, and then slipped an old, tattered fold of brown envelope out from the back pages; there were slanted, handwritten notes all over it. 'Have you got any idea what you want for them? What they could be worth?'

'Only going by what other Breguet watches have gone for?' Francis said.

Avram studied him, 'You mean at auction?' Francis nodded. Avram hunched his shoulders. 'Naturally, we'd make more if we could legitimise the sale, but as always for you and I that luxury seldom comes around twice in one life.' He smiled, consulting his scrap of paper. 'Even so, provided I can get in touch with the right people, I should still be able to get you a handsome ransom for them.'

Francis didn't react.

'Of course,' Avram went on, 'it's the story of these watches which makes them remarkable, not the price they've got on their head.' He sat down, the high, red leather back of the chair swaddling him. Francis regarded him with patience. 'They've been missing for decades,' Avram said. 'Apparently after having been buried, dug up, smuggled, stolen, and then counterfeited. The fakes were sold on in New York years ago; so if what you've got here is kosher – and I've known you long enough now to know you wouldn't bother being here if you didn't already know that that was case – then exactly how *you* came by them is a tale I think is best kept close to your chest for now. It's safer, at least until the deal is done. And I'd prefer if you took this one with you until Monday, I'd rather it not be directly under my nose while I make my phone calls. After all, walls are thin and I'm only half the warrior that I used to be.'

Francis gave him another slanted smile.

'What I *can* tell you though,' Avram said, waving the scrap of paper in his left hand, 'is *my* small role in proceedings –' He broke off, slowing himself down. 'But before I do that, it's probably wise if I explain where the watches came from in the first place, no?'

'By all means,' Francis said, ready to listen.

Avram clapped his hands together. 'Okay,' he said, organising his thoughts. 'The watches were originally commissioned by a wealthy banker in Switzerland, a Mr Yousef Goldrein, as gifts for his new born twin sons; hence the inscriptions.' He gestured at the desk. 'But that much you can find out in the book; it's not until later on that things get noteworthy. As is usually the case with these things, they were passed down through the family, from fathers to their sons, for generations, until they eventually ended up with a man named Yonah Goldrein – this would have been sometime before the Second World War. Now, because Yonah was his father's only male issue, he had to take sole responsibility for the pair. Luckily, with Europe on the verge of the Holocaust,

Yonah – along with a good few other members of his friends and family – had the good sense to have his valuables buried somewhere in a secret vault to protect his inheritance.' Avram's eyebrows made two triumphant arches. 'It was the only way he could be certain that his birthright didn't wind up decorating some fat SS officers' dress uniform. Obviously, I wouldn't have a clue as to the whereabouts of that vault, but the fact that that watch is sitting there on my desk today, is proof enough that one existed. And that makes me happy.' A swell of enthusiasm got him back to his feet and Francis had to watch the spit balls flying excitedly from the corners of his mouth. His speech was speeding up, becoming the childish prattle of someone who still believes they're whispering. 'At some point, God only knows how, our hero Yonah survives the death camps, flees Europe, and during peace time resurfaces in the states where he remarries and produces some children; two of which are boys. Now, this is the important part: as soon as those two boys came of age they were each given a letter from their father, who by then was no longer of this earth, in which he explained everything they needed to know to regain their birthright.' He flapped the envelope again. 'And that's how we ended up here,' he said, grandly. 'It was meant to be.'

Furrowed, Francis looked at him. 'What do you mean?

There was silence, Avram smoothing down the few strands of hair on his head and considering the squiggles on the paper. 'Well,' he muttered, concentrating. 'These are the people I need to get in touch with to help you sell your goods. I thought it was peculiar at the time, but now that it transpires that you've got this watch, perhaps it wasn't.' His pupils were flickering, back and forth – from the desk to the piece of paper in his hand, and back again.

'I don't follow,' Francis said. 'What was peculiar?'

'The phone call in sixty one,' Avram said.

He closed his eyes and counted backwards. 'I received a phone call from an American. He was asking me about a pair of Breguet pocket watches which he was adamant were floating about on this side of the pond, in particular London.' He opened his eyes and shook the piece of paper. 'That's what this is, the information he gave me; who to contact if they should ever crop up.'

'Why you though?'

'Like I said, they were convinced that the stuff either had been, or still was, somewhere in our great capital city.' Avram answered. 'Subsequently I've found out that they'd approached a couple of friends of mine who were also trading in shiny things at the time –' He barked out a laugh in a single syllable. 'It's been a while, but now that you've shown me this, I can't say that I blame them.' He paused, wiping his mouth and showing a ridiculous grin. 'You see, there was, and still is if you know the right people, a tremendous market for Holocaust jewellery. And what had happened was, a few months prior to that phone call, upon receiving their father's instructions, the Goldrein brothers out there in New York had made arrangements to have their family's vault dug up and all of its contents smuggled on over to the good old USA. Presumably they were trying to avoid some sort of bureaucracy, taxes or red tape at customs or something, but unfortunately for them – although not for you it would seem – the entire cache was hijacked in transit from Antwerp.' Still grinning, Avram paused again, this time to see if Francis's face would show cracks; it didn't, and so he carried on: 'The way I understood it, these Yankees wouldn't have had a clue where their watches had got to, not if a pair of fakes hadn't surfaced at Christies. The way it worked out, an Asian gentleman, a collector, was having a few of his pieces valued and the experts there informed him that his Abram Louis Breguet watches were forgeries. When they asked him where he'd bought them, he said that he'd purchased them from an Englishman who'd claimed to be working on behalf of the Goldrein estate. That in turn gave the Goldreins the nugget of information they'd needed. And I wouldn't imagine it took them long to discover that they had a probate lawyer working for them who'd studied at an English university and therefore had connections over here. The lawyer must have spilled the beans because the man I spoke to on the telephone that day gave me a name, the name of the bloke their lawyer was in cahoots with in London. He said that I should check any potential items against that name to verify that they were probably the originals. The thing was I had never heard of him in all my life.'

'What was the name?' Francis asked.

Avram took a breather to confer one final time with his scrap of paper. 'Pollitt,' he said. 'Ori Pollitt. Does it mean anything to you?'

Francis measured his answer. 'Put it this way, I'd be lying if I said it didn't ring a bell.'

By midday the Daimler was away from York and heading further north. It was raining, pissing down, frown lines on the windscreen and the motorway licking through the countryside and splitting the horizon down the middle like a long, liquorice-blackened tongue.

Palm up, the pocket watch flat and heavy on his hand, Lewis couldn't leave it alone. He also couldn't stop asking questions.

'Having big ears is almost as bad as having a big mouth,' Francis said, preoccupied. 'Once we've got to where we're going and I can sit down and tell you about it properly, I will.' He turned his head. 'What did your mum say?'

'Nothing,' Lewis said quickly, unwilling to change the subject. 'But how comes you didn't even tell Avram?'

Francis smoothed down the back of his hair and left his hand on his neck. 'Because,' he said, 'If I've learned anything, it's that you should never show your hand too early, even when you're playing with friends.'

Lewis rolled his eyes. After wiping it down with his cuff, he put the watch inside its velvet box and slipped it back into his grandfather's coat on the backseat. The thing was a craft of art; embellished Roman numerals and daggered hands. Opened up, its guts were a working of tiny, overlapped cogs and gilded wheels. He wondered how long ago it had stopped telling time. Outside, the rain was visible. Lewis stared at a herd of Friesian cows, black and white in a field, half of them lying down. Inside the car's quiet, he suddenly felt that maybe he shouldn't have listened – that he shouldn't have asked; he'd heard his grandfather before saying that earwigging was only one step ahead of grassing, so how did that make him look? He thought about it, sinking down with heat in his cheeks, worried that something might've changed. 'What about the other stuff?' he said, edging into it, not fully coming away from the window. His grandfather squinted over at him, the overcast sky greying one whole side of him.

'What other stuff?'

'The stuff you telling me about over breakfast,' Lewis said. 'What happened with Oliver after you chopped off his thumb?'

Francis pondered it, looking like his mind was working on two things at once; just as Lewis was beginning to believe he wasn't going to answer, he said: 'To be honest I'm not a hundred percent sure. I know that they had four years off me for what I did though.'

'You went to prison for it?'

Francis smiled at him, Lewis's concerns about his grandfather thinking less of him spent in an instant. 'Don't be so surprised,' he said, 'I did do it with my face showing.'

Lewis lifted himself up, aggrieved. 'Yeah, but how can he go running to the police after what *he* did to you?'

Francis bunched his shoulders. 'Some people are just like that,' he levelled, pleased that his grandson was worth a little salt. 'To be fair to him though, I got the impression that it was his family who saw that the charges got pressed.'

'Still,' Lewis said, disgusted, 'what a dick 'ed.'

Francis agreed. 'It's funny though, just as I was about done with my time that Riley Baker came in. I didn't see him, I only heard. But he was on remand awaiting trial for murder; he'd hit some youngster from Mitcham over the head one too many times with a bar stool and wound up looking at the long one.'

'Life?' Lewis asked.

'Yep,' Francis said, remaking an earlier point with his eyes. 'I couldn't tell you if he ever saw the other side of it or not. When I came out Harris had all but disappeared, I saw his brother a couple of times here and there but by then we'd moved to better things and weren't much interested. Years and years later though, I was told by a good friend of your grandmother's that Oliver threw himself in front of a train at Earl's Court station. So I'm guessing that that was his lot.'

On Monday the 5th of January 1981, a man named Terry Bennett strolled along the underground tracks at Earl's Court station with a torch in one hand and a clipboard in the other. His face was the same shade of nothing as the station tiles. Behind him on the platform, another man, one who'd seen the whole thing, gave a statement to a police officer, his hands shaking, holding onto a cold can from the vending machine. He told them that he'd stood and watched as a big-bellied stranger wearing a denim jacket had paced up and down the edge of the platform, one foot on either side of the yellow safety line. He'd appeared antsy – that was the word he'd used – and like he might've hurt someone because his fists looked scarred. When he'd heard the train coming, he'd shouted something and jumped. It was a sound he said would always stick with him, not the shout or the impact, but the chinking of copper coins flying against the walls as they burst from his pockets. Other witnesses said they weren't sure if the man had gone too late or too early, but somehow he had managed to get himself wedged between the carriages and platform and been dragged the length of the station. When his body had fallen low enough to be chewed by the wheels, his torso had wrapped around the undercarriage and pieces of him had been scattered amongst the litter on the track.

When Terry Bennett, whose job it was to identify and collect all of the strewn body parts, turned the upper section of the torso over, he found a mangled suicide note in the chest pocket. In it, the deceased, who would later be recognised as Oliver Brian Harris, apologised to his wife Judith for the debts and to his mother for losing the demolition business his father had left to him and his brother. When Judith Harris eventually read her husband's parting words, after the initial outpouring of emotion, a large part of her couldn't help but rejoice the fact that her and her children would suffer no more beatings.

Eventually, with the warm wind from the tunnel blowing into his face and rustling the papers on his clipboard, Terry found what he was looking for: roughly eighteen feet inside the mouth of the tunnel, half buried in soot and crisp packets,

Barley Sugar

was a severed right hand with its thumb missing.

JACK MANNERS

1959

Jotted in pencil on the outside of the envelope, faded and almost three year's old, was a date: *September 1956*. When it had first arrived, like all the others, the smell of perfume had been ripe; but now, after being strapped with elastic bands and bundled up underneath the mattress of his bunk, that smell had long mixed with the stale scent of prison. Francis spread open the dog-eared envelope and sniffed; she was still in there but faint. He had more recent letters in the pile, ones still splendid with Connie's aroma and clearly hallmarked by her lipstick kiss, but the old ones meant more. He had read and reread everything, umpteen times, always imagining her with her knees up under the blanket scribbling on her lap, her painted nails looping and crossing the page to make smiles on her Y's.

He skimmed over the first few lines and then slowed his reading:

...everybody hopes you are well. I met Micky's new girlfriend, Carrie, tonight. She's really nice. She laughs a lot, but then again I suppose you would have to if you were going to put up with Micky bless him. We all went to the pictures together. Marcia couldn't go so Winston took me instead; I thought that was sweet of him. Did you ask him to take me to get me out the house? We went to see that new film, Rock Around the Clock, over at the Elephant and

Castle. The place went crazy; it was like a dance in there, everybody up and jiving in the isles as soon as the music started. It's been like that everywhere it's showed, have you read about it in the papers? They say it'll be banned soon. People started flicking cigarettes and matches up in the air and ripping up seats and throwing them. When the manager ordered the film to be stopped, it made it worse. Outside was wild; there were girls dancing in the middle of the road, and boys were all throwing bottles and kicking all the cars. The police came. I didn't like it, some lads started saying stuff to Winston and calling me names because they thought that I was with him. He wanted to fight with them over it but I made him stop and take me home. It made it worse that you weren't there because I think he felt like he had to protect me. I felt bad for him. It made me wonder what Marcia goes through when she's out with him. I feel sorry for them. Anyway, I said that I would write you when I got in and Micky told me to tell you, 'that he's had a word with Guvnor and they are willing to let you back on the choir as long as you keep doing special favours for the Vicar'. At first I thought he was telling me some sort of code that you might understand, it was only when I looked at his face that I realised he was taking the pea...

A cell door clanged somewhere along the prison landing. Keys jangled under voices and boots wrangled under keys. Francis stared fixedly at the letter, no longer reading. He closed his eyes and concentrated on the face embossed on the inside of his lids. He squeezed, trying to force his tiny world into perspective so he could get away to somewhere else. Trapped, cocooned inside his room, he thought about Connie, about the horse-chestnut hair which fell in angles around her chin. He thought about the warmth beneath her blouse, about how she looked on her visits, and about the ghost he couldn't touch. He thought about the passing winters and the cold which made his shoulder ache where the axe had struck. He asked himself about the worth of revenge; thinking about pride and about scars. He thought about lust and lives, dreaming about home for half a minute, imagining his mother sitting and missing his father while he was out shaving men clean and making women dirty. He marvelled at trust, questioning the reality of time. He thought about clocks and about distance, and then about nothing – nothing except how Jack managed to pull off his card tricks. The chilled sunlight on the barred window played shadowed piano keys on the far wall. The wire mesh in the mattress yawned under his weight and the cold metal bedframe iced his ankle in the gap between his sock and trouser.

He opened his eyes and moved a little higher up the bed. A moment more, and Francis folded the letter, slipped that one back into its envelope and selected another from the pile.

Oct 11th 1955,

Francis, I don't know what to say. What can I say? I asked your barrister if I could borrow a sheet of paper so I could write something to you in the hope they give it to you once you've been sentenced. The thing is, now he's given it to me, I'm not sure what to write.

I can see you. I'm looking right at you from the gallery as the court is going about the business of taking you away from me. My heart is breaking. I can't believe the things they're saying about you, the way they're making you look. I'm sure plenty of girls and women have sat where I am, probably in this seat. It's somewhere I never thought I'd be. Thank God Marcia is here with me. She asked me a minute ago whether I thought I would feel better if Winston and Micky were with you, or at least one of them. I said that's not the way you would want it. Oliver's mum is only a few seats away and she keeps giving me looks, staring and shaking her head. She's probably wondering what I'm writing. You should have seen her turning up her nose when the barrister was speaking on your behalf. I hate her and her double standards. I've got half a mind to tell her exactly what her precious son did to you so she can stop muttering about what a monster you are to her friend. I won't, not in here anyway. It might make things worse for you if I cause a scene. So, I'm sitting here minding my P's and Q's and trying to bottle it up and stay quiet. She just sliced her eyes at me again.

I know I've told you before but I want to tell you again that I'm not angry with you for doing what you did. I thought I was, but now I know I'm not. As much as I wish none of it happened, it's not right for me to be angry with you for standing up for yourself. I know what you will think when you read this, but I can't help but think that if you had never got involved with me, or if I had never been involved with him, then this wouldn't of happened and you wouldn't be standing down there now. From where I'm sitting it looks like I've ruined your life and I'm sorry. You could have met another girl, one who wouldn't have dragged you into this sort of mess. Oh my God, I don't even know what I'm trying to say. Of course I wouldn't want that but I just feel so guilty. This is awful. You are only standing a few meters away from me but already I'm not allowed to speak to you. It feels so long since I kissed you. I miss you. The judge looks so stern. The way he talks is so cruel. This whole thing feels so cruel. I'm waiting for you to look up at me again. I know it's not, but if it's any consolation you look handsome standing down there in your suit. I love you. If you must go, I want you to go knowing that you never have to doubt me Francis. I am yours and yours only. A girl with two hearts couldn't love you more properly than I do, right now and forever. No clock, no time, no anything can change that. I promise.

Do you remember that day that you took me to London Zoo? When all the others had walked on you took my hand and led me back to see that great big lion again, do you remember what you said to me? You were fascinated by him, how magnificent he was, how strong and brave. I said that I thought he looked sad sitting behind those bars, and you said that he was but it didn't matter because, even though he was in a cage, people still had no choice but to respect him. You said he still held his head up at the people staring, and that even though they'd locked him up they couldn't stop him acting like a king. I hope you remember that lion, Francis. You need to always remember that lion.

I'm going to stop writing now, before that judge bangs down his stick. And when they sentence you, I know you

*will wink at me push your shoulders back so that I won't be
sad. I am going to try and smile back, for you, but I will be
sad anyway.*

The words tickled the back of his neck as much now as
the first time that he'd ever read them. He tipped his head
back and rested it on the wall, his hair making a glossy
stain on the whitewashed bricks behind him. He stayed
that way for a while, spotting the difference between the
empty bunk opposite and his own, paying simple attention
to the noise clamouring around him; to the stupid squawks
and scarecrows who were playing cops and robbers on
the landings.

When at last Francis heard footfalls directly outside his door,
he smiled. He understood before the lock clanked that Jack
was back, bright eyed and bushy tailed.

'Happy birthday, Frankie,' Jack said, waiting for the door
to swing all the way back before swanning in. 'You feeling
any older?'

Francis sat up and collected his letters together. 'That was
two days ago.'

'Does that mean I missed the party?' Jack mocked, his eyes
skimming lightly over the scene he'd walked in on. 'Why so
jumpy?' he said. 'Did we catch you with your pants down?'

Francis laughed.

Jack beamed at him. 'Hang on a sec,' he said, inhaling
through his nose. 'I can smell perfume.' He turned to the

prison officer who'd walked him to the cell. 'Can you smell that, Guv? I think he's had a bird in 'ere while I was away.'

Francis held his hands up. 'You've got me,' he said, 'she just left. If you run, you might be able to catch her at the gate, Guv.'

'Stay where you are,' Jack said, his voice doing a comic impression of authority. He placed a long arm around the prison officer's shoulders, tapped him gently on the top of the chest with one hand and deftly removed a pack of cigarettes from his trouser pocket with the other. 'I doubt whether she would be worth the jog. Not if she's hanging around in a place like this.' He wiggled his eyebrows suggestively. 'I would say a man such as your good self would probably have better tastes than the likes of young Frankie here.' The guard frowned as Jack stepped away from him. 'Correct me if I'm mistaken, but going by the look of you Guv, I'd be as bold as to say that you like your women a little more well-nourished.' Jack took the imaginary weight of a huge breast in one hand and showed it to the guard – behind his back he flipped the cigarettes over to Francis.

'Cheers!' Francis said, catching them.

'Call it a birthday present,' Jack replied.

The guard's keychain rattled. Stood in the doorway, he patted himself down and checked his pockets to see what was missing.

Mr Jack Manners, confidence trickster and paper crook, sauntered over towards his bunk. He was an image, a showman, his eyes two individual actors. He had an accent from everywhere and ten years on Francis's twenty two; only his hairline showed his age, it ebbed backwards from his face in a slick widow's peak which lent to him being believable as anyone – even as a convict. He swished about the prison like a black cat's tail, winning at cards and making marbles disappear underneath cups. *Sleight of hand* he called it, by law it was thieving.

Francis carefully procured a couple of fags from the packet and then, taking pity on the befuddled guard, tossed the box back to him. 'Here you go, Guv. Catch!'

The guard caught the packet, fumbled it, and then squashed it against his chest. 'You're a sly git, Manners,' he said, shaking his head. 'You're a blooming liability.'

Jack grinned. 'I have my uses,' he said. 'Which reminds me –' He straightened up, prepping them for a performance. 'Ready?' When he'd made sure Francis and the guard were both watching, he waved his hands to show they were empty, clapped his hands together, and then, with a quick movement, whipped a red envelope out of thin air. 'Connie says happy birthday,' he announced. 'Unless of course she's changed her fragrance. In which case, I don't know who it's from.'

The guard snorted in appreciation.

'How did *you* get it?' Francis asked, confused.

Jack flicked the red letter over to Francis and then lay back on his bunk. 'Whoever they had doing the mail this week delivered it to me in the hospital wing instead of bringing it here to you,' he explained. 'There I was, on holiday, minding my own business and indulging in the bed service and a smelly red envelope with your name on it falls into my lap.'

He rested his hands behind his head and crossed his ankles. 'Being that I stay vaguely aware of the date, I assumed it was your birthday card.'

'Nice one,' Francis said, balancing a cigarette on the end of his smile. He tucked the card under his pillow for later and sparked a match. 'I appreciate the gesture,' he said, impressed by Jack's talents – he couldn't have known it then, but Jack's sleight of hand would one day make all the difference.

Once, when they had still been boys, Francis, Micky, and Winston had scaled the wall of the local allotments and raided the unattended sheds. On their way out, climbing the back fence, carrying the single pair of binoculars they'd found dangling on an old man's coat peg, Francis had taken a funny turn and fainted. His eyes had rolled back into his head and he'd lost his grip. Micky had been too busy talking to notice; it had been Winston who'd stuck out an arm and caught hold of him. It had been Winston who had stopped him hitting the ground.

And in the June of '59, when Francis walked out of Wormwood Scrubs, it was Winston who was waiting.

'How did you know it was today?' Francis asked, surprised to see him. 'I didn't think I told anyone.'

Winston came towards him, his eyes almost completely hidden by merry creases. 'Your mum sent me,' he said, opening his arms. 'I kept it to myself; she didn't think you'd want a fuss made. It weren't easy keeping it from Connie.' He embraced his friend firmly – bull-shouldered – and clapped him on the back.

Behind them, the red and white brickwork on the gatehouse of the Scrubs looked more befitting to a palace. The sun ducked below the silver lining in the clouds and Francis didn't look back. Why would he? Things only matter while they're happening, and even then, most don't matter enough.

The park adjacent to the jail was rolled out like an unkempt garden. Free and laughing, Francis strolled across the grass and listened to Winston retelling the story of how, a few years back, Micky had avoided doing his national service by buying and forging medical records from a neighbour whose son had been born with a hole in his heart. The birds sang, slinging insults from the trees at the dogs running rings around their masters. The conversation bonded, skipping over months and meanings, flowing amongst the silences; the way they do when two people who have known each other their whole lives.

'I haven't seen as much of him as I'd like,' Winston said when the talk came back around to Micky. 'Ever since Marge started knocking about with a new crowd and mixing in bigger circles, it's like Mick's got something to prove. He's out robbing whatever he can get his hands on – anything and everything. Don't get me wrong I went on a few bits of work with him, just recently I've been leaving him to it.' He sniggered through his nose. 'You know what he's like, France; he's fucking reckless. Not that I'm knocking him, it ain't like he's doing badly out of it.'

Francis threw his head back and took in the sky. 'Good for him,' he said genuinely.

'That reminds me,' Winston said, digging a handful of crumpled pound notes out of his pocket. 'How are you holding for money?'

There was no need for Francis to answer; he accepted them gratefully and without a word, nodding his appreciation. They stayed dumb for a few seconds, the pair of them skint, soundlessly putting their heads together to think up a new way to make means. The rich green levelled out beneath their feet, hind legs cocking in the distance and marking the tree line. For a moment it appeared that the whole world was a wide open snooker table, a game to be played; a velvet green full of easy angles and possibilities for young men who had pockets to fill.

From a distance on Derby day, the white fences of Epsom racecourse appear like a flush grin across the Downs.

Micky Meehan's shell green Austin veered into one of the scuffed, faraway parking areas on the hillside, dry dust clouding his tyres. 'I'm getting married,' he shouted, head and shoulders hanging out the window.

The sun was shining, the rays turning the multi-coloured roofs of the parked cars into a cluster of boiled sweets. Francis and Winston were waiting where he'd told them to, dressed smart, Connie, Marcia, and the others girls they were with, standing off to the side, flapping in their floral frocks and chatting amongst themselves. Heads turned. The car stopped. Micky hopped out and grabbed hold of Francis; it was the first time that he'd seen him.

'Are you having us on?'

Winston stuck a hand and tried to ruffle his hair. 'Nope,' Micky said, too fast, ducking out of reach. 'I've told you before, boys: I love her.'

Apparently now that she was Micky's fiancée, behind him, Carrie Andrews had to open her own door. Donning a bashful expression, she rose on the far side of the car wearing a face full of blush. Even with her light brown hair heaped up on top of her head, she was short; the kind of girl whose lips usually wore the reminiscence of a giggle and who easily forgot that she probably would've liked to have been able to buy her dresses a size smaller. 'Charming,' she said, bright as a daisy and as common as muck. She peered over at the girls. 'You'd think he would at least wait for me to get out the car, so we could announce it properly.'

Slightly bewildered, Francis waved a hand at her, hoping to make her acquaintance before the girls swallowed her up in a rush of excitement. He looked at Winston, and then back at Micky who was now fixing the creases in his clothes and checking his reflection in the car window. 'Congratulations then,' he said, still unsure if Micky was serious. 'How comes you didn't say anything?'

'I just did.'

'Well, how did it happen?' Winston asked.

Micky stopped what he was doing to give him a look.

'What do you mean, *how?*' he mocked. 'I asked, and then she said, 'oh yes please Micky, you're the best thing that ever happened to me.' His face lit up. 'That's why I've been grafting so much. I'm saving up so we can move in together.'

On the road running up the hill, a car – a pristine, white Jaguar towing a horse box – had slowed down and stopped at the entrance of the car park. At first Francis thought the driver was watching the girls, but the longer he looked it became obvious the man was staring at Micky.

'Who's he?' Francis said, gesturing. 'What's he goggling at you for?'

Micky turned full circle to see. 'Nobody,' he said uninterested. 'I over-took him and scared his horse. He almost tipped his trailer.' He waved it away. 'Fuck him, anyway. Wait until you see what I've got in the boot.' He poked Winston in the chest to regain his attention. 'But before you go getting yourself all over-excited, I'll just tell you now Wince, it ain't a bunch of Bibles.'

'Keep on,' Winston replied, wrapping his arms around him in a bear hug and planting a noisy kiss on his cheek. 'One of these days them jokes will get you chinned.'

The girls laughed.

Chuckling, Micky wiped his face and led them around to the back of his car. Francis was one step behind; watching the white car until at last it pulled away and disappeared over the crest of the hill. He couldn't quite place the face...

'Begging your pardon ladies,' Micky was saying, 'but we are in need of a little privacy.' He tilted an imaginary hat towards Carrie as if he were an old-fashioned stagecoach driver. 'I'll catch you up. We just need to take care of a bit of boy's stuff.' The girls exchanged some amused glances before they left, meandering, Connie raising her eyebrows at Francis and making her point. 'Thanking you kindly Madams, thanking you kindly.'

When he was sure the girls had made enough ground, Micky popped the lock and lifted the boot lid. Inside there were two brown cardboard boxes, flaps open, both overflowing with frilly knickers, lacy smalls, and long, luxurious hold-ups'. 'French,' he whispered, pointing out the foreign lettering on the label. 'Carrie would kill me if she knew I was driving about with these in here.' He double-checked how far the girls had got. 'I have to keep them handy though, they've been going like hot cakes. I took them up to the hairdresser's yesterday and got rid of two whole crates. This is all I've got left.' He dipped a hand in and pulled out a pair of fishnet stockings. 'These are best sellers,' he said, wide-eyed.

'Where did you get them?'

'They were left unattended in a warehouse,' Micky said. 'A whole load of 'em, this is all I could carry.'

Winston looked at him. 'Why didn't you tell me where you were going?'

'It weren't planned.' Micky answered. 'I just went in on the off chance.' Winston shook his head at him and turned away. 'Fucking 'ell, sorry, mum.' He rolled his eyes at Francis. 'That's why I'm showing you now,' Micky said, 'so you can both grab a couple of pairs for yourselves.' Winston screwed up his face. 'Not for *yourselves*,' he said laughing, 'for the girls. You can gift wrap them and make out you bought them as a present. They'll love it.' He winked at Francis. 'You can't go wrong; Carrie's had one of everything.'

'Don't mind if I do,' Francis said.

Micky slapped him on the back. 'Good man,' he said, looking only at Winston. 'Go on,' he encouraged, 'stop acting like a little girl and pick yourself out a pair of knickers.' A bray of laughter echoed under the car's boot-lid. Winston's face pulled into a gradual smile. 'That's better. Besides,' Micky said, 'this is all small potatoes. I've got something proper lined up for us. If it comes off, we'll *all* be quids in.'

'What is it?' Francis asked, delving into the boot.

Micky moved side on, his voice an octave lower. 'We're blaggin' ourselves a bank,' he said. 'That's why we're here; Marge wants to talk to you both about it.'

'Marge?'

'I weren't supposed to say nothing,' Micky went on, 'so act like it's the first you've heard of it when he sits you down, otherwise he'll throw a fucking wobbler.'

Francis and Winston exchanged a look. 'Whose idea was this?'

'Mine,' Micky said. 'It came about by accident. *I* was only planning on robbing the brewery for the wage packets.' Winston caught Francis's eyes again, both of them knowing that to Micky, who could only think in straight lines, this probably all sounded like it made sense. Micky sighed, realising he was losing them. 'Right,' he said, impatiently explaining. 'Some bird I know who works in a bank, she put me on to the fact that the brewery near us does it's banking in Clapham. The boss – manager or whoever he is – goes in every Friday to pick up the cash to fill the wage packets. Then the silly bastard takes a bag of money back with him to pay his workers. All I was going to do was get her to point him out, follow him, and then grab it off him and blah, blah, blah.

'None of that matters now. Because when I mentioned it to Marge, he went and spoke to her and found out something better: it's not only the brewery, but several businesses what do their banking there on the same day. She told him that they *all* keep their takings there in a safe over the weekend to be collected.' He raised his eyebrows. 'Once he'd heard that, Marge said that if we're doing it we might as well do it properly and break the safe.' Micky stepped back for his big reveal and shrugged shoulders to prove how simple it was. 'So that's what we're going to do. We were on for last week but seeing as it was my thing, I told him to wait until Francis was out.'

The pause which followed didn't last as long as it should've.

'Cheers,' Francis said, 'but how the fuck are we supposed to crack a safe?'

'That's why I let Marge take over,' Micky clarified. 'He knows people.'

Seeing that Francis was considering it, Winston said: 'Hold on. What about the bank? How's he planning on getting in there in the first place?'

'Fuck knows?' Micky answered. 'Like I said, Marge has got it all straightened out.'

The girls hadn't taken the blindest bit of notice. They had dawdled ahead into the apricot sunshine, their conversation concerning themselves. When the boys caught up, they were the ones left out.

Gently, Francis pulled Connie by the arm and let the others go on without them. Before he had a chance to speak, Connie said: 'What does he want you to do with him?'

Francis laughed. 'Nothing,' he lied. 'It will probably never happen.' He ran a careful fingertip along the bow of her jaw and kissed her. 'I've got more important things to think about,' he said, withdrawing a stringy, black suspender belt from his pocket and dangling it in front of her.

'My God,' she said, snatching so she could hide it. 'Where did you get –'

'Don't ask,' Francis smiled. 'Open your bag.'

'By the way,' she said, watching him stuff lingerie into her purse, 'my mum and dad want you to come for dinner next weekend. Will you?'

Barley Sugar

GEORGE KING

Bertie Crogan drove on, rough hands on the wooden wheel.

Roy Easter was asleep in the seat beside him, his heavy, ginger head lolled back like a dead man's, white daylight burning the windscreen and singeing the hair in his nose. Bertie looked over his shoulder to check on the animal, the bleary silver stripe between his eyes just visible through the hole in the horsebox. He was good with faces; he'd learned to be, a blade in the back as a bairn being a blunt lesson. When you'd done as much and to as many people as he had, regardless of introductions, he made a point of remembering masks. If the day came, and he was face down in the dirt being stuck and fucked again, this time he wanted to know who was sticking the boot in and riding him.

Another shaft of sunlight split the bushes. He shaded his eyes, thinking of the beast behind him, of his violent speed. He admired the Horse – *the Stallion* – nature's perfect creation of muscle. As a boy he's seen men mating them, their hooves high, that unfathomable size tearing the mare and making mice of men. That day, for those minutes, he'd wished to become one, to be able to run, to be able to be strong and feel the weight of his sack slapping against the bare blue skin on the inside of his thigh.

His thoughts overlapped, out of context, moving pictures and images winding down the road. Then it came to him, rising up attached to the Punch and Judy face of Arthur Cox. He remembered where he'd seen them before: it had been years ago, in a pub, Arthur had had them with him. They'd stood out, even then, three wee cunts; one tall, one small, and one coon. The wee shite, the one who'd swerved him on the hill and scared the steed, was a Meehan. And now he could see the resemblance, just like his older brother and their bastard father, the boy had been born with a mouth too big for his mother's teat.

Knowing that, his neck relaxed. For a moment he could only hear his pulse in his temples. He looked down at Roy, at the fermented breaths blowing slowly from his bulk. The expression on Bertie's face didn't change; only once they'd reached the racecourse did he decide to wake him.

'I've never screamed so much in all my life,' Carrie squeaked, flushed and spinning in giggles. Her horse had come in first. Micky hung his head, knowing what was coming: Francis, Winston, and Marge all erupted together in boyish laughter. She didn't realise she'd been misinterpreted until she turned and saw Connie and Marcia joining in. 'Oh, no,' she said, flapping to correct them. 'I didn't mean that.'

The quintessential Teddy Boy had graduated into a short back and sides and a Savile Row suit. Smiling, Marge Meehan forced his little brother down onto one knee and made him propose properly, a grandstand of elaborate hats ascending behind him. He looked older, he was, twenty eight, but the sureness which had settled around his eyes since the last time Francis had seen him grew beyond that.

He'd welcomed Francis home as a grown-up, shaking his hand and buying him a drink.

Pretending to keep her winning race stub out of reach and blushing, Carrie offered her hand. To cheers and whistles, Micky kissed the ring on her finger and then stood up and twirled her around in the applause.

'Congratulations!' Marge shouted, kissing her on both cheeks. 'And I can't believe you've picked a winner on the day you got engaged,' he added, 'that's luck for a lifetime.'

Marge knew where he was going. He led the way, cutting a path through the crowds, Winston and Francis carrying Micky on their shoulders over the threshold of a summer coloured gazebo tent and sitting him down at one of the camping tables. The marquee was packed, walled in by male backs, all standing sideways to let the ladies pass, everyone in full dress. A loud, booze-filled gabble was trapped beneath the canopy; bottles clinking between rounds and half full glasses being emptied over mismatched lawn sets and deck chairs.

'We should have a toast,' Marge said, coming back from the bar accompanied by a waitress and drinks. He handed Carrie her winnings, a wedge of notes in a roll. 'Don't let Micky spend it all for you,' he said smiling, and then picked up a glass from the table. 'Oi!' he shouted, raising his hand along with his voice. 'Listen up!' One by one people's faces started to turn towards him. 'If you would be so kind,' he went on, 'I would like to ask everyone to raise their glasses and give a toast to my little brother and his bride to be. They were engaged today.'

Carrie gaped at Connie for help, 'What is he doing?' she whispered, seeing glass after glass going up around them.

'On your feet, Mick,' Marge said, gently pulling Carrie up out of her chair and placing her hand in Micky's. 'Soon to be, Mr and Mrs Meehan, everybody!' he announced, presenting them together.

Micky just had time to take a hit from his hip flask and slip it back inside his jacket before he was surrounded and shaking hands in every direction. Carrie was separated, obscured by swishing fabric, Connie and Marcia following her around like bridesmaids holding onto a dress trail; trapped inside a circle of women, she was being passed from pillar to post, modelling her ring.

Once Micky had finally regained his seat, he leaned across the table, slurring slightly, and said: 'I reckon I pulled off the greatest caper of my life to make sure she was happy with that ring.' His cheeks were burning. 'Shall I tell you what I done?'

Francis, Winston and Marge, who had been quietly discussing something, looked at him, amused. 'Go on then,' Marge said, humouring him, 'but if you're going to tell us that Nan borrowed you one of hers so you could impress your missus, save it for later on.'

Micky fucked his brother off with two fingers and then smiled at the others. 'This could come in handy for one of you lot one day,' he advised, unable to contain his enthusiasm for what he was about to say. 'Right,' he began, 'this is what you do. As soon as you've convinced yourself to pop the question, you find yourself a nice little jewellers somewhere – I went up town so it would look the part, but it don't matter where it is. Then, a day or two before you're going to ask her – this can't be done off the cuff, you need to plan a particular day so you can know what you're doing. Then what you do is, pop in, pick out the ring you want and pay for it like normal, only you ask him to hold it there until you come back the next day with your missus.' He held up his hand and silenced Marge before he could cut him off. 'But this is the clever bit,' he said, full of promise. 'Once you've done that, you have a quiet word with the geezer behind the counter; tell him that there's a drink in it for him if he'll change the price tag on the ring *you've* picked out with another one in the case which is twice as expensive.' He stifled a laugh, proud of himself. 'The old bloke done it for me no problem; what does he care? He's still getting the price he wanted for it, it just means that when you go in with your bird, she comes walking out thinking she's got a right old result on her finger. Everyone's a winner, it's perfect.' He looked around to make sure Carrie was out of earshot. 'I love her and all of that, but it ain't as if the girl knows her diamonds is it?'

It took a couple of seconds for what Micky had actually said to translate. When it did, Francis, Winston and Marge burst out laughing, in hysterics, slapping the shaky table-top and grabbing hold of one another's jackets. They shook their heads at him, at his craftiness knowing no bounds.

'Bless her,' Winston said, sniggering in disbelief. 'You're a little cunt, mate.'

Micky threw his head back and cackled heartily, 'That I am,' he said, 'but don't try and pretend that *you* ain't. The difference being, I'm also a fucking genius for thinking of it in the first place.'

They all laughed harder, coughing, choking on their humour and washing it down with whisky.

From out of the hum, from nowhere, another waitress turned up and tapped Marge on the arm. 'This is from George,' she said uncertainly, waiting until she had his full attention before setting a large champagne bottle down on the table. 'They told me to send your brother his best wishes.'

Marge offered her his appreciation, and then immediately turned in his chair and held a hand up in salute towards the far side of the tent. Noticeable amongst the other men there, buttoned into a herringbone waistcoat, his shirt sleeves folded back on his forearms, George King raised his reply and waved Marge over.

'Is that who I think it is?' Micky asked.

Standing up from the table, Marge nodded. 'Drink up,' he said. 'Once you've finished with that I'll call you over and introduce you.' He walked away, his little brother watching him in awe now he knew whose bottle he was drinking from.

Francis nudged Winston under the table. 'Oi,' he said curiously. 'Ain't that the bloke from earlier, the one with the horse-box?'

Winston followed his gaze. 'Fuck me,' he said, realising someone was staring at them, his eyes stalking between the bodies. 'I knew I recognised him.' he said, sitting up. Francis frowned at him. 'He's that nutcase Scotsman who tried to tax us on that silver we stole that time. Don't you remember? Arthur was shit scared of him.'

Francis's face brightened. 'I thought he was familiar,' he said, memory serving. 'What's up with him, why's he looking like that?'

Micky reached over and tipped some more champagne into his whisky glass. He supped the fizz off of the top. 'Who fucking cares?'

George King was one of the gentry; a distinguished member of what the newspaper men like to call *London's underworld*. Now in his fifties, his name had long been soaked in liquor, surfacing in backwashed pint glasses everywhere south of the river. Speak be believed, he had once separated a man at the neck and got rid of his body in the brown waters off of the coast; the head, skinned to the skull by the undercurrent in the channel, had anonymously washed up at Tilbury a month later. Since the second of the great wars he had flourished, profiting from every crime punishable but most of the money coming from the importing of timber from Scandinavia. He knew boats and loved them, presiding over most of his country – the docklands – from a vantage point at Surrey Quays. A sturdy man, handsome, he was the owner of a smile which sat none too well on the countenance of a crook. Nevertheless, the people who needed to know knew, and everybody else went to work underneath an umbrella.

'My middle brother, Micky,' Marge said, doing the introductions.

All of a sudden feeling backed in, small and self-conscious, Micky nodded. 'Thanks for the bottle.'

'The least I can do for a man who's about to cuff himself to a ball and chain,' George said, taking Micky's hand inside two of his. He had an unexpectedly gruff voice. Micky smiled and tried to keep a firm handshake. George winked at him. 'Mind you,' he said, 'judging by that little pile the girl won earlier, it seems as if she knows how to back herself a good horse.' Keeping hold of Micky's hand, he looked at Marge. 'Will she make an honest man of him?'

Marge chuckled. 'She'd have to be an angel from heaven to manage that.'

'No chance,' Micky said. 'I'm my own man.'

George laughed. 'So are all this lot, son,' he said, leaning in closer. 'But let me let you in on a little secret: no matter who he is, villain or vicar, a bloke can only ever be as naughty as his old lady allows him to be.' He let go of Micky's hand and slapped him on the top of his arm. 'You could do a lot worse than to remember that.' Well-handled by the bubbly and unsure how to respond, Micky nodded. Turning to where Francis and Winston were standing, George said: 'Are these two your pals?' He eyed Winston's shoulders before shaking him his hand. 'Stone me,' he said, 'this one's got some width on him. Are you a fighter, son?'

Winston shook his head, '… good to meet you.'

'And you,' George said, humble, recounting his name

as if the boy didn't already know who he was. 'You look to me like you might take to it,' he said. 'You ever fought in the ring?'

'Nah,' Winston said, 'never in a ring.'

George grinned. 'Well if you fancy trying on some gloves, have words with that man there…' he pointed to a bald man who was standing behind them. 'He's a good man, he trains fighters.'

Around them, men were smoking and joking about backing lousy nags. Francis could no longer see the Scotsman, there were too many hat brims trimming the features in the crowd.

'So this must be, Francis?' George said, glancing at Marge. He took Francis's hand, giving him a preconceived look of recognition; as if, at some point, Marge must've mentioned what he'd done to someone's thumbs.

In the background, camouflaged by the foliage of faces, Bertie Crogan was listening. A man willing to sin for his pride must learn to listen to laughter, to pick apart its layers and hear the hidden message or sly meaning. He finds the spite in it, the intent, the same way a dog must teach itself to recognise the intention in a stranger's footsteps long before they meet. He hadn't liked their laughter – not then and not now – those cock-sure big gobs, opening wide and mouthing off through their whisky-stained railings. They were laughing far too loudly.

'Ye owe me an apology,' he barked, his lip appearing before he did. He pushed his way out of the throng, the gold buckles on his braces weighing down his shirt. He stopped a chair length in front of Micky. 'This wee ned nearly hurt ma pony.'

'Is this geezer a friend of yours, George?' Micky wagged a thumb at the man in front of him.

Smirking at the kid's nerve, George nodded.

There was a titter of laughter.

'In that case,' Micky said, 'I didn't mean to scare you...' he left a deliberate pause, long enough for another snicker from someone, '...frighten your horse, I mean.'

Marge chucked his brother a warning, a little shake of the head.

'Margie,' Bertie called, without looking away. 'What's wrong wi yer wee brother here? Didnae yer mammy ever teach him how he should talk tae men?'

Marge's face flattened. 'What the fuck is that supposed to mean?'

Eyes up, everybody took a step.

'Now, now,' George said, intervening. He put a hand on Bertie's chest. 'Whatever all this is about, today ain't the right day for it; we didn't all turn out in our best for a fucking carry on.' He glanced at everyone and no one. 'Let's all back up a bit so we don't ruin each other's shoes shall we? Look around, people are trying to enjoy themselves.'

Bertie stayed as he was. 'He owes me a fucking apology, Georgie?'

'He just fucking give you one,' Marge said, standing in front of his brother.

Bertie showed his teeth. 'Careful, Margie, I'll nae tell you again.'

George looked over his shoulder at Marge. 'Quiet,' he

said, cutting off his reply. Calmly, he leaned into Bertie's ear and spoke: 'Listen to me, that there is Margie's kid brother. Their father is a friend of mine. Now, how am I ever going to be able to look him in his eye if I stand by drinking my drink while you open one of them up?' He pulled his head back. 'Let's just leave this where we found it, it's fuck all –'

'It's fine, George,' Micky said, swerved around Marge. He held his hands up in apology. 'Honestly, he's right, I should've said sorry. Fair's fair; it was my fault. I was out of order.' He pulled the hip flask out of his inside pocket, a shot of silver ahead of a grin. 'I don't know if you know or not,' he said, looking at Bertie, 'but I got engaged today, we were just celebrating.' He tipped his head back, exaggerating, swallowing a swig and wincing at the taste. 'What do you say that me and you have a little drink together and put all of this behind us?' He held the flask out in front of him, just out of reach. 'Call it a peace offering.'

The moment moved ahead of time, whole seconds had to be dragged back for the others to understand what was happening – what was being said. Bertie, with George King's hand still pressing on his chest, didn't stir. He stood, unable to hear or do anything. His pupils were loch black, their vision now nothing more than dark cuts in the sallow skin which was stretched across his cheekbones. Inside his mouth, warm blood had begun to seep onto his tongue and flavour his temper with red meat.

Barley Sugar

MR WHITAKER

Edith Ellis heard it again and got up out of bed. Without her glasses, she could hardly make out the clock face but she knew it was mocking her; the lights in the homes opposite had gone out over an hour ago. She poked her nose underneath the net curtain in front of her bedroom window, seeing only the shape and shadow of a moggy on the coal shed. There was nothing wrong with her ears mind you, and perhaps that was the problem because there it was again, a little further away this time – a ruddy motor engine, racing around the neighbourhood, skidding, backfiring, and making all manner of racket whilst decent people were trying to rest.

No peace for the wicked, she thought, hunching her bed-coat around her shoulders. *If it's not fireworks in the winter, then it's racing cars in the summer. Men* (the pronunciation scornful, the way her mother had said it) *if they're not making a noise they're not happy.* She pulled her head back, the net running over the back of her neck and falling in front of her eyes and for a split second reminding her of being a bride. For fifty four years she had been listening to Eric Ellis's nasal troubles, and now that she was awake it occurred to her that for once he was miraculously quiet. He was likely pretending, laying there with one eye open and hoping she wouldn't speak to him. Another one of her mother's favourites came to mind, but she left him to it and padded back to her own bed. *They're like overgrown babies,* she thought, enjoying her private slur as she goggled at the lump he was making beneath his sheet. Her husband's bed creaked; and as if he could somehow read her mind, he rolled over and passed wind in response.

Precisely five minutes later, Micky Meehan thundered back along the same residential roads in Clapham, screeching around corners and making as much noise as possible, heading towards the high street. This time Edith didn't bother getting up; she merely opened one eye, covered her mouth with the blanket, and uttered the only word her mother had ever forbidden her to use.

Francis and Winston were hidden behind a whitewashed window of a disused shop, waiting to see Micky's break lights shoot past and create the distraction for the final explosion. In the basement below, crouching like soldiers, their boots scrambling over brick dust and rubble, four other men scurried through a hole in the wall. On the other side, the last man through blocked it up by hoisting a soggy mattress in front of it. 'Thirty seconds,' he whispered, and then hunkered down and covered his ears.

Detective Inspector Harvey Welsh hadn't said anything since leaving the station. His moustache had mainly been raised in protest to the bitter taste of breakfast tea and Marmite he had in his mouth. It was early, clearly too early for the report he'd been given to have visited a typewriter; the sodding thing was handwritten. Rather than try to decipher it, he sat there posturing, wondering how much the bastards had got away with, only lifting his eyes to check the constable was still driving in the right direction.

Clapham Common flashed past, green eyed. Three minutes later the constable was pulled up outside the bank, a silent Harvey Welsh breathing down his neck. The Detective screwed up the report, tossed it onto the back seat, and got out without closing his door. He stood a moment surveying the building, looking like a pallbearer. He wiped his mouth with the back of his hand, snorting up the faint soapy smell. He waited for the constable to catch up and then strode on ahead of him.

'How much have we lost?' Welsh asked, without breaking stride.

Posted at the entrance, another officer held the door for him. 'They're not quite sure yet, sir.' Welsh sniffed at him and then passed, the iron clad creases in his trousers going in in front of him. Watching the prick out of earshot, the officer let the constable through and then remarked: 'He's taking it all a bit personal, ain't he?'

The constable carried on.

Paunchy, the bank manager was waiting for them at the end of the hall. 'I'll be in charge,' Welsh told him, skipping the handshake to introduce his credentials. He looked at him quizzically, a brief twitch. 'Do we know what was taken?'

'That I'm still trying to find out,' the manager answered.

He made a pass at what he'd been given and handed it back. 'It's difficult to tell, you see. My clerk is attempting to round up the exact figure as we speak.'

'Quick as he can, then. It's pivotal,' Welsh said. 'Knowing exactly *what* I'm dealing with is usually the cleanest way of finding out *who* I'm dealing with.' Having left it trembling in the little man's grip, he accepted his property back and then stowed it. 'Now, I understand that the strong room was breached. Correct?'

'I'm afraid so. They blew the blasted door off.'

'What about the safe?'

'Empty,' the manager said, sounding somewhat inadequate. 'Except for some of the coin bags, they left some of those behind.' He rubbed his brow. 'I'm sure you would probably have a better idea than me, but by the looks of it down there I'd suggest that they must've cut it open somehow...' Welsh looked at him and he readjusted. 'Maybe I should just show you?'

'Please,' Welsh grunted. He beckoned to the constable to keep up and then allowed himself to be led along another corridor, his focus all the time working over the back of the simple man's head. When the manager finally stopped, he was on the brink of a narrow flight of concrete steps. He gestured nervously – *after you* – and then moved aside. 'Remember,' Welsh said before descending, 'sharpish on that number.'

'What is that smell?'

'Thievery,' Welsh answered.

It was bad air, singed; the burnt-out odour hanging around the tips of the strip bulbs on the basement ceiling. For Welsh, these subterranean lairs full of filing cabinets, currency and strong armed secrets, tended to provoke photographic images of war bunkers. They echoed oddly. And for him, as long as he'd been working robberies, he'd never found himself used to the way footsteps echoed in a crime scene, a place which was preferably private. It was like disturbing a tomb which would rather be left alone; a place only to be graced by the dusty footprints of unholy ghosts.

Welsh sniffed, walking forwards. 'Gelignite,' he said.

'I beg your pardon, sir?'

'Gelignite, that's what they've used. It's an explosive.'

Behind them, the bank manager reached the bottom of the stairs. 'That's where the rascals came in,' he said, pointing out the obvious. Adjacent to the foot of the steps, beyond a splintered door, there was a small office space with a hole blown out of its far wall. 'It used to be one of our filing rooms.'

To begin with Welsh didn't acknowledge that anyone had spoken, then he inquired: 'What do you have next door to you?' He was treading carefully, taking the trouble to place his shoes between the sheets of white paper which were littering the floor. Blankly, the manager looked at him – 'On that side of you,' Welsh insisted. 'What do you have on that side of you?'

The manager flinched a little. 'Nothing ... that is to say, it's just a shop space. I believe it's vacant.'

The bank manger was right: the hole in the wall easily big enough for a man to crawl through. Welsh crouched, peering through to the basement on the other side. Past the overturned cabinets and scattered brick piles, he could just see the corner of a chequered mattress.

'That's how they usually do it,' Welsh said, his fingers roaming to find a single pound note amongst the debris. He rescued it, handing it off to the constable who was standing beside him. 'It all counts,' he said seriously. 'Make sure you deduct a quid from the final count when they give it to us.' His knees clicked as he stood up. 'You were spot-on about how they got in.' He sighed, not giving the bank manager the compliment of any eye contact. 'Constable, this is our entry point. We're going to need somebody topside to gain entry to the building next door, so run up and tell them to do something about it.' The constable started to go – 'Without making a mess, Constable,' Welsh added. 'And then get yourself back down here. Oh, and if you should happen to run into any of this man's employees, show them how to do their sums. I want that count.'

The bank manager watched the constable up the stairs and then, needing to say something, said: 'Is that a mattress I can see?' He chortled, making conversation. 'What a curious thing to keep in a shop basement.'

'It belongs to our friendly neighbourhood bank robbers,' Welsh responded, patronising him with a brief study. 'What they do is, soak it through and then stick it over the hole to muffle the blast. It also saves them having to swallow any of the bricks they've just blown up.'

'Right you are.'

Welsh moved to the end of the passage. 'I take it that that there is your strong-room?'

'Yes it is, if one can still call it that.'

The door to the room was a hung-over, a twisted steel drunk clinging onto the doorway. The walls were indented with shrapnel, and inside, hiding in plain sight, was the huge safe. It was just sitting there, squat and hollow and olive green, looking like a fat and overfed war criminal that had just been disembowelled, the roughly cut hole in his gut big enough for the rats to roll in. The detective moved in, his eyes finding everything. A discarded gas cylinder rolled over and clinked. He wondered about the men who'd been here, pictured them scrounging for the neatly bound batches of notes. Laughing; humming themselves a merry little tune and dancing themselves a dandy little dance while they filled they're boots and packed their sacks. *Fathered by drunks and mothered by whores*, he thought, and then noticed that the bank manager was watching him, impartial, the way a child watches a man work.

'It seems an awful lot to carry through a hole in a wall,' he said, analysing the gas cylinder and cutting equipment on the floor. 'And what with that mattress, how many of them would you say there were?'

'Well, we certainly can't call them lazy, can we?' Welsh replied. 'Most of this would've been brought along as a last resort. Whoever their Jelly-man was, I'd say that your safe was a bridge too far for him.'

'...Jelly-man?'

'The explosives man,' Welsh explained. 'They call them that because of the gelignite they use. Half of them haven't got a clue what they're doing; I've been saved from more than one investigation before now because one of these fools has brought the roof down on top of him and his cronies. No such luck here though.' He grimaced, tapping his toe on the safe. 'Nah, whoever this fella was, he did a good enough job on the wall and your big door but he was pushing it with this. All he managed to do was jamb the locks. That's why they've had to cut it open.'

The constable's footfalls were coming back down the stairs.

'Believe it or not, that's a good thing,' Welsh continued. 'It tells me two things: Number one, that the Jelly-man wasn't a professional and probably won't have any previous for this sort of thing. If he did, the gang wouldn't have deemed it necessary to lug along all that cutting equipment. It's more than likely that he just works in quarry somewhere.' He held up another finger. 'And number two: whoever cut that hole in the safe does know what he's doing, especially with a heat gun. That means that we're more than likely looking for a bloke who works with metal, probably a welder.'

The bank manager smiled, impressed. The constable arrived out of breath and handed him a folded piece of paper.

'Another thing,' Welsh added, 'In the report I was given, it said that there were reports from local residents of a vehicle driving around the area at unsociable hours.' He turned to the constable. 'Your next job is to get me a description of the car, or better of the driver.' The constable nodded. 'What these gangs often do is send somebody to out to drive around and make a commotion. That way, any loud bangs or small explosions get marked down as engine noise. People pay no attention. They're clever, but not clever enough.'

'I certainly hope so Detective,' the bank manager said, his eyes bulging at the piece of paper the constable had given him. He sighed. 'This is the total of what they stole.'

Polite silence...

Francis's knife and fork screeched against the good china, the pitch note scoring the scene. Prompted underneath the table, he spoke: 'Thank you, Mrs Whitaker. That was lovely.' He rested his cutlery in the shallow gravy. 'I have to say,' he said, 'that was one of the best meals I've had in a long time.' He didn't need another nudge from Connie to realise how it had sounded. 'I don't mean just because I was in –'

'I know what you meant, love.' Mrs Whitaker smiled at him the same warm way her daughter did. 'Don't worry so much,' she said, 'you're not on trial here; you don't have to mind what you say in this house.' Francis bowed his head a little. 'We'll have to see if we can't have you over again, start feeding you up.'

'I'd like that,' Francis said, tittering along with her, unsure what to do with his hands now that he'd stopped eating.

In the space where it would have been helpful for Mr Whitaker to say something, a secret passed between Connie and her mother. Mrs Whitaker stood to clear the table. 'So,' she said, 'Who would like a slice of cake?' To Francis she looked the way he supposed Connie would if she were corked and allowed to age appropriately. She was a woman of good taste – her and her husband both; they were what

Francis's own parents might've called *decent, hardworking people*, the backbone of a nation: no fools, simply quiet in prayer and conservative in their bedroom practice.

'Have some,' Connie instructed, wrapping her red hair around her neck in a comforting gesture. Francis looked at her and then at her mother, who was already on her way to the kitchen whether he liked it or not.

'I've got a surprise for you,' Connie added, her leg finding his beneath the tablecloth.

Almost laughing: 'What is it?'

'Wait and see,' Connie said, forgetting that her father was sitting in front of them. 'You'll like it.'

Mr Whitaker was a gracious man; he appeared the way he should do in order to sell furniture for a living. Francis had watched him eating, using his utensils. He had musicians' hands, slender, the kind that, given the time to rehearse, might've been savvy at plucking strings or playing chords. He hadn't talked much; the only noticeable thing Francis could recall him saying during the meal, was that a wise man would never trust somebody who didn't like football and have an interest in boxing with the wellbeing of his daughter. It had been a joke but even in jest it had told Francis all he needed to know: that even if the man didn't particularly like it, or him, he was at least willing to give Connie the chance to make her own mistake.

Mrs Whitaker came in backwards, bumping open the door, carrying a tray. 'Connie made this herself,' she announced, and then set down the scent of cinnamon and sultanas in front of him.

'Homemade fruitcake,' Connie said. 'In your letter you said it was your favourite.'

Francis blushed, wanting to cup her smile. 'I did,' he said, 'and it is. Thank you. It looks beautiful.'

Connie's mother was beaming at them, and was about to make a noise when Mr Whitaker suddenly spoke: 'Do you smoke, Francis?'

Francis considered him, now apparently not the same man as he used to be, as he was inside the frame on the mantelpiece. In the photograph he was stood in the middle of his three daughters on Putney Heath, wearing a sunbeam smile and trying to hold onto his little girls in a summer's breeze. The man in the picture was yet to realise that a day would come when he would be sat opposite an ex-con in his own dining room, a Teddy Boy who was about to change the whole scene; who threatened to peel that loving arm from around his daughter's shoulder and tuck her against his own velvet lapel. Francis wondered what he might've said had he known Connie was baking cakes for a bank robber...

Seeing no reason to lie, Francis nodded.

Richard Whitaker reciprocated, appreciating the young man's honesty. 'Perhaps, once you've finished your afters, you'd like to join me in the garden then...?' He waited for Francis to nod a second time and then excused himself and walked outside, stopping to rest a supportive hand on Connie's shoulder.

'Not too much,' Mrs Whitaker nagged, calling after him. 'It will sit on your chest.' She turned back to the table. 'Well,' she said, 'there's not much use in me sitting here and gawking at you, I may as well make a start on those dishes.' She opened up to her daughter. 'That way you two can have a minute to yourselves.' She stopped before the door had swung all the way shut. 'Francis, love, if you are going out to smoke, the garden is through the kitchen, okay?' Her hair vanished.

'What was all that about?' Francis asked, furrowed.

Connie cut the cake and then sat back down beside him, 'What?'

'Your old man, is he alright?'

'He wasn't being shirty,' Connie said, 'that's just how he is. I think they both wanted to give us some time to ourselves.' She checked to make sure the kitchen door was fully closed. 'I'm glad, anyway.' She was whispering now. 'I haven't shown you your surprise.'

'I thought it was the cake.'

Connie shook her head, her hair falling loose from her shoulder as she wriggled her chair out from the table. Posing, playing, she hoisted three or four handfuls of her skirt above her knees, kicking her heels out and pouting, guiding his eyes down at her French lingerie.

'You want to behave yourself,' Francis remarked, laughing. 'If your dad walks in on you like that he'll have me put back in stir.'

'Do you like them?' She giggled, going high enough that the lacy pull of her suspender belt was making archway displays on her thighs.

'You look fucking unbelievable,' Francis slurred, his speech trailing off and becoming the moment. He kissed the side of her face and neck, his lips forming letters as he went, 'Honestly … it … ain't... fair...' He reached underneath the tablecloth and began a long stroke of her; his touch going over her knee and then pausing, picking at the tiny dimple in her skin where the tight stocking-top pinched into her thigh. She closed her eyes and searched for his hand on her final third, the back of his knuckles brushing over the swollen V in her underskirt –

She pressed his hand down where it was and held it hard on the mesh of her knickers. 'That's far enough,' she hushed, taking a breath and then kissing him. 'I want you to try your cake.'

Night time was showing off its decorations.

The rich smell of tobacco smoke flowered over the lawn. Francis stepped down off the patio and onto the grass, eyes running backwards along the wooden fence from the bushes at the bottom of the garden. There was an opaque shed shape in the brambles, two sides of a sloping roof poking up in worship. Mr Whitaker was next to it, gazing up at the astronomy smoking his pipe.

Walking towards him, Francis shook a cigarette out of his packet and eased it between his lips. Seemingly concentrated on the taste of his pipe, Mr Whitaker didn't look at him until he was within arm's reach. He puffed a while and then drew a match from his box and struck it for Francis. Francis hung out his chin and let the flame take to his fag; it glowed, burning the silence.

'Mother Nature's ball gown,' Mr Whitaker said. 'That's what my aunt used to call it.' Francis could tell he was smiling without looking at him. 'She told us that those stars we can see are her sequins catching the light from the moon, and that the moon is really the brooch she's got pinned to her chest.'

Francis sucked in a lungful of smoke and let it escape slowly. 'That's a nice way of looking at it,' he said.

Nothing...

Another cloud of scented fog filled the space between them; the background falling out of focus, exposing everything, real ranks and standings, stripping the world back to cave days, to ritual: men and fire.

Mr Whitaker held his eyes for long enough to see him properly, to try and understand the young man in front of him. 'Are you serious about her?' he said, adjusting his pipe.

'Yes.'

Mr Whitaker gauged him a moment longer before going back to the sky. 'So you will want to get married at some point?'

'Definitely,' Francis said, flicking his ash onto the grass, standing his ground.

Mr Whitaker heard him. He took his pipe from his mouth, glancing sideways and finding what he wanted to see; the courage in the lad's eye, the aggressive intention which he was waiting for. Assured, his face opened up.

Francis took another drag on his cigarette and smiled back.

'I haven't brought you out here so I can quiz you on what

you do for a living,' Mr Whitaker said. 'I'm already aware – Connie tells me things.' He grinned at Francis's reaction. 'Nor do I want to embarrass you. I'm also not going to tell you that I don't think you're good enough for my daughter. What good would that do?' He was holding the bowl of his pipe now, using it to illustrate his points. 'What I will say is that as her father, naturally, I'm not over the moon about some of the things she's told me – hold on, let me finish...' He hesitated, regaining his train of thought. 'I trust my daughter Francis, which means to say that to some extent I trust her judgment. She says that she loves you, so I take her at her word. That's how it works – Constance is no younger now than her mother was when she first decided on me; call me mawkish but I like to think that there was something in it, so why should this be any different? What I'm trying to say is that trying to control your little girl's heart is pointless. It has a mind of its own. If I stopped her seeing you on account of what you get up to for money it will only be me that's breaking her heart. I rather that it wasn't; I rather, that if it has to be anyone, that it be you.'

Francis smoked and listened.

'A father's job – his only job – is to protect his family. And that is what I'm doing, the best way I can.' Mr Whitaker said. 'I'm an honest man, personally I've found it easier to be, but that's not to say that I haven't had my scrapes. I'm not going to attempt to alter the way you are because I'm not of the opinion that what a man does to feed himself necessarily defines him as a person – certainly not at twenty one it doesn't, anyhow. What I prefer to do is make sure that we're both facing the same goal.' The pipe had gone out; he turned it over, tapping the bottom. 'I don't want her involved, Francis. Not in anything.' His stare was watery from the smoke, sincere. 'Connie is now our concern. For as long as she loves you, we now have a mutual responsibility to look out for her wellbeing. Do I have your word that you won't let her be mixed up in anything?'

Francis took his time to contemplate what he was being asked and by whom; he got rid of his cigarette and pressed it into the earth. 'Honestly,' he said, 'I would never...' He broke off, starting again, looking him in the eye. 'I give you my word.'

'Do you love her?'

'I wouldn't be out here with you if I didn't,' Francis said genuinely.

'No,' Mr Whitaker remarked, 'I don't think that you would.' The handshake came away in its own time, Connie's father absorbing what had been said and then making up his mind. 'I've got something I'd like you to have,' he said. 'Call it a gesture, in keeping with our little talk.' He tilted his brow, his demeanour ranging from earnest to business-like in a beat. Francis measured him carefully. 'Wait here.'

Slipping another cigarette out of his pack, Francis stood on the lawn and watched Mr Whitaker's stooped silhouette being swallowed by the shed. The door hinges creaked. He found his own matches, lit up, and then let the flame burn down to his thumb. From inside the shed came the unmistakable sound of a lid popping off a biscuit tin.

'I won't tell you where I got this,' Mr Whitaker said,

ducking his head in the dark, closing the door, and then striding back over the grass. 'I've had it a long time. It hasn't been taken care of very well; it's mostly lived in there.' He was holding something out on his palm; instantly Francis knew what it was. 'I've kept it dry and everything so I would've thought that it still works. I only fired it once, years ago now just to test it. It's still loaded.'

Francis was eyeing him – and the pistol. 'Fucking 'ell; I weren't expecting that.'

'It's not for silly stuff,' Mr Whitaker said, withdrawing his hand slightly. 'I'm not giving it to you to earn with. It's symbolic, understand? Between us – you and me – nobody else need know.'

Francis held out his hand and took responsibility. The gun was heavy, a burden loaded with individual implications. He admired its dense weight, its callous black metal and worn wooden handle, the long barrel pointing out like an accusing finger. He turned it over, feeling its pull and wondering if it were possible for a man or boy to ever forget the first time he held a gun.

'You don't have to say anything, just keep it under your belt, okay?' Mr Whitaker fixed Francis with a blunt gaze. 'I don't mean that literally of course; find a shoebox or a loose floorboard for it. As long as you're not unnecessary with it, then I'm happy.'

Francis agreed dutifully. 'I don't know what to say,' he admitted. 'Other than thank you … and I'll take care of it.'

'I'll go and grab your jacket so you can keep it out of sight until you're home.' Mr Whitaker drew himself up. 'Make sure Connie doesn't lay eyes on it, won't you?' he added. 'The women in this family can be fond of their own voices.' Francis smiled. Mr Whitaker patted him on the shoulder, almost starting away and then not. 'By the way,' he said, 'how did that arm of yours heal up in the end?'

Francis rolled it in its socket, 'Fine.'

'I respect you for what you did, you know?' Mr Whitaker told him. 'For what that chap did to *you*, he deserved it.' Satisfied with what he'd said, and with *back-in-a-jiffy* enthusiasm he turned on his heel and headed for the house.

The second cigarette had almost smoked itself without any help, a tiny orange bud in a blotted world. Francis stood there like a relic, captured in still life, an iconic image of his time: a Teddy Boy, alone beneath the stars, a fag butt in one hand and a luger pistol in the other.

ORI POLLITT

High above Greenland Docks, sailing in the midmorning sunshine, a lone seagull arched its wings, glided downwards and settled itself on the rim of the ship's funnel. He flapped, lowering his head and defining his balance to take in the view. There were men below – human birds – two of them, squawking and ruffling one another's feathers.

'You're winding *yourself* up,' George King said, frustrated. 'I don't understand what you're getting so excited about, Bertie.' He turned away and peered out over the water.

'Are yer fucking deaf…?'

George closed his eyes, taking a breath before coming about. 'I think I must be,' he said glaring, his face bronze. 'But once I stop trying to listen altogether, once I give up, that's when it becomes bad news for the both of us. So, calm the fuck down!'

Unkempt and fuming, Bertie Crogan watched him.

The gull took off, circled, and then landed again. He edged himself along the rusted harpoon gun mounted on the ship's bow, small-minded and tiny-eyed. The boat, a retired Norwegian whaling vessel, was the jewel in George's crown; beloved but no longer seaworthy, it now kept to the quayside, decaying, bobbing in the brown like a body in a bathtub. In the background the racket of clattering wood, brick and bone carried on regardless; the sound of stacking timber and men hoisting ropes, of a thousand pairs of grubby hands shedding their skins.

'Yer not hearing me, Georgie,' Bertie said, choosing his words.

'Nah, I ain't,' George said, standing square on, the sun casting his gigantic shadow across the deck. Toying with the idea... Bertie offered him the curve of a smile and twisted slightly so he could take in the men at work on the dockside. He was pale in spite of summer, the blue veins showing on the backs of his hands.

The monotonous hammer banging started again.

George stayed put, his white shirt unbuttoned and sculpting his chest hair. 'Now,' he said, 'Don't worry about Leonard, he's a good man. He knows how to keep a secret; it's not as if he's anywhere he hasn't been before.' He smoothed his thick fingers over his hair, relaxing a little. 'I'll see that his family are right for his share. He knows that we'll make sure they don't starve.'

Bertie sniggered. 'I'm nae worried aboot *Leonard*, Georgie.'

'Why the fuck do you keep throwing his name about, then?'

'Because he owes me money...'

George scowled. 'What for, getting caught?'

'Nae,' Bertie said. 'Because the coppers came through one of ma doors tae get the stupid bastard, that's why.' He stuck his finger into his front. 'The fucking place is shut doon.'

Harvey Welsh had found his Jelly-man: he'd arrested Leonard Humphreys a day ago in a raid on an illegal betting shop, an enterprise which belonged to Crogan on the Fulham Road. Leonard had had his collar felt for one simple reason: his name was one of five with previous convictions on an employee record at a quarry near Dartford. As George had foretold, Leonard knew the drill, he'd sat in the interview room with his head in his hands and said nothing.

George looked unsympathetic. 'That's the name of the game, mate,' he said. 'It ain't Leonard's fault; if *you* don't pay the right people then they'll knock at your door.' He shook his head, mocking. 'What are you suggesting, that he asked them to nick him at one of your places just to piss you off?'

'I dinnae know, did he?' Bertie said seriously. 'Or maybe somebody else did and fucked the pair of us…?'

'Who?'

'Margie.'

'Bollocks.'

'Why?' Bertie spat and wiped his mouth on his sleeve. 'Flash prick! Maybe that wee shite *is* paying the right people –'

'Oh, for fuck's sake,' George sighed. 'What are you, a fucking schoolgirl? Calling people names and squabbling over petty nonsense: It gets fucking boring, you and him.' Bertie spat again and swatted the air in between them. 'That's what this is all about, ain't it?' George went on, 'it's all about that bee you've got in your bonnet over Marge. What is it with you, eh? What are you really fucked off about, the old bill turning over one of your places or Marge making a few quid?' George chased down Bertie's gaze. 'That's what this is: you're trying to lean on Leonard because you can't stick it on Marge.'

Bertie rocked back and forth on his heels. 'What do yer mean, I cannae?' he growled, his face questioning George's, trying his eyes. 'I can dae as I please, Georgie … and I can fucking well dae it wi God's will.'

George ignored him. 'I've told you already, Marge asked me if I could put him in touch with anybody who might be able to help out on a job he was doing. I gave him Leonard, so there should be no problem. End of.'

Bertie reasserted his feet, his stare rolling over black. 'There's one wee problem, Georgie: ye should've asked me before using one of ma donkeys for somebody else's work – especially when it leaves me oot of pocket and every other *cunt* makes on it.' He let out a short cackle, seething, reaching around and slapping himself on his backside. 'Am I a lassie, Georgie? Am I a queer? Dae yer want me tae hold ma cheeks apart for yer wee boy Margie tae come along and stick his dick in ma wee arse-hole...?'

George eyed him...

Bertie Crogan had killed his first man by the time he'd earned a dozen candles on a birthday cake. *'I was already a murderer when I lost ma virginity,'* he had once confessed to George laughing. *'Ma mother was a bonnie lass but a whore. I used to watch her with her Johns in the alley behind our hoose.'* He had said it like he was proud. *'The first man I ever killed was an Englishman: hurting her, he was. Grabbing her tits and twisting 'em off – they are vicious people the English. Ye should've seen me Georgie, sneaking up behind him holding the breadknife in ma hand. I was only a bairn, still scared of ma own shadow, I was clever nae tae piss ma pants. The silly bastard didnae even know I was there. He was still at it, even after I stabbed him in the back his wee cock didnae fall oot. The more I cut the bastard the faster he fucked her. I swear tae ye, even once the prick knew he*

was dying he was still sticking it tae her, even with me on his
fucking back. Hard as yer like, he was, doing it tae spite me.
And the bastard finished the job before he took a last gob of
air, I'm sure of it. Can ye believe it? I didnae get off him until
he'd stopped moving, and even when I went round the front
tae get a look at his face, the wee prick still had hold of her
tits. Ma poor mother had tae dig his dead dick oot of her just
so I could drag the bastard's body away for the fucking rats,'

'...One of *your* donkeys?' George said. 'Am I now supposed
to ask *you* before I speak to one of my own people?' Crogan
didn't react. 'He's a grown man. Whether he's doing bits-
and-bobs for you is neither here nor there, Bertie. He doesn't
need you to pat his head and watch him out the door every
time he goes on a bit of work.'

'I'm nae losing money, Georgie. Why should ma business
suffer? Specially if he was working for *ye*? One way or the
other, I'm nae losing a fucking penny.'

'Now it's my fault, is it?' George said, sarcastically. 'Now *I*
owe you the money, do I? If that's what you're here for I can't
tell you no plainer than this: you ain't fucking getting it.'

Bertie laughed maliciously. 'I dinnae want *your* money,
Georgie. Not when Margie boy has just robbed a bank. I'll
have his; Marge can pass me Leonard's divvy.'

George pinched the bridge on his nose, losing patience.
'Make your fucking mind up, will you? By the sounds of it,
you've got it in for the lot of us.' Mastering himself, he took
a stern step closer. 'Look,' he said, 'Marge is coming in on
a venture with *me*, so that means that all that money they
raised from that bank is going in under *my* roof.' Bertie's

tongue began to taste like iron filings. 'You're going to have to wipe your mouth on this one,' George was saying. 'Take a loss, reopen that betting shop at the other end of the street and this time make sure you throw some change at the law, save them bursting in on you again.'

'What venture?'

'A club,' George said. '*My* roof,' he reiterated, making himself clear.

Unmoved, Bertie took his time... 'I dinnae understand why yer letting him get above himself – or his wee brother and the little shags he's got wi him –'

'That's my business,' George said.

'Good for him,' Bertie said treading backwards. He narrowed his sights suspiciously, suddenly believing that he'd worked it out. He grinned. 'Yer keeping it for yerself aren't ye, Georgie?'

'No,' George said. 'I'm just keeping it where I can see it.'

'Argh,' Bertie chuckled, slipping out of his temper like it was a costume. 'Yer should hae said; ye let me get all worked up over nothing.' As he talked, behind his back, his let his palm deliberate with the handle of the hunting knife tucked into his trousers, liking that it was there, precarious under the cloth like a second erection. 'I apologise tae ye, Georgie? Dea ye accept?' The counterfeit grin was static, Bertie's mind was making diabolical speeches to him in morse code, double daring him to do it. 'I'll tell yer what, I'll make a deal wi ye: I'll nae mention it tae Margie, I'll only see Leonard about it when he gets oot.'

George looked at him slate-faced; he never trusted the way

Crogan swung the way he did, the way he flew in and out of moods, laughing with his hands behind his back. 'Suit yourself,' he said, 'but if you're still collecting the losses on that betting shop when Leonard walks out of the nick, you can't be doing as well as I thought you was.' Brooding, George started to turn away and then stopped, reading Bertie's mind. 'That doesn't mean his wife,' he added flatly. 'Stay away from the man's home while he ain't there.'

The gull perched on the harpoon opened and closed its yellow beak and cawed.

'Ye know, Georgie, if ye keep stepping in the way of these wee cunts, one day ye and me might meet in the middle.' He was still grinning. 'God forbid that should happen, eh?'

Finished with the discussion, George showed him his back, half goading him, expecting to feel Bertie creep up behind him, blade between his peekaboo fingers. 'So be it,' he said, 'whatever will be, will be.' He listened for the direction of the footsteps on the metal decking – Crogan was walking away. George smiled, raising his voice over his shoulder. 'I would have thought that you'd take better care of yourself than that, Bertie. Have a look about, mate: there's no heather on the hills round 'ere.'

Crossing the gangplank to the quayside, Bertie was already singing, his tone a drunken uncle: 'Scots, whae hae wi Wallace bled…Scots, wham Bruce has aften led…welcome tae yer gory bed…or tae victory…' He lifted his fist in farewell. 'I'll see yer at the club, Georgie!' he shouted. 'Opening night … yer can buy me a drink.'

George let him go. He was watching the water, pondering

fag ends, caught in the drift, huddling against the hull like little men overboard in terracotta lifejackets. The gull took off, answering the call to prayer, soaring in search of the ocean.

On the 5th of August 1958 Carrie Andrews became an honest woman. Lacy and white, wearing an icing sugar smile and pearl earrings, she wedded her love inside Wandsworth town hall. Worse for wear and clad in his favourite drape jacket and brothel creeper shoes, her groom managed to recite his vows earnestly despite a thumping hangover. They cut their cake and sang a chorus for an avalanche of well-wishers. And in the evening, after a couple of broken barrels, they left the pub dancing, beer cans on a string playing a wedding march behind their bumper. Mr and Mrs Meehan – Micky and Carrie – were now husband and wife.

Standing on the pavement, tiptoeing alongside the leggy blonde who'd accompanied him to the festivities, Mr Ori Pollitt waved amongst those who were seeing them on their way.

Three days later, sat like a tangerine on top of a fruit bowl and still overdressed, Ori Pollitt was stuck behind his desk.

Speaking into the telephone: 'Honestly, old boy,' he said, his expressive face glowing beneath a dry sweep of ginger hair, 'I'm telling you: most of these so-called villains are as thick as two planks.' He rolled a long laugh off his tongue, only slowing down when he heard voices outside. 'On that note, Matthew, I shall have to bid you farewell; I think there's somebody here to see me.' He sat up a little straighter. 'Right you are friend, cheerio!' There was no knock; the office door opened. The telephone receiver went down with a *ding*. 'Margie!' Ori exclaimed, jubilantly jumping up from his chair. 'To what do I owe the pleasure?'

Ori Pollitt, Chartered Accountant – the man who used to rent out dirty photographs to the other lads in the dormitory back when he was a public school boy – was now practically related to Marge; or so he was fond of saying. The two had first rubbed shoulders thanks to a certain leggy blonde who happened to be the sister of Marge's then girlfriend. Marge had introduced Ori to George and Mr King had put him to work: he had his uses, primarily making numbers get bigger, land somewhere else and sometimes disappear altogether. He made the money make itself – unbalancing books, doing snide stock receipts, loaning against moody businesses, cheque frauds, and setting up long firm deals – easy pickings for his porky little fingers in his Chelsea office.

'Thought I'd drop by and see how you're managing,' Marge said, shaking Ori's hand.

'Sit tight,' he said, closing the door on whoever he'd arrived with. 'I'll be a minute.'

'I spoke to Georgie boy yesterday,' Ori said. 'Did he

not tell you?'

'I ain't seen him. I've been running about here-there-and-everywhere, trying to sort –'

'It's all sorted,' Ori professed. 'No problems whatsoever … well, tell a lie, there was one fellow down at the council who had his knickers in a twist over the licensing but that's all taken care of now; he's happy.'

'What about the bank business?'

'All wrapped up with a polka-dot bow,' Ori bragged, leaning back against the front of his desk, fiddling with his cravat. 'You know how people are: we had to lay out the odd bob or two to oil a few palms but it's all done now.' He shuffled his eyebrows. 'The money's safe; the investments were all made through falsified accounts by fictitious investors. It's easier. That way, if any of you should fall foul of the law in the future they won't be able to touch it because none of you are on the actual paperwork –' He noticed the way Marge was studying him. 'There's no need for the frown old boy, naturally, you will all have access to the personal accounts; I've set them up in the same names. George is having identification documents mocked up for each of you.' Smiling, he stood up off the desk and pinched Marge's cheek roguishly. 'You're in good hands,' he said, already on his way over to the bookshelves in the corner. 'We can go over all the details once the place is open; the only thing you need worry about is how to stop Micky and his mates drinking the bloody place dry now they've been made shareholders.' He chortled, a glass brandy decanter clinking in his hand. 'If you can keep a lid on them, in six months' time we should all be strolling around with pockets as full as a poof's arsehole.'

Marge laughed. 'Look, if you want to handle that kind of cash that's your own look-out, mate. If it's all the same, I'd rather keep mine clean and tidy.'

'You know me Margie boy,' Ori said, chuckling, 'soiled or otherwise, I'm not bothered how it comes.' Beaming, he handed Marge his glass and toasted himself. 'Another?' Marge nodded. Ori went back to the bookcase. 'By the way,' he said, pausing. 'Who have you got hiding outside?'

'My kid brother,' Marge said, 'the youngest one, Nippy.'

'Didn't I meet him at the wedding?' Ori asked, thinking on it and then answering himself. 'I did; isn't he the one who shares my blessings?' He made his ginger fringe fall into his face.

'That's him,' Marge said. 'I've got him running errands with me today.'

'Well, how old is he?'

'Fifteen, I think,' Marge answered.

'For heaven's sake man,' Ori cried, incredulous. 'That's plenty old enough. Bring him in and give him a drink, we can't leave him sitting out there like a stray cat.'

'I'll call him in when we've finished talking,' Marge compromised.

'But there's nothing left to say, old boy,' Ori said dismissively, going ahead and fishing out a third glass. 'It's like I said: we've had no problems. Honestly, the vast majority of these bankers and officials are as thick as two planks.'

Barley Sugar

CASSELS

2004

Around the same time on Sunday afternoon that Lewis and his Grandfather were driving through a storm in north Yorkshire and Deborah Coles was rushing out the door of her lover's flat in search of new underwear, Alistair Cassels was deep in thought and making changes.

Upright and bespectacled in his mother's old armchair, he was perusing the reworked opening of his manuscript. It was finally finished – the *whole* thing – the *novel* – all four hundred and fifty pages of it painstakingly plotted and transcribed from the lip of his imagination. 'Done!' he said aloud, glancing down at *Tolstoy* his pet tortoise. He was a writer now, more so than ever; the white rustle of unfilled pages was now somebody else's plague. He lifted his eyes, smirking at a bijou wooden plaque standing atop the gas fire; it had been a witty little reminder from the school faculty last Christmas: *those who can't do, teach.*

The book, *this* book, the first one – a non-masterpiece involving a super sleuth detective, a band of inner city youth, and the mysterious murder of a scout leader – was only supposed to breathe new life into a beloved but much hacked-at genre.

He unsettled his papers so he could hear his happy sound and then got up, careful not to tread on Tolstoy. His mother's collection of porcelain wildlife tracked him around the room. The house, a three bedroom end of terrace which his parents had prised from the council during Thatcher's reign, still echoed of songs of praise and still whiffed of the lady who'd lived here last. And he supposed that this house he had inherited was what Juliet had been waiting for in order to leave him; his ever-thoughtful ex-wife had been biding her time. That way he would at least have somewhere to live. How good of her to think of him, to be so considerate before moving her lady-friend into their marital bed. He thought that he'd married a teacher, not a *lesbian*. The best part was that she'd used a cucumber from the fridge as a paperweight to pin the note to the sideboard:

Alistair,

Please excuse the crudeness of the note. I couldn't bring myself to see you just now, hence this, but you need to move back to your family home. I've met someone and I'm in love with her. Please try and refrain from telephoning me to squabble, I think we both can admit this has been coming. However, should you need me for anything constructive, I will be staying with Sarah until you are gone.

PS. I don't wish to go through the hullaballoo of a divorce just now, so maybe we should address that in due time.

It had been as simple as that; nothing more to discuss. His wife was in love with the music teacher and he was back at his deceased mother's. He hated this house, all four walls and the roof. It had been sold to his parents with ideals, as their own little piece of England in an 'up and coming area'. Only Thatcher hadn't worked out, had she? And the so-called up-and-coming area never materialised. Labour had taken over and let in the lowlife landlords.

He took off his spectacles, polished the lenses, and then slid them back onto his nose; the hooked stems brushed against the grey above his ears. He understood now that this is why he wrote and had written, and perhaps why so feverishly. That stack of paper on the armchair was his ticket. Once he was published he could give up teaching – a vocation he found to be increasingly pointless; it was more in tune with supervising the dross than educating young minds. In the time it took to sell this God-awful house, he could churn out a follow up, another crime thriller starring the same detective in a different setting; it would be something just to tide him over until he moved on to a better place. Then, once he'd bought himself a little hovel in the country – something on a dusty lane opposite a meadow – he could start work on something real: a piece of literature.

He stalked once more around the room and then went back to his chair and his manuscript. He thought about nothing else. Not about Lewis or Sammy. Not about the wallet on his dresser or the keys on the hook. Not once did he question the lie he'd told or even why he'd told it. Even if he had, it wouldn't have rankled.

Butterflies…

Belly Fairies; that's what her mother had called them: tiny, magical visitors which played in a girl's tummy to let her know whether or not she liked a boy. If Deborah had been seesawing this morning in James's flat, she was now riding high at full tilt. James had sprung it on her while she was showering, calling through the door: *'I've just got off the phone to mum,'* he'd said. She hadn't responded, only anticipated what might come next. *'Hear this,'* he'd gone on, *'I told her I was with you and she asked me to bring you for Sunday dinner.'* – A surprised chuckle – *'Do you fancy it? The whole family will be there.'* A day before she wouldn't have believed she would have spent the night, now she was considering meeting his parents. It was almost moving too fast, flying before her eyes, pinning and spinning her like the hearts and diamonds ride at the fair.

She was now rushing, unprepared in minimal make up, bouncing along the high street wearing last night's dress. The previous evening she had left home equipped only for a dinner: mascara, lippie, and half a bottle of perfume in her bag. Now all this had happened and she'd found herself caught short. She needed an appropriate outfit – at the very least some clean underwear. If this thing with James was to all of a sudden decide to go somewhere, then first impressions counted. Her thoughts were merry, going round too fast. Even if sex didn't clarify the beginning of something, surely an invite for Sunday dinner did?

The shopping centre's revolving doors sucked her in, twirled her round, and then blew her inside on a positive wind. Not so much recently, but at one point, places like these had become no-go zones. At the same time as she became a widow, Deborah had also made the unconscious conversion to catalogue mum. Retail therapy for the single parent: licking one's thumbs and flicking through crate paper pages, going on a strategic shopping spree from the sofa by taking down the item number and conveniently spreading out the cost in easy monthly payments. Phil Collins' version of the Supremes hit, *You Can't Hurry Love,* was coming out of the centre's Tannoy system. Deborah hummed along in an optimistic rush, rerunning her list in her mind: *foundation and blusher ... something to wear ... and last but not least, clean pants.* Her credit card suddenly felt as pliable as her body. Lubricated, she pushed amongst the clothing rails. She found something quickly; something she liked, something suitable: a pair of navy fitted trousers and a detailed cream blouse. She could wear it with last night's heels. It was perfect for a first impression, femme as well as unashamedly covered up: in other words, no cleavage. If James's mother was anything like how she imagined, she certainly didn't think she would appreciate another woman attempting to gain favour at her dinner table.

As Deborah wandered through the cosmetics counters, it occurred to her that it was going to be difficult to find a colour match amongst the shades of tan and taupe, *less is more she thought*, feeling marvellous. In a childish, fingers crossed behind her back kind of way, she realised that she was now hopeful. This afternoon was another unknown, another step closer towards ... *moving on without forgetting.*

Outside the car, green England was nothing but a mythical

shape hidden behind a sheet of torrential rain and tyre splash. Lewis squinted at the electronic traffic-sign as they passed; dotty yellow bulbs glinting like something rich: INCIDENT AHEAD. SLOW DOWN.

'That's bound to be a jack-knifed lorry,' Francis commented, adding a second hand to the steering-wheel.

Lewis stooped forwards and peered out of the windscreen. 'Whatever it is, it don't look good,' he said expertly, blowing out his cheeks and sighing, mimicking a cynical man.

'Nothing ever does,' Francis said, philosophising. Without knowing he was, he was smiling – his grandson pulling the exact same face that his father used to. He slowed the Daimler down to thirty.

Lewis sat back in his seat, pausing, staring at the side of his grandfather's face. 'Have you ever shot someone?' he said, his first thought (the Lugar pistol) coming out as a question.

Francis glanced at him briefly. 'Once,' he said, answering without any difficulty. 'But I shouldn't have. It was one of –'

'I *knew* it!' Lewis shouted, excitement lighting him up. 'Shit, man, I knew it … you was a proper *Gangster!*'

Francis laughed. 'And what's one of them, then?'

'Whatever,' Lewis dismissed, refusing to feel silly. 'You know what I mean, everything you're saying … *guns* … *robberies* … *nightclubs* … it sounds like one of them old gangster films.'

Francis shook his head. 'That's just a fictional word,' he said, calmly. 'Think about it: they're only *Gangsters* if you're looking at them from the outside; otherwise, they're just a bloke who gets a runny nose and a sore throat like the rest of us.' He shifted to Lewis, then back to the road. 'Not that I'm saying there ain't dangerous people around, of course there are – some might even be successful criminals. But you only have to pick up a history book to see that the men who go chasing made up titles are usually the first ones to lose their heads.'

Undeterred, Lewis measured him. 'Stop trying *not* to glamourise it,' he said flippantly, distracted by the blues and twos on the side of the road. The traffic was crawling, break lights burning in the damp. Up ahead, an articulator lorry had crash landed across two lanes, its hide peeled halfway back, the fire crew and their equipment cutting the dead driver out of his crushed cab. The Daimler rolled by the wreck harmlessly, splashing up puddles like an old pair of Cherry Reds. Thinking that his grandfather had been right about the lorry, Lewis was going to say something and then decided to keep his mouth shut.

Francis hardly looked. 'The club was George and Margie's thing,' he said. 'We all stuck a few quid into it but mainly we stayed in the background. They took care of it; all that razzmatazz bit was their bag, not mine. I was happy with whatever they gave me.' Whirling, the emergency service lights bathed his face in cold water. 'We opened on New Year's Eve, 1959...' he said. '... My God! Micky was proud as punch; he couldn't believe that we owned something on the King's Road.' He sighed reminiscently, shying away from the light. He blinked. 'I'll never forget it for as long as I live,' he said regrettably. 'That was the night when our whole world changed.'

Barley Sugar

NIPPY

New Year's Eve, 1959

Moving on champagne heels, Marcia Blake climbed the empty stairwell at the back of the club one step at a time, the lofty chill lifting the hem of her sparkly cocktail dress. Her temples thumped, the thin air waving and helping her offer a flat palm to the wall. The stairs creaked like weathered decking. She took a deep breath and puffed into her bobbed fringe. The place reeked of fresh paint and perfume. Behind her – below – beyond a second set of doors, the club insisted on having a good time. And why not, it was opening night: dickey bows and feathers all round. Everybody they knew (*he* knew) was out and wearing fur, celebrating the boys' marvellous *fucking* achievement.

She felt nauseous, like she was full of soup. She thought about screaming, about calling out his name at the top of her voice and giving him a chance – she stopped herself. She couldn't do it, couldn't bear to get no reply; she'd feel like one of those poor fools who call a man's name into an empty house only to realise that the hard silence means that he's gone. That he's with another – *better* – woman, a prettier girl. Quivering, drunk, wondering if he might hear her if she cried. She could never find him anymore; he was gone, always *gone*. Marcia tottered back over her shoulder, hoping for someone. There was nobody coming to stop her, nobody running out into the hall and telling her to come back, reassuring her that she was being silly, that she was imagining it. But why would they? Not one of them had noticed her leaving; not Connie, not Carrie, or any of the other girlfriends and wives, they were all too busy perching around tables in dramatic dresses and admiring their men. *Their* men, who were where they could see them, swanning about in fine suits and showing off their new club. She snuffed a dry, bitter, spit-filled laugh to herself: to think, she was the muggins who had starched his shirt. The back of her throat burned. Why her? Why couldn't it be somebody else's turn to walk the back stairs? It echoed here, with that strange loneliness which blows through the back of places, the jazz band's smoky notes wafting underneath the double doors from the main lounge. Nobody cared. Marcia turned her head purposefully, the movement tinkling her earrings like miniature wind chimes. She took a step higher ... then another, treading in violet vertigo. From the top step she could no longer hear anything else; only the passionate, frantic noise coming from the upstairs office – the sound of a woman making a meal of a man. The door on the landing was open a crack, teasing slim pickings for the voyeur. Clenched, she approached it furrowed, wary like a mother doe. Her body was now a single nerve, everything finding a pulse. They were fucking; she could hear it. She hitched, crudely aware that her vagina was throbbing – *tightening* – as if making one last attempt at holding on to him.

She didn't register the door hitting the wall behind its hinges after she'd kicked it open. The scene in front of her was a medley of movement: Winston, trousers around his ankles, pulled out and fell backwards, folding in half, his feet caught up in fabric. On the desk, the girl's legs stayed spread like a pair of welcoming arms. She peeked over her chest apologetically.

Marcia wailed and then ran; her tears not making it to her chin.

Beyond the club's main entrance, the King's Road beeped and glittered under shadow and gloss.

'...Forget about all that, for now,' George said, staying calm. He fixed his tie in one of the foyer mirrors. 'First thing's first: you need to go and get yourself stitched up, son.'

Using Davey for support, Marge leaned back against the wall; the square tablecloth he had pressed to the wound on the side of his head soaked and oversized. 'It's only a nick,' he slurred, screwing up his face in pain. 'I tell you what though, George; I'm fucking well having him for it this time. The cunt could've taken my fucking eye out.'

George put a hand on his shoulder. 'Fair enough; he's brought it on himself.'

Only Ori had actually seen it happen; he and Marge had been alone with some girls on a private table. By the time any of the others had got through the screaming and commotion, they'd found him laid out with a chair on top of him and Bertie Crogan's champagne flute sticking out of his scalp.

'Shame you ducked,' Micky said, joking. 'If you'd lost

an eye, you'd finally have an excuse to fucking – what?' he said, shrugging at the way Francis was looking. 'Why you looking at me like that? That's what it says in the Bible: an eye for an eye.'

'That's *not* what it means...' Ori said, his pompous voice interjecting. He had his head down, blotting spots of Marge's blood into his buff coloured trousers.

Micky wheeled around on him. 'Don't fucking open your mouth now you *prick*, a minute ago you was hiding behind that lanky bird of yours. Do us all a favour: next time somebody glasses a friend of yours in front of you, scream. That way somebody else might be able to stop the bastard strolling away -'

'Alright ... alright...' George said, stepping in, 'save all that bollocks for another day.' He looked at Ori, prompting him. 'Go and fetch a motor,' he told him. 'You and Davey get Marge up the hospital.'

Micky took a step backwards and let Ori slip past him and out of the doors to the street. 'It's raining,' Ori said. 'Somebody might want to find him an umbrella.'

'He's just had his noggin opened up Ori, mate; I doubt a little bit of water will hurt him.' Watching him go up the road, agitated, Micky turned in a circle. 'And where the fuck is *Winston?*'

Behind them, a consoling arm wrapped around Marcia, Connie pushed open the club's double doors. 'He's upstairs,' she said. Marcia tucked herself deeper into her friend's bosom, mascara etched into her face.

'*Mind out!*' Francis said, getting the backs up of the

bystanders who hadn't noticed the two women. He moved to help her, concerned. 'What's happened?'

'Your friend,' Connie answered. She bowed her head and whispered something soft in Marcia's ear. 'Can you get us our coats please, Francis? We're leaving.' She glanced up at Micky and George – who were now helping Davey shuffle Marge outside into a waiting car – and then regarded Francis. 'I'm not talking about this here,' she hissed quietly. 'Marcia needs to go home.'

Without instruction, the cloakroom attendant obliged Connie's request. One by one, she handed Francis two fur-collared coats over the counter. Opening the first one up for Marcia to slip into, he fished into his pocket for his money clip. 'Well, hold on a second,' he said, pushing paper into her hand. 'I'll get someone to flag you a taxi.'

In the road, engine running, Ori flashed his headlights. Micky banged his hand twice on the car's roof to wish them well, and then stood back next to George to watch it drive away.

Connie stopped what she was doing. 'Is Marge okay?'

Francis nodded, shrouding her in her coat. 'Once they've seen to him with a needle and thread, he should be fine.' He tried again to find out what had happened, this time discreetly mouthing silently behind Marcia's back … *what's going on?*

Imploring him with her eyes, Connie shook her head and returned an arm to Marcia's shoulder.

Inside the lounge, one of the two young pals Nippy Meehan had been allowed to bring to the club keeled over the bar and threw up all over his shoes. He picked his head up, wiped his mouth, and then carried on drinking. Struggling to stand straight, Nippy and his other friend gave him a round of applause, erupting in brutal laughter. Winston bought them all another drink, knocked back one more for the road, and headed towards the world. He hadn't bothered to ask about Marge; on his way downstairs and through the bar, three people had stopped him and he'd been told.

Leaving, Winston hesitated, only spotting Carrie in the crowd. The doors flapped outwards, the brass butterfly handles getting away from him. Coming in out of the cold, George King slapped him on the back as he passed.

'Where the fuck did *you* go?' Micky's voice bombarded him as soon as the door was wide enough to make him visible.

Winston took a tactical glance over to where Connie and Marcia were huddled by the wall. 'It don't matter,' he replied, urging Micky to leave the subject alone. 'Where's Marge? Was he cut bad?'

Micky looked over at the girls and then back to Winston, a strange joy in his expression. 'He'll live,' he answered. 'They've took him up the hospital. His problem was that he only had Ori with him, Crogan had *Roy Easter* –'

'*Micky…?*' Carrie's loud, brassy voice interrupted. She came up behind Winston, leading Nippy by the wrist and shimmying her pregnant belly through the crowd inside. 'You need to have a word with your little brother,' she said. 'They're in here causing trouble for no reason; they've just started on some bloke at the bar.'

Stupidly drunk, Nippy beamed about it. 'I thought he was one of the geezers Marge was rowing with.'

'I think it's time for them to go,' Carrie insisted.

Winston, who'd been pulled to one side by Francis, spoke without turning around: 'They can come with me. I'm fucking off home in a minute, anyway.'

Micky took over; grabbing his little brother's arm and slinging him out the door. 'And you two can piss off an' all,' he said, aiming a false tirade at Nippy's two staggering pals. 'How bloody well dare you start a to-do in front of my lovely wife … she's not in any condition to have to deal with the likes of you young ruffians. Go on, sling your hooks.' He shoved them playfully, pushing until they'd tumbled legless out onto the street and fallen on top of Nippy. Noticing Marcia crying, Carrie side-stepped her husband and went to her. 'Fucking charming,' Micky commented, dusting down his suit. 'She makes me kick out my own brother and then turns her back on me.' Hands splayed, he turned back to Winston. 'I might as well drive you home with them, then. Look at the fucking state they're in, I'd better get them back to my mum's before they start bumming each other where people can see.'

'I'm walking,' Winston said. 'I need to clear my head.'

Micky stared at him, confused. 'What for,' he said, 'it's fucking *raining*…' But Winston was already going, glazed, brushing past him and swaying unsteadily out onto the pavement, raindrops skidding off of his hair oil.

Francis and Micky regarded one another.

'Go with him, Mick,' Francis said.

'He just said he was walking. Sod that it's pissin' down.'

'Take an umbrella!'

Micky laughed. 'Who am I, Ori fucking Pollitt?'

'Go with him.' Francis said, careful to keep his voice away from the girls. 'He ain't right, I can tell.' Nippy and his friends were now rolling over, play-fighting on the curb. 'Take them along as well; it'll sober them up.'

Micky stuck his head out of the door to see how far Winston had got up the road. Having thought about it, he barked at his brother: 'Nippy! Stop playing with your boyfriends and get up. We're walking with Winston.' He stepped across the foyer and tugged on Carrie's sleeve – he could hear Francis behind him, reassuring Nippy that once they were across the bridge they'd be in Battersea, practically home. 'I'm going for a stroll with Wince,' he told her; and then, unable to resist stirring: '*Francis* reckons I should go with him and make sure he's okay.'

From under Connie's arm, Marcia glared at him.

'You're not going after that bloke who hit Marge, are you?' Carrie touched his arm, 'Promise me...'

'I promise,' Micky said smiling.

'I mean it, Micky. You got a pregnant wife who needs your concern. Let Marge take care of his own problems. Please.'

'Listen,' Micky said, smiling and rubbing her belly. 'You go home with these two and see Marcia right. As soon as I've got Nip back at mum's I'll run straight round the corner and dive in under the covers with you. If I go anywhere else, you can...' She gave in, pursing her lips and inviting him to kiss her.

Sandwiched between two other parked cars, Bertie Crogan's white Jaguar sat perfectly still on the side of the road like a spot on a domino. He had left the club almost in jest; disappearing not because George had said so – the respect there had worn thin – but because men who move in straight lines are easier to see coming. He recited the mantra to himself, in his head, his mind churning it over and over as if to settle something with itself. His face ached. He twisted, flexing his jaw; the shadowed rendering of him in the window grimacing grotesque, the blood between its teeth canine. He swallowed bitterly, drinking a shot of the coppery gloop from under his tongue and reassuring himself. He watched his ghost, nodding, muttering incoherent orders underneath his breath and moving the battlefield. The eyes were already at war, stoned, tuning in and out from between his ears, unblinking. Beside him, crushing the passenger seat, Roy Easter's lumpy, ruddy face was minding the other wing mirror.

Bertie's voice cracked the silence, blood and mucus spraying the windscreen: 'Aye…' he said, suddenly responding to Easter's grumbled breathing. 'What dae ye expect, he's a fucking Englishman; the man favours the meek.'

Easter hardly heard. He had his brawny head lowered, swollen knuckles rubbing the window to get a clearer picture of the figures that were crossing the road. It was Nippy and his two friends, blundering about and shouting, staging a pantomime fight.

Bertie scowled into the rear-view. From a distance, the club entrance was only a hazy glow, distorted by the rain-smeared windows of the cars behind. The boys had gone over to Roy's side leaving two shapes, Micky and Winston, lagging on the opposite pavement. Roy pulled something from underneath his seat and silently nudged open the car door.

Roy's voice, an Irish whisper: 'If that there's Micky and the coloured boy on yer side, who are these coming up?'

'It's nae Margie,' Bertie said, hunkering down and checking both sides – both mirrors. 'Looks tae me like the wee brother and his pals.'

Nippy took a dive, got up, and then tripped again. He scampered ahead, laughing, rounding on his friends and beckoning them on. No more than ten feet from the car, loud and unaware, arms wide, he bawled something at Micky on the other side of the road. With no idea what was behind him, he stepped backwards and rested his hand on the parked car, waiting for directions. Easter opened the door another inch, ready and heavy-handed, so close he could reach out and pick the lose threads out the back of the boy's jacket.

A cold march stomping his chest, Bertie swallowed another mouthful of blood and checked how far Micky and Winston were behind. 'Leave 'em be,' he hissed through a clogged breath. He sank lower, touching himself. Nippy's hand lifted off of the paint and he went running, his friends catching up, charging and swinging their blazers above their heads. Easter didn't move; his hand and whatever was in it only a glass width away when the boys bumbled past his window none the wiser. They jogged on, raucous, yelling and whipping one another with their jackets until they vanished around the corner. 'That's it...' Bertie whispered cajoling himself, cradle-singing. '...Let the wee bastards go. Wait for Margie. I want Margie.'

Eventually, chatting, Micky and Winston strolled in and out of the frame of the windows. Like Hunters in a hive, Bertie Crogan and Roy Easter noiselessly observed them crossing over the road and turning the corner.

'You shouldn't feel too fucking bad mate, that little blonde tart was a peach.' Micky flicked his wet hair back, laughing. 'I just can't believe she burst in and nabbed you at it; no wonder the girls had their cat claws out.'

Battersea Bridge was rolled out before them, low lit, the Victorian lampposts lining its trim burning orange wells in the dark water. Up ahead, halfway across and three sheets to the wind, Nippy had climbed the railings to aim a stream of piss into the river.

'Oi, Nip!' Micky shouted. 'If you fall in, make sure you tuck that away before you hit the water; whatever's swimming about down there might eat tiddlers.'

Balancing, Nippy stuck two fingers up.

'I'm done with her anyway,' Winston said.

'Who, that tart?' Micky asked, distracted.

'Nah, Marcia. She's a fucking pretender.'

Micky sounded surprised: 'What do you mean? She ain't been sleeping around as well, has she?'

Winston frowned at him. 'She been pretending the whole time I've known her,' he conceded. 'She don't love *me* – she never fucking has, mate. It's all been bollocks: wanting to get married and have a family and all that...' He scoffed. 'The bird only lets me fuck her if she's wearing one of them ladies' fucking prophylactics.' Micky's face twisted. 'It's like a condom for women,' Winston clarified before he could ask. 'It's like sticking your dick in a fucking sock.'

Micky cackled. 'Why, what's the matter with her? Has she got a disease or something?'

'Nope,' Winston said plainly. 'She wears it because she's shit-scared of having my baby.' Micky looked at him, knowing Winston, knowing what that meant. 'At first I went along with it. But after this long – after supposedly falling in love with me – it ain't fucking right; it can't be right, can it?'

Micky shrugged. 'I don't get it, mate. Why? It ain't as if you're skint and can't look after her.'

Winston stopped. He rubbed his face with his hand and then showed Micky a clean set of fingers. 'Because *this* don't come off,' he said, solemnly. 'She stuffs a plastic bag up her crotch to make sure none of me gets in her. That fucking thing catches my babies before they can grow.' Micky looked away from the demonstration. 'Marcia told me, she said her mother warned her from the start not to give her any funny coloured grandkids. When we was first together she used to say that she didn't care what people said, that it went in one ear and out the other.' He smiled weakly. 'For her to still be wearing those fanny sacks though, she was obviously lying, weren't she?'

'Fuck her then,' Micky said defiantly. 'And her stuck-up mother. The bird's a wrong'un, it's just took us this long to suss her out.' He bumped his shoulder into Winston's and laughed. 'At least now we can fuck her off and find you a new nice little sort, one who loves herself a big bit of black...' He nudged him again. 'Not that blonde tart though, once was enough for her. She don't deserve you either.'

Winston nudged him back, harder. 'Fuck it! Micky, one day when I'm all grown up, I wanna be just like you!'

'Who fucking don't?' Micky joked, spreading his arms to take in the city. Ahead, Nippy had clambered down and carried on; the youngsters were almost across. Pointing, Micky called out to them: 'Oi, Nippy you silly prick! Go right! Cut through the estate at Surrey Lane...'

Winston's face, the wet air stretching across it, had firmed up. He had eyes on his friend, 'You're a lucky little cunt, Mick,' he said, smiling. 'What you've got with Carrie is worth way more than any of this other shit we've got going on. Make sure you keep that in mind.' He rested his arm over Micky's shoulder and patted him on the back. 'Whatever you do, don't fuck it up...don't let anything fuck it up. You're about to be someone's old man. That's what this whole thing is about...it's all part of God's plan.'

There were quickening footfalls on the King's Road, undone

shoelaces lashing along beside the slight man in the grey suit. Panting, he skidded alongside the Jaguar and rapped on the glass. 'You've missed him,' he said, speaking before Roy could wind down the window. 'Marge ain't there no more, they've took him up the hospital already.'

'Where did they take him?'

'Fucked if I know,' the man said. 'George has had me running errands up and down the stairs all bloody night.'

'Well why the *fuck* didnae ye tell us, yer wee fuck.' Bertie spat, leaning over Roy's lap. He smashed a fist against the dashboard. 'Are yer fucking certain? I didnae see them.'

Standing back, the man gave a nod. 'I'm sorry Bertie, mate, I just couldn't –'

The car barked into life. Growling, it swung out into the road and sped away.

The bedroom was spinning, still pungent with the pumps and grunts Silvia's husband had just given her before sleep – for once, the *'good-seeing-to'* had materialised after the drinking. She peeled herself out from under him and stood up off the bed. She went to the window, pussyfooting naked, wondering whether or not it would still be raining. Nipples sniffing upwards for fresh air, she slid open the window.

Spirited voices outside: *'Go on girl, Give us a flash! Show us your fropneys!'* They cheered, demanding an encore, catcalling, pitching in with bells and whistles. The curtains curtseyed; the wind blowing and giving the boys their show.

Silvia jumped back, startled, her breasts doing a delightful little swing step in time with the applause.

Dennis Duffy opened his eyes, seeing red. 'Who the fuck's that, Silvia?' he rasped, squirming out from the blanket and struggling with his vowels. On his feet, he swung a backhand to get her out of his way, a bellied man moving like a dead animal. He regarded her standing there with her arms pinned across her chest, her femaleness suddenly a nuisance now that he'd shot his bolt. Fuming, accusing her of inviting the attention – the way she always did, the way she *fucking* breathed – he bowed his tubby head and took a look outside.

The racket grew louder...

Outside the ground floor flat, one of Nippy's pals had unbuttoned his trousers and pulled down his pants. 'I'll show you mine, if you show me yours,' he cooed, tossing his hips, his pink cock twitching like a snout beneath a bush of black hair.

'Piss off!' Dennis Duffy had to slide the window all the way up to get his bare chest over the sill. 'Have some fucking respect; put that away before I come down there and hack it off.'

Shouts and laughter ... disappointed groans.

'It weren't *your* tits what we wanted to see, mate,' Nippy jeered. 'Do us a favour: go inside and send your bird back out.'

Nippy's pal wagged his piece in disagreement. 'Nah, leave him where he is, he's got bigger boobs than she has.'

'You bloody what?' Duffy snapped. He glared down at them, his gut bubbling gin and beer. 'I fucking wouldn't if I was you – don't you fucking try *me*. Fuck off on your way or else I'll –'

'Oh, shut up mate!' Nippy heckled, heckling. 'It'll take you five minutes to get down the stairs you fat cunt. Just send your missus out instead.'

'Fucking wait there then,' Duffy threatened, his low brow sitting down on his nose. 'I hope you can back up that gob once I open my door.'

'C'mon then, giddy up, we ain't got all night!' Nippy teased, goading him.

Inside the bedroom, now wrapped in a bath towel, Silvia Duffy watched her husband's broad back come in from the window. 'Where's my fucking boots?' he raged, stomping around the bed and knocking her over again.

Traveling on the night's quiet, Nippy's voice bounced along the bricks. Lagging behind, Micky and Winston quickened their stride.

In a flat upstairs, another man stuck his head beneath his blind to see what was going on…

'And you can fuck off an' all,' Nippy shouted, seeing him appear as a pale wipe behind his window. 'Get back in bed you nosey bastard.'

The light went on. The blind reeled and the window opened, the voice inside it punchy: 'What's the fucking problem? You alright down there, Den? Are these little pricks giving you headache?' Stubbornly built, Dennis Duffy's upstairs neighbour and drinking chum, Clyde Graham, leaned his two fists and worn features out of his window.

'What's it to you?' Nippy's pal spat, tucking himself back into his pants. 'Mind your own business.'

'I'm fucking going out there and ironing 'em out,' Duffy's voice replied. 'They're a couple of sex cases, Clyde. I caught 'em flashing Silvia.'

Nippy sneered, two fingers up on each hand. 'Hurry up then, dick 'ed. We're still waiting.'

Clyde Graham need hear no more. He was still (always) playing by prison rules: Jacks on twos, Queen's a slag, and Nonces are fair game. He pointed at Nippy's friend who was still doing up his trousers. '*You're* first,' he swore, and then banged his window shut.

Hunting, the white Jaguar crawled across Battersea Bridge, its headlamps thrown into a wild gaze. The downpour was masking their scent. There was nothing moving, no shadows. Copper-headed, Crogan's face was fixed fierce, ravenous, talons dug in. Scowling, he had to avert his eyes from the glare of an oncoming car. He veered right after the bridge, following his nose. The lights planed across the mouth of Surrey Lane, embarrassing it, showing up its flaws. Seeing the cracks in the pavement, the moss, the slow loop of the lamp, it reminded him of trying to catch hares as a boy – of shining his torch into a field and finding those frightened eyes in the dark. He eased his hands around the wheel, softly, softly, turning slowly to float the beams from side to side, reaching into those shadowy places on the pavements that the street lamps left blind. He knew – was *sure* – that sooner or later he would find them. All of a sudden they'd just be there, flashing; those frightened eyes shining in the dark.

On the sodden patch of grass outside of the flats Nippy was pacing, riling himself up. He looked at his two friends edging away. 'You ready?' he said, muffling a gassy burp with his fist.

Bottling it, the froth having now flattened out on the piss taking, Nippy's pals were backing out. Still fiddling with his top button, one of them said:

'Let's push off, Nip,' he said. 'It was only meant as a giggle; this is all getting out of hand.'

'It's true,' agreed the other one. 'And I've got a dickie belly as it is.' He gestured down at the vomit which had dried into his turn-ups. 'C'mon, let's have it away.' He tugged on Nippy's sleeve. 'It ain't worth it, Nip.'

Hiding it better than his friends, Nippy stood his ground and watched them both. He posed there, holding his nerve, acting like he was reluctant to leave. 'Bollocks!' he said. 'I ain't fucking having that; what am I, some sort of soft touch?' He strode over towards the flats again with his arms swinging, wanting to put on a show, knowing Micky and Winston would see. The downstairs lights were still off. Nippy honed in on the metal dustbin which was standing beneath the kitchen window, its lid askew. He seized it with both hands, double checking over his shoulder before raising it above his head. Pieces of loose rubbish clanged inside. The lid toppled off and gonged down on the floor. Poised with his arms extended, high-handedly, Nippy took a short run up and let go.

The sound of a large pane of glass breaking; then an unmusical, metallic bashing of a steel drum rolling on a dish-rack and denting a kitchen sink.

'Have that you fat Cunt!' Nippy bawled triumphantly. He took in the destruction and then ran. Hysterical laughter followed him; clapping heels, running away; boys scattering with friends like winners.

From further down the street, looking on at what was happening, Micky shouted: 'Nippy, you little prick! What you playing at? You trying to get everyone nicked, or what?' Impulsively, sticking his hip flask back inside his pocket, he loped into a gradual jog, an old dog unable to resist a chase – an older brother, always half serious, pretending he wanted to administer discipline ahead of joining in.

Full of thought, Winston didn't bother. He carried on as he was, uninvolved, walking and watching without intent.

Clyde Graham heard the crash come from the flat downstairs and halted briefly, his hand still rattling around inside his *own* kitchen drawer. Stupidly expressionless, he snatched at handfuls of utensils and cutlery, weighing up a couple of potentials and then tossing them aside. Head steaming, wearing only the jeans he'd passed out in, he fell against the side of the sink and took hold of his cock. He had the feeling that he needed to do something; either piss or be sick or shit on the floor. He staggered on his tiptoes, a slanted jet of invisible urine cleaning the gravy off of the dirty dinner plates in the washing-up bowl. And that's when he found it – the thing missing from the drawer – the black handle with the brass studs, sticking out of the crockery like a wooden limb in a bomb site. He pulled it free – the sword in the stone – plodding backwards and dribbling soap suds down his front.

Not until he was halfway out of his front door and he stopped to dry the blade on his jeans did he realise he'd picked up a carving fork.

Micky gave up; Nippy was too quick for him. Leaning on his thighs, he looked back at Winston from half a street and a world away. A man from the flats was talking to him, not happy, more than likely gobbing off about the window.

At a distance, stood on the grass in his short trousers and work boots, an open shirt billowing back off of his stomach, Dennis Duffy appeared more like a fat child who'd dressed up to play war on his front lawn than a threat. He had even picked up the dustbin lid to hold as a makeshift shield.

'Just bung him a couple of quid to shut him up, Wince.' Micky called back along the road. 'Give him enough so he can have a drink after he's paid for the window.' He waved a hand at it, then, turning his head, searched for Nippy. 'I hope you know he'll want you to pay him that back. Dick 'ed!' He was smiling, unfocused. Winston was behind him, delving into his pockets, the dustbin lid taking him by surprise and whacking into the side of his face.

And then the second man was there, something in his hand, Winston underneath him, going down, the man stabbing at the back of him.

The carving fork punctured the skin on Winston's back; again, it slid coolly between his ribs and reached into him, long fingered, pointing at his organs. It was blow after blow, punching and kicking, spikes nipping at his arms and legs. He covered his head, unable to see; the dustbin lid was slaughtering him, each time he managed to get a snippet of a picture it struck him again, over and over. There were sharp pains in his side, cold strikes, skewers jabbing below the flesh and chipping at the bone. More agony – delirium – trying to get up and fight back, dropping his arms to protect his stomach and getting dents to the head. Ears ringing, a manic tune played on out-of-tune keys. The perspective dwindled, small lights in black dresses, and then his mind started to twist too fast to keep hold of, his wits dying in darkness. The swirling thought was one of hope: *if I can just get up from the mud.* That was what was stopping him; the thick, gloopy liquid all over him wasn't allowing him to put any weight down. His knees and elbows kept sliding out from under him, his face writhing in a warm bath. If he could just reach the concrete, he thought, he would be able to find his feet.

By the time Micky's head had untangled what was happening, he was sprinting, eyes all the way forwards, treading on adrenalin. He called out to Winston, the words drowning in panic, being dragged under and held down by frantic breathing. The run was soundless; grim reality with hot hands cupped over his ears. Winston lay limp, the two men still attacking him – savaging him, a dustbin lid trouncing his unseen face in the dirt. Micky's vision tunnelled, sucking him back towards his friend. He couldn't move any faster. Winston was unconscious, he had to be; he wasn't fighting back.

Further up the road, a way beyond, Nippy froze, his legs stubbornly waiting for an instruction which wouldn't come. The young, inconsiderate smile had dropped out of his mouth. He shook, looking around for his two friends who were gone. He was scared stiff, petrified by the oncoming headlights in the road.

Silvia Duffy peeped out of her window again. She tightened the towel around her body, seeing yellow car light spilling over both sides of the road. *Thank God somebody's called the law*, she thought, shaking, watching her husband and Clyde scarper from the roar of the approaching engine. They lumbered away and disappeared somewhere around the back of the flats. In the growing glow she could now see the man face down on the grass; he was motionless, dead looking, his blood pooling out around him and feeding the soil.

The Jaguar had a rabbit in the headlights.

Bertie Crogan never noticed the lump on the grass, he'd seen Micky, mouth open, his short arms and legs working, the light catching on his frightened eyes. Within a rush he'd decided, instinct taking over, his teeth biting into the pink meat on the inside of his cheek. *One in the hand is worth two in the bush*, was the non-thought, his stained claws dug in to the steering-wheel. The scuffed toe of his shoe sank on the accelerator. Roy Easter grabbed on, the Jag snarling, a big bonnet hunkering down ready to pounce, its lights – eyes – shooting holes in the road. Crogan howled …

… It was the wild, midnight sound of two foxes fighting.

The vehicle swerved ferociously, changing direction,

wailing in the turn and gaining speed. On the other side of the windscreen, doggedly trying to get back to Winston, Micky kept coming. The bulbs were burning hell's fire into his face. The car shook – the bodies inside jolting as it banged the curb, mounted the pavement, and then ruined the life in front of it. Micky bucked like a deer in the sight of a rifle. He went nowhere; the Jaguar's nose taking him with it through the low brick wall beyond the bushes.

Pinned there, dying, Micky Meehan stared past the shattered glass. He saw what had killed him. Bertie Crogan stared back at him; he was crying … jaws wide and red, vowing something in a still-born scream.

Nippy covered his eyes, the universe revolving and pressing in to stifle him. He couldn't see, think or feel; he was drifting.

In the beyond the car was reversing, dragging its kill with it into the road. It bumped down the curb, bringing up bricks and purring. Someone – some *Thing* – was yowling inside the metal beast. Micky flopped from the front bumper and became a dead weight on the road, sprawled out, his silver hip flask totting away from him and resting on its own.

A loud revving…the car, barely a white line, hammered away, one of its headlights closed in a wink.

When Nippy took his hands away from his face he was alone; nothing out there but an empty street singing a black hymn. Now he ran, almost skating, the ground unknown beneath him. He went towards the debris hushed. Dry, he called his name… and then stopped a few feet from his body. Quaking, scared to see, he reached down and lifted the hip flask from the tar. He shook it limply; the drip left inside it making a wish against the walls. He opened it and vibrated the final swig onto his gloved tongue. He swallowed, tasting the tears at the bottom of the bottle, and then he took the last steps forward.

Micky was looking past him, his porcelain death mask fixed on the heavens. It was the happy-sad face of a bone china clown – one with a painted tear on his cheek and an untold joke rested on his lips.

Barley Sugar

BUNNY

January, 1960.

Winston was under, way under, sunken between sleep and living, fathoms shy of the surface. There were no visions that far down, only voices, high up and outside of him, soft like psalms in a chapel loft.

'Your friend has more than enough to worry about,' the doctor had told Francis testily, placing his hands inside the pockets of his white coat. 'He has *twenty seven* stab wounds. His internal bleeding was some of the worst I've ever had the misfortune of treating...*And*, he still has a partially collapsed lung. Why not allow his body to concentrate on breathing normally before burdening it with bereavement?'

And so, Winton was kept in the dark; even when, a week later he awoke in hospital swaddled up to his armpits in bandages, nobody told him about Micky. They left it as long as they could. Eventually it fell to Francis to break the news – against doctor's orders – a day or so before the funeral. By then, in truth, as weak as Winston still was, Francis needed his support.

Even with Francis's help Winston couldn't get off the mattress; bloodshot and stuck, he had no choice but to whisper his prayers and goodbyes into his pillow. Up to his ears in stiff cotton sheets, he lay that morning drifting in and out of grief, watching the clock for the time the ceremony started. The hospital ward hummed with the slow ticking of a tired mind mulling things over, the dying air carrying stifled, wheezy coughs around the cold void. It was a long space, tall, full of astute windows; the daylight elongating the patients in their beds and making them look more useless. There were no answers – no cures – only the drugged mutterings of stiff faces and bad card players.

When Francis finally arrived he was alone. He walked on to the ward looking like he hadn't slept, a rolled up newspaper in one hand. There was a chair beside Winston's bed already waiting for him; without speaking, he tossed the paper on to the foot of the bed and sat down, his grave suit creased around the elbows.

'How was it?'

'Difficult,' Francis answered. He sighed, sore-eyed. 'How did you get on here?'

'I've had better days,' Winston said. 'One of the nurses came and sat with me for a while and let me tell her about Mick...' he choked and coughed away the rest. When he'd finished, he peered at Francis, suffocated, and said: 'Each time them bloody doors go I keep thinking –'

Francis nodded to save Winston the labour of going on.

'Did you tell his family that if I could've been there I would've...' Winston broke off again, this time shaking his head to stop the tears coming. He took a breath. 'Did he get a good send-off?'

Francis closed his eyes, a hand going to his face to cover

his mouth before he returned a watery smile. He glanced away, staring at nothing, looking around for a way out of a feeling, the spare feet between him and Winston suddenly seeming vast. Together they let the moment travel, the length of the walls, the floor falling away and filling in again before, wiping his eyes and composing himself, Winston said something:

'Least he died honourably … trying to save me. I can tell you one thing: there ain't no dignity in a fucking bed pan.' His gaze redirected towards one of the nurses at the far end of the ward; she was pulling the curtain around another patient's bed to give him some privacy. Francis looked over. 'Every time I have to have a shit in one of them things, all I can think about is what Mick would've been saying if he could see me.'

Francis tilted his head back to let a sore throated, emotional cackle escape. 'He never would have let you live it down, I know that much.' Winston chuckled. Their best friend, the small blonde boy who scaled railings and pinched cars, who stole as much from life as he could, was always most alive in laughter.

'Oi,' Winston said, remembering, 'it ain't funny; the other night I was desperate. I thought I was going to mess myself.' He sniggered. 'I woke up and started looking around for the bloody shit dish and I could've sworn I could see the bastard standing over me, that cocky little grin slapped all over his face. I'm not sure if I was still dreaming or what, but it felt proper real.'

'It wouldn't surprise me,' Francis said seriously. He

straightened up. 'I still keep having the same dream about him every night. It's the same one, over and over. It happened last night.'

'The one with the statue?'

Francis nodded.

Winston reflected on it for a few seconds and then said: 'It's crazy; your mind can do strange things. It makes you think you're off your nut. The other day this lot in here thought I was losing my marbles, I reckon.' He shook his head in disbelief. 'I couldn't stop laughing. I was just laying here pissing myself, thinking about that time when we found all them cans of paint when we was kids.' He grinned painfully. 'Do you remember that?'

The memory had emerged over Francis's face. 'Micky's mum was just talking about that at the pub after the funeral,' he said fondly. 'She was telling everyone how she dragged the three of us home and stood us naked in the tub outside her house.'

'The neighbours were all out,' Winston pitched in, laughing. 'And she wouldn't stop belting us round the legs while she was trying to scrub us down.'

Francis folded over his knees and clapped his hands together. 'Micky was pissing himself,' he said, panting. 'He didn't care that we was in trouble; he just kept pointing down at your bare brown bum with all that paint running off it. He was in fits.'

'It was the *white spirit*,' Winston said. He rubbed his glassy eyes, squinting, joyful. 'The prick was acting like it was the funniest thing he'd ever seen: *me* being drowned in white spirit.'

'Yeah,' Francis recalled. 'He called you *White Spirit* for ages after that. He said it suited you.'

Winston nodded amused. 'He was a *cunt*; always on a wind up.'

'I'll give you that; the boy did have a gob on him.' Francis rocked back in the chair. 'Fuck me though,' he said, 'God help anyone else who dared say anything about you. Do you remember that brother and sister who lived on the end of our street?'

'The Talbot twins,' Winston clarified.

'That's them. Remember when the sister piped up and started calling you names? Micky whacked the pair of them before anyone else knew what she'd said.'

'Fuckin' 'ell,' Winston said, taken back. 'I remember: he said he wasn't allowed to hit girls so he thumped her brother instead...' he sniggered. 'And then he turns round and chins her anyway for trying to grass on him.'

They laughed again, harder; the pause coming after the giggles and tears. Francis rested a blue gaze on his friend:

'He loved you, Wince.'

Winston bowed his head, fingers fidgeting with his bandages. He took stock in silence. Evasively, he asked: 'How's Carrie holding up?'

'She's doing better than I am, I think,' Francis answered. 'She keeps trying to comfort everyone else, bless her.'

Winston adjusted his position, his powerful arms pushing him higher on the pillows. He breathed easier. 'I suppose she's keeping strong for the baby's sake,' he said. 'It must be killing her.' He turned thoughtfully, reaching over and lifting a glass of water from his nightstand. The bruising on the side of his face had flowered into a deep purple.

'Connie's been over there most days,' Francis said. 'Marcia has as well.'

As if to ignore Marcia's name, Winston sipped his water over parched lips. 'It makes better sense of everything,' he said, 'puts your – *our* – own mortality into perspective. I keep going over a conversation me and Mick had that night; he told me that if he had to sum up his life, even after all the silly bollocks he'd pulled off, the thing he was best proud of was the chance of starting a family with Carrie. For all his sins I think he really loved her. She made him a baby, she should be happy for that. I reckon that the moment he knew his number was up – *if* he did? – knowing that he was leaving a piece of him behind with her would've made it easier for him to go.' Winston took another sip of water and placed the glass back where it was, Francis looking at him mournfully. 'When he died he was happy doing what he was doing,' he continued. 'He was proud. Carrie was right in what she said: Mick would want us all to carry on until we are all as happy and proud of what *we're* doing as he was. It ain't like our time won't run out one day, maybe sooner than we think; we need to get on with it.' Winston's attention had settled forcefully on Francis. 'I can't stop thinking about what I would've left behind if I hadn't woken up – I keep seeing myself laid out in one of these places with the sheet pulled right up over my face.' He motioned to his wounds. 'I was *this* close, mate.' He pinched his fingertips together.

'And what would I have left? Nothing … apart from an expensive suit and a big stain on the ground –'

'Shut up!'

'Nah, I mean it,' Winston replied seriously. 'We've got to get it now, France, while the getting's good.' His face had turned and he'd shifted his focus over to the nurse who was now doing her round of bed checks. 'That way we can concentrate on raising some kids and being happy. I already know Connie is ready to be a mum; I've heard her tell Marcia enough times.' He browsed Francis's reaction and then went back to studying the nurse. 'How is she?'

Francis laughed a little, charting Winston's angle. 'She's bearing up,' he said. 'Sometimes I think they're tougher than *us* – women I mean. They've got something inside them that we don't, they know how to nurture people and give them what they need. They're able to maintain even when the chips are down. To be honest I think Connie's just determined to get me through this more than anything else.'

'I know what you're getting at,' Winston said, distracted.

'She's also adamant that someone's been in the house,' Francis stated.

'What?'

'She's convinced that we got burgled.'

'Why? What did they take?'

'That's the thing,' Francis shrugged, 'I couldn't find nothing missing. But she said she came home – in the daytime – and just had a feeling that someone had been in there. She said she checked all the windows and one of the ones at the back was wide open.'

Winston frowned. 'You didn't open it?'

Francis shook his head. 'I thought she was imagining it, but then she showed me that one of our photo frames had been moved: it was a picture of me, you and Micky, taken years ago.'

'It's probably the Old Bill then,' Winston said, his swollen cheek lifting in disgust.

'That's what I was thinking –'

'They can never fucking leave off, can they,' Winston said, raising his voice. 'Soulless fucking bastards, they could at least let people bury their dead before they go snooping in the bedroom drawers.'

Francis agreed. 'Fuck knows what they was after if they were?'

'*Us!*' Winston said, shortly. He fell quiet, winded, having to inhale to steady his breathing. The tall walk of the slender nurse was now heading their way; Winston averted his eyes to see how long they had before she arrived. 'There was something else Micky was going on about that night,' Winston rushed, gasping. '*Antwerp,*' he puffed. 'He thought we should do it.'

Francis scoffed sarcastically. 'This is Micky we're talking about, Wince: he wanted us to do *everything*.' He grinned and stood up to leave. 'First of all, you need to get fixed.'

A pair of long stockings laddered up her legs and hid under the hem of her stiff, white uniform. Francis shot Winston a wink and headed for the door. The nurse recovered the newspaper from the foot of the bed and placed it beside Winston on the table.

Beatrice Warren – or *Bunny*, as she'd insisted Winston call her – was *herself* feeling something. And the same as Winston's smile the thing had evolved; first shy, then tentative, a growing taboo, an inquisitive inclination which had moved over the days from bud to bloom. She was attracted to him, that much she'd been happy to admit. Handling his severe, muscled body had forced her to daydream in spite of herself. She had played her part in healing him, in redressing his wounds and listening to him talk, her ears laying soft comfort to his pain. During the days and nights they had spoken often and he had told her things, real things, worse for wear when he'd woken in sweats.

He'd taken her in and around a world which was invisible to her, walking her through the miles of his life. He'd opened up on a raw page: a mother who'd lost him; a father who'd stolen and smuggled him to a cold country and then died to defend it; a grandmother who'd felt shame in raising him. He told her about three boys – one of whom was now gone – that had grown up to become men together – about how now there was only fear that followed. It was overwhelming; never in all her twenty two years had she heard a man – boy – sound so true. To be so brave and so scared. She had now seen him, below the surface, hurting in the secret cave beneath his ribs. He'd wept. And this morning, when his best friend was being buried, he'd left a beautiful mark on her, safe in the secrecy of the bed-curtain. She had reached out and touched his hand, unprofessionally, and then opened her arms and held him and allowed his impression to be made quaking against her. And now, thinking about it as she fussed over his sheets, it dawned on her that it had been inside today's clammy, muffled embrace when she'd realised – as lustily as her previous idea – that what she was feeling was maybe more than *something*.

'I hope he didn't leave on my account...?'

Winston watched Francis until he was out of sight. 'He's got somewhere to be,' he said, looking back at Bunny. She hovered down onto the side of his mattress, her strong, blonde plait coiled up underneath her nurses' cap.

'It's good to see you laughing,' Bunny said gently. '*And* crying, it's good for you. Much better to let it out, believe me.'

Winston wasn't sure what to say ... he thought that compared to his, her voice sounded like classical notes. He dropped his eyes down over the slender breast plate on her tunic. 'Did you see that, then?' he muttered, smiling, avoiding her by following the soft bow of her throat up only as far as her lips.

'You and your friend have a special bond. It's unusual to see two men be like that with each other. It's wonderful that you have someone like that in your life, someone to look out for you.' Her gaze brushed the sentiment over him, over the berry colours which had settled in bruises through his skin. His face edged into a smile. She mirrored him; the Scandinavian airs which she'd inherited from her mother resting on her cheek bones and expressing the same embarrassed glow.

...Silent questions...no answers...

Winston wondered whether she would or not? And whether she'd like to as much as him? He thought about how lewd it would be to pursue her before he could even walk, to chase her while he was still strewn. He knew what Micky would have said: '*Why not? Worst they can do is laugh!*' ... And then – just as he was considering placing a bid and asking what she would reckon to letting him take her out for dinner once he was back on his feet – a loud matronly call poked its nose in:

'Nurse Warren! A little help, if you please...?'

Startled, Bunny jumped up and stood to attention. 'Be right with you,' she said, appeasing the voice but without taking her eyes off Winston. She stooped over for the newspaper and handed it to him as if that had been the reason she was there. 'I'll come and see you later,' she whispered to him, promising. 'We can talk properly then.'

Winston nodded at her, watching her go, a butterfly which had crossed his path and then disappeared.

Winston's heart leapt, stiff bristles combing over his back. He sat up straighter on the pillows, winded; the newspaper spread open across his lap.

The sweat from his fingers had rubbed off some of the ink, but the headline still read: **Battersea Shooting: Nazi Gun for Hire**. Winston studied the picture: not a photograph, a sketch, like a diagram of the weapon recovered at the scene.

The caption said: A German Mauser Luger. Obviously there had to be hundreds of those floating about in London since the war ended, people brought them back as souvenirs, he knew that but it was the article, not the fact that Francis owned one of those pistols which made it too much of a coincidence. He skimmed over it again:

A man was found in a critical condition after being shot three times on his South London doorstep. The weapon, a German Luger pistol, was recovered at the scene on the Surrey Lane housing estate in the early hours of yesterday morning, after the would-be assassin discarded it and fled on foot. Clyde Graham, 43, is currently receiving treatment in hospital after undergoing surgery. The Police Inspector on the case has quoted, 'We have not yet made any arrests, but are working quickly to apprehend a suspect.' He went on to say that the investigation was also yet to conclude a motive for the attack and could not rule out a case of mistaken identity. The police are appealing to any members of the public who may have information about the crime, or knowledge of the weapon used, to come forward and aid the investigation.

He tore his eyes away, racing. The name Clyde Graham meant nothing, but it was the same bloke, it had to be – it was the same *street* – and on the night before Micky's funeral. *That's why he brought me the sodding paper,* Winston thought, stunned, *He fucking shot the bastard.* His breathing rattled, whistling on the exhalation. He could think of no reason why Francis wouldn't have just told him other than he thought it wasn't the place, too many ears, that's why he'd sided with print. Winston coughed and called for the nurse:

'Bunny?' he spluttered, beckoning. 'Come here, I need a favour.'

At a distance, shuffling along behind a trolley and refilling water jugs, Bunny frowned at him. 'What is it?'

'I need you to telephone Francis for me,' Winston replied, urging her to come.

'He left not even an hour ago,' she said, confused and coming towards him.

'It's important.'

She looked at him, trying to understand his eyes. 'Well, what do you want me to say?'

'He probably ain't home yet,' Winston babbled, thinking out loud. 'You might have to leave a message with Connie.'

Bunny stopped at the side of the bed and looked down at the newspaper. 'Winston, is everything okay?'

'Hopefully,' Winston said distracted. 'Listen, tell him I said … tell him I said thank you for bringing me the paper today. Say that I read it, and that it means a lot to me.'

'You want me to ring up and leave a message, just to tell him *that?*'

'Don't worry,' Winston smiled, crumpling the newspaper to blur the lines. 'He'll understand.'

Connie had taken the message gladly; she even humoured the polite female voice on the other end of the telephone when it suggested that she write it down because Winston was being so stubborn about its importance. She scribbled the words, joined up in her untidy handwriting on the back of an unopened envelope she found on the hallway table, drew a flower around it to grab Francis's attention and then waited for him to come home, not thinking about it, her mind rehashing something Carrie had said to her earlier in the day. She drank tea and pottered, sober, the remnants of the *one* (a whisky chaser) she'd given herself at the wake long gone like the afternoon.

At nightfall, still waiting, she filled up a hot-water bottle, climbed into their bed, and huddled beneath the duvet. From there she slept, easy and dreamless until the sound of fabric rolling inside out and coming off at the end of the bed woke her. Francis undressed in silence, the familiar shape of him edged by the moon. She didn't say anything, simply held up the corner of the cover and then kissed him on his naked shoulder as he lay down.

She waited ... drifted ... and then woke again suddenly at midnight when Francis's legs began to flinch. He was dreaming again, the same as every night, crying in his sleep. Connie sat up frightened, watching him and trying to make out what he was murmuring. She listened, hoping it would come again, wanting to wake him ... but then not. There were tears falling out of his closed eyes and wetting the dark. He writhed, this time his fingertips flickering.

Inside his dreamscape Francis was walking a slow road leading anywhere. The outline of a person was carved into the view ahead of him; the statue of a man. There were no lights on in the houses; the windows were dark hollows, the scooped-out sockets of skulls. He had an overwhelming urge to touch the statue, to move his feet faster and get there. He couldn't reach it. He stared at the figure blearily now seeing lights creeping up behind it, two of them, slits to begin with but then widening and opening like eyes. He wiped his face, running, the ground running out. The statue was growing, coming closer. There were cat-eye's on the other side, white and fiery, seeing through him. The lights raged, growling, thunder on the remote banks of a mountain. Whatever it was, it was hunting, the lights casting the road into pale shades and slithers of brightness. In the shine, chasing, Francis could at last distinguish the figure: it was Micky, expressionless like a fairy-tale prince turned to stone. And now he could hear that his friend was calling to him, high-pitched and scared, his shaking voice breathing frantically and pleading with some sort of God for mercy. The eyes and the mouth were closing in. Francis got there, his heart rattling, his feet plunging through pallid streams. The statue – Micky – was ancient; the surface chipped and filled with mossy cracks like a graveyard stone. Francis screamed, weeping, the cold lights shooting towards him from the other side, perfectly round now. He reached out his hand, praying, speaking in a foreign language, trying to move him, desperate to save him from those lights. Micky's effigy ogled him helplessly, the lights nearly on top of them, Francis clawing to shift the weight and Micky starting to crumble. He was falling apart, piece by piece, handful after handful, becoming broken the more Francis tried to pry him out of the path of what was coming.

His face was ruined, half destroyed, shards of it shattering in the road. Francis wailed uselessly, the lights too near, too rabid, to hungry everywhere around him. He closed his eyes, fistfuls of Micky's crushed soul slicing into his hands …

And then it was nothing, bright black, Connie's voice burrowing through the dark.

'Francis…? Francis ..?' She placed a hot palm on his skin and shook him awake.

His face was damp, eyes somewhere else – to him, propped up on her elbow next to him, her hair coaxed over her neck, she looked ghostly. He watched her reaching over him to turn on the bedside lamp. 'Leave it off for a minute,' he said, touching her to settle her beside him, her breasts lolling in her nightdress. He hung out a hand and found his cigarettes on the nightstand and lit one, vibrating. He didn't put it to his lips; instead just held it and let it smoulder, the smoke curling upwards like strands of grey hair. After a minute he said, 'I love you.'

Connie looked at him, her palm sweeping away the fallen ash on the duvet. 'What was the dream?' she asked softly. 'Was it the same one?'

'Do you know when I knew?' Francis said, ignoring her question. 'It was that night when Oliver hit me with the axe. Not because he hurt me, but because I was so scared that I couldn't get up and stop him hurting you. All I could think about was what he might have done to you. It was the helplessness that hurt, that's what was painful.' He moved his eyes over hers, vulnerable. 'That's what this dream is about: helplessness. Because Micky's dead and there was nothing I could do to stop it happening – because I wasn't there to protect him. Winston could've died as well...' His voice cracked into a low sob, forcing him to wrestle with it. 'I should've gone with them – I should've *fucking* been there to do something, Con.' He looked away, eyes stinging in the glow of his cigarette. 'We've always looked after ourselves – the *three* of us – our whole lives. But the one real time they needed me I was fucking nowhere...' Connie began to weep next to him. 'I feel *so* guilty, Connie. I can't stop feeling fucking *guilty*.'

'But why, Francis? How could you have known?' She held his chin, wanting to tell him that she was glad he hadn't gone, needing him to know that he was exactly where he should be, and that neither Winston nor Micky would want him to be in their place. She wanted to tell him how much she loved him and that she wished he could see himself as she did – as *they* did. Instead she kissed him, his lips quaking beneath her, his tears pressed against hers as she held him and whispered into his mouth. They stayed that way, weeping, until long after the cigarette had burnt out and their vigil had ended and their words were cried out. Eventually she folded and nestled her head against his chest.

'Did you see the message from Winston?' she sighed, not asleep. She felt him shake his head. 'He got a nurse to phone for him; I left the note on the hallway table.'

'Is he okay?'

She nodded, her hair stroking him. 'He wanted to thank you for taking him the newspaper.' Francis opened his eyes, furrowed. Connie lifted her head to see him. 'That's what I thought. He told her to tell you that it meant a lot to him.'

Francis rolled her off him gently so he could sit up. 'What? He told her to telephone just to say that?'

'She said he *insisted*.'

For a moment Francis fixed a confused stare on the bedroom door. 'Where did you say you put it?' He got up and padded out of the room naked. 'Do you think something's wrong?' Connie called. When she got no answer, she said, 'It's on the hallway table, but I can tell you, that's what it said.' She sat, waiting and flattening down the duvet on Francis's side of the mattress, then deciding, that this time she should go through with switching on the bedside lamp.

Francis's voice came back: 'Did you buy a paper today?' He'd turned the light on in the kitchen.

'Yes, but I didn't read it. I think it's in the waste-basket.'

A cupboard banged shut and Francis's footsteps came back along the hall, accompanied by the sound of turning pages. 'This is what he's on about,' he announced from the doorway. He stalked forwards, still reading, and then passed Connie the paper so she could see the story.

The paper rattled. She looked at the headline, at the illustration of the gun, her heart beating. 'Did you have something to do with this?' She didn't get a reply; Francis was crouched, his hands rifling for something underneath the bed. 'Francis, you're scaring me...'

Digging his fingernails under the little tin rim, Francis popped the lid off of a metal lunch box. He gaped distrustfully at what he was seeing: the Lugar was gone, and in its place was Micky's silver hip flask. He exhaled and let himself topple backwards onto his bum. 'Shit! I know who was in here. It was Nippy.'

Connie went from the hip flask to Francis's face. 'What do you mean, it was *Nippy*? Nippy who what ... who *burgled* us?'

'Remember your old man give me that old war pistol he had?' Connie nodded. 'I reckon it might be the same one from that shooting.'

'I don't understand...'

Francis shook his head, not quite believing how it could be possible. 'I knew something weren't right when you said Winston got that nurse to phone,' he observed. 'He must think I had something to do with it. That's why he mentioned the fucking newspaper.'

'And *did* you?'

'Nah, I didn't even know the gun was gone.' He held a hand out towards her. 'Pass me the paper a sec,' he said, taking it and scanning the text. 'Clyde Graham; that bloke's name. He must be one of the geezers who troubled Winston.'

'I'm not following, Francis.' There were now more tears running down her cheeks. 'Are you telling me that Nippy came in here and stole that gun from you? How would *he* know that you had that bloody thing under our bed?'

'I ain't got a clue,' Francis answered, hoarse. 'But it was him who last had Micky's hip flask; he showed it to me at the hospital. I told him he should keep hold of it for his brother.' Connie wiped her face on the duvet, still looking at Francis; he was staring at himself in the side of the hip flask, the reflection long and sombre. 'The last thing he said to me was that he was going to redeem himself. He was fucked – so was *I* – I didn't really take in what he was saying. He must've left *this* here so we'd know it was him.'

'But it wasn't *his* fault,' Connie snivelled. 'It was a horrible accident. Somebody was driving drunk and hit Micky on the pavement; that's what the police said.'

'But Micky was *only* running back to help Winston,' Francis said, siding with and against Nippy. 'And Winston was only being attacked because of what Nippy had done. He started it. If it weren't for him and his pals acting up, nothing would've happened...' Francis's voice trailed off thickly, pain in his throat. The hip flask rolled out of his grasp. He dropped his head, sobbing, screwing up the words on the page in front of him.

Connie reached out a hand to touch him but this time he moved. She sat for a second, waiting, and then turned off the light.

On the night before Micky's funeral Nippy Meehan went back to Surrey Lane.

Silvia Duffy had to hold her husband by the arm to stop him answering the door. The two of them, ears peeled, stood in the hallway in the dark and watched their letterbox flapping. When the knocking ceased they stayed put, not talking, listening to the footsteps climbing the concrete steps to the floor above.

Clyde Graham had nobody to hold him back. In the

soundless holes between the banging at his door, his sightless footfalls resounded through the ceiling. The latch opened, his annoyance muffled by the three gunshots which clapped on his arrival. The echoes boomed in the high corners of the block, and the next sound was of escaping paces thudding down the staircase and out onto the road. Clyde Graham – *the man upstairs* – flopped in his doorway bleeding.

Nippy Meehan dropped the gun and sprinted away in search of redemption.

Barley Sugar

LOUIS BREGUET

2004

Avram Abrahams had closed the shop early and hurried home. By first dark he was reading again, toiling away as he had been for the past hour; stretched out on the leather beaten settee inside his living room. He'd lost a slipper. From the opposite side of the rug, his partner – a taxidermy black Border collie mounted on a wooden plinth – shared its thoughts with him. Avram looked up, considering him (and his opinion) before spreading the pages and holding up the book so the dog could better see. After all, collies - even the stuffed ones - are clever, clever canines. Motionless, the dog concurred, offering him the same friendly grin it had apparently died with until Avram broke the connection. Speaking out loud, he let go of the book and began to fumble underneath cushions for his address book. When he'd found it – a wad of discoloured paper, held together by elastic bands – he slapped it against his thigh and spilled sheets onto the floor. He combed through, intent, stopping every so often to match one of the numbers against the brown envelope he'd showed Francis that afternoon. He gave no mind to the sound of things falling as he looped an arm behind the sofa, snatched up the telephone, and then dragged the whole thing over onto his lap. He shot a wink at the dog and started to dial, his finger having to wait for the numbers to click back around on themselves before he could punch in the next digit; during these interims, to get ready for whoever might answer, he practiced his Hebrew pronunciations under his breath.

Lewis was quite content to get lost in the hum; the wobble in his grandfather's vocal cords when he'd last spoken had demanded that they both look away.

Passing blurrily, the signs said: Durham 20 Miles. The Daimler exited the motorway and picked up an unlit lane. Lewis wasn't sure; he honed in on the Bed and Breakfast boards lashed to the posts of the roadside cottages. He'd never seen his grandfather the way he had just now. He felt sorry for him – for his loss. Not least because after listening to all the crazy stories about him, *Micky* would've been his best bet as to where the fabled pocket watches had come from. He'd been expecting to hear how Micky had pulled off some sort of ridiculous raid on a jewellers, not how he'd been murdered. It had caught him off guard. And so, unseeing, he sat undoing the question on the tip of his tongue, thinking it would be better to stay quiet for a while.

'I don't know about you, but myself, I'm looking forward to a drink…?' Francis revealed, when the beginnings of a village began materialising around the windows. The Daimler slowed, almost to a stop, and then made a right turn. Green-fingered bushes scraped the sides of the car as it started up the track towards the dignified stone building beyond the gatepost, tyres on gravel. The courtyard car park – at one time a playground – opened out and offered a resting-place. The handbrake yawned. Lewis cast his eyes over the thick ivy beard growing up the walls and thought that up close, lit by the uplighters in the flower beds, the place looked like something out of a Sherlock Holmes story. The sign read: The Schoolboys' Bell.

'Are we staying here?'

Francis turned off the engine. 'I've stayed here before, a few times,' he said. 'They do some good food.'

'It looks like something out of a murder mystery,' Lewis said.

Francis smiled. 'Before it was ever a hotel, it used to be an old schoolhouse,' he said … then paused to hear the hail hitting the roof. 'Right,' he added, collecting his thoughts, 'This is the plan: *You* grab the bags out the boot, and *I'll* make a run for cover. You can meet me inside.'

Lewis rolled his eyes, popped open his door, and then set his white trainers down in the wet gravel. '*Very* funny,' he said, hunching forwards and collecting hail stones in the hood of his sweatshirt.

Deborah was nearly home, the tower blocks standing guard on either side, moon coloured within odd patches of green like grubby umpires eager to call an end to the game. She'd decided, at some point during the meal probably, that she wouldn't be inviting him up, or *in*. And not because of impressions – she'd been doing a good one of herself all afternoon.

'You can just drop me at the petrol station if you like? I can walk from there; I've got to get a few bits anyway.' That had been the suggestion which had set off the silence. And now, a full three minutes later, Deborah supposed that what it had done was slaughter any tom-cat ideas James may or may not have been having of fucking on the floor of her flat, his first time in a tower block. But she wasn't sure what he thought or what he was thinking; from side on – only a guess – he now seemed to have resorted to trying to find a right word to describe the goings on of last 24 hours. Deborah looked at him, trying to read his mind and landing on … *Satisfactory.*

'I've got a confession to make,' Deborah said, breaching the peace, 'I just sat through an entire dinner with your parents without any underwear on.' It wasn't designed to be seductive; she smiled at him, amused.

James double took – her, the road, then back to her. 'Are you serious?'

'It wasn't done on purpose or anything, it just worked out that way.'

'Really…? I can't tell if you're joking.' The little grin faded, making her feel a little bare. James looked away. He was trying to hide it but it was there, a tide mark around his iris, that same patronising cut away he'd given her when she'd mocked him for showering before sex. 'Why would you do that?'

'I was rushing around,' Deborah said, not feeling she should explain herself, 'I forgot to buy any new ones and mine were dirty.' She scoffed, 'Why, does it bother you?'

Unconvinced the lie would carry in tones; James shook his head … and then couldn't help himself. 'Well,' he said quietly. 'I think it's a bit *much*.'

Deborah's arms had folded defensively over her chest. Forcing some humour into her voice, she repeated the phrase back to him, '*A bit much…?*'

James glimpsed at her and then overly concentrated on where he was supposed to be going. 'Look, it doesn't matter or anything,' he said not comfortable enough to argue with her. 'It's not like it's a big deal. It was just a shock to hear you say it out loud.' He tried to brush it aside by smiling and touching something in the dashboard. 'How about the weekend as a whole,' he asked, changing the subject, 'Has it been a good time? I mean, no knickers aside, have you enjoyed yourself?'

The pastel pin-stripes on his shirt were suddenly aggravating. Deborah nodded, outwardly calm, her insides slowly tying a knot. 'Can I ask you something?' She said politely. James' head turned, briefing her. 'Do you think that asking somebody that you've just met how they became a single mother is, a *bit much*? Because that's what your mum did. When we were alone in the kitchen.'

James furrowed, needing the distraction of the big red light on the petrol station which was coming up on their left. 'Sorry,' he said honestly. 'She can sometimes be … well, *rude*.' He shrugged at her. 'Were you offended?'

'No. I just found it uncomfortable.'

'What did you say?'

'I told her that I considered myself lucky, that a lot of women lose the fathers of their children to a lot less than death; and that nevertheless, the vast majority go on to do a wonderful job of raising their sons and daughters against some of the toughest odds.' She sighed. 'I also told her that single mothers are a special kind of people who deserve admiration, and one day, if she's lucky, *she* might finally topple down off of her high horse into the real world where she can actually meet some.'

James spent a second staring. 'You said *all* that?'

Deborah didn't bother keeping him in suspense. 'Of course not,' she said, 'but I bloody should've.'

'I can only apologise, Deb. In all honesty, I can't imagine she meant anything by it.'

'You mean, in the same way that I didn't mean anything by forgetting to buy myself some new knickers…?' Deborah smirked at him theatrically, making her point.

James chuckled and raised a hand in surrender. 'Match point,' he said. 'You win!' He pulled the car into the petrol station. 'I don't mind waiting and then taking you home,' he said, eyeing the rear view mirror. 'It doesn't feel gentlemanly leaving you here like this. It doesn't look safe.'

Deborah watched him watching a group of teenage boys stalking between the petrol pumps, rustling crisp packets and dropping them on the forecourt – two of them were boys she recognised, Lewis's friends. 'Don't be silly,' she said. 'This is practically on my doorstep.' Fiddling with her handbag, she unlocked the door but didn't get out.

James tempted her: 'Last chance; its freezing cold and I've

got heated seats –'

Deborah kissed him … quickly, and then opened her door and got out of the car. *The only thing more awkward than a first kiss is a first kiss goodbye*, she thought, twisting around and stooping down to see his face. He was looking at her, lips lingering. 'Thank you for a lovely night and day,' she said.

'You're welcome – but make sure you call me when you get in; I'll feel better when I know you're safely home.' She nodded, starting to close the door. 'Before you go, Debs…' He was muddling in his seat. '… In spite of your *pants* and my *mother*, I think I'd like it if we could do this again.'

'Then, we will,' Deborah said, pleased, believing that they would. 'I'll speak to you in a bit. Bye…'

The car door closed.

James shifted gears and went back the way he came, Deborah waving through the window, watching him go from the cover of the confectionery shelves inside the petrol station. She already knew that she wasn't going home, not so soon afterwards, not to be alone with herself. As backward as it sounded to her, especially after where she'd been and what she'd been doing for the last two days, the one and only person whose company she needed was Connie's, her mother-in-law. The pull was overwhelming, so she thought that that's where she should go. Refusing to think, she picked up a farmhouse fruit cake from the bottom shelf, paid for it with change, and then walked the short distance back to where her own car was parked.

The clock ticking was loudest.

Keeping her knees together, Constance Coles was sitting dead centre on the settee wrapped in a luxurious cardigan, her pale face set to a vacant pose. She'd been weeping, the redness in her eyes supping away at her husband's best bottle without touching a drop. She was undecided, the whisky bottle staring her down from the coffee table, its potion wakeless and the colour of chestnut rust. Next to her was a shoebox coffin, the old, handwritten letters she'd resurrected from inside fanned out around her feet, decades of dust on the carpet. Connie had gone through the lot, something she couldn't recall doing in years, since maybe '85. And that, then, had left her feeling much the same way as she did now: like she could do with a drink to take the edge off. But she hadn't taken one, not yet, purely because on the last occasion, when she did, poor Francis and Charlie had come home to find her collapsed and unable to stand. She wasn't a drinker, never had been, she usually saved her tipples for birthdays and weddings, and certainly not when Francis wasn't around – not except that is, for the times when she elected to sit alone and reopen old wounds. And it had been that way forever … ever since *that* day … ever since she had been made too frightened of letting go without knowing Francis was home to catch her before she hit the hallway floor, before the fragile truth showed up in red rings on her cheeks and the scars came out beneath her skin. *(The Devil makes work for idle thumbs).* So Connie pinned her hands between her thighs.

Tudor wandered in from his patrol, cast a glance her way, and then settled down beside the coffee table. The dog was unnerved; he could sense – in the way nature allows dogs to pick up on these things – that there was something unhealthy about his mistress. He rested his huge, sandy head on his paws and kept one eye open. Connie wiggled her toes inside her house loafers to remind herself that she was still kicking. She thought about making a noise, saying something out loud, for the sake of it, just to have something to do other than sit there. Tudor raised his head and an ear, listening; to him the sound was definitely there, a faint rumble outside … a car coming. He sprang up on his haunches, jowls wobbling, and coughed as if to warm up his vocal cords.

'My God dog! You made me jump!' Connie's first words were a croaky slur. She clutched her breast. 'What is it?' she said. 'What's the matter?'

Deborah turned into the driveway with one hand protecting the fruitcake from sliding off the passenger seat. Immediately she wondered why she didn't come here more often. The house – the one Charlie had grown up in, the one he and her had first made love under the roof of, and the one the son they had made once upon a time toddled barefooted – was right where it always had been, still, holding fast like a doorstop propping open the entrance to what has always been her *real* life. The familiar warmth steamed the creases out of the

November chill. In that moment, more so than before, her and James suddenly seemed ridiculous. She steered around the flower beds and stopped the car. The dog was barking, breath and bone on the inside of the living room window. Seeing him, widening her eyes to keep them from leaking, it occurred to her that Tudor had been a puppy only four years ago, that to him, who'd never met Charlie, the true champion of this castle was probably nothing more than a vague scent somewhere around the skirting boards.

Connie appeared at the curtain and then vanished, meticulously clearing the letters from the table and hiding the bottle before answering the door.

'I didn't expect to see you here, Love – Tudor, you silly dog. It's okay.' Connie let go of the dog's collar and he went bounding over the doorstep wagging his mood behind him.

Arm in the air to keep the cake out of reach, Deborah bumped the car closed and greeted the dog. 'With all the men away, I thought you might fancy some tea and cake…?'

'More than you could ever imagine, sweetheart.'

Deborah sent her a washed out little smile. Usually it never ceased to amaze her how good her mother-in-law always looked; she was timeless, one of those fictions who was able to wear her mid-sixties without letting out the waist. Not tonight though, not this evening; standing there abandoned on the threshold of her home, she looked sallow, ill, like she had just swallowed a mouthful of something which made her sick.

The two women tucked themselves in on either side of Connie's kitchen table, Tudor asleep at their feet.

Deborah cast eyes over the room, 'I love this house; it always feels like a proper home.'

Connie touched her fingers to her warm mug. 'That's why, despite all the skeletons in the closets, I've never been able to bring myself to leave.' Deborah looked at her strangely. 'Oh, I'm not saying it's haunted or anything,' Connie smiled. 'I just mean that we've got some bad memories living here with us. That's all...'

The Schoolboy's Bell, with its wood panelled walls, didn't need the eerie sepia expressions in the old class photographs framed along the hall to preserve the echo of a schoolhouse. It was all around them, blaring quiet: reading, writing, and arithmetic.

Francis checked them in, Lewis ringing himself out next to him, taking off his hoodie and flicking the hail stones out of his hair. The lounge was decorated in the style of an old-fashioned smoking room; comfortable chairs and chess tables angled around a noble fireplace. The arch windows were smooth black, the only view a reflection of the faces in the fire. They ordered their drinks – a coke, a pint, and a whisky chaser – and then plotted down in a pair of tartan armchairs.

'What kind of gun is that,' Lewis asked, attention drawn

by what was mounted over the mantelpiece. Barely having touched down, he was on his feet and striding over for a closer look.

Francis watched him over the rim of his pint glass. 'It's a blunderbuss,' he said. 'That one's a shotgun. See how wide the barrel is…?' Lewis was trailing a hand along the length of the polished brass, funnel-shaped barrel. He nodded. 'That's because they load that way, like a cannon. It'll fire almost anything that'll fit; just stuff it down with a bit of gunpowder and shoot.' Lewis touched the handle, wanting to take it down and hold it. Francis took another sip. 'Come over here, anyway. I've got something more important to show you.'

Lewis turned around, stretching his T-shirt out to try and relieve some of the wrinkles. 'Is that what I think it is?' he said, spotting what his grandfather had set on the table. 'We've had that with us the whole time and you didn't show me?'

Francis hung his coat back over the chair next to him. 'I'm showing now.'

'Can I hold it?'

'Course you can.'

Cradling it with his palms, Lewis lifted Micky's hip flask up and gave it a little shake. It was half full. He gaped at it, at the fleur de lis patterns in the corners and the scratches on the silver. It was proof of everything. 'I can't believe he died,' he remarked, flopping back into his chair. 'Did that Scottish man get away with it?'

'Does anybody ever *really* get away with anything? One

way or the other, it all costs us something.'

'Nippy should have shot *him* instead of that other bloke.'

Francis swallowed another philosophical mouthful. 'At the time, none of us knew he was even involved. And anyway, even back then it wasn't so easy that you could just go round shooting people.'

'But you did,' Lewis argued. 'You already told me that you shot someone.'

Francis's eyes scolded him for talking too loud. He tipped his head towards a mixed group of mountain bikers who were sitting just the other side of the fireplace, and then said:

'I did, and it was one of the things I regret most about my life. It never should have happened.'

'Why? Who was he?'

'I don't know much about him,' Francis spoke softly, 'except that his name was Gerald Best, and that he was a copper.'

'It was a *policeman?*' Lewis hissed, shocked. 'Did he die?'

Francis looked at him. 'Like I said, everything we do costs us something. Lots of people have killed, Lewis. Over all sorts: lust, pride, revenge, money, sometimes even by mistake. And believe me; it's taken something from each of them. Only when it's too late can we find out if we were forgiven.' He sat forwards and placed his drink on the table. 'In my case, I try to tell myself that Gerald must've done someone a horrible mischief – or that he would've done if he'd lived. All I know is that the bloke never did me any harm. He just turned up where he shouldn't have.' Holding the hip flask as a talisman, Lewis stared at him, silenced. Francis stood up and kicked his feet to make sure his trousers fell straight, losing what looked like a necklace from his pocket.

'What are those?' Lewis asked curiously.

'Prayer beads,' Francis said, bending down. 'They were a gift.'

'Anyway,' He said, brushing it off. 'I thought you were interested in finding out about the pocket watches...?'

'I was, but I didn't think you wanted to tell me.'

Francis smiled. 'Just not while I was driving,' he said. 'It's better to sit down and tell you properly.' There was a sudden flare up of laughter from the other table. 'First thing's first though,' Francis added, minding his business. 'Splash a bit of that into your coke so we can have a toast when I get back from ordering something to eat.' He glanced at the food menu, 'I'm going for the lamb shanks.'

'Same,' Lewis said, sounding like a boy. He was fishing the lemon slice out of his tall glass with the straw. He raised the hip flask to make sure his grandfather was serious. 'What's in this?'

'Whisky,' Francis answered, walking to the bar.

Lewis had goose-bumps. He twisted the cap free and started to pour, the grown-up smell stinging his nose. He watched as the firelight from the hearth behind him and the liquor mingled in the bottom of his glass. This wasn't his first drink – he and Sammy had stolen a crate of beers from the back of the off licence for a party someone was having in the summer – but it would be the first one that counted. Later he would remember this night and that drink, the sweet sugar and the rub of too much spirit.

Francis came back and sat down. 'I ordered us apple crumble and custard for afters,' he said, picking the shot glass up from the table. 'You ready?' Lewis nodded and chinked his glass against his grandfather's. 'To Charlie and Micky...'

'To dad and Micky,' Lewis said, and then knocked back a mouthful and swallowed. He coughed.

'Well done,' Francis winked, slamming the bottom of his glass on the wooden table. 'Taste any good?' Lewis nodded, not daring to wipe the whisky mist out of his eye. 'Right then,' Francis began, feeling the spirit in his chest: 'The watches. Bear in mind, I'm piecing some of this together with what Avram told me earlier because we didn't know it at the time –' He raised his index finger. '– And, none of *us* had the foggiest it was even about those watches in the beginning. Only Ori did; the whole thing was *his* caper.' He shook his head comically and went back to his beer. 'What had happened was, Pollitt had been shopping that bit of work about for a while – he'd actually gone to George and Marge with it, it was them that brought us on board. This would've been just around the time before Micky passed because I remember him getting all excited about wanting to do it.' He laughed. 'To be honest I didn't buy into it too much. The way it was put to us was that a good friend of Ori's, one of his accountant or lawyer pals from university, was working for a wealthy Jewish family over in the States. Apparently, according to Pollitt's mate, it had come down the pipe that these New York bankers had a load of jewels over in Belgium that they were planning on bringing through England on their way over to America. I only found out when I spoke to Avram today that the stuff was so-called, Holocaust jewellery. What they'd said to me was that this friend of Ori's didn't know exactly what was coming, or what it was worth; he just knew that there would be gold and silver and stones and that it was part of an inheritance.

'I could see what George and Marge were saying: if it was worth these people smuggling, then it must be worth nicking. And I could see why they were interested: no bank to think about, no safe, no digging tunnels and dynamiting walls...' He was counting off the pros on his fingers. '...And it was potentially a big earner for everybody. But me, myself, I looked at it another way...' His fingers were going again. '...We didn't have enough information, we knew sod-all about what this stuff even was or who it belonged to, and the main thing: we had no clue where it was going to be at any given time – all they knew was that it would be coming through England on its journey.' He took another drink, pausing. 'Knowing what I know now though, in hindsight, Ori and his mate must've known exactly what was in that vault; they just weren't letting on. And going by what Avram said, I reckon they probably already had a buyer lined up – that collector from the Far East he was going on about.' He chuckled. 'The truth was though; I'd be lying if I said I actually thought any of it was even going to happen. And even when it did, more than for money, I only really went along on it for Winston's sake.'

'Why for Winston's sake?'

'Because, when it eventually came around to doing it, Micky wasn't there anymore. It had been almost a year; we finally did it, December 1960, right before the following Christmas. I think Winston felt like we owed it to Mick to pull it off, because he had been so excited by the prospect of doing it himself.' Francis pondered it. 'All I can remember is how unprepared we was,' he said, thinking. 'One night Ori turns up at George's and tells him that he'd had a call from New York and the stuff was floating.' His eyes closed at the ludicrousness of what he was about to say. 'When I turned up, all they knew was that it was being smuggled out of Antwerp and over to England on a fishing trawler; all they had was the name of the boat, not a clue where the bloody thing was docking. It was ridiculous. I couldn't believe what I was hearing, George goes: *'we'll have to take it at sea'*.' Lewis looked at him sceptically. 'That's exactly what I was thinking,' Francis chuckled. 'He reckoned that in the time it took for their boat to reach British waters, he could sort out a couple of speedboats, and we could go after it in the Channel.'

'Oh shit!'

'And these vessels of his weren't what you're thinking,' Francis said. 'When we got there they were basically a couple of row boats with outboard motors stuck on the back.' Lewis laughed. 'It has to be the most dangerous thing I've ever done in my life, that *any* of us have. The waves were coming over the sides and it was fucking freezing; God only knows how George managed to find that trawler way out there in the dark, but he did. Two boat loads of us wearing wet woolly hats boarded that trawler like a bunch of swashbucklers who'd been at it all their lives. Only Davey Thomson fell in.

I remember him splashing about and George screaming for us to hurry up because the boats kept drifting away; why we didn't just leave them and all sail home on the trawler I'll never know, but there you go.'

'It don't matter,' Lewis said, grinning. 'Either way, it worked out alright in the end.'

'*I* was the only one who ever doubted it.' Francis said, reaching for his pint.

'What did you do with the people on the trawler?'

'Nothing. Why, were you hoping that we threw them overboard?' Lewis scrunched up his nose in reply. 'I think someone must've untied the captain so he could take them home,' Francis said. 'They were good as gold, mate. I'd say, being out there, we were probably more scared than they were. I know I was. Crammed into them wooden tubs with suitcases of jewellery on our feet, all any of us could think about were our little boats sinking. You should've heard the cheer that went up when we saw land. It was daybreak by then; we burst into song the moment we spotted the cliffs coming through the fog. I couldn't tell you where we was – some remote shingle beach somewhere – but right before we hopped over the side to wade in, Winston turned to me and said, '*Micky would've loved this*'.'

Pupils darting, Lewis listened to himself think, taking no notice of the young waitress or the food on her tray. Francis slid the empty glasses aside so she could set their dinner down. When she'd walked away, Lewis asked:

'And that's how you got the watches...?'

Francis answered, unravelling his knife and fork from his

napkin. 'Pretty much,' he said. 'I'm not sure why, probably because they were a pair, but when we were all divvying up, everybody picking bits and pieces for their wives and girlfriends, Marge just plucked them out the pile and handed them to me and Winston. None of *us* knew what they were; we just stuck them in our pockets and carried on. It's only knowing what I do now, that I realise *Ori* knew. But at the time, he was keeping quiet in the corner.'

'And that was it ... as simple as that?'

Francis laughed with his mouthful. 'Yeah' he said, '*As simple as that*. I'll tell you what though: they were far easier to get than to keep hold of.'

Barley Sugar

DICKIE DORRANCE

December, 1960

'No, no. Honestly. Not even in a month of Sundays, old boy. I've told you: they're ignorant; they'll *never* even notice the difference.' The telephone cord was trailing from Ori Pollitt's desk to the office window behind it. 'I understand your concern Matthew, but have faith, the forger came highly recommended. Besides, they have absolutely no idea what they *had*; the moment I mentioned I might have a buyer they handed them straight over, no problem … people like these understand how it all works. It's always a risk.' He paused to listen to Matthew fretting from long distance. 'Okay,' Ori said. 'Let me put it to you this way: I had the fakes made, less an insurance policy and more a gesture of goodwill on our behalf; more than likely, I could've had them refashioned in silver for all the bloody difference it would've made. These types we're talking about Matthew, they don't care about details; they're always more interested in what they've made rather than what they've lost. They're used to occasionally missing out. And even if they do cotton on, I shouldn't imagine they'll anti up too much over a pair of pocket watches which are completely insignificant to them. No way, they'll be far too drunk on the profits of the other stuff to muster more than a yawn…' Beaming crookedly down at the passers-by in the street, Ori blew an airy little wineglass laugh into the mouthpiece of the telephone. 'Trust me, old boy, you're worrying about nothing. I'd much prefer to hear how things are going on your end with the Orientals...'

Matthew crackled down the line from New York and Ori paced, his gaudy tie matching the arrogance of his shoes and the five-fingered, Broadway grin across his chops. On his desktop, the Louis Breguet originals lay staged inside a velvet-lined box.

After listening and humming over the finer details, Ori clapped his hand against his thigh, 'Let's leave it there then, shall we? End on a high note. We can discuss the rest next week in the Big Apple.' He simpered at Matthew's response, twirling to a curtsey back behind his desk. 'Okay ... yes ...I certainly will ... and you old boy, all the best until then.' When the telephone receiver went down, Ori congratulated himself by stooping to his chair's level and working his pupils over the box on his desk. *It's true what they say*, he thought, *Time is money*. Eventually, he snapped the box shut, stuffed it back into the drawer, and rang for assistance.

'Enter...' he mocked, when the knock sounded on the door. 'Oh, Meredith, glad it's you. I've got some little jobs need doing.'

Meredith nudged the door with her tea-and-biscuits bottom and lifted her pen. 'What are they?'

Ori flashed at her, exaggerating the whisper. 'First,' he said. 'What do you say we do it one last time over the desk, for old times' sake?' She narrowed her eyes. 'Oh, yes, that's right, you have a boyfriend now.' He grinned, little teeth behind big lips. 'I take it it's going well then...tell me – just between you and me – which is worse, being bored or being lonely?'

Doing well to hold onto the preconceived smile she'd walked in with, Meredith huffed, unmoved. 'I'm only joshing,' Ori sang. 'Never mind, listen, there's a couple of small favours I'd like you to do for me, if you wouldn't mind? If you could keep a low tone about it, much the better: you know how people are. I don't want any fuss made.' Meredith tossed her brows, prodding him to get on with it. 'Right, well, it's nothing dramatic, I just need you to get onto a shipping company for me; I'm going to be abroad for a while and I've got some boxes of belongings I'd like to follow me over.'

'Which destination?' she asked, pen poised.

'The Big Apple,' he said, sounding caviller. 'I'd also think you were marvellous if you could find me a seat on British Airways for early next week – First Class if they've got it.'

Meredith peered up from her notes. 'So soon; how long are you planning on staying?'

'Who knows? I'm not entirely certain that I'll be coming back.'

'About fucking time...' The voice in the corner grumbled, upon finally hearing footfalls on the landing. Barry Horace – an associate of George King's who'd earned a share from the boat – was lolling on a misplaced dining chair, pinching at the wrinkle on the back of his bald head. 'Make sure you keep my stuff separate.'

Francis and Winston didn't have time to acknowledge him ...

The lank, upright figure of Dickie Dorrance sailed into the

nightclub's office like a warm breeze through an open door. A piece of high art society, he was well at home on the King's Road, his steep nose and sticky beak speaking for itself. He stopped, publicising himself to the man in the corner. 'There really is no need to gawk, sweetie,' he said. 'Everything's okay, I'm just *queer.*'

Barry snorted. 'Never would've guessed.'

Dickie stomped one of his riding boots down like a matador, smiling and modelling his jodhpurs. 'Why, thank you very much for noticing,' he said. 'Do you like it? It's Napoleonic…' He splayed his arms in order to show off the military tunic he was wearing: navy blue with red cuffs and gold buttons. Incorporating it into a twirl, he extended a hand and beckoned to the little lady he'd left loitering in the hallway. 'Don't be shy,' he told her. 'His type are all bark and baby balls.'

Starting to get up, Barry gaped over at Francis. *'Is he fucking serious?'*

'Leave him,' Winston said, laughing.

Turning his back on the man in the corner, Dickie kissed both of Francis's cheeks in a belated greeting. 'You're looking dashing, as always,' he cooed, joyously. 'Please tell me you're still clinging onto that tremendous girlfriend of yours…the gorgeous red head.'

'Connie…'

Dickie pouted. 'How is she? I didn't see her dancing downstairs, is she not here tonight?'

'Nah, I tend to leave her at home when studs like Barry are about.'

'A wise move,' Dickie said, exaggerating a wink and then turning his attention to Winston. 'Winston love, tell me, are you back in full working order?' His eyes made a clean sweep of Winston's physique and then settled on his crotch until Winston shoved him away playfully. 'Gosh, I haven't seen either of you since the wedding.' He paused, unpinning the white flower from his lapel and handing it to Winston. 'For the funniest of our friends,' he toasted, 'may he forever keep the angels laughing.' Allowing for a moment of silence, he added: 'And what about Marge, how is he managing?'

'He's doing okay.'

Dickie squinted at the mound of jewellery on the desk. 'Indeed! Right, then,' he said, clearing his throat and pressing on, 'shall we get on down to business? I hope you don't mind that I haven't come alone. If it had been paintings again I would have, but seeing as this lot glitters, I thought I'd prove my wisdom by bringing someone who knows what they're doing.'

Dickie got behind his lady-friend and presented her: 'This is milady Vienna. Wonderful name isn't it? Daddy's German, mummy's Austrian. We met years ago at an exhibition in Munich and have been lovers ever since.' He gave her shoulders a little shake, making her curls fall out from her hat. 'Do listen to her boys, she certainly knows her stuff.'

'I'm very much pleased to meet vit you,' Vienna said, lifting her gaze for the first time, her eyes creasing as the smile spread beneath her brim. 'How do you do…?'

'We're all fine, love,' Francis said, moving forward to take her hand. 'And thank you for coming to see us.' With a light hold on her fingers, he showed her the desk. 'As you can see, we've got a good few bits and pieces here that need an opinion.'

In the corner, Barry tipped his head back.

Winston smiled his hello. 'Yeah, even old Barry over there has got something he'd like you to take a look at before you go.'

'Is that so?' Dickie tittered. 'Well, what are you waiting for, Barry? Whip it out and pop it up on the desk, *I'll* make sure it gets a good seeing to.'

Barry spat on the carpet.

'…I'll be interested in what you think of these,' Francis was saying, passing Vienna one of the pocket watches. 'I'm not sure what to do with them; I've just been given them back by a friend of mine who thought he'd found a buyer. It looks like that's fallen through though, so if they ain't worth much, we'll just hang on to them.'

Vienna took an excited breath, nostrils fogging the gold. With delicate, gloved fingers she inspected the watch; the mechanism, the numerals, the beautifully fashioned dagger tipped hands. 'Faschugen,' she muttered, looking disappointed. 'Sorry, I mean to say: fake or false?' She peered at Dickie to double check her English. Francis and Winston frowned at one another. 'Sorry,' Vienna said, placing the watch back in Francis's palm, 'of this I am certain, das are counterfeit.'

'How can you tell?'

'I know vat I'm talking,' she said, smiling regrettably. 'Please excuse, but it's as mine furher liked to say: if I vas deaf I could no longer hear a lie … but, if I vas blind, I vould still see *dis* one. There is no engraving. Dis should have inscription.'

'There is an inscription,' Francis said. 'I've seen it; it's written in a foreign language…' He trailed off, his thumb finding nothing but smooth gold plate.

Vienna gave him an unfortunate wince, and then continued tucking her hair back into her hat.

Ori Pollitt's telephone rang on...

At first light, Francis and Winston picked up Nippy and drove him over to the mansion flat which Ori rented on Barnes Common.

(There was no answer...)

Nippy dropped to one knee and thumbed the brass keyhole cover to one side. The thin barrel of Ori's hall was sparse – no swishing night robe, no sleeping beauty. The only clue to movement was that the bedroom door was ajar, a pale shaft of daylight, one of the dawn's pathways to heaven, pulling diagonally across the parquet floor.

'No sign of him,' Nippy said, blinking up at Winston. 'Shall I go round the back and see if I can get in?'

'Only if you can do it quietly...?'

In a matter of minutes Nippy had found a drainpipe, shinned up it to the second floor, smashed the bathroom window with his elbow, and scrambled through. Covered in anti-climbing paint and brick dust, he worked his way through the flat. Everything which could be carried was gone, yet there was no mess; the bed was made, the curtains tied, and the furniture still steadfast in position. The only evidence anything had been disturbed was the dust marks on the surfaces, square rings and footprints; that, and a few forgotten books on the shelves.

'I reckon he's looked lively and scarpered,' Nippy said, opening the front door with his hand tucked inside his cuff. 'He ain't here, and it don't look like he's coming back.'

The heavy bags underneath Francis's eyes were punch drunk. At 9:15am – straightening his tie for the want of something less obvious to do with his hands – he walked into Ori's Chelsea office and asked for his accountant.

'I'm afraid Mr Pollitt isn't here, sir. If it's a matter of importance though, I'd be happy to find somebody else who might be able to help you.'

Francis smiled. 'I'd rather wait,' he said, checking his wrist. 'Do you mind? It's only just after nine; perhaps he's running late…?'

Meredith sucked in her stomach beneath her desk. She regarded his face, absently fingering the brooch on her jumper. 'I'm *sorry*. It's my fault,' she said, flushing. 'I don't think I made myself very clear. What I meant to say was Mr Pollitt is *away*. His clients have been passed over to one of his colleagues.'

'I see,' Francis said, outwardly cordial, inwardly cursing him. 'Then, do you have any idea when he'll be returning?'

'Not for a fair while, I don't think. But as I said, I'd be more than happy to –'

Francis dismissed her graciously. 'Mr Pollitt is my business accountant, you see. I've been with him since the beginning;

he knows the books inside out. I'd prefer to speak to him if I may. Did he leave a contact number, a forwarding address, somewhere I can reach him?'

Meredith shrugged regretfully, her painted thumbnail stroking the corner of the ledger and making the pages flap. 'There's nothing here,' she said. 'But don't worry, he had me ship most of his more important things over there for him, so if he has personal business with you, I'm sure you'll hear from him as soon as he gets settled.'

'Over *there*? He's *abroad*?'

'It was all a bit sudden,' Meredith said. 'I'm not sure many people were made aware that he was going.'

Francis looked at her, 'Wow, good for him...any idea where?'

'New York,' she said. 'But he doesn't leave until Monday morning, so if it's that imperative that you catch up with him, what I could do is give you his home address and you try and catch up with him there.'

'Not until *Monday*,' Francis repeated. 'Are you certain?'

'I'm positive,' Meredith said, 'I booked his flight for him.'

Sitting on his principles, Winston only stopped ranting once he'd spotted Francis hurrying back towards the car.

'British Airways, ten o'clock, Monday morning,' Francis said, sliding in behind the wheel and slamming the door. 'He's flying from Heathrow to New York; the little bastard's emigrating on us, he's already has his stuff shipped.'

Nippy stuck his head between the front seats. 'Emigrating?'

'It means he's fucking off.' Winston explained. 'What a *cunt!*' he spat. 'He's tucked us right up.'

The car away from the curb and Nippy flopped back onto the rear seat. 'Stone me!' he mused. 'Them pocket watches must be worth a mint.'

A fist hit the dashboard. 'What the fuck do we do now?'

Francis answered through a yawn, 'For starters, go home and get some rest.'

'*Sleep…?* You want us to kip while that little prick makes mugs of us?'

'I'm fucking shattered, Wince.'

'What and I ain't…?' Winston was eye-balling the side of Francis's face. 'Bollocks to that,' he said. 'I ain't letting him get away with it.'

'Who said anything about letting him get away with it?'

'You…'

'Did I? I said I was going home to rest,' Francis argued. 'Then I'm thinking to phone George and see if he can't nobble someone down at that shipyard and have Ori's crates opened up.' Winston rolled his eyes and let his head bounce back off of the headrest. Francis cut away to look at the road. 'Have you got a better idea?'

'Yep,' Winston said, irritated. 'We keep on searching for him until Monday, and if we ain't found him, we go to the fucking airport and wrap him up.'

'Grab him in the middle of Heathrow airport, is *that* your plan?' Francis sneered. 'And how likely is it we'll get nicked doing that? And what, one of us just walks up and bundles him away in front of all those people? Think about it: if he has got the watches on him, it will just look like we've robbed him. And once we're banged up, the law will give them back to him anyway.'

'Oh, but *George* is going to save the day, is he?' Winston turned in his seat to get this off his chest. 'He doesn't give a toss if we got ripped off, Francis. For all we know he was probably in on it with the little prick. He's the one he fucking works for.'

Francis didn't entertain the idea. 'Talk sense ... why would George have let Marge give us the watches in the first place if he knew they were worth something? He was right there in the room with us.'

'And so was Ori.'

'Yeah, but Ori ain't George, is he?'

'Just as fucking well, because when I catch up to that snide little cunt I'm –'

'In the middle of an airport...?' Francis questioned, peering ahead. 'For fuck's sake, Wince, let's try and use our heads...'

Winston unfolded his arms. 'By doing what, lying down and going to fucking sleep?'

'Hello, Jack ... its Francis ... yeah, that's right, Francis Coles...' He chuckled into the telephone. '...I know, I know, it's been a while, how's tricks?' Grinning, 'I thought as much. Good stuff. Listen, I might need a favour from you ... nah, nah, nothing like that, I just need to borrow you for a morning. There's something you might be able to help me with...'

Francis had arrived home to an empty house, his eyes bloodshot blue, the inner rings of marbles. After hanging up, he made another call to George, and then crashed out on his bed. And there he slept, jealous but free from dreams and grateful for the tricks up his sleeve.

The rustle of shopping bags woke him in the afternoon – Connie closing the front door and slipping off her shoes. On her stockings, she carried on into the kitchen and put the bags down. Francis shuffled up behind her and placed his hands on her waist; he rested there, warm in the curves her mother's mother had left her. He could remember Connie telling him once, that as a little girl, her grandmother had promised her that when she grew into a woman, she too would have baby-making hips.

'Sleep well...?' Connie asked gently, feeling Francis pressing his face into the back of her hair. Rather than answer, he kissed her head. She wanted to tell him how long the night had been without him, without the toss and turn in the small hours – instead, she closed her eyes until he'd let go. Sleep creased, he moved to the kitchen table and sat down. 'Do you want to tell me, or is it something I'm better off not knowing?' She closed the cupboard before turning to look at him. She reciprocated his smile, sculpting hers into an even more loving shape.

Francis started the saga: the story of Ori Pollitt and the Big Apple. She listened attentively, a sight for sore eyes, a green meadow gaze with rose pinched cheeks, who wasn't the least bit surprised. When he'd finished talking, she placed a short glass of milk and some buttered toast down in front of him. 'You're right about Winston,' she said, somehow only attaching any significance to what Francis had said about the two of them arguing. 'He probably has been acting funny.' She sat down opposite him and handed him the pot of strawberry jam. 'But it's not because of you, Francis. It's Bunny. She's pregnant.'

'What?' Francis stopped chewing. 'Why didn't he tell me?'

'He did – I mean, he meant to … that's why he came round the other day, so you two could talk.'

'When was this?'

'A few days ago,' Connie said, 'when you were running around with George. He was distraught. He sat right where you are now and we cried together.'

Francis looked baffled. 'Cried? Why?'

'Because he said that Bunny doesn't think she wants to see it through. He was worried she might have it taken care of it already. It was awful to see him like that.'

'Why didn't you tell me?'

'I haven't seen you, Francis.'

'Fuck!' Francis said severely. 'And that's why they've been having problems?' Connie responded with a series of sensitive little nods. 'Shit, no wonder he's acting up. I better go over and see him tonight.'

Connie sat and watched him eat in silence, seeing sadness building around the edges of his mouth. For a flicker she thought about telling him, about taking his hand and blurting out that *she* too had missed one of her monthlies.

That for the last two mornings in a row she had thrown up in the washbasin. But instead, she stayed quiet.

Morning had broken. When Francis answered the telephone in the hallway, it was George King's voice coming down the wire. Ori Pollitt's shipment of personal affects had been ransacked and left strewn across a warehouse floor.

'No joy,' George said. 'Marge took Clarky over there with him and they went through everything with his name on it. Nothing turned up, nothing that resembles what you're talking about.'

'Cheers. It was worth a try, anyway.'

After a brief quiet, George said: 'Have you considered that he might have got shot of them already?'

Francis held the phone away from his ear and made a face at Connie who was standing in the doorway. 'Nah, he's definitely taking them abroad with him.'

'Do you want me to send someone out to scout for him?'

'Winston's already looking,' Francis said. There was a pause; Marge saying something to George in the background. 'Okay,' George said, when he came back. 'Well, let us know if there's anything we can do. And if you need a hand getting rid of any other bits, just let me know. I wouldn't want to see you boys come up short.'

'Will do,' Francis said.

He put down the telephone disappointed and then saw that Connie was still looking at him.

On the Monday morning the plan came together.

Early enough to catch the worm – or in his case, a giant metal bird with engines on the sides – Ori Pollitt gulped the last dregs of a badly made Bloody Mary and let the hotel room materialise. So he'd been told Mary was the best thing for a champagne hangover. She didn't work; he still felt like his head was half hanging off. But, it had been a sweet dream: counting money on his back with the Empire State Building between his legs. He got up, stood, and then stalked into the royalist bathroom to wash the prostitute stink off of him before getting dressed. *Travel light and go far,* he thought ten minutes later, slinging his leather satchel over his shoulder and making his way down to the lobby to check out.

By quarter to eight, as the city of London was starting to stir up another soggy sod of a morning, Pollitt was in a taxi and on his way. When the driver tried to blather about never having been on an aeroplane, Ori cut him off by pursing his lips and whistling the star spangled banner. Conversation killed, he burped up some tomato flavoured gas and then spent the rest of the drive to Heathrow thinking about the glittering leap he was about to take. He was proud of himself; today, *he* was the man who could step over oceans without wetting his shoes. He was the man who'd rolled the dice and won the raffle, the guy who'd looked after number one and therefore was entitled to celebrate. And he did, by crooning the words to *I'll be seeing you*, under his breath until the airport turned up.

Then…the paranoia started, a doctor's dose to begin with – a bitter mouthful on a silver spoon. As the taxi pulled up next to the terminal building, Ori could have sworn that he recognised the lad leaning on the railings outside. He did, he'd be willing to bet both of the balls in his bag on it; it was the youngest Meehan brother. The driver muttered something. Ori whipped round and paid the fare, only averting his eyes for a second, but when he looked back the boy was gone. *I need to bloody well eat something before I fly*, he thought, hesitating before getting out of the car, blaming his swirly state of mind on his liquid breakfast. But when the cab pulled away he was left exposed. He was visible, a sore thumb dressed in a herringbone jacket and tartan tie. Singular thuds burst in his chest, speeding and slowing, shooting for pheasant. Clutching his satchel he turned in a complete circle, taking in everyone and everything. *See, old boy*, he told himself, *you're being ridiculous, how would they know?*

He got going, acutely aware that he was frightened. Across the concourse and into the terminal, anxious, a sweaty palm nervously sticking to his leather satchel, the original pocket watches stuffed deep down inside. He checked the flight board. It occurred to him then, for the second time, that his imagination might be getting away from him; that it could be feasting on the empty bubbles and winged insects in his stomach. A man brushed his shoulder … then another, rushing past. Walking, his legs were no longer under his head's direction. He thought he saw another face, badly scarred, *Davey Thompson* in the crowd behind him. A large group of long-haired music fans crossed his path in a blur of colours ... then two men in bowler hats. Ori stared through the funnel of space they left desperate to see what he'd seen ... Davey, if that's who it was, had disappeared too. His heart thumped once, and he moved quicker, knees up. More people were coming towards him, men and women, laughing and roaring. A Tannoy speaker perforated the madness. There were blue and red letters, straight ahead: BRITISH AIRWAYS. He jerked his neck, daring to check over his shoulder. That was when he saw Winston, a brown face in a white flock, less than twenty feet away, not following fast but gaining. Ori broke into a slippery run, tripping when Davey suddenly popped up again on his right hand side. He bleated, a wary sheep being herded by dogs, spotting and reaching for the saving grace of the policeman standing at the check-in desk ahead of him. Staggering and knocking other passengers aside, Ori fell down in front him and tugged on his sleeve:

'Help me, please help me, they're trying to swipe my bag officer...'

'Steady on there, Boyo!' The policeman grabbed hold of him and helped him to his feet. 'What's that you say?'

Ori's immediate concern was with who was behind him; his eyes darted, desperately searching for a sight of Winston or Davey. 'Two men,' he said breathless, the words a rushed verse. 'At least I think there were two, there could've been *more*. But I definitely saw two: one coloured and one with cuts on his face – I mean scars. He has scars all over his face.'

The lady behind the check-in desk implored the rest of the queue to remain calm.

'Can anybody see these men?' The policeman asked loudly. He tucked Ori behind him and surveyed the onlookers. 'If anyone can see someone of the like this man is describing, just point them out.' There was a murmur as people started to turn and search for the culprits, but nobody pointed a finger.

'They were there,' Ori explained. 'Right there, just behind me.' There was nothing there, no faces, coloured or scarred, no harm doing; it was as if Winston and Davey – and even the lad outside – had been nothing but hallucinations and paranoid vapour. Charting the terminal, one hand still holding on to the back of the policeman's jacket and his eyeballs hurrying in every direction, Ori began to feel a little lunatic, as if he'd swallowed the smelling salts instead of sniffing them. Shamefaced, he giggled. 'They must have seen me reach you and then vanished,' he said.

Ever vigilant, the policeman beamed at him. 'It wouldn't be the first time, sir.' He raised a palm of apology to the rest of the queue, 'Nothing to worry about now boys and girls, you can carry on about your flying.' It was only then that Ori realised that his saviour had a thick Welsh accent.

Pulling himself together, Ori waited for the queue to begin milling around before deciding to lie: 'My Grandmother was Welsh,' he said. 'Which part are you from?'

The policeman slapped Ori on the back. 'In that case,' he said, 'I'm happy to have been of service to a fellow countryman. I'm from a town called Rhyl in the north.'

'You're joking,' Ori gushed. 'That's where my grandmother

was born. Fancy that … a big stroke of luck you being here when you were, I'd say. It's certainly saved *my* bacon. I don't know how I could ever thank you.' He leaned in close to whisper. 'I happen to be carrying valuables, you see. I dare say that's what they got wind of.'

The policeman tucked him a wink. 'Like I say, I'm glad to be of service. No need for thanks.'

'But I wonder,' Ori mused, double checking what was around him, 'do you think I could be a devil and ask a further favour?'

'Go ahead. I'll certainly see what I can do.'

'Well, would it be at all possible … or rather, would you mind, just staying with me – just until I'm through customs and onto the other side?' Ori searched him pleadingly. 'I've got a terrible fear that they might come back, you see.'

True to his word the policeman stayed where he was, keeping an eye out and making small talk until it was Ori's turn at the desk. Given a little less on his mind, Ori might have noticed that the tall man with the combed back widows' peak of black hair didn't much look like Wales. The bridge of his nose was too high; a countenance bred for a card table sooner than one from a coal mine. Once the lady had handed him his boarding pass, the policeman hung an arm around his shoulder and walked him in the direction of the boarding gates.

'Now listen, it's nothing personal, boyo, but I'd be grateful if you'd allow those customs officers there to have a sly peep inside that satchel of yours. It's not that I'm saying I don't believe you or anything like that, it's just those are the rules, see.' Being led, Ori smiled reluctantly, the policeman – a puppeteer – persuading him over to the table, all the time touching and nudging him with little bumps and instructions.

Preoccupied, a red-headed marionette on a string, Ori did as he was shown and laid his satchel down in front of two pale-faced officials. He opened it up and bared its fruit.

'Two men tried to steal this gentleman's bag.' The policeman said. 'Be warned; one was a coloured fellow, the other had some sort of scarring on his face –'

'Would you please be careful with those,' Ori said, seeing the watch box coming out of the bag. The officer slowly lifted the lid, the pocket watches appearing like gold coins, like the first two stepping stones toward a golden future. 'My grandfather's timepieces,' Ori explained. 'Antique. They're on their way to New York to be auctioned.'

'…You can never be too careful,' the policeman was saying, over- extending his long, friendly drawl. 'You can bet your life they're still around…' He tapped Ori lightly on the back. '…I'm pretty certain I spotted one of the buggers when we was on our way over; watching us from behind that barrier there, he was.' Prodded by a hot breath in his ear, Ori whipped around on himself, hearing sirens. Knowing both of the officials would follow the bluff, the policeman skilfully picked the watch box up from the table, performing his trick. 'As soon as I get my friend here safely through passport control, I'll be straight over there and seeing about getting a hand on them.' He touched Ori on the back again. 'Wow! I should expect you'll be asking quite a price from these.' The policeman added cheerily, admiring the pocket watches before handing them over.

Ori snatched the box back possessively and began repacking his satchel. 'Are we quite finished here?'

'Free to go, I'd say,' the policeman suggested. The two customs officials nodded. 'Lovely! I'll leave you here then boyo, nobody's getting past either of these two. Don't you worry; they'll watch you all the way until you've shown your ticket.' He thrust his hand out. 'I didn't get your name...?'

'Pollitt...' Ori said absently. '...Mr Pollitt.'

'Officer, Jack Manners,' the policeman responded, grinning. 'If you should ever find yourself back in Rhyl visiting, Mr Pollitt, you be sure to tell everyone about the good work I'm doing down here in the big smoke.' He winked at him, still shaking his hand. 'And good luck with the auction.'

Assessing each and every one of the bystanders beyond the barrier, Ori Pollitt joined the other queue and flashed his passport. He shuffled like a man expecting a stab in the back. When he turned around on the other side, the police officer, Jack Manners, was still smiling and waving.

Not until Ori was belted safely into this aeroplane seat, high above the clouds, would the policeman's face and far-fetched accent begin to bother him. A pink face trapped in an oval window, he still had hours ahead of him to ponder. And by then it was already too late.

Barley Sugar

As the British Airways flight to New York city left the runway, Jack Manners, confidence trickster and petty thief, strolled through Heathrow airport dressed in uniform. The grin was now a Gin rummy flush across his facade. The accent was a nice touch, he thought, as he stepped out into the wide open car park and began cutting diagonally across it like a chess piece.

Squashed inside a black Ford by the boundary fence, Francis and the others were waiting for him. Nobody need ask, the la-di-da smile was a give away. Once Jack was close enough to be sure that he had their attention, he stopped, rolled his shoulders, and then flicked his sleeves ... one by one, as if by magic, the Louis Breguet originals appeared in his palms like gold dust.

MARGE

January, 1961

'No word of a lie,' Francis said. 'Jack switched them right underneath his toffee nose. He flew off with his own set of fakes.'

The men around the club table – friends of friends – burst simultaneously into a loud bully of laughter: clapping hands and rolling glasses. George whooped a cough through a smoke ring. 'You better watch *this* one,' he said, addressing the long beaks of the men opposite. 'Our Francis is a smart fish. You mark my words: give it a year and he'll have us all out of work.' Being lorded, the pocket watch was being passed around the table, backhanded from one person to the next.

'I thought there were two…? What's happened to the other one?'

'Winston's got it,' Francis answered, looking along the faces to work out who was asking. 'It's his.'

'Well, how much you asking on *yours? –*'

Another voice piped up from somewhere: 'Don't bother with him Francis, mate. He's fucking skint. Take it from me, *I* pay his wages.'

The table rocked on more laughter…

'They ain't for sale anyway,' Francis told the table before the bidding could start. 'Least not singularly, they come or go as a pair.'

'What the fuck does anyone want with *two* identical pocket watches?' Somebody put in. 'It ain't like you can wear 'em both, is it?'

Ignoring everybody, George laid a hand on Francis's shoulder. 'Where is Winston, by the way? I ain't seen him?'

'He didn't feel like celebrating,' Francis said. 'Nothing to do with all this stuff; I think he's still having a carry on with that bird he's been seeing.'

George tipped him a knowing look and then let it lie. He leaned backwards on his chair and swallowed another drink, thumping himself on the chest and coughing. Besides the talk, the pocket watch had made its way back round; George extended a hand, took it from the man next to him, and slipped it back into the front of Francis's waistcoat. 'A piece of advice: make sure you and Winston find out exactly what you've got here ... *And* exactly what they're worth. I've got a good feeling for you both. I'm proud of you.' No longer hearing anyone else, Francis nodded. 'Take your time ... always think.' George looked at him, varnished. 'You're a thinker, Francis ... And the best thing you can ever be in *this* business is a thinker.' Hand still on his shoulder, he pulled Francis towards him and kissed his forehead. '...The world will always need more thinkers.'

That night would be the final time Francis would ever see George King alive. The hard-earned, learned look in his eye would be his lasting memory – that and the glorious race day in the summer. Three days later, George was arrested at his home and charged with several frauds and laundering offences; parting gifts attributed to his accountant, Mr Ori

Pollitt. On the morning of the twenty ninth of January 1961, during the first round of cell checks at Pentonville Prison where he was awaiting trail, he was discovered dead inside the segregation unit. The only explanation for his passing came in the coroner's crude handwriting: *Natural causes*, and then in brackets *(sudden)*. He was fifty eight years old.

George Arthur King, loving husband and father, left behind a wife and three sons, a good name, and a dilapidated old whaling boat moored at Greenland Docks.

A taught man with a reclining chin, Dr Huff remained impartial; a tone of chalkboard English. 'I'm afraid that your hunch was correct, Constance,' he said, retaking his seat. 'You do *indeed*, find yourself with child.'

Unaware that they were even closed, Connie opened her eyes. She marvelled down at her belly, everything swimming in warm water and television fuzz. 'My goodness!' she said, the small hairs of her imagination receiving a broadcast; a black and white vision of a shirtless Francis leaning and gently placing their baby on her breast to feed...

'I know it's news, but I really must ask a few questions regarding the –'

'Sorry, what..?' Connie's hand had covered her mouth. 'Am I *really?*'

Making a note on his pad, the doctor nodded impatiently. 'Am I right in saying that you are currently in your twenty-third year?' He glanced up at her non-response.

'Oh!' Connie smiled away her distraction. 'Yes, yes, I'm twenty three.'

'And the father, is he –'

'Yes,' Connie answered quickly. 'He's the same age.'

'No, no, dear … I was simply endeavouring to find out whether or not he was still *around?*'

Connie looked up at him. 'Of course he is,' she said. 'He'll be over the moon.'

'I see…But I *would* be exact in thinking that the two of you are currently unmarried?' Connie had crossed her arms defensively over her stomach. 'Is it a new relationship?' Connie shook her head. Huff frowned. 'Well, do you at least have a desire – plans maybe – to make it a proper family?'

'I don't know; we haven't discussed it much.'

The doctor's pencil drew a line through something on his paper, the leaden sound working hard, scratching the polish off the moment. 'But you would describe the relationship as a loving one?' His eyes rose from the page. 'The two of you are, in *love?*'

Connie scoffed; offended by the way he'd regurgitated the word, by the summit of his unpicked nose. 'I'm sorry,' she said, 'but I find that a little intrusive?'

The pencil swirled another note. 'For that I apologise,' the doctor retorted. 'I assure you, I'm merely trying to determine and diagnose your situation.'

'My, *situation…?*'

Huff sighed. 'Surely you can grasp how this looks? You've come in today to discover whether or not you're pregnant, and you're alone and *unmarried*. As a humanist and a medical professional, it is my duty – both to you and the child – to not only confirm your condition, but also to ascertain your mental state and consider your personal circumstances.'

'I understand that,' Connie said, 'but you're making me feel as if I've done something wrong.'

The doctor extended a close-lipped grin. 'Not at all,' he said, tapping. 'But if you were to be frank with me, it would put me in a much stronger position to help you.'

Despising that it had even occurred to this man that she might be lying to him, Connie said: 'In that case, I'll make my *situation* as clear as I can so you can rest assured: my unborn child – the one you've just informed me I'm expecting – was conceived in complete, real and heart beating *love*. My partner and I live together and have done for a while. And if our marital status is of such great importance, then I should tell you, the reason we've as yet not married is because I have been told repeatedly – by *medical professionals* – that my body couldn't carry or bear children...' Her voice trembled '...And I didn't think it was fair for me to marry a man if I was unable to give him a family...' Straining against tears, she added: 'So if I came across surprised or overwhelmed when you told me, that's why; *not* because I was disappointed.'

Dr Huff waited... 'I've been around a long time,' he said, handing her a tissue, unmoved. 'And over the years I've treated and advised a great number of girls and women who may or may not have backed themselves into what you might call a corner.' He winced regrettably. 'In such cases, wherever they occur, I like my patients to be well informed –

or to put it another way: to be aware of their options.'

Connie dabbed her eyes. '*Options…?*'

The doctor gave her a collected look. 'Adoption,' he said matter-of-factly, '*Or,* if necessary, a possible termination.'

Winston wiped spittle on the back of his hand. 'What the fuck do you mean an *abortion?*'

'You know what I mean, Winston. Why do you want me to say it?' Bunny exhaled, a fall of blonde hair on the mauve sofa in front of him. 'Why make this harder than it needs to be? I've asked you – *told you* – already. I don't want to talk about it. Please. Can we not just let it be?' She reached out a hand and fell short, shaking.

Winston was standing and glaring at her, looking in loving horror, red-eyed with wet hatred. 'Let it fucking *be*…are you off your head? It's fucking sick, Beatrice. *You're* fucking sick. How the fuck could you do it?' He was speaking, screaming, in a pious rage, limbs losing themselves. The coffee table flipped over – kicked – vase and ashtray on the carpet. Bunny recoiled, the standard lamp going over the sideboard, a fist through the bell shade. Fractured china, weeping, poignant silence… 'You spiteful little cow!'

Bunny cowered and curled up against the arm of the settee, a Golden Retriever bitch in a ball. She was frightened of him; this low down he was gargantuan, unrecognisable from the lover who'd brought her flowers. Her pulse started, in surges, the fear, the turn on, the reason he and she were here in the first place. That's what it had been – what it *still* was; the taboo violence of allowing someone so rough to bunch up her skirts with his fists, of wanting him on top of her, weight bearing down, her writhing around with her legs wide and crushing her bones upwards. It was that idea of him, the animal scent and satisfaction of the forbidden fruit. Scared, her tail tucked, she could feel herself throbbing slightly, squeezing drips of memory.

Winston wobbled, staring down at her disgusted. 'What's the fucking matter with you...?' He said. 'I never thought you could be so cold hearted.'

Bunny braved a glance up at him; he looked poisoned, rabid. 'One of us had to be,' she said, flicking her hair back. 'What kind of parents would we make together?'

'Don't smile,' Winston snapped; his forehead was thick with creases. 'You need your fucking head checked; why would you rob yourself of the chance of having a family?'

'*A family...?* What sort of a family would we be, Winston, one that you go out stealing and beating people up to put food on the table for?' Bunny kept eye contact, Scandinavian blue. 'You're a criminal, and so are all of your friends. *I'm* not the devil just because I don't want the father of my children to be a –'

'Go on, say it...'

She shook her head, 'I was going to say *thief.*'

Winston's face contorted. 'Course you fucking was...' He stooped to get closer to her. 'Well maybe you should've said something. Maybe you should've told me – maybe you should've stopped and shouted out that you didn't want a brown baby instead of opening your legs and screaming about how good the colour of my cock looked going inside you.' He stepped backwards, hurting, turning and driving his foot into one of the coffee table's upturned legs: it splintered and broke off in pieces: a wooden slap. Bunny gasped, her own hand covering her mouth. 'You horrible fucking bitch,' he said, weakening. 'You might as well have just shot me in the heart.' ...And then he came back towards her, cracking and breathing hard, his useful right hand purposeful.

Bunny turned her cheek, watching him with one eye and trembling. 'Don't hit me...please...not my face!'

Winston stopped and walked towards the door, *'Hit you?'* he sobbed. 'Who the *fuck* do you think I am?'

Two pairs of black shoes climbed the frost-covered steps outside Marge Meehan's town house. He wasn't expecting visitors; not this late, not with the kids in bed and his wife Kay snuggled downstairs with the television, waiting for him to finish in the bath.

The doorbell... (Too long a ring)

The voices transmitted in submarine, bath-tones. Soaking up to his chin, the haste coming up the stairs could've been Kay on her way to see about one of the babies' bad dreams. He flinched, his toe touching the hot tap. With pruned fingers he pulled himself up, sitting and mopping the sodden hair out of his face, warm water draining from his lug-holes. *'Kay...?'*

A sarcastic, one-knuckled tap on the bathroom door...

Marge started to his feet, slipped, and then jumped up, soap suds belly flopping over the side of the tub. A moment of recognition, his brain having to catch up with what it was seeing: Bertie Crogan dressed in death robes, a felt fedora hat and an overcoat, a shadow on the wall.

'Before ye ask, Margie ... she's fine.' Bertie smiled at him through drug sized pupils. 'She's seeing tae the wee pups.'

'KAY...?' Marge shrieked, desperate for a response. Her voice came back, more inconvenienced than alarmed: *They've woken the children, Thomas. Get rid of them. What's so important that it couldn't wait?'*

Keeping one arm behind his back, Bertie quietly closed the door so they could be alone. Marge watched him, his chest heaving naked thuds. 'Calm yerself doon, Margie. Naebody will hurt her.' He paused to study Marge's flaccid, dripping penis. 'I told her that we had some urgent business tae discuss, that's all.'

Marge could feel his testicles bunching up underneath him, defensive reflex pressuring him to cover his genitals. Pride kept his hands by his sides. 'Who's downstairs?'

'Only, Roy,' Bertie said, shushing, speaking as if he were cajoling a child. His eyes didn't lift. 'I left everybody else outside; I didnae wan tae mess up yer carpets, Margie. That would be disrespectful.'

Listening with heightened hearing to the house, Marge weighed his chances; he was stuck, somewhere between fight and flight, the bathwater stilling around his ankles. Readying himself, not daring to take his eyes of Bertie's hidden hand, he said: 'What the fuck are you here for…*me?*'

'I didnae come for love, if that's what yer thinking, Margie.' Crogan tittered. 'I'm here for my inheritances.'

Marge could feel his tongue gumming on the roof of his mouth. '*What?*'

Ignoring the two folded bath towels waiting on the chair in the corner, Bertie reached over and plucked a scrunched face flannel up off of the edge of the sink. 'First cover yerself up, Margie. I nae like tae see ye embarrassed.' Marge didn't move; the flannel hit him in the stomach and slid lifelessly down into the water. Bertie tipped his hat, sharp with unshaven grey. 'I'll tell ye what I'll dae for ye, Margie: seeing as I've disturbed yer home, I'll make my point so ye can finish scrubbing behind yer ears.' Gaze slowly rising, his mouth flattened. 'George left me *everything*,' he said, stating it as fact. 'And I'm starting wi the clubs.' Marge looked at him confused. '*King's Road*, Margie; I'm having his share.'

'You must be off of your nut,' Marge said, inwardly relieved to finally have an understanding of what was happening; even in Scottish the rules of extortion were crystal.

'Mibbies,' Bertie said. 'But if you'd rather put the responsibility on yer wee wife, I'll be happy tae take it from her each week.'

Marge exploded, spitting through his teeth. 'Who the *fuck* do you think you're fucking talking to –'

Bertie whipped his hunting knife out from behind his back and stabbed the air in a mock charge, regaining control. Marge wobbled, his feet making slippery squeaks on the surface of the tub, the water sloshed, his hands spreading out to brace him against the clammy tiles. He froze; the blade poised and pointing at his cock. He could hear Kay's muttering, comforting the children down the hall.

'Whoa there horsey,' Bertie soothed, 'Remember Margie, George isnae around tae keep the wolves in the hills anymore. They're right outside on yer doorstep and they're hungry.' He barked a single syllable of laughter and lowered the knife a little. 'Ye cannae scare me off, Margie. Not now I've seen yer wee bawbag.'

The lights along the Putney side of the river sparkled, as individual as the spaced-out dreams trailing a lullaby. Connie had stopped, a lamppost for support, the rustle of chip wrappings covering her nerves before she spoke. She had told him, the river running, the winter water carrying the words away somewhere unseen. She watched as he took a long drain from the neck of the wine bottle he was holding. Catching the ruby drips on the back of his fist, Francis smiled. When he placed his palm against her stomach, Connie nourished his mouth with another kiss.

Winston lowered his head and interlocked his fingers, the way his grandmother had shown him as a boy. Wordlessly, he recited the verse she'd composed for him to copy out and learn by heart:

Barley Sugar

Almighty God, I come before you, a sinner and thief, to ask forgiveness. I pray not only for my own soul, but for the spirits of those who I've loved and have already been called. I beg we be cleaned Lord, washed by the grace of your hand, punished for that which we do knowingly and without repent. I thank you selfishly for that which I receive daily, the sustenance and shelter I ignore, the blessings I take for granted, the truth which I've been shown but will not heed. I seek only to be better Lord, and I pray that you not forsake those who have been gracious to me because of my sin. Only that you may reward them with a place in thy kingdom, protected by thy watchful gaze, their loving souls' safe beneath the wings of thy angels. Save us Lord, in this life and our next, keep the demons within us idle, and those who would mean or do us harm always a hundred steps behind us and a mile from our door. Gift us thy blessing, Lord. In thy name I pray. Amen.

It was to the point, short and sweet, one wretched soul begging *to* and *for* its betters. Not much but all he had; it was something to say, a muttering to break the silence in between waking and making the next mistake, the plea of a bitter old woman frightened of how a boy's brown shadow could reflect on her: not much but all he had.

He held on for a moment longer, clutching to the nothing until his eyes had dried. The world restored as it had been, pale grey, the afternoon crystallising the cemetery headstones whilst the gothic carvings lent their ears to frosty birdsong. He was still sat at Micky's graveside, cross-legged in his Sunday best, only now there was the respectful crunch of fallen leaves coming up behind him.

'I've been looking for you everywhere, Wince.' Francis stopped, his coat blowing open over his brogues. 'Where you been?'

'I went to church,' Winston mumbled, glancing up. 'Fuck knows why, I just felt like I should.' He shrugged. 'I ain't even fucking sure if I believe in heaven anymore, but I thought I might as well come and see what Mick reckons.'

'And what did he say?'

Winston smiled, a little boy who's just found a wobbly tooth. 'Nothing, yet...'

Francis placed a hand on the headstone, 'Well it must be good if *he's* keeping it quiet.' Winston snorted, a plume of breath covering the wreath petals he had on his lap. 'What you got with you there?'

'This...? It's just an old picture.' Winston opened his fist and showed Francis a torn photograph.

Francis studied it, 'Is that you and your mum?' he asked, surprised. 'I thought you only had the *one* picture of her, where did you dig this out from?' The grainy photograph showed a young Caribbean woman with a yellow scarf tied around her hair, the ends of it finding a breeze. Balanced naked on her hip, wide eyed with awe, was a chubby baby boy. Behind them was the bow of a ship, and the only remnants of whoever had been torn out of the picture was the pleat of a shirt sleeve and a shadow on the sand.

'It was my old man's,' Winston told him. 'My nan didn't even show *me* it until I was about twelve. My dad was in it with us, but she ripped him out before she'd let me have it.' Something small happened behind Winston's eyes. 'She said that it wouldn't do me any good to get ideas that we could've ever been a family.'

Francis ran a finger along the jagged white tear, and then handed it back. 'I can't believe you never showed me this one, it's a nice picture.'

'I was probably embarrassed,' Winston said. 'I used to keep it under my pillow.' He smiled, distracted again by the last line on Micky's epitaph. 'I showed him once,' he said. 'I had to, he knocked on my door one time right when I'd just started rummaging through my nan's stuff to try and find the missing section with my dad in it. She must've gone up the shops or something, I can't remember, but I know I was looking for it so I could stick it all back together.'

'I take it you never found it...?'

Winston dropped his head and then raised it in a full smile. 'No chance,' he laughed. 'She came back and caught Micky in the kitchen going through the tins on top of the cupboard. I heard her clip him round the ear all the way from upstairs.'

Francis laughed, Winston joining in, a buoyant noise in a dead landscape of red berries and crow caws. Ahead of them another gust of wind took a bouquet of dried flowers across the pathway. When it had quietened, Winston said:

'How comes you came looking for me, anyway?'

'No one ain't seen you in days,' Francis answered honestly. 'I called up at Bunny's to see if she knew where you was. She told me what happened. She said she thought you might be in a bad way.'

'Yeah, well, Bunny's a wrong'un,' Winston replied calmly, wishing to, but not being quite able to leave it. 'Fuck it anyway,' he added, 'there's nothing I can do about it. She made the decision. There ain't no point in me even thinking about it, is there?'

Francis stepped across the grave to touch Winston's shoulder. 'It weren't just that.' he said. 'Marge had a spot of bother over at his house last night; I wanted to check and make sure nobody ain't paid you a visit.'

Marge was holding court in his parents' living room, two of his uncles and his father watching from the arms of the armchairs. Winston and Francis arrived halfway through; Micky's mum kissing their cheeks and Kay waving to them from the staircase, midway to investigating the child-sized footfalls on the landing.

'Did he tell you what happened?' Marge asked, directing the question at Winston as soon as he saw him – he looked at Francis to make sure that he had. Nippy, who was moving between rooms, pilfering what he could from the kitchen, bumped into Winston's back. '...The lairy cunt had that fucking knife of his right underneath my bollocks,' Marge echoed animated. 'I'm standing there, sopping wet, trying to make up my mind if I should just scrap it out with him. The only fucking reason I never, was because I kept thinking about Kay and the kids down the hall. I told him – I looked straight at him and said: coming here, doing this what he's doing, it's going to get us both fucking killed. Stupid bastard...' He clapped his hands in a manic gesture, remembering something else. 'Do you know what else he fucking did, Wince? Before he fucked off singing that fucking song he sings, he turned around at the door and offered his fucking condolences for Mick –'

Micky's father raised his cane, the ivory eagle head pointed at his eldest son. 'That's enough of all that,' he barked. 'It's no bleedin' good keep going over and over what was said, is it? The short of it is that Crogan's leaning on you.' He glanced at Winston and Francis, a father from their own, a stout London Irishman who'd grown the wilted look of a man who'd aged greatly over a short time. 'What have I always taught you boys? What's important ain't what was done; it's what you lot are willing to do about it.' He whacked his cane against the ground, going around the room, face to face. 'From where I am, there's two ways you can go if he's squeezing you,' he said. 'Do something to warn him off; and when that don't work, drown him in a puddle and fling him in the fucking Thames.'

Francis eyed Winston, then Marge.

One of the uncles got up from his armchair. 'Bertie won't piss in his pants, Thomas. You might have to –'

'Maybe not...?' The second uncle interjected. 'What's Crogan got in the way of businesses and such?'

Marge folded his lip, vaguely thinking. 'From what I know of him, I think he moves a fair few pills about. He's got a couple of betting shops; and I think he owns a car service in west London somewhere.'

'That's it then! Knock over the betting shops and have a few quid off of *him*. That way, next time he comes calling you can pay him with his *own* money.'

'...Hold up,' Marge said, snubbing out his chuckling uncle. 'I remember George saying once that Bertie's big thing was breeding horses. He fucking loves them. He's got his own stable somewhere up country.'

'It's no good if you don't know *where* though, is it?'

'*I* can *find* that out,' Mr Meehan said, poking his brother with his cane. 'We'll go and ask old Freddie Sellers. He'll know; he's spent a life at the bloody races.'

Winston stepped in and volunteered: 'If you give me an address, I'll drive there tonight and burn the whole fucking place to the ground.' He looked at Francis and Marge, 'And before any of you say anything about coming along, you both need to be at home in case he decides to start knocking on any more doors.'

Mr Meehan smiled and nodded in agreement. 'Well, there you go then,' he said. 'You can't say any fairer than that.'

Silhouetted and muddied up to their calves, Winston and Nippy watched from a field as the high flames they'd created strained upward like long golden fingers feeling for the stars. The neighing, desperate and pleading, cried out beneath the crackle of the blazing stable wood. To God in Heaven it would've looked as if Hell had opened one eye, the imperial blackness set alight with the stench of burning horse hair and brutal bucking death.

Barley Sugar

BERTIE CROGAN

2004

Still talking about the house, Connie said: 'I didn't even see *this* place until after Francis had already bought it. He just picked me up and drove me over here one day to surprise me; I didn't know what to say, it wasn't but a matter of weeks since I'd found out I was expecting.' She waved a hand at the idea. 'The explanation was, *that it came up and he couldn't resist.*' She smiled thinly. 'Sometimes it's just easier to let them get on with it. Not that I'm complaining; I just wasn't over the moon about him doing the sort of things that he was doing at the time, especially not for some bricks and mortar. I would've been quite happy in the flat we were renting if it meant he couldn't have got into trouble. There was no telling him though; his response was that if we were going to be a family then we needed a home of our own, somewhere that he knew me and the baby would be safe...' With that she peered downward, picking at her slice of cake for solace, her lips becoming an apprehensive line.

On the kitchen floor Tudor wet his chops, sighed, and then went on dreaming beneath the table. Wriggling, Deborah slipped off one of her heels and rubbed a bare foot along the dog's fur. Sipping her tea, lost in concentration, she gazed past Connie at the artwork displayed on the refrigerator door: it was a child's painting showing a father and son standing side by side at a football match. In the bottom corner, half obscured by one of the magnets holding it in place, was a rectangle of white card which accredited the artist: Lewis Coles. Absorbed, Deborah admired it with a mother's attention; the brightly coloured, clumsy little finger splodges moving her far beyond anything she'd ever seen hung on a gallery wall.

'Lewis did that right after Charlie died,' Connie told her, grateful for a point of interest. 'He gave it to me because I promised I'd hang it forever. Do you remember?'

'Shame on me,' Deborah said, meditating on it, her face showing the drain of keeping from weeping. 'I've never really properly looked at it before. It's beautiful.'

Connie turned back and observed her. 'Deborah, love, you'll drive yourself crazy. You mustn't worry about him too much; all this business with the school is just one of those phases they go through. Charlie was the same; God knows he gave me enough sleepless nights.'

Underneath the table Tudor rolled over onto his back. Deborah excused her eyes and glanced at him. 'It's not Lewis...' she said, only watching the dog. Her heart building it up, her great truth rushed out as an admission. 'I've started seeing someone,' she revealed. 'I was with him today. Just now, before I came here. He took me to meet his family. I haven't told Lewis anything; he has no idea.' She allowed herself a breath and shook her head. 'Neither do I, I don't think. I thought I was okay about it. Ready. Now I'm not so sure.' Finding the courage to bring her eyes up, she added: 'I think that's why I'm here. I needed to see how it would feel – what *you* would say...?'

Connie reached a comforting touch across the table and covered Deborah's hand. 'Well,' she said softly. 'Is he a nice man?'

'I don't know – I mean, I *do*, he is, but it's just not as simple as that, is it?'

'Nothing's ever *simple*,' Connie said. 'Especially deciding to take off your wedding ring –' As if she'd been bitten, Deborah pulled back her hand and covered her ring finger. 'That's not an accusation, love. That can't have been easy for you.'

Defensive, Deborah pushed her chair out and hobbled over to the sideboard on one heel. She tore off a sheet of kitchen towel and blotted her mascara. 'I feel like a *shitty* wife and a *bad* mother. It's bloody embarrassing.'

'Well that's daft for starters,' Connie said. 'If that were true, you wouldn't be here telling *me* about it, would you?'

'I feel like I've *betrayed* everyone,' Deborah went on, cursing herself. 'Especially Lewis; he'd absolutely *hate* me if he knew.'

Wondering how much strength she had left, Connie stood up and made the trip over to her daughter in law. 'Listen to me,' she said positively. 'It's not your fault Charlie died, sweetheart. Now I'm not saying that you have to share a pillow with the very next man who happens along, but you're still young love, nobody expects you to live out your days all by yourself – not if you *don't* want to. You mustn't worry about us; we love you; we *want* to see you happy. And that goes for Charlie as well – you take it from *me*, I'm his *mother* – he wouldn't begrudge you a life, love.' Connie brushed a tear from Deborah's cheek. 'Trust me on this,' she insisted. 'Lewis is still a boy; you only need tell him what you're sure of yourself. He'll understand eventually, and even if he doesn't know it yet, he'll always only want the best for you. Whether that be with *this* man or somebody else.'

Sensing something lifting, Deborah squeezed Connie's palm and exhaled a timid smile. Having watched and waited for them to finish, behind them, the dog laboured himself up to a courteous sitting position and began sniffing at the cake crumbs on the table.

The tartan chairs and stools inside The Schoolboy's Bell were none the busier. Lewis hadn't noticed; finding the late drama of the watch swap at the airport more satisfying than his dinner. He'd listened privately, between forkfuls, a rapt smile becoming a mashed potato leer upon hearing that *his* side had won. When the waitress returned, the story ceased – dying horses burning in the stable.

'Have you finished with these?' The girl asked, taking their plates. 'And would you like me to bring you your dessert?'

'I wouldn't say no.'

Lewis mirrored his grandfather's sentiments, waiting for the girl to turn and leave before speaking: 'So the pocket watch that *we're* carrying is definitely the real thing? And who's got the other one then, Winston?'

'Insha'Allah,' Francis answered under his breath.

'What? What does *that* mean?' Lewis asked baffled by his

grandfather's change of tongue.

'If God wills it,' Francis said. 'It's what Winston would say.' Francis chuckled, one eye on the direction their pudding was coming from. 'But we won't know until we get there.'

'Is that what we're doing, going to meet *Winston?*' Lewis looked at him confused. 'I didn't think he would still be alive.'

Francis smiled.

'And what, he lives all the way *up here?*'

'I suppose you could say that, yeah...' the waitress sat two crusts of crumble and a warm jug of yellow custard on the table, '...at least, for the last few years he's been up here anyway.'

Tudor drooled unapologetically.

'The dog's just polished off what was left of your cake, love.'

Deborah shrugged her shoulders, aches and pains across her lips. 'He's welcome to it,' she said. 'I feel sick...' She extended the tissue in her hand to show Connie how much she was shaking.

Connie covered her with another warm look. 'Let me tell you what Francis's grandmother told me on the morning of our wedding. She took me over to one side and said: husbands are really no different to sweeties; if you pick carefully from the bag, one at a time, you'll be fine. It's only when you rush in and start grabbing by the handful that they make you *sick*.' Deborah blew her nose in understanding. 'And *then* she said...' Connie smiled, '...That if I was to find out over time that I had a particularly sweet tooth and I couldn't help myself, that

I should always remember to make sure nobody could see the sugar on my lips.'

Deborah tittered, 'My *God!*'

'I *know,*' Connie agreed. 'And that was supposedly coming from *'a woman of the world'*. So there's no need for *you* to feel sick. Not when a lot of women don't wait to be widowed.'

Blotting her eyes, Deborah puffed out her cheeks and tried to accept herself: a disorganised mess inside a finger painting. She hiccuped into a teary laugh, 'I don't know what I was thinking bringing cake; I should have brought a *bottle.*'

Moving slowly back over towards the table, Connie gave her a telling little nod and then sat down. 'Before you turned up and rescued me, I was sat in the other room undressing some of Francis's whisky with my eyes.' She said regrettably. 'I'm sometimes visited by a few ghosts when he isn't here. Mind you, knowing where he's going is probably making it worse.'

'Aren't we the pair...?' Deborah said dryly. 'I did think you looked a bit pale when I arrived.' She sat down, concerned. 'Is everything okay, Connie? That's the second time I've heard you mention ghosts since I've been here. What did you mean, about where Francis is going...?'

Connie considered the cold cup of tea on the table in front of her. For what felt a long time she didn't speak, seemingly making up her mind about something. 'Wait here,' she said eventually, pushing back her chair and starting to stand. 'I think, maybe, there's something I should show you first.'

Francis gave a subtle shake of his head in return to Lewis's question: no, setting fire to the stable didn't do any good. 'In hindsight,' he said, 'I'm not even sure we expected it to. It was more about us seeing how far we were willing to go to stand up for ourselves.'

Lewis moved his spoon around his dessert bowl, doodling in the custard. He glanced over at the fireplace, at the spittle and hiss of the dead horses leaping through the flames. His grandfather's face had deepened, firelight – *the orange moon* – scuffing over the leather and lengthening the lines.

'What it did do though,' Francis said, 'was spark the events which would determine pretty much all of our lives. Right up until now: me sitting *here* with *you*. Whether or not it would've always gone the way it did, who knows? But once we sent those stables up, those flames engulfed every single one of us.'

'Did he know it was you lot straight away?'

'No. By then, he was fighting on so many fronts it could've been anybody. I reckon with it being horses he assumed it was something to do with a few of the racing people he had debts with. It wasn't until Marge's dad's pal, Freddie Sellers, told him that it was us that he found out.'

'He grassed…?'

Francis shook his head. 'Not *really*; the whole point was that he knew it was us, weren't it? We knew he'd tell him. As soon as Freddie found out we'd slaughtered a stall full of thoroughbreds, he was straight over at Marge's wanting to set up a meet, to save things from getting further out of hand.'

'What did Marge say?'

'He told him to go back and tell Bertie, that trying to get money out of us or our club was like *flogging a dead horse*.'

Lewis grinned. 'Then what...?'

'Two nights later, the club on the King's Road was torched,' Francis said gravely. 'We *weren't* open or nothing; the place was all but destroyed before the fire brigade even got there.' Lewis opened his mouth – but before he could say what he was about to, his grandfather went on: 'And as if that wasn't enough of a message, Crogan then went back and broke into Marge's house. It was empty, Marge had Kay and the kids at his mum's with him; the bastard went from bedroom to bedroom and fired a shotgun shell into each and every mattress.'

...Seeing the scraps of fabric and feathers flying up from the children's bedding, Lewis widened his eyes.

'They must have been out of their bloody boxes on some sort of drugs,' Francis said, 'because the next day the Old Bill arrested Roy Easter in Battersea Park. They found him comatose and soaking wet on the back seat of a car.' He arched his back, tired, a complement to a good meal...then exhaled. 'What had happened was, after the two of them had run through Marge's, they must've shot over to Earls Court to pick themselves up a rent-boy and then taken him over to the park with them.' Francis didn't explain ... Lewis was already curling his lip. 'Once they'd *finished* with the poor sod, they turned him over and tried to drown him in the boating lake. Whether or not they thought they'd killed him, I don't know, but they hadn't. Someone found the kid amongst the reeds in the morning; and when the police turned up, Easter was still asleep in his motor. He got remanded on an attempted murder.'

Lewis stared back at him unbelievingly.

'Not until the story made the paper, did we find any of this out,' Francis said. He shrugged heavily. 'I'll never fucking forget it: I remember, being over at the club assessing the fire damage and Nippy running in and handing me the paper. The telephone was ringing – God knows how it was working, but it was – and just as I turned to answer it, Nip goes: 'It's *good news*, France. That means Bertie boy's out there somewhere on his lonesome…'

Deborah peeled back the brown parcel-paper Connie had just given her, not entirely certain of what she was seeing: beneath the second layer, were four folds of thick fabric, light blue, printed with what were unmistakably fluffy, white playschool clouds.

'I don't know if you know …whether Charlie ever told you about what happened to me…?' Connie had returned to the table, not only with the paper package, but also the old shoebox she'd been rummaging through on the coffee table.

The package crumpled quietly. Looking vague, Deborah smoothed out a corner of cloth.

Connie watched her, rigid, her shoebox squirreled away on her lap. She was different, resolute, as if, during her little trip outside the room, she'd tried to thicken her skin. 'Just after Francis and I moved in here, I lost our first child,' she said. 'I miscarried…' Her eyes closed briefly and then reopened. 'The nursery was the first room that we decorated; *those* curtains were supposed to be the final touch. You might think it's a little morbid, but I could never bring myself to chuck them away.' She glanced around the space they were sitting in. 'It's exactly the same way I feel about this house; even after everything that happened I couldn't abandon it. I felt like I *shouldn't*. Francis bought it so it could be our family home, if I were to let go of that then...' She didn't allow herself to go any further, as if she wanted to keep a distance from her words. Her eyes were now standing with tears. Deborah watched her, slightly bemused, not sure when she should speak. 'It was pouring with rain,' Connie recalled, hurrying, telling it now like it was something she *needed* to tell. 'I don't remember anything of the morning. It's just disappeared. I know where I was: North End Road. My friend Marcia had stood me up so I was going around the shop windows by myself, picking out bits and pieces we needed for the house. I went into the curtain makers, and when I came out it had started pouring. I've got a vivid memory of me running up the street and knocking on the glass of a phone-box, trying to get two little lads to come on out so I could use it to call Francis and get him to pick me up.' Connie paused, reliving it, the back of her hand touching her cheek as though to feel if there was any colour left. 'He wasn't himself when he answered, he was distracted. It's funny; I remember being surprised that the phone-line was even in operation because a night or so beforehand there'd been a big fire at their club. Francis had gone to see the amount of damage. He told me I would be better off jumping in a taxi and letting him meet me at home. He said that he wasn't going to be finished there for a good while – those were the exact words he used. He said, '*a good while*'.'

There was now an echo to her. Unconsciously Connie's hand came away from her face … It drifted downwards, tapping apprehensively on the lid of the shoebox in her lap…

'It was *such* a long time ago,' she continued, vacant, completely unaware of what her fingers were playing, 'it's like seeing myself as somebody else. Someone that I know was me, but at the same time *isn't*. Does that make sense?'

'Perfect sense,' Deborah said, not knowing that she meant it. She had to clear her throat, her own emotions still bobbing for air. Tap…tap…tap…Connie's nervous fingers kept going, counting down…

Connie said: 'I have this image – one I'm convinced is *real*. I'm hurrying along and trying to stop my brolly from blowing behind me. It was my favourite one; pink and blue Japanese blossoms across the top and a bamboo handle.' (Tap…tap…tap…) 'There was a taxi with his light on but he didn't stop when I flagged. Just to get out of the rain I ducked into a shop doorway – I don't know why because I was already drenched. Across the road, directly ahead of me was a betting shop. Next to it, on a kind of side door, hardly even noticeable, there was a sign saying: Car Service.' (Tap… tap…tap…) Tudor fidgeted restlessly. He paced in a circle then came back to Connie's side, pawing at her leg. 'I've been over it so many times,' she said. 'And each time I've searched for a way out of it for myself, for an alternative route that might keep it from happening to me.' She grimaced down at the dog pitifully. 'At the time it seemed like a Godsend. I didn't think twice; I just dragged my bag and brolly across the road and went in.' (The tapping quickened...) 'I shouldn't have. I could already hear his voice from outside; it was *so* loud, *so* coarse. I shouldn't have gone in – maybe if the weather wasn't so bad, I don't know, maybe I wouldn't have, maybe I could've saved it from happening I don't know...' Connie broke off, choking. 'His *voice*,' she slurred, sickened. 'I've been hearing it ever since. It's been *forty* odd years and it's never left me. Any time I turn on the television or overhear a man talking with a Scottish accent somewhere, it gets me – it *scares* me...'

Connie shook a desperate, please-let-me-finish gesture at Deborah across the table, the anguish sagging from her pallet, half mooning her mouth.

'The only thing I noticed about him was his hat; he tipped it at me when I walked in. He was getting ready to leave, putting on his coat. If I'd known who he was I *never* would've accepted the offer. I didn't know, he introduced himself as the owner of a car firm. He said, rather than me wait around in wet clothes for another driver, that he didn't mind doing the fare himself. He said he was heading on to Surrey and that Putney wasn't out of his way. I had no reason to be afraid of him; I didn't know who he was. I didn't recognise him. I just wanted to get home. I was thinking about hanging the curtains in the nursery.'

Tudor nudged the shoebox on Connie's lap. *He knows*, Deborah thought, watching his tongue curl out and try to comfort her tapping fingers, *he knows that something's coming.* Even with the uplighters along the underside of the kitchen cupboards throwing a rich glow over their faces, Connie's complexion had all but washed off.

'He didn't say or do anything untoward, not at first, not even once we were alone in the car.' The tapping had now become an incessant drumming. 'I can remember exactly where we were when I saw something change in him. We were coming over Hammersmith Bridge onto the Barnes side and he asked me if I ever liked to go out dancing. Me and Francis weren't married then but I thought it would put him off, so I told him that I did but only at my husband's club. But as soon as the words came out of my mouth, he changed; I was sitting in the back and I could feel him looking at me in the mirror, sharp, staring at me as if he could tell everything about me all at once. His eyes were completely black. I don't know why but I hadn't seen them until then; I couldn't, not until I was scared. All of a sudden he was wild; as soon as I gave him the name of the club and told him I was with Francis, he made this sound. It was horrible, like an animal call, and then he just burst out laughing.' Tiny, frightened breaths had created an undertone to Connie's speech. She hitched, gazing at her fingers, for the first time aware of their constant drumming on the cardboard. 'His voice was *so* overbearing,' she said, unable to control her hand. 'It smothered me – *trapped* me. I did try and speak up; I asked him why he was laughing because I couldn't understand it. I'll never forget what he did: he showed me his teeth in the mirror and told me that he'd always believed it to be true but now he was certain that God was a Scotsman.'

The talking fractured. Deborah suddenly realised that her heart was pattering, that it was matching Connie's tapping for pace. The atmosphere tightened; as if their tea for two had shrunk to a dolls house scene, everything plastic, everything on edge and waiting to break. Connie and Deborah lingered there together, like two girls about to share a terrible secret and dreading it. On his haunches beside them, Tudor kept his vigil.

'That's when I panicked. He started driving faster, jolting the wheel so I was tossed about in the back. He was questioning me, over and over, repeating things and shouting over himself. His voice was *so* violent. He was speaking through his teeth, all at once, cursing about Francis and his friends. I couldn't hear half of what he was saying, I kept on trying to focus on what was outside of the window because everything was getting away from me. I could see it all leaving me behind. And then he came out and started *singing*.'

Tudor dropped his chin onto her knee. Connie tried to catch her breath, still talking, the two things becoming unrelated, the story picking up a downhill roll of its own.

'It just went on and on,' she said. 'I got desperate. I dug everything out of my purse and took off my necklace so I would have something to offer him to let me out.' She closed her eyes on her tears, banishing pictures. 'That's when I think I knew what he wanted. He laughed at me. He said that jewellery wasn't precious enough a thing to pay what Francis owed. He said what Francis had done would cost him everything.'

Hearing it in horror now, Deborah tried to remember the

daytime: the daytime, when the world was a finger painting in primary colours and the bad men from the bad dreams came in crayon. *My God, he tried to rape her*, Deborah thought obscenely, clinging to the word *'tried'*, recalling the daytime memory of the first time Charlie had led her by the hand into this very kitchen and introduced her to his mother. *It can only be tried; please God, let it only have been tried.* The idea that the beautiful lady Deborah had met that day, the woman who'd not only welcomed her into her home but into her heart and family, the idea that she could have been dealing and living with a thing like this was unbearable. The thought that Charlie's mother could have been suffering the continuous, reoccurring pain of a scar, of a lifelong tattoo, which had been bleeding beneath the skin since before he or she had even been born, was just too cruel. *Please God, it has to be tried…*

'We always pretend we know what we'd do, how we'd react in a situation,' Connie said. She shuddered, wiping her eyes. 'The truth is, I froze. I did almost nothing. I don't think I even tried the handle on the door. I just sat there, rocking about and thinking about my mother. I kept imagining how heartbroken she'd be, that how on the day she'd given birth to me and held me in my shawl, she never could have fathomed that somebody would one day want to hurt me. That someone could just decide to invade my body, something *she'd* made; just for the sake of spoiling it. That somebody would choose to steal some of my soul from me. I kept thinking how the thought of that happening to her little girl would have been unfathomable.' Her small muscles ached. Dry tears, like empty spirits, trickled over the bulbs of her cheeks and bleached the low shadow of her former self. (Tap...tap...tap...) 'I just did *nothing*,' she said again softly. 'I knew what he was going to do but I did nothing. I had already succumbed. I couldn't fight. I didn't want to. I didn't dare because of the baby I had inside me. I was willing to sacrifice my body if it meant that our baby could live. That was all that was important.' She stared at the thought from far away. 'Waiting for that car to stop were the longest, most *vicious* minutes of my life. I knew where I was – I'm not sure if that made it worse. I was within reach of home; he'd pulled over on Putney Common, on one of those bushy little through lanes. The rain stopped, the trees were shutting out the sky. I remember watching the water beads on the windows, wishing I could run that fast. When he turned the engine off, he just turned around in his seat and looked at me; it felt like a long time, like he wanted to defeat me with his eyes first. I couldn't talk, my mouth was stuck, I was just trying to breathe for the baby. He tossed his hat at me. I didn't even move. I just let it hit me. And when he started talking I couldn't hear him anymore.'

Tudor set off on another lap around the table, the relentless tapping driving him to fidget.

'I don't know if I was unconscious but once he leaned over and hit me I couldn't see him. Not until he was on top of me. I stayed still. I could feel him dragging at me under my skirt. And he kept talking, the whole time he never stopped talking. The spit from his mouth was hitting me in the face. Everything was ringing and his fingers were so painful. I wasn't listening to him. He had a hold of my hair – *down there* – and he was shaking it and shaking it, he wouldn't let go until I would open my eyes and look at him. He was gripping me by the throat and saying something about Francis. His trousers were already undone; his filthy parts were pushing against me. He was forcing it with one hand and choking me with the other. I had no strength. I couldn't keep my legs closed. When I finally managed to open my mouth I was already shouting. I was pleading with him, screaming over and over that I was pregnant. I could already feel myself bleeding … I was *sure* I was bleeding. I *begged* him not to anymore. I cried at him to stop but it made him angrier. He bit me; I could feel his teeth going through the skin on my shoulder. He was crushing my neck, pressing down and taking the life out of me. There was just no air. No smell. There was nothing but a washy picture of him over me, like I was looking at him through cling film.' Connie was wheezing, taking beating breaths, the words jamming her throat. She shuddered and tried to shake the vision away. 'I thought he was going to kill me,' she sobbed. 'And then, when everything stopped and weight lifted, I could see the raindrops running on the windows again. He was just staring at me, not moving. He was humming that song through his teeth. Then he put his hand over my eyes; in the blackness I felt him lose grip and fall out of me. When he took his hand away he was fixing up his trousers. The only thing I did was try to check how much I was bleeding. But when I looked at my hand there was no blood. It was just him I could feel, dripping out of me.'

Although she knew Connie's fingers were still moving, Deborah could no longer register the Morse code they were tapping. There was cold blowing in her ears and making her numb, like evil frost on raw bones, hurting her from the inside out.

'He was watching me and waiting,' Connie said. 'When I looked at my fingers, he grabbed my wrist and made me taste him. I didn't care or know; I was just praying that now he had it out of him he would leave me alone. He was still raving about Francis as he shoved my fingers into my mouth. He forced them down my throat until I retched and then opened the car door and hung me out by my hair. He must have chucked me out because I fell into the mud on the side of the road.' (Tap...tap...tap...) Whining, Tudor impatiently circled. 'I crawled over to the bushes being sick, trying to get away. I heard the car door slam. I can remember squeezing my eyes shut, waiting for the engine to start, hoping he'd go. It did but the car didn't pull away. It stayed there, growling, making a sound like an animal, as if there was a predator behind me. And then he was howling again, singing that song. I had no clue he was standing right beside me. It was so loud; the rain was coming down again as well as the bushes – the bushes were blowing and scratching me as I crawled in the mud. He must have got back out of the car because his voice shouted in my ear, close, and then he knocked me senseless again. He was kicking me,' Connie said, stifled. 'He was kicking me in the *stomach*.'

Tudor barked, the tension snapping in a lonely echo. Connie's chest was heaving; she held a hand out to Deborah, dreamlike and afraid.

'The next thing I remember was coughing up muddy puddle water. The car was gone. I don't know how long I laid there but I had black spots in my eyes. I kept on telling myself to breathe but I couldn't get any air in. I tried but it was too thin. Nobody knew I was there, and nobody came. He'd thrown all my bags out further up the road. When I finally managed to stand, those curtains were the only thing I picked up. To passers-by it must have looked as if I'd just fallen over because nobody pulled over to help me. I was petrified for the baby; I was too frightened to check if I was bleeding so I just pulled my skirt down and started stumbling towards the house. I knew Francis wouldn't be home but I just wanted to get there and turn a light on, everything was so dark. Even with my coat over my head I could still hear him, his voice, singing and shouting inside my ears. He was telling me that he'd killed my baby; he was telling me that it was because of what Francis had done. I *knew* he was right, I could feel the dead weight I was carrying home with me. By the time I got here my will was already gone. I collapsed in the hall. My body had given up. I've been telling myself for years that it was my fault for not fighting more, for not *breathing* more, but in the end all I could do was lay there on the floor and let my baby bleed out of me.'

The drumming stopped, suddenly, the final heartbeat nothing more than a lifeless tap on a cardboard box-top.

Again Tudor barked, this time rearing, his paws landing on Connie's lap. The shoebox toppled, lidless, the old letters inside fluttering down and double coating the floor. For a long time Connie clung to him, arms around his collar, her sadness wetting his fur.

Lewis was sitting uncomfortably, not wanting to move. Fifteen years of wisdom was more than enough to tell him when to keep quiet…

Francis cleared his throat and stood up. He made his way towards the gents in silence, supposing that the boy would find it easier to look at the space he'd left behind for a while. He'd told him the truth, save the detail, because however hard it had been to say, wrapping the boy in cotton wool would only serve to make him a fluffy man. The cubicle door closed behind him, the skin on his face stretched. He would take as much time as he needed … longer. And then, when he eventually returned to his grandson, he would be ready to tell him the rest.

GERALD BEST

1961

Gerald Best was awake to witness the dawn crack. He cut a large, harmless figure in his vest and pants; his well-slept, pink face at home in the pastel window. As always, his mother was already up and dressed and praising the day from downstairs. He barely made a creak getting to the bathroom; a big man, he had one of those lofty, toe-ended strides which tilted him onto the balls of his feet. *Dopey,* is what they called it down at the station; they said it was all the sawdust he had between his ears tipping him over. Not that his mother minded them joking, as long as it wasn't mean-spirited. Besides, *she* happened to be very fond of the way he walked because it reminded her of his father. He had stood at six feet six inches tall on the day they'd measured him for his coffin. Gerald was just short of that, but according to Mrs Best, what with him only being twenty seven years old, he may yet still have some growing to do.

Gerald washed his face with soap, scrubbed his teeth with toothpaste, and then tidied his hair. When he walked back into his room freshly pressed, he found his uniform waiting for him on the end of his single bed, steam still rising from the cuffs. He dressed, concentrating, careful not to miss a single button. He was beaming, his mind going slowly over the things which had occurred yesterday evening. And he had every reason to be pleased: his mother and some of the other ladies in their church group had finally convinced Sallyanne Elmer that it would be perfectly fine for her to accompany him to the picture show. Gerald had heeded their advice and behaved like a gentleman, taking her to see a long and windy romance film, full of lots of music. He'd enjoyed it; and he'd remembered all the things his mother had told him about girls. So, he'd led the conversation, told a few jokes, and then walked her home afterwards. He'd been patient, the way he'd been told to, and sure enough by the time the stroll was at an end, Sallyanne had kissed him on the lips and agreed to go out again the following weekend. Now, sitting down on the edge of his bed and pulling on his socks, he wondered if she too had still been able to feel their kiss this morning…

Drying her hands on her apron, his mother was waiting for him at the foot of the stairs. Gerald ate his breakfast with her watching him: two poached eggs, a slice of bread with raspberry jam, and a mug of tea. He answered her questions shyly, making her smile, allowing her to dust the crumbs off his chest and double check his uniform before she handed him his sandwiches. He kissed her cheek and waved goodbye on his way to work, his toes clipping the pavement with his daily purpose. She watched him from the doorstep, proud, hoping that her neighbours might peek out and see how grand her boy was. She couldn't have known then, there would only ever be two more mornings like that one. In seventy two short hours, the spare pair of shoes she kept polished for Gerald at the foot of her stairs would stay empty until the day the Good Lord called for her to bring them to him.

Walking to work, Gerald had no idea about what had happened to Connie Whitaker on the day before that one, and nor would he ever. Still, the repercussions from it would ultimately, somehow, cost him his life. And he would never kiss Sallyanne Elmer again.

The house – Francis and Connie's new home – stood momentarily still and molested. Nothing was where it should be; the furniture, still disjointed and half moved in, was squashed between totems of unpacked boxes. The sour smell of washing up liquid and lineage had since soaked into the skirtings. Only two nights ago, Francis and Connie had made love beneath the bay of the living room window, their naked bodies drawing calligraphy in the moon dust on the floor. But already that was a memory; an apparition of her as she was, as she had been before yesterday, before Francis had walked in and found her collapsed in the hallway, shaking, cupping handfuls of her own blood up from between her legs. Before Francis's shoes had pressed prints in the crimson and she'd flinched from him. Before he'd lifted the veil of her hair and seen the bruises beneath her skin. Before she'd screamed and before he'd asked. Before all the vague words and hysteria and her begging him to make her a promise: *'Please don't take me to the hospital, Francis. I don't want anybody to know, please don't take me there.'*

It had taken less than a minute for him to go back on

his word. *'I'm taking you to your Mum and Dad's and getting you a doctor,'* he'd whispered, scooping her up in his arms and carrying her out to the car, *'I have to, there's too much blood.'*

After what seemed like hours of rancid, whirling explanation, the doctor's pills finally helped her sleep. Francis had lay there beside her teenage bed, in a state of vicious consciousness, listening to her painful breathing. He'd prayed that they were good dreams, numb and forgetting, not like the ghastly visions of reliving. He'd heard Mrs Whitaker weeping for her baby, muffled sobs leaking through the walls from next door. Alert in his drowsiness, Francis had felt the animal inside him twisting in its pit. The beast was of the same species as the monster who'd hurt her, a primate with a murderous voice. Beyond the net was blackness; no moon, just stars. They winked down at him arrogantly, like avid gamblers who'd placed bets on each and every one of the tiny little cock fights going on in the world of men that night. They were mocking him; not just because they could, but because up where they were, everything made beautiful stayed that way forever.

The morning had come along with the same achy screams and breathlessness of birth. Connie had awoken, calling for her mother. Mrs Whitaker, dressing gown flailing, had propped her daughter up on the toilet and pressed a cold flannel to her forehead. Worthlessly, Francis had listened to the jagged daggers of urine, stop-starting, trickling out of Connie's body and into the bowl. Bloodshot and pale, his stomach had punched each time he held out a hand to her and she'd cowered away from him. '*I think it's best if you leave for a while,*' Mrs Whitaker had said. '*Take yourself home and sort yourself out. You can come back tomorrow. For now, at least, she needs her mother.*'

So, reluctantly, Francis had gone home – to their new home, blotted and unlived in. On the way he'd stopped at a payphone, the tremors in his voice summoning his friend. Winston had been waiting for him when he got there.

Now, in the late afternoon, the only real light either of them could recognise was coming from a lamp Winston had stood on a dining chair next to the far wall. The two men were sat at either end of a sideboard unit which was askew across the middle of the living room, wallpaper rolls and paint cans between them. Barefoot, his dishevelled shirt hanging open, Francis ran a dirty hand through his hair. He'd taken off his shoes and socks after cleaning up the hallway. The bucket and sponge, yellow of all the colours in the rainbow, stood soiled and reeking in the corner of their broken dream.

'I have to kill him,' Francis said. The words were spoken without upheaval, just the simple recognition of the inevitable. 'Whatever happens, I *have* to. I won't be able to live with myself if I don't...*or* with Connie.'

His own problems seeming dwarfed in comparison, Winston waited until there was almost silence again, and then said: 'You need to wait, France. If only for Connie's sake, you need to wait. Do it properly.'

'I can't just sit here and do fuck all. This happened to her because of *me*. I was the one who fucking told her to get a taxi; it's *my* fault.' His voice broke into bits and he stifled himself angrily. 'I couldn't protect her. That *cunt* had hold of her and I couldn't protect her from him. *He* told her that, he laughed at her, he said he was only doing it because –'

'He did it because he's a fucking sex case, Francis. It weren't for no murdered horses, I'll tell you that.' Winston looked at him.

Francis shook his head helplessly. 'She won't let me touch her,' he said, his face red calm. 'She pulls away like she don't know me, like she don't trust that I won't hurt her. She blames me, I know she does. And so do her parents; that's why her mother sent me away. They think I can't protect her.'

'This is what I'm on about,' Winston said. 'You need to help her get better before you go chasing him. What happens if you get nicked…? She's scared as it is; imagine how she'll be if you go and leave her on her own.'

Francis tried to hold his head on straight. 'But what else can I do?'

'Stay put,' Winston answered earnestly. 'Sit on your hands for a few days – for as long as it takes. You need to be where she can see you; where you can soak up some of the hurt for her. *I* can start looking for him; let me chase him.' Francis was crying. 'Connie knows you love her … God knows, we all do. And she knows that you'd give your life to look after hers. But right now, after all what's happened, you have to show your strength by staying still.'

Francis's head was still in his hands, his fingers caging his face. Winston looked around at the festering sadness, at the shadows stalking the walls.

'I'm staying here with you.' Winton told him quietly.

'We'll go over and check on Connie again tomorrow, no matter what her mother says. We can find out properly what the doctor's said and see if there's anything she needs. Then we'll come back here and sit tight ... start patching the place up a bit. It'll give us something to do.' He exhaled. 'Then, like I said, I'll start hunting for him.'

Pressed and sweaty, Francis slowly took his hands away from his face. 'She was pregnant, Wince,' he confessed, eyes fixed in apology. 'I didn't tell you because of what just happened with, Bunny. Connie said it wouldn't be fair so soon after; she knew how much it meant to you...' He was wiping furiously at his tears. '*That's* what's in that fucking bucket,' he wept. '*That's* what that cunt done; he made her lose our baby. He killed my fucking family, Winston. What's in that bucket is all that's left of it...'

Disbelieving and discoloured, Winston's face pulled. He stood up and went to where his friend was sitting, an angel on his shoulder. Francis leant on him and let go...

There were no more words.

Two and a half days later, Carrie Meehan didn't know she was looking at the man who'd killed her husband in the mirror. He ghosted across the width of the glass, the brim of his black hat jutting sideways. A vague recollection tapped her on the back as he passed, her eyes following him. He was stepping lightly, a loud mouth talking its way across a room. Carrie watched, the radio playing and the show going on, the bright, pop-art shade of the salon wall lending a peculiar backdrop. The ladies gossiped on around her, snipped hair falling in all colours, the high street throwing and fetching cars on the other side of the shop-front window.

Unobstructed, the man strutted towards the service counter, his long coat tail swishing behind his knees. Immediately, scissors in hand, Carrie's hairdresser, Poppy, turned and started towards the till. She looked uncomfortable; the man playing with his cigarette, two thick curtains of smoke rising from his nostrils while he waited for her to open the cash drawer. Poppy handed him some notes and bumped the till closed with her hip. Crooning, the man shoved the money into his trouser pocket, his coat opening and flashing the buckles on his braces. He revolved in a slow circle, wired eyes scavenging from the women around him. When he reached Carrie, his cigarette levitated on his lips. She cut away, hunkering in the chair and turned back to the mirror. He drifted past, this time going the other way, a sleepless face crazily brazen. It was hard to tell with the hat on ... *The races,* she thought suddenly, *he's the Scottish bloke from the races...the one Marge was fighting with that night at the club.*

Carrie craned to get a better glimpse, but the bell above the door tolled and he was gone.

Poppy came back, mouth in a straight line; a twiggy woman, her heavily made up eyelids. 'Fucking arsehole,' she said, snapping her scissors against her comb.

'What did he do?'

Poppy blinked at her in the mirror. 'Oh, not *him*,' she

said, stabbing her nose towards the door. '*He's* an arsehole, but my stupid brother is a bigger one. It's Stuart who owes him money, not me. He reckons he paid him ages ago, but because that bloke knows Stuart is scared of him, he just keeps coming in and helping himself whenever he feels like it.' She scowled. 'Stuart is petrified of him; he's even let the lairy sod bully him out of his own house. He won't do nothing about it. '

Carrie frowned. 'How do you mean?'

'He just turned up on Stuart's doorstep about a week ago and told him he needed somewhere to stay. He said he was wanted by the police for something.' Poppy relaxed her shoulders, beginning to open up about her problems. 'Stuart won't tell me how he knows him, but you can bet it's something to do with that stuff he pushes…' She waited for Carrie to catch up, and then mouthed the word '*pills*' into the mirror. 'I'm guessing that's why Stu owed him money in the first place. Serves him right,' she nagged. 'Stu's scared to set foot in his own house; the silly sod's spent the last couple of evenings on my couch upstairs.' She blinked, her eyes vanishing behind bold colours. 'Stuart reckons he's had a prostitute staying over there with him; the night before last, he phoned my flat at two o'clock in the morning and made Stuart drive over there to deliver him another bag of pills.'

Carrie's soft, buttercream cheeks rounded. 'If it's the same bloke, then I think Marge's wife, Kay, was talking to me about him the other day.'

Poppy puckered. 'Who's Marge?'

'Mick's older brother,' Carrie answered, as if Poppy should

already know. 'If that bloke is who I think he is, then, apparently, he set a fire at Marge's club and almost burned the place to the ground. They're all looking for him.' Taken aback, Poppy's eyebrows peeked. 'Do you know his name?' Carrie inquired.

'Bertie,' Poppy said immediately. 'His name's Berties something or other...'

'I bloody knew I recognised his face,' Carrie said, uncertain why she was smiling. 'That's him! Micky couldn't fucking stand him.'

Davey Thompson's hand was steady. He pressed the sharp tongue of his straight-razor flat against the tired, puffy bag just below the man's left eye. 'Listen to me, you tubby bastard,' he said, hissing in his ear. 'If I find out you've been talking bollocks to us, I'll come straight back here, cut your fat fucking face open, and then ask you again while your eyeball is rolling about between your shoes. Do you hear me?'

The man groaned to indicate he'd understood. 'I swear I am,' he said, peering up with bulbous eyes, frightened to jog the razor. He carefully placed a hand over his heart, 'Honestly, I'm telling you gospels.'

Amused by the turn of phrase, Davey's scarred skin tore into a grin as he looked up at Marge and Winton. Marge nodded, convinced, and Davey withdrew the blade. The man – a simple cab controller – spluttered something agreeable, sucking in his relief and shifting on his stool. Marge scrutinised him.

'So what are you telling us, that Crogan only ever comes in here to collect money?' There had been no mention of Connie or of what had happened to her; that was none of the controller's concern. Although, he supposed, red-faced and hapless on his little stool, that whatever these three gentleman where chasing Bertie for, it was probably worth it.

'Honest to God, I ain't lying,' the controller repeated. 'I don't know where he lives or anything. He's only a silent partner; I run this place on my own.' He clasped his palms together in appeal. 'If you'll let me look, I can probably find you a telephone number for him.'

'We ain't interested in fucking *speaking* to him,' Davey sneered.

'How often does he come in?' Marge said.

'Not often, it's only a small business. I wouldn't expect to see him now for a while; he came in a few days back and cleaned out the safe. There's sod all in there. I can open it up and prove it if you like.'

Marge swatted the offer away, looking at Winston who'd heard enough and was heading towards the door.

'What about next door?' Davey probed, not giving up. 'How long have they been shut?'

'Most of the week,' the controller answered. 'Bertie shows his face in there a lot more than here. The betting takes much more money than the cars, you see. I go as far as to say, the staff in there would likely be more use to you, they're more familiar with him than I am.'

Davey glared at him, disgusted. 'I'll tell them that you said that when we find them,' he warned, slipping his razor back into his pocket, having just noticed that the others were leaving. 'You mind how you go now, won't you. And remember what I've said.'

'What now?'

'I'd say our best bet is talking to some of George's people,' Marge said. He sauntered over to where his car was parked and stood by the open door. 'Thing is, off the top of my head, I can only think of one or two who might know anything.'

Winston stooped to squeeze into the backseat. 'Drop me off back at *my* motor then,' he said. 'I'll meet you back at your mum's after.'

Marge looked at him surprised. 'Ain't you coming?'

'You two go,' Winston replied. 'I'm going over to see your dad's pal, Freddie Sellers.' Marge bent down and made a face at him over the seat. 'It's worth a try,' Winston said. 'The old git seemed to know enough about the cunt last time, didn't he?'

'If you say so,' Marge said, trying to see the sense in it. He slid in behind the wheel and waited for Davey to walk around to the passenger side. Both doors slammed, and then the engine smothered the conversation.

Francis found himself alone in their new home, daylight capturing the dust motes floating over the hall. Balancing the small pile of fresh shirts on one arm, he kicked the front door closed with his heel and let the dust vanish back into the dim loneliness. The house was holding its breath.

He trod into what was supposed to be their new living room and dumped the shirts on top of a step-ladder. *'These should see you through…'* Mrs Whitaker's words when she'd given him first the shirts and then some advice. *'Francis, I want you to listen to me.'* She'd hesitated, reaching out and touching his sleeve before he could leave. *'I want you to try and remember that this awful thing was done to Constance, not to you.'* She'd taken a quick glance over her shoulder to check Connie wasn't up and out of bed, standing at the top of the stairs. *'There's no sense in asking her what she's not willing to tell. I'd like you to try and keep that in mind when you two are talking.'* Her voice had become a laboured whisper. *'Also, I don't want you going cavaliering after the man who did this. Lord knows I'd like to see him strung up as much as you for this, but it isn't for you to solve. Getting yourself into more trouble won't do anybody any good. When she's ready, Connie can decide whether or not to talk to the police; if so, then we'll let the law handle it. And if not, well, we'll cross that bridge when we…'* But then the look had come from behind her back, untraceable, Connie's father avid and burning. Francis had seen it before; Mr Whitaker in his garden, the same earnest demands on his face. On his eyes, Francis had promised to protect his daughter and he'd flaked on his word. The Lugar meant nothing – the Lugar was gone. He'd let him down; and it was his fault. The man's little girl was upstairs right now, folded in half, lying under her bedding like a broken string, surviving on single mouthfuls of canned soup. And it was killing him, the same way it was killing her, that her womb had been looted. That she wouldn't talk. That the one time she'd allowed him to touch her, her hand had felt cold and dead and not hers at all. Francis couldn't shake it, that fiery image of the man's face: Mr Whitaker asking him if he was ever going to keep his promise.

For an unknown time, gaping at the gormless room around him, Francis unpacked boxes. He was placing things, then changing his mind and replacing them with other things. He was moving in pointless circles. Despite the effort – or perhaps in spite of it – his mind wouldn't rest. It was gnashing at him, rendering the walls with the obscene images of Connie's torture. He could see it all, a mural of suffering scribed in oils, her frightened body being choked and fucked and ruined until there was no life in her left and she was barren in the bushes. The angels were hiding behind their harps, behind sponged clouds high above a dungeon floor covered in blooded swaddling. And there was no saviour coming, only Crogan cackling with his dick out. He was kilted, spitting and warring. He was something sculpted, something grown out of stone and thunder, something which was bladed to wage scorn on the daughters of Eve and to eat their infants up from inside their bellies.

A cupboard opened, its heavy, ornate door releasing the fresh coffin smell of carpentry into the room. Francis stared at the pieces of broken china inside, wondering about the unborn baby, about whether it's tiny, underwater ears would have been aware of the stranger's voice who was suffocating its mother...

The doorbell was ringing, shrill and unabashed, the sound of a fire bell startling him out of his numbness. Francis cowered a little; as if he'd been caught somewhere he shouldn't have been, thinking that if he stayed completely still the intruder might disappear. The bell warbled again, this time dragging an involuntary walk out of him. Drunk and sober, he swooned into the hall, the half-moon glass in the front door giving him no clues.

A loud voice chirped: 'Surprise...' Before the daylight had even finished making its mathematical shape on the hallway floor, Carrie Meehan had clicked her bon-bon coloured heels together on the doorstep and come forward to kiss his cheek.

Francis stiffened, holding his ground so she couldn't pass, looking better than he had yesterday but still nowhere near well.

Carrie took a step back and surveyed him strangely. 'You left the keys in the lock! I would've let myself in, but I thought I might catch you two at it; you should never wait too long to christen a new place.' She pouted suggestively ... and then when Francis didn't cotton on, she pointed at the bunch of door keys hanging from the lock behind him, the estate agent's cardboard address tag still tied to the ring. 'You'd better take that tag off for a start,' she said, 'otherwise, if you lose them, whoever picks them up will know exactly where you live.' She beamed at him, joking. 'You'll have to watch out for burglars now that you've got a posh post code, Francis.'

Ashen-faced, Francis tried to smile.

Carrie persevered: 'I knew this was the right one,' she said, marvelling at the façade of the house. 'Even so, I had to walk up and down the street *three* times before I spotted your car.' She took another step backwards, eyes exploring. 'Big, ain't it...?'

Furrowed, and not meaning to sound as rude as he did, Francis asked: 'How comes you're here, Car?'

Carrie examined the peculiar look on his face; there was something missing, something which normally shone there. 'I did tell Connie I would try and pop by today,' she said, slightly defensive. 'She's been dying to show me the new place, so I said I would drop in on my way back from the hairdressers.' Francis squinted over the top of her head. 'Thanks for fucking noticing,' she giggled, slapping him on the arm playfully, and then modelling her new hair do anyway.

...Francis, who would have been happy for the conversation to die on the doorstep, gazed away down the street, drawing cold air in through his nostrils, no longer alive...

'Well,' Carrie said awkwardly, snapping him out of his sleep. 'Is Connie home?'

Francis flickered, wanting to sound casual: 'Nah, she must've forgotten you were coming. She's gone over to her mum's to collect some more bits.'

Carrie rolled her eyes – and then, pondering it, she poked an accusing finger at him. 'Some bloody *Mr* you are,' she said humorously, 'why didn't you drive her?'

'Because I can't bear it over there at the moment,' Francis

said, making the truth sound harmless.

Carrie concentrated on him, on the unnatural smile he was performing. 'Are you okay, Francis? I mean, is everything alright in there? You look a bit peaky.'

Francis nodded. 'I'm just tired, Car. And I've still got so much to do. Sorry, I would invite you in, but she'll kill me if I show you around before she's had a chance to properly put her touch on things.'

'Save the apologies,' Carrie said, smiling, 'I know where I'm not wanted.' Her tone a posh mockery. 'Besides,' she pretended, 'I've been turned away from far grander front doors than this in my time.' She gave him a royal wave. 'By all means, I shall leave you to your toil on one condition, sir...' Francis was already waiting to close the door. '...when her ladyship returns, will you be sure to inform her that I called?' Carrie was now half way towards the end of the drive. 'Oh, before I bid you farewell,' she said, suddenly reverting back to her usual self. 'I saw that Scottish bloke that Marge was looking for today. The one he thinks set the fire at the club.'

The reaction was not instantaneous; it took time for Francis's mind to slice the sentence into small, manageable mouthfuls and chew it over. His whole body tensed, nerves boiling, his chest cavity frothing over with adrenaline and smut. His ears filled with blood, heartbeats drowning the sound of his own voice: 'Where?' He heard himself speak, felt it, the word spiked on his tongue.

Caught off guard by the sudden passion in his voice, Carrie wheeled around. 'At the hair salon,' she said. 'I couldn't believe it; he just walked in while I was sitting there.'

'Are you sure it was him?'

'One hundred percent; my hairdresser, Poppy, she said that he's been staying in her brother's house.'

'Where does her brother live?'

'I don't know, I didn't ask,' Carrie admitted. 'But Poppy's salon is on Surbiton high street.'

'What's the place called?' Francis demanded, yanking his keys out of the front door behind him. By the time Carrie could answer, he was already on his way towards his car, his dirty white shirt billowing out behind him.

The only thing Arthur Cox wouldn't sell is his fucking moustache... Something Micky had said once, moons ago.

Francis bumped two wheels up on the pavement, got out of his car, and then walked around to the back of the pub as arranged. Lost in anger, head marching ahead of him, he forced open the wooden gate with his shoulder; stubborn, the splintered timber scraped over the cobbles and gave onto a stack of beer barrels in the rear courtyard. It was late afternoon, everything already one colour. The cellar doors, set into the ground at the back of the building, were still closed; Arthur wasn't there yet.

Francis waited, pacing impatiently, tucking his shirt into his trousers until he heard the clunk of a padlock. A wheezy cough echoed underground. The cellar doors struggled, groaning on rusty hinges and then falling flat. Francis grabbed hold of both handles and heaved; the doors rose, spread open, and then flapped down hard on either side like a pair of dead wings.

The top of Arthur's head, aged and terminal, came slowly up the metal steps. He stopped, half in and half out of the hole, sniffing the air above ground like a wary animal. He coughed again, spitting, the collection of phlegm plopping between his feet and landing on the cellar floor.

'Like I told you on the phone,' Arthur spluttered, reaching up to hand Francis a pistol swathed in an oily cloth, 'I don't want it back once you've dirtied it. If that's the case, you'll have to give me its worth.'

Francis snatched it and stuffed a fistful of notes into his hand. 'You might as well take this now then.'

Arthur counted, busy fingers smoothing the money out on his palm. 'You know the apple,' he said, looking up. 'If anyone should enquire...'

The old man, Freddy Sellers, proved to be as unenlightened as the controller at the car service. Turning his car around on a leafy lane and muddying the bumpers, Winston wondered if Marge might be having more joy.

He spent the drive home thinking about Francis. He imagined him, helpless at Connie's bedside, every impulse inside him being quietened by her breathing. He thought about the non-choice he'd be given, about the differences between Man's law and God's. He theologised over the rules, over the dogmata drawn by nature, bestowing each and every living thing with the inclination to mark a patch of earth and defend it, with the will to fight and to protect its own. Surely, only in a handwritten, man-made rulebook could any honourable creature be expected to turn the other cheek and allow another beast to bear its teeth at his family. After all, it was Man who made cages; and it was only him, rather than God, who would see fit to punish an animal for its given disposition. It was only in a man's world where natural instincts should cost, where the price of retribution was set as high as a noose or as low as a lifetime's freedom.

Thou shall not kill... the commandment, bleating in his grandmother's drone, floated somewhere in the back of Winston's mind as he drove.

Winston lifted the door knocker outside the Meehan house, the brass sound familiar, All Farthing Lane laid out behind him like a lifelong memory.

'I would've thought you'd be with Francis,' Carrie said, opening the door. Winston wasn't surprised to see her, or the blonde toddler who was riding her hip. He regarded them, dozens of thoughts running concurrently.

'What you on about?' he asked, realising immediately that she couldn't have yet heard about Connie, if she had she wouldn't have been smiling.

'He drove off so fast, I assumed he was going to pick you up or something,' Carrie said. And then, seeing that she wasn't making any sense: 'I stopped by their new house on my way home from the hairdressers earlier on. I was hoping for a tour of the new place, but as soon as I mentioned that I'd seen that Scottish bloke who Marge has been wanting words with, Francis just rushed off and left me standing there. I *assumed* that he'd gone to get you. Did he not then?'

Winston was already racing back towards his car. 'Where was he heading?'

'I'm guessing, Surbiton,' Carrie said, suddenly aware that something was happening. 'That's where I saw that bloke... In *Poppy's* hair salon. It's on the high street.'

Poppy was busy sweeping up the last ringlets of hair from the salon floor, when the copper bell above the door chimed. The man who appeared behind her was tall and straight-faced; a lucid pair of eyes which were both black and blue. The instructions were patient. She did as he asked, under only a little duress, carefully printing her brother's address in clear capitals and then handing it to him on a scrap of paper.

And then, after she'd watched him leave, the telephone on the service counter started to ring.

Now that he knew where he was going, Francis was no longer moving at pace. Mechanically, he touched the brake and slowed the car for a red light. He waited, the contents of an empty stomach pushing down on his bowels and making it uncomfortable to sit. His wits were almost painful, half blind after sucking in every road sign and lamppost that he'd passed. Perspiring, he tried to get hold of his mind and master it, to tend the noxious hate inside him into something with a more methodical function. Slowing the blood, he rechecked the address and then placed his hand back on the pistol in his lap, as if he could somehow feel his way there.

It was dark outside, the purple before the black.

Twenty minutes after Francis had come and gone, Winston's knuckles rapped on the same salon window. Inside, still on the telephone to Carrie, Poppy dropped the receiver and came forward to open the door; both of her hands were shaking.

TANSY

1961

Wearing only an unbuttoned shirt and his underpants, Bertie Crogan was celebrating his birthday, he was making no effort to hide his erection. The volume on the television set was turned all the way down so he could concentrate better on the pictures. *Fifty six*, he thought distantly, his mouth twisting under a wooden-horse memory from boyhood. He glanced at the ashtray which was teetering on the arm of his chair, then sucked the last life out of another cigarette, pinched it between his fingernails, and finally snuffed it out. In the blue haze of the TV, the smoke easily resembled a soul rising towards the afterlife.

Treading egg shells into the carpet, his company came in from the kitchen. She was balancing a cake, a lot of what hadn't been baked smeared down the front of her dress. Probably not yet twenty one, she and *he* had both been calling her Tansy. It sounded nice and she liked it, far better than the name her mother gave her. She was walking forcibly slow, a narrow, ordinarily faced girl with hay bale hair, and breasts that should've belonged on another. Only Bertie's pupils stirred; his only concerns braless beneath her dress. He watched her clearing a space to set her creation down, too conscious. The coffee table looked prepped for suicide: a double-barrelled shotgun, surrounded by torn out pages of *The Racing Post* and forty something violet pills, all lined up along one side, close to the edge, like contemplative jumpers.

'Use this tae cut it,' Bertie grumbled. He slipped his trusted hunting knife out from underneath the armchair's cushion and pointed it at her.

Tansy took it from him, coiling, plunging it into the sponge and then delicately handing him a chunk. White, melted sugar dripped through her fingers, the cake never cooling before she'd iced it. She stood with her knees together, zigzagging, performing a clumsy ritual with the blade: licking it clean before dropping it onto the table to pluck up another pill to swallow.

'It's nae bad,' Bertie told her, his gaze below her armpits. 'Now, then,' he said. 'I want tae watch ye. Take off yer dress an' dance for me while I eat.'

Her face brightened over his comment about the cake. 'But there isn't any music,' she said, unzipping.

'I'll sing tae ye,' Bertie replied, wiping sweetness from his lips and beginning to hum. Covered in cake crumbs, the song rolled out like a long dream, all the way from the top of some hillside in his mind.

Tansy's breasts toppled out, unsupported, her hips wiggling her out of her dress. She swayed, using old tricks, things she'd developed way before she could ever shoulder the responsibility. Her arms folded across her middle, squeezing her cleavage together to hold his attention while she stepped nimbly away from the ring of cloth around her feet. She let go, each bosom separating from its twin and drooping, a crease smile grinning underneath. Writhing, her hands covered in jam and cream filling, she brushed the spread off her nipples and began cutting jerky, uncouth shapes into the blue with her waist. She leaned forwards, flesh knocking together, and then slowly peeled off her knickers.

Bertie drew in a thick breath, wanting to pick up the scent she was secreting. Ferociously, his eyes crawled in and out of the spaces on her body, the sharp bones of her hips standing out like speech marks on either side of the bushy triangle between her legs. He observed – cock twitching – penned in by the running track seam on his Y fronts.

'That's loaded,' he said, seeing her reaching for the shotgun on the table.

As if she were a novice actress remembering her prop training, she lifted it gracefully, smiling, kissing the tips of both barrels. 'I'm not frightened of it,' she whispered suggestively, flashing wonder at the sawn-off length.

Bertie had stopped humming. He stiffened, studying her pale fingers handling the dangerous weight. 'Touch yerself wi it…' She heeded his instruction, laying the cold metal, rigid and oily, first against her chest, and then guiding it gradually downwards until it was flattening the tight curls of her pubic patch like an iron tongue. For her, holding the exaggerated rapture on her face and pressing it between her lips, it felt like a powerful thing. Bertie prodded her, hissing: 'See how much o' it ye can fit in tae yer wee quimmie…'

Mouth slightly agape, Tansy obliged him, opening herself up and feeling the rough, sawn-off metal scratching hideously at her. She winced, desperately disguising a brief moan as pleasurable. Performing, she pulled it away, spitting a luscious mouthful of saliva into her palm and rubbing it over the business end of the gun. She tried again, pouting, painfully cocking a leg and coaxing it inside her...

Bertie gritted his teeth and gripped himself.

The house was detached; a thin, fenced slither of alleyway divorcing it from its neighbour. The road was golden; most, if not all, of the other homes on the row still with their lights on. This one was dead, curtains drawn; the kitchen window having just snapped back to blackness as Francis watched.

On foot now, he crept onto the adjacent property, thoughtless, his head drifting past the ongoing lives and amber lamps around him: dozens of strangers loving and arguing as they sat down to their evening meals or waited for their baths to run. Hunched, he moved across the neighbouring drive and slipped down the side of the building. He sidestepped, feeling his way, the damp odour of weathered wood sweating out of the partition fence behind him. The pistol in his hand had taken on the weight of David's first stone. He tripped; a stack of bicycles toppling over unseen in the murk. He froze, ducking, letting the rattles shake away, straddling the handlebars and shuffling on. Out of sight, he could hear a door slamming and the jabber of excited voices. Without looking over his shoulder, he squatted once he'd reached the rear gardens. More lights baffled him, further away, beyond the washing lines and the hedges. With a knee in the dirt, everything looked the same. He steadied himself; his ears full of distrusted whispers, his swallow the texture of rusted nails. He tilted his head back to breathe and saw four, flour-white paws stepping across his periphery. The tomcat slinked along the top of the fence, his glowing, murderous, hunter's stare fixed on the man-shape crouching below his walkway. Francis watched him, taking him on board; thinking that to think now would be to act less. The cat disappeared into the dark, stalking away to find fresh food and new enemies. Soon the cat-fighting would start; that awful, wild, howling which plagues the suburban dreamers.

Purposefully mindless, keeping the pistol loose in his palm, Francis scaled the six foot fence. Up and over, momentarily on high, dropping onto the other side and into the consequence of an entire life. The remnants of a berry bush nicked at the skin beneath his trousers as he landed. From behind, the house appeared as opaque as it had from the front; only in the margin around the French doors was there any life: the soft hue of a flickering television set.

Francis cut through the overgrown grass, flying and seeing almost solely in black and white. His mind was made up for him. Each moment, too quick, occurring whether he lived it or not. It was bigger than him, travelling forward of its own accord, tightening his fingers around the gun and swinging it against his thigh after every step. Ears pricked, he approached noiselessly and peeped through a break in the drapes. Without his notice, his heartbeat like his breathing, had all but evaporated. From then on, he was surviving purely on instinct and red rage.

Barley Sugar

The French doors caved inwards, a single kick splintering the lock. They separated and flapped amongst the floor length drapes. Two shots banged out ... the bullets ghosting, hitting nothing but fresh air and fabric.

Tansy fell and flipped the coffee table over, scrambling to avoid the noise, covered in pills and cake cream. She crawled towards the kitchen screaming, tail between her legs, the barrel of the shotgun hanging half out of her and dragging along the carpet. It detached before she got there, when her knees touched the lino, pulling out like a big bee sting and falling a foot from the doorway. Without looking back, she crabbed through the kitchen and into the hall panicking. She wasn't upright until she was free of the front door and running, her bare, pale body, a streak of white to the naked eye.

Acting on reflex, Bertie's hand clutched for an old friend that wasn't there; thanks to the girl, his knife was now lost amid cake slop and papers. A cornered animal, he bared his teeth, ears flat, greasy hair ploughed straight back from his forehead in ragged paths. Automatically, he sprang at what was coming towards him, eyes shining, his socks snatching for grab on the carpet. He looked almost pleased, fearless, a vague recognition hitting him within the mayhem; as if, for it to have been anybody other than Francis, would've made it a disappointment.

Francis didn't fire again. He was on him in a stride, swinging the pistol and smashing it into the side of Bertie's head. The blow sent the gun flying into the rubble, a discarded toy in a boy's playroom. Crogan kept coming, scalped, a whole cliff of his face opened and flowing with black blood. Losing his balance, he lashed out; pounding and pulling, gouging at whatever was in front of him. There was no timing in the attack, just frenzy. Untethered, twisting in their skins for better angles, the two men came together in perfect violence. They were now two wolves warring over a dead deer, thrashing at one another without etiquette. There was no speech, no vowels. They were using only honest language, the panting groans of labour; strained, human growls which escape through bitten teeth. It was the sound of fighting which has no end. It was two men covered in one another, beasts breathing in, sharing the same final moments. It was the noise of not dying, of a mortal's primal impulse to defy nature's thunder. It was the music of living, of striving and hunting, of killing and surviving, even, if for just one more day.

Francis hit him again, his knuckles shattering against sharp enamel, Crogan's teeth bedding in and shredding the nerves in his fist. He felt Bertie's legs buckle. The two of them tumbled once more, screwed together, landing hard somewhere at the edge of the room. Neither could feel the damage, the spiked chemicals inside their bodies still challenging them to endure. Muscles heaving, Francis pulled himself up and pinned Bertie under his weight. He was squashing his throat, driving his tattered fist down over and over, striking him anywhere he could. Bertie writhed, his hands clawing and scratching at Francis's hair and face. His grimace was a tired, beaten mark; a stubborn pair of warrior eyes refusing to look at the dark spots which were blotting them. He pawed desperately, tugging at Francis's clothes. He was frisking everything, almost unconscious, his fingers somehow picking Francis's trouser pocket and closing around a bunch of keys. He raked them out, his only weapon, their steely texture good enough. Frantic, he swung his arm and began digging them into Francis's ribs.

Francis's left arm – which had been stretching for the discarded knife he'd spotted beside the overturned coffee table – recoiled back to his side. He tried again, reaching and fingering the cold handle, the pain in his side stabbing in and starting him over. Bertie had almost bucked him off, his arm jousting, the jagged metal puncturing Francis's skin and taking toothy bites at his lung. They were rapid wounds, frantic, sawing at the soft flesh and fabric. Francis let out a brutal bawl and pummelled harder at Crogan's skull, hearing nothing of his noise, only the ragged slaps of his fists and forearms as they cracked the bone beneath him. Black blood sprayed out the nose and eye sockets, spattering into Francis's open and roaring mouth. He swallowed, the hot coppery taste of rape and murder boiling down within his chest. Red and blurry, he made another snatch at the knife. This time the carpet handed it to him. He held on to it, unbalanced, the wooden handle slippery in his grip as he speared it into Bertie's cheek. The hole let the air out with a high pitched note. Savagely, Francis started to carve; butchering the neck, shoulder and stomach of the half dead thing underneath him.

Bertie gurgled; his ravaged body not letting go. He seized Francis's face with one of his hands, a bloodied thumb smearing death across his eyelids. Francis pulled back and slipped lower on the carcass, needing to feed undisturbed. This was the man who'd hurt Connie – who, in a single moment, had taken hold of her and destroyed her heart and child. Speaking now, hissing in unrecognisable phrases composed of hatred, Francis plunged the knife into Bertie's underwear. He watched as the white cotton ran wild, the colour spreading and filling up the baggy pouch. The hunting blade twisted, readily licking and eager, going in again, faster and faster, raping Crogan's soul, mutilating the part of him that Francis loathed most.

Suffering in purgatory, the only distinguishable light left splashed over Bertie's head and flooded his nose. He stared at Francis, slicked with blood, his vision now coming in the watery smudges of a drowning boy. He tried to speak, saying something, most of the words bubbling beneath his liquid. He spluttered … and then forced a dying smile.

Exhausted, Francis had already stopped – *God give me strength* – his face now anaemic. *'Micky…I ate his heart…'* were the only words Francis had been able to make out.

Francis gazed down in disbelief; as Bertie Crogan went under with his mouth open. He was still singing.

DETECTIVE HARVEY WELSH

Had he have known what would happen, Gerald still would've professed it as God's will.

He was already within a mile of the address when the call came in, the Police Operator's instructions fuzzing down the line. He listened obediently, responded, and then returned the radio to its mount beneath the dash. Out of sight, the wires constricted and shrank silently back into their coils.

Without hesitation, prompt and correct, Gerald Best turned his panda car around and put his foot down.

A man, a neighbour, who'd identified himself only as Mr Shepard, had a stark naked girl hiding in his hedgerow. He telephoned the police station after peering out of his window and discovering her there; judging by the state she was in, one could reasonably deduce that she was bound to be either the victim of a domestic assault, or some sort of strange sex game. But whichever way round it was, he'd also stated, quite clearly, that it wasn't *his* job to go out there and find out; reporting it was as much as he was willing to do.

Gerald went about his work decidedly, his starched uniform stiff across the small of his back. His countenance was sour, the mere comprehension of any man laying an aggressive hand on a lady was too much for him to bear. He thought about Sallyanne, and how he would never even –

His brow softened at the thought of her. It had been that way all day; whatever nastiness he'd encountered, the slightest mental note of her smile and smell had seemed to somehow lessen it. It was spiritual, he was certain of that. How else could he explain it? And he understood that it was probably inappropriate to be spending his time daydreaming about a woman whilst he was working – especially now, whilst attending a disturbance where one may indeed need his assistance – but he just couldn't help it. The celestial vision of Sallyanne Elmer wouldn't leave … and he supposed that he didn't want it to. The hint of a doting grin began to fathom over the breadth of his jaw. Privately, just one more time, he decided to remember their kiss.

Then, double checking the street sign, Gerald realised that he'd arrived.

All was well and quiet; there was no Mr Shepard and no naked girl. Gerald drove slowly along the row of houses, the odd bedroom lights, above and beyond, smouldering delicately and reminding him of church candles.

He stopped the car and got out.

The house was almost completely black, as if it were under a cloak, only a faint hum-blue glowing from somewhere inside. The front door had been left ajar. From the doorstep he announced himself, walking watchfully, his shiny shoes making up careful ground. There was no reply ... only a blank, eulogy silence. Gently, Gerald pushed the door back with his fingertips and stepped inside.

If he'd hesitated for thirty more seconds, he might have seen Winston's headlights pulling up outside the same address.

Despite keeping an eye out for it, Winston didn't notice Francis's car parked at the top of the road. He passed it by, solely focused on the police panda car halfway down the street in front of him. Instinctively, he dipped his lights, slowing and craning his neck to see. The house was giving nothing away; it looked forsaken, as if nobody had ever been home. He drove a little further down before pulling over, stepping out of his car, and then noiselessly creeping back along the opposite pavement. He stopped, heart changing gear, trepidation knocking at the open front door. This was the place; and he knew it before he took another step – the address Poppy had given him was now irrelevant. Francis had found him – whether he was in there dead or alive, it was already too late.

Francis had tried to stand, staggered, and then collapsed a few feet from Bertie's body. The wounds in his side were streaming, bubbling up through the jagged little holes in his crust like underground red-river springs. He'd fallen where he lay now, close to the kitchen, halfway between passed out and dreaming.

There was a heavy voice, inaudible, calling through the blue. And then footsteps; cautious, one at a time footsteps, bringing with them the pungent scent of shoe polish. Francis roused slightly, delirious, still belonging to the indigo dream: he could see himself as a little boy climbing the allotment fence, his eyes the colour of raddled denim and his young head filled with dizzy red spots. Fast, without warning, he was mind backwards, falling through the bright summer and into a blackout, all the way, until Winston's arms had stopped him hitting the soiled ground. Micky was laughing, teasing him for fainting...

And that was all, the scene ceased, those heavy footfalls overlapping the childish clamour.

Francis opened his eyes, feeling another presence in the foggy pallor but not seeing one. The voice called out again. Impulsively, without having even acknowledged that the shotgun was there before he felt for it, Francis reached out a hand, as if some part of his subconscious had seen and remembered where the thing had fallen. He dragged it over the carpet towards him, gathering it in and wedging it beneath his chest. The footfalls were louder, coming closer. Out of one warbled eye, in double vision, he could see a huge figure in the dim. It was moving through the kitchen, two legs looking like six, long soles sticking and then slowly peeling up off the lino. Inside an age of time which acted as a second, the name *Roy Easter* pronounced itself illogically from within the lifeless blue shade of his psyche. He was repeating it ludicrously, over and over until his mind was convinced: Roy Easter had been there all along. There had been no arrest, no remand in prison, and no newspaper article; Easter had just been here forever, waiting alongside Crogan for him to come.

Each step now trembled like a shocking truth, the drowsy shouting falling on deaf ears. The figure, vast in its threat, was almost on top of him, and time was too close to gone. Without conscious thought, Francis shifted a little, wriggling on his stomach, lifting the shotgun barrel and pulling both of its triggers at the same time...

The shot burst the blue, every single thing being corrupted. The kick from the weapon sent all senses out of range. Francis's body moved, more of his blood being shaken out of him. Behind his eyes, he dreamed that the figure was falling, hit in the thighs, taken off its polished feet and thrown backwards into the trap of the kitchen.

The blast banged off the ear drums.

Winston went towards it, the open front door sucking away the twinkling street behind him. The hallway burned with the fired stink of gunpowder. His eyes adjusted quickly, and through the gap by the hinges he could see a shadow low down in the television-lit kitchen, silver uniform buttons blinking at an angle. The copper was making a wet noise, his slippery limbs searching for lost purchase. He was propped up, his back against the kitchen cupboards, the tops of his legs splattered in his lap. He was choking on death rattle breaths, his head large and lolling.

Winston watched for a second, the smooth, timid blue light appearing to part along the floor to let the blood run into a lake. He stepped back and squinted down the length of the hall at a second door; the one which he reasoned must lead to the living room. He crept to it, hearing nothing, cracking it open just an inch with the toe of his shoe.

The Technicolor flicker was brighter. Francis was sprawled out on his side, the dark length of a shotgun barrel poking out from underneath him like a lance. Winston widened the door, keeping as much of himself out of shot as he could, calling to him in a hoarse whisper. Prudently, he leaned around the frame and eventually went in, forgetting about where Crogan might be; it wasn't until he was crouched down, desperately trying to revive Francis, that his eyes finally found Bertie's corpse: he was prostrate, face up and a rugs length away, a thick wooden knife-handle standing out of his underwear.

One of Francis's bloodied hands twitched, and then it sprang up and took hold of Winston, as if wanting to cling on to a dream. He could hear his name echoing, it was breaking into his consciousness and beckoning him round. He forced open a frightened eye and saw Winston, the brown boy underneath the allotment fence.

Francis tried to mumble, wheezed … and then: 'I can stand.'

'Where are you hurt?'

Groggily, Francis examined his stained palms. 'I can

stand,' he repeated. 'It's not all my blood.'

From inside the kitchen a groan murmured. Gerald whimpered, his legs making what sounded like mushy sweeps across the floor.

'Let me see,' Winston urged, casing Francis's ribs for wounds. 'We need to move, France.'

'Get me up. I can walk.' Francis's voice was disabled but convinced. 'They're just scratches.' He pulled against Winston's clothes and hoisted himself up. Winston took his weight, exhaling, his whole body working on preserving his friend and his freedom. He stood, racing in panicked calm, hooking Francis's arm over his shoulder and dragging him towards the door.

Behind them, a spluttered moan came from the kitchen.

Francis took his first steps in the hallway, his feet touching down in uncoordinated, brief meetings with the floor. Winston kept hold of him and kept them moving, one foot in front of the other, until they stumbled, bandy-legged over the front doorstep.

Francis tipped his head back, the wallpaper walls suddenly being replaced by a starred sky and a line of lit windows around the edge of the world. 'Take me to Connie,' he rasped, finding a single thought. 'If they nick me at the hospital, I won't get to see her. *Please*, Wince. Take me to her.'

'You need a doctor.' Observing the street, Winston adjusted his grip around Francis's torso, paranoid about all the on looking curtains. 'You need someone who can stop the bleeding.'

'I need to see Connie,' Francis slurred. 'I'll live; it's just a few scratches.' He planted his feet to stop their momentum. 'She can look after me, Wince. She can find me a doctor. Take me there.' He looked into Winston's face, an upward, pleading expression. 'If they get me at the hospital everything will be fucked. I can't leave her like that. I *need* to see her.'

Winston propped him against the side of his car, opened the lock, and then bundled him onto the back seat. 'Pull your legs in,' he said, slamming the door on Francis's soles. He opened the driver's door and then hesitated, his eyes gazing back over the car's roof at the house behind them. 'Stay here,' he said, speaking through the glass. The jolt of fear which had struck him was mature; grown up enough to understand the consequences of their actions. What happens if the copper wasn't dead? What if he'd seen their faces … heard their names?

Heartbeat battering his temples, Winston started to run back along the street.

Winston burst back inside the house and into the shambolic silence. He padded into the living room, looming over the body there. Bertie was as he was: a red stare amongst the cake and carpet. Winston stooped until they were face to face, holding his breath to hear. He swallowed nervously, his mind doing too much too fast. He took hold of the knife handle protruding from Crogan's loins and jerked it; it came free, smooth and untroubled. He kicked him, the corpse wallowing in its own juice, something chinking in its closed fist...

Another deep, guttural moan groaned from the kitchen.

Winston spun around on the spot, feeling someone behind him. The room was still; the sweaty blue haze settled throughout. On the floor, inside the crimson divot where Francis had been, a shotgun lay idle. Winston stepped over it, rushing, working his way into the kitchen doorway.

The copper was still breathing, his large, buttoned chest heaving like a billow press. He hadn't moved much, his shot legs unable to dislodge his lower back from the cupboard doors. The blood had taken over the floor, an oil spillage, the white birds printed on the lino coated by the spread.

Winston took the necessary steps to get close enough. The man – the copper – sighed and lifted his head. Winston froze, his shoes disturbing the perfect surface of red sea like two dirty ships at anchor. The copper's – Gerald's – eyes were open, fluttering, praying in Morse code. Winston watched him, time roaring on and forcing a judgment. He knelt down and cupped his left palm over the man's eyes. Bertie's hunting knife was light in his right hand. There was no resistance, the copper's arms stayed wilted where they were. Not allowing himself to think, to choose otherwise, Winston placed the tip of the blade over the man's defenceless heart and then, shaking, thrust it powerfully into the stiff uniform fabric. It slid in up to the handle, easy. Winston let go and stood up. He backed away, his heels turning the tide in the dark swell. The man's – Gerald's

– body gasped … and then his chest fell flat.

Without taking his eyes off him, Winston backed away until he was on dry land – until his feet were back on the carpet. Feverish, taking a last look around him, he snatched up the shotgun and then ran.

The fear was nauseous now.

Driving, Winston peered over at Francis on the back seat. 'Take your clothes off,' he said. 'If you get seen like that, we've got no chance.' Struggling to keep the car from bolting away like a frightened pony, Winston took one of his hands off the steering-wheel and began to tear open his shirt; the buttons popped, flying against the inside of the windscreen. He tossed it over his shoulder. 'Mine's cleaner than yours, press it down on your cuts.'

Francis didn't argue; wincing, he sat himself up and started to scrape himself out of his clothes.

'Hide those under the seat.' Winston glanced back at the road. 'There's a coat in the boot. If you can, reach over and put it on.'

Francis did as he was told; grimacing in pain, he undressed and stuffed his sodden clothes underneath the seat in front of him. Stripped down, he managed to wrap his ribcage in the shirt Winston had given him, and then drag the overcoat out of the boot and button it up. He straightened, panting slowly, his eyes folding closed as his head rolled back.

Winston banged his fist against the steering-wheel in

frustration. 'What the fuck happened in there?' he said reproachfully. 'Why didn't you wait?' He was watching Francis in the mirror. 'You should've told me that you knew where he was. We could've planned it properly.'

'I fucking killed him,' Francis replied, dry spit tacking his tongue to his pallet. 'I done him with my own two hands.'

'Yeah, and you left a half shot copper behind to tell everyone that it was you an' all.'

Francis forced his eyes open. 'I thought it was *Easter*.'

'What?'

'I thought it was Roy Easter,' Francis said, struggling for breath. His head rocked forwards to check on his wounds: the bleeding had eased a little under the pressure. 'Is he dead?'

Winston didn't answer him – there was a vehicle, a black car, coming towards them, headlights in horrific clarity. 'Take this,' he ordered, steadying the wheel before reaching across to the seat next to him and grabbing the shotgun. He passed it discreetly between the seats, the muscles in his arm showing in shadow. 'If that's Old Bill, wave it out the window when I take off. Give them something to think about before they chase us.'

The distance closed, the other car's lights creating complete sightlessness and squeezing time. There were no turns in the white out; it was straight forward, straight ahead. Blinded, Winston could smell the salt in his sweat. He sat and listened, the fear eccentric, the sound of Francis's trapped breathing almost as bad as captured. Out of body and sky high on electric adrenaline, Winston had to watch with his eyes closed as the car approached. Things darkened; the two cars passing without acknowledgment, too close, the red warning fading to black behind the tail lights.

Francis was the first to speak: 'Crogan...' he mumbled, delirious and barely making sense. 'He told me, Winton. *He* was Micky... Micky was *him*...'

'We're here.' Winston pulled up on Whitlock Drive and cut the engine. He swivelled round and looked at Francis slouched on the back seat. 'You still breathing okay?' Francis nodded, budging painfully, trying to get up. 'Hold on,' Winston said, scrutinising the congealed blood pockmarking his friend's abdomen. 'I want you to listen to me before you go in there.'

Francis opened his eyes groggily.

Winston's face was concentrated. 'We can still get away with this, France. The Old Bill will have a fucking job on just to work out what happened back there. If we're careful and we look out for ourselves properly, we might be able to wear this one.' He took a quick look at the queue of painted front doors on the other side of the glass. 'Now,' he said intently, 'this is what we do: you stay here and keep your nut down for a few days and see the doctor; just pay him and tell him that a stranger from over the East End poked you a few times but you'd rather he be discreet about it.'

Francis screwed up his nose and inhaled; to him, now that he was here, the thought of being caught didn't matter anymore. He'd done what he had to; and as long as the consequences could wait until morning, he would live with whatever had to happen next. He didn't mention the naked girl in the house, in all honesty, he wasn't sure if she had even been there at all.

'... I'm going to go and stay at the Putney house like before,' Winston was saying. 'The neighbours have got used to seeing me there, moving bits and bobs in and out; if I keep painting and shifting boxes about, everything will look normal.' He thought for a second, ad-libbing. 'What I will do is set a bonfire in the garden to get rid of some of the rubbish and chuck all those stained clothes in...' He trailed off, something else occurring to him. 'What happened to your motor, where did you leave it?'

'At the top of the road that house was on,' Francis answered weakly.

'Well that's what we'll go by then,' Winston said. 'I can send Nippy over there to have a look for it in a day or two; if it's still there and it ain't been tampered with, we'll know that they don't have a clue who they're looking for.' The shotgun rolled off Francis's lap and landed in the rear foot well. 'Leave it there,' Winston said. 'I'll stroll down and lob in the river tomorrow.' He leaned over the seat and closed Francis's coat over his chest. 'Where are your house keys?'

Francis patted himself down pointlessly. 'In my trousers,' he said, 'under the seat.'

Winston nodded back at him, and then he opened the car door and got out.

Connie struggled out from underneath her duvet and hobbled over to her bedroom window. Feeling only a feeling, she'd imagined that she could hear Francis outside; the tone all trampled, as if he were somehow hurt and trapped between dragging footfalls. She touched the windowsill, shaking, her nocturnal eyes still swirling with the patterns of the artex ceiling. There was pitch silence … and then a tiny, terrified squeal. She wheeled around, panicking, treading the boards with her nightdress catching beneath her feet, rushing as best she could, out of her room and down the stairs towards the front door...

Her mother called out to her from the landing...

'It's Francis, mum. Something's happened to him. Phone the doctor.'

Somebody had finally found the main light switch on the wall; under the harsh scrutiny of the bare bulb swinging in the centre of the ceiling, the scene was suddenly less artistic.

Detective Inspector Harvey Walsh – a man who once crawled through a hole blown in the basement wall of a bank vault, and had by then investigated enough robberies and frauds to be considered capable of dealing with death – was standing over corpse number one when the light came on. He hadn't changed much during the intervening years, save the yellow insignia embroidered on his tie and the wire frames he now wore.

He stooped, straightened up, walked a circle around the

body, and then crouched to fastidiously examine the mess in the poor chap's crotch. 'Have we found out who I'm looking at yet?'

'No, sir.'

Welsh glanced up at the officers around him, his moustache rigid. 'And what was it I was told about a naked girl in someone's garden?

The constable twitched. 'That was a report from one of the neighbours,' he answered, sifting the pages of his notepad. 'From a ... Mr Shepard ... I believe.'

'Is Mr Shepard available for comment?' Welsh inquired, gripping the dead man's wrist and turning his hand over. He hesitated, considering something ... and then, reaching down carefully with his other hand, he plucked a bunch of door keys from inside the deceased's clenched fingers.

'No, sir,' the constable responded, perusing what his superior was doing. 'I don't believe anyone's spoken to him yet, sir.'

'Well, he needs to be spoken to, so I suggest somebody goes and knocks on his sodding door.'

'Yes, sir,' the constable conceded, snapping his heels and turning straight into another man who was rushing towards him –

'Harvey, we've got a description.' The small man revealed calmly. 'One of the neighbours is saying he saw a coloured fella running away up the street. And wait for it ... the numpty was only carrying a sodding shotgun.'

Harvey Welsh poked his finger through the key-ring and let the bunch dangle with great significance; they jingled lightly, their jagged teeth stained to a rosy copper colour, the thin cardboard address tag twirling on the end of its string. '*Mr Shepard*...?' he asked perceptively. The small man affirmed with a nod of the head. Welsh focused back on the keys – more importantly on the bloodied address tag. 'Looks like we're already onto a winner then,' he said, eventually peering up. 'And he's certain that he saw a coloured man...?'

'That's what he said. He sounded positive enough to me.'

Welsh stood up slowly, passing his colleague the bunch of keys for consideration. 'Call that address in and find out who lives there,' he said. 'Putney seems a strange place to go looking for a black man, but it will do as a place to start.'

Winston turned onto the driveway of Francis and Connie's new home and murdered the engine. He sat still, waiting for his nerves to settle, the night's madness mercilessly orbiting within a long minute. The mute prayers which he'd seen flickering from the dead copper's eyes wouldn't die.

Eventually, Winston stepped out of the car and opened its back door. He reached into the foot-well behind the front seat, shifted the shotgun to one side, and then felt around for Francis's clothes. The trousers, twisted into a damp ball, pulled free – there was no sound, no jingle of keys. Winston checked the pockets, then turned away and shook them out, bitty moisture sprayed across half of his face. He ducked back inside the car and swept a palm across the floor – no keys, only a bloody shirt and a hollow shoe. He stuffed the trousers back under the seat and left the shotgun where it was. Mindful of being overlooked, and with the thought of having to break-in draining the last leg of strength out of him, Winston nudged the car door closed and then skulked around to the back of the house.

Floating now, preoccupied, he drove his elbow through one of the small study windows and clambered over the ledge. The broken glass cut him; tiny shards of shimmer tinkling his hair and shoulders. Without turning any of the lights on, guided by the wooden banister, he trounced through the darkness and up the staircase. Standing on the landing, already not completely recalling how he'd got up there, Winston pushed open one of the bedroom doors. There was a double mattress on the floor beneath the bare window, a hill of ruffled sheets in its middle. Winston began to turn himself out of his clothes, not yet feeling the sting in his fingers. Naked, he tripped and sprawled out across the bedding, only moving, wriggling, to tug a crushed cigarette box from underneath his back. He dangled an arm over the side until he found a lighter – it sparked, the low flame loaning a little holy warmth to the cracked plaster in the corners. He inhaled ... two long, reassuring pulls before he coughed, rolled over, and then threw up over the side of the mattress.

Weary, and with the taste of bile gumming his lips, Winston flopped backwards and yielded. His eyelids shuttered, again showing him those wordless wishes which had died in that policeman's eyes. Then he drifted into the smoke, seeing only single thoughts falling through the hole in the cloud, sucking in the tobacco-flavoured air until it had drugged him and he slept.

The sleep that arrived was cloaked and dressed as Death – an all-black figure amongst the blue hue of television light inside *that* house. He had brought Micky with him, crying and laughing, still too far away, still lost behind those headlights.

His wounds dressed, Francis lay within Connie's arms, a broken hand across her stomach, sobbing against her breasts. They stayed that way – as they were – as they had been – seemingly unaltered inside the room where she'd slept as a child; the room next door to her parents', where she'd first learned to love and to believe, with complete faith, in the secrets adults told to one another of a night-time.

She whispered to him, speaking in simple words. They made vows ... and then they loved and slept and dreamed together, frightened to let go, as if in all their lives this would never happen again.

It was almost dawn when Winston awoke. He knew that there were people in the house; the stamping thunder was running up the stairs in jackboots. They crashed through the bedroom door with tense voices ... *'Murder! We're arresting you for Murder!'* And before he could even sit, the weight of three men was on top of him.

Uniformed shouts: 'You killed a copper, you dark bastard. You've fucking had it…' Throughout the house, more doors were coming off their hinges. More voices, making demands of empty spaces. Fists and knees whacked into Winston's head and shoulders, the strong arms of the overbearing bodies pinning him. His vision disappeared, springing in and out of reality, bouncing on the buoyancy of the mattress. The police batons were dishing him leather blows, taking his skin off. His eyes were closing up; all the colours of the fruit bowl swelling across his temple. He writhed, suffocating – a netted fish stealing a last sup of throttled air before drowning on dry land. It was all blue, as far as his one eye could see, the precious greying daylight – the television shade of his dream – flickering from the bare window behind him and numbing the stirrup kicks in his back. It was almost blissful, the officers' heels returning him to sleep, his fear steadily resigning to calm as the burden of him was being taken away. He was now out of his own hands; his fortune was now somebody else's to grant.

'That's enough!' The order came from the bedroom doorway. 'Stand him up. I want him on his feet –'

Another of the policemen took his turn to hit Winston with his truncheon, 'you murderin' bastard.'

Winston was hooked under his armpits and dragged to his feet, the ground beneath him a doused wobble which he couldn't feel. His eyes rolled slowly out of their flinch, the entire geography of the room jumping on a grotesque merry-go-round…

'We let ourselves in,' Detective Walsh told him. He was jangling a bunch of keys at the end of his arm. He was unexcited – a man who held an insurmountable upper hand. Slowly, waiting for Winston's bruised focus to land on his, he raised the shotgun he'd found in the back of the car on the drive and showed it to him. 'Just as well that you left this where it was,' he said. 'If I'd found you in bed with it, I could've found an excuse to fire my pistol.'

Winston didn't respond.

'Give me your name...' Welsh took a step towards him. Winston bowed his head. 'Have it your way,' Welsh said, and then brought the shotgun up by the barrel and drove the stock into Winston's stomach. His arms held by the officers on either side, Winston's body slumped to its knees, crucified. Welsh regarded his nakedness for a moment, and then said: 'Find something to cover him up with before you bring him out; we found his clothes in the car.'

VICTOR

2004

Connie talked until the day came, until the armoured black outside the window had rolled over and shown its pale underbelly. The night had passed in an almost continuous monologue; the pauses coming in moments, her hands sifting through the lifetime of letters she had kept in her shoebox.

'So that's where Francis is taking Lewis?' Deborah asked, watching Connie opening the back door to let Tudor out into the garden. 'This morning...? He's taking him to a prison?'

Connie nodded before she kissed Deborah's cheek and started up the stairs, a smile lifting each side of her face into a gentle curtsey.

Through sore eyes, and without a word, Deborah stood by and watched her go, the night's indelible mark tired across her brow. Once Connie's feet had creaked across the landing, Deborah turned back into the living room and sat sleeplessly for a while. She reread some of the letters Connie had shown her, skimming over the lifetime of dates in the corners, analysing the blocky hand writing and the same loopy W which returned at the bottom to sign each page. Unthinkably, the man who'd penned all these letters had been in prison longer than she'd been alive. She glanced at the clock on the wall, at the pendulum making its brief swings, the relevance of time, more or less, inconceivable. She stared at the hour hand, hypnotised, reprogramming until without even realising that she was doing it, she had begun to rehearse the lie she was going to have to tell when she got home and called in sick at work.

The old man dropped his legs over the side of his bunk and sat up. He smiled somewhere in the dark; a weathered brown face amused by the dim shape on the calendar. Morning still hadn't broken; the birds yet to leave their nests.

He looked down at his hands and spread his fingers, the markers of a man's life. Today the arthritis was worthwhile. He'd earned it, going the rounds – twenty-four a day for forty-odd years – and only now could he raise his fist at the bell. He'd done the distance, on four legs, an old dog whose new trick was living an entire life behind a wall – squeezing four decades in to the same room using only smoke and mirrors – going in a young man and re-emerging at sixty eight – all in the blink of an eye.

Enjoying the subtle silence, Winston made a few rough passes over the bushy trimmings of his silver beard. Only those rising for Fajr prayer were making motions; the rest of the prison would have an itchy blanket over its head for at least another hour. The dream, or recollection, or whatever it was, had come again last night; one last time before he could go, one last time to remind him. In it, as always, Winston saw himself as he *had* been, standing in court, wearing the new suit which Francis had had made and sent to him for his sentencing. Winston's hands were nervous, sweaty, fidgeting with the gold pocket watch which had been attached to his waistcoat. He was listening; trying hard to fathom the things being said, the judge addressing the guilty with vigorous silence. Each of the other faces had now become blurred, muted, the honourable gentleman's mouth cutting disproportionate holes out of the script. The whole court room strained, not a single word finding a single soul. It was a mime, a puppet show; an ongoing act of agony which would go on until morning, until the shade was broken by the banging gavel and Winston could wake. Only then could he hear him, the judge, his Honour, speaking with spikey intent, as clear and as dull as day, as if he were inside the cell with him...

'*Winston McDaniels... Before I go on, I wish to make it ardently clear, both to you and to this court that the leniency which this court is affording you was not reached upon lightly. Neither should it be taken for granted – be it by you or anyone else who is here in attendance today. It is due purely to your forthcoming guilty plea – as well as the visible remorse which you've shown throughout the duration of these proceedings – which even makes it feasible for me to allow you to avoid the rope. However, leaving you with your life is as far as I find myself or my mercy willing and able to bend. Therefore, coupled with handing you a life sentence for your crimes, it will be recommended by this court that you should serve a minimum of thirty years in custody. Further to that, it will remain to be seen and then decided by a future Home Secretary whether or not you will ever be released. But again, I feel it is my duty – both to this court and the good public – to stress upon you the unlikelihood of that day ever arriving.'*

Winston stood up from his bunk and stretched and pulled his sweatshirt on over his head, the judge's prose seemingly reverberating off the four small walls like the first stones cast. He slipped his feet into his slippers and took the two short steps over to the sink, his stomach protruding the elastic on his waistband. He doubted if his *man-judge* – after all a mere mortal – was any longer of this world; it was only his words which were left, in rank echo, four decades on, still smelling like stubbed cigars and cognac. Winston smiled, enjoying the selfish satisfaction of simply standing up on a day like this – a day he would have to go backwards through time to even remember imagining – a day so far into the inconceivable future it had had to be forgotten about.

Forty four years was sod's law, but for Winston there had never been any decision to make. As the great man-judge had once spelt out from his high bench, Winston's wretched life could well have been swinging at the end of a rope – so to still be here was in itself proof of an afterlife. And there had never been any resentment, despite Francis always having maintained that it should have been *him* who took on the burden of that policeman's life, that he'd been already dying when Winston had got there, that it was *him* and not Winston who had killed Gerald Best, Winston knew different. Winston had seen him, still breathing, the soft, blue television light reviving the life in his eyes and illuminating his prayers; those had always been the toughest dreams to abide, the dreams when Gerald spoke to him. For Winston there was no grey in it: Crogan's life had never counted. So, however much Francis protested and remonstrated with him not to take the fall for both of the dead men, it was beside the point; pleading guilty and holding his hands up to the lot was the only proper thing he could do, if not for Francis then for Gerald; because, rightly or wrongly, Winston had only killed him in order to try and protect Francis, therefore, to give him up would do nothing but rub out any minuscule meaning that there might be in the innocent man's death. That was what Francis had never been able to understand. And what good would it have done anyway? He, Winston, had already been caught, bang to rights, shotgun in the car; whatever he'd told them, it wasn't as if they were going to undo his handcuffs and let him go; speaking even half of the truth would only have meant that they drag Francis in and strung him up alongside him on the gallows. Bollocks to 'em, had been Winston's thinking; if they swung him, they swung him, but why should they get two bad lives in receipt for just one of their good?

The tap groaned under pressure. Making his intention, Winston rolled his sleeves up above his elbows. '*Bismillah,*' he said, and then ran his palms under the cold water, performing Wadu. With an open heart, in all humility and gratitude, he rolled out his mat and began – *Alhamdulillah* – the last prayer he would ever have to pray in prison.

There were boot-steps outside on the landing, a keychain

playing the same melancholy music he'd been hearing for years – a tambourine-man busking in a tube station.

The eye flap on the cell door opened, and then the lock.

'One of the mysteries of the job that is...'

'What's that then, Guv?'

'Why these doors have to make as much bloody noise when they open as when they close.' Victor, an old hand of a prison officer, stood in the doorway, his bald, northern grin nearly as big as his uniform.

'I reckon that depends on what side of it you're standing on.'

Victor conceded to Winston's point; he sighed. 'Either way,' he said, 'I've seen to it that you'll be the first out today. It should give yer more daylight to travel by. Are yer going all the way down to London in one hop?'

'With any luck, I will, yeah. I'm being picked up'

Victor glanced around the cell. 'Well, you only need pack what can't be burned,' he said cheerily, and then stepped forward and handed Winston a transparent plastic sack for his belongings. 'You'll have to excuse the finger marks; my wife keeps insisting on me using hand-cream, she thinks it'll keep me from going home to her with chapped knuckles.'

'You ought to be more careful with your prints, Vic,' Winston chuckled. 'Otherwise you'll end up in here for good.'

'I already have,' Victor said cynically. 'And *I'll* still be here long after you've gone, so don't expect me to feel sorry for yer. By the time the system has finished with me, I'll have done almost as long as you.'

Clearing the narrow shelf above his writing table, Winston said: 'Well then, for such long and loyal service, let me be the first to congratulate your distinguished career choice by offering you this unopened packet of Ginger Nut biscuits as a small token of Her Majesty's gratitude, mate.'

'Not my cuppa, I'm afraid,' Victor said. He winked, removing the black clip-on tie from his collar and then refitting it. 'I'd be happy to donate them to the staff office but I know you wouldn't like them falling into the wrong hands.' Regretfully, Winston shrugged and tossed the orange packet over onto his bunk. 'I'll tell you what I'll do,' Victor added, 'if you leave those there, I'll make sure that somebody worthy finds a use for 'em...'

'Perfect!' Winston said, carefully placing the things he was taking with him into the bottom of the plastic sack; his photographs, letters, and a long lasting copy of the Qur'an. Victor watched him until there was a knot in the end of the sack, and then he found some professionalism...

'Right then, McDaniels,' he said, his voice now a bugle. 'I'll be back in thirty minutes. Then we can see about getting you on yer way.'

'I can't believe he took the blame,' Lewis said; he was walking beside his grandfather, adjusting the hood of his sweatshirt so it sat, just right, over the collar of his jacket. 'And they could've hanged him. That must've took some heart.'

'It was the single bravest act I've ever even heard of,' Francis told him, glassy eyed, fully focused on the structure they were approaching, on the rising brickwork, 'because it wasn't done to save his own life, he did it to save mine. Also your grandmother's; he knew what was at stake for her. I will love him eternally for that.'

Francis squinted at his wristwatch: 8:50 am. Thick, dour clouds had already begun to eclipse the bright morning rise over County Durham. The two of them stopped walking, red-nosed, the wind gossiping around their ears, keeping them burning. Lewis gaped ahead at the prison gates, elephantine, tall walls and barbed wire rings. He was enamoured, his face that of a boy catching his first glimpse of a big football ground and finally being able to comprehend the magnitude of the thing. And there it was in front of him, cathedral-like, old and full of souls.

'Did you ever tell him not to do it?'

'Of course,' Francis answered, sounding like he was exonerating himself whether he liked it or not. 'But it made no difference; Winston had signed a confession within a couple of hours of his arrest. By the time I got to see him, it was already done and dusted. I was devastated. It sounds fucking ridiculous saying it while I'm standing here with you on this side of the wall, but at the time...' He scoffed resentfully at what he was about to say. '...at the time I couldn't help feeling as if he hadn't allowed me my glory.' Lewis looked at him. 'I mean, I done what I'd done fully aware of the consequences. I was more than happy to face up to them and take my lumps; I think I might have even *wanted* to.' He shook his head. 'I did what I did for your grandmother. It was *my* revenge, my sacrifice to make. I never planned on dragging him into it. So like I said, at the time, I couldn't understand why he was doing what he was doing. He was adamant about it, it was like he understood something that I couldn't; I thought I'd done it all for your grandmother, to protect her, because she needed me to. In reality, I'd done it because of how much I needed *her*. I need her to be okay, to be beside me, as she was, as herself, the way she always had been. I didn't know how to mend her...I was desperate. And Winston could see that; he protected me from myself. He knew that I would never find any kind of peace without her...he saved me and gave me that. I owe him. He wanted us to have the opportunity to build a family. He said that even if he died in there, knowing that he'd given us that chance, after what had happened, would mean that he at least stood for something.' Francis savoured a deep breath. 'I've never really been able to get my head around what he did for us, or why, and I'll never agree with the things he said to me that day – the world didn't need me anymore than it needed him.' Francis sighed. 'But that ain't to say I'm not grateful or that I haven't lived my life the best way I could to honour what he did. I've tried to do as he asked: I've loved your grandmother, and I've tried to find peace and be grateful for every single day God's given us.'

'Yeah, but if things had been the other way around, you would've done the same thing for him, wouldn't you?'

Francis smiled, appreciating his grandson's faith in him. 'I like to think I would of,' he said, speaking with the practice of a man who'd pondered the same question over many nights. 'In all truthfulness, though, I don't know if I was ever as brave as Winston.'

Lewis shifted his feet, uneasy, turning away in a half circle, fully understanding either everything or nothing of what his grandfather was saying. He thought that his grandfather had the look of someone else, someone who'd arrived somewhere that he wanted to be, but now wished he were happier to be there. He looked suddenly vulnerable to the cold, as if overnight he'd grown old. A car moved somewhere behind them, subdued, the imperfect silence as unyielding as the great wall in front of them. Lewis pushed his hands into his pockets, thinking up a million questions but having nothing to say. The fingers of his left hand found something, a cigarette, bowed by the seam of his jacket, a broken matchstick splintered with it in two halves. He pulled it out and gently straightened it. It felt natural, like something which had been put there long ago for this exact moment, something he could offer, something he could share...

He did it nonchalantly and without a word, holding the white paper stick and offering it as something needed.

Francis – who had waged and won a war of wills with tobacco five years earlier – accepted it in the manner it was intended. No questions asked; it passed between their hands with only a measured glance. The broken, pink match head flared against Francis's thumbnail. He curled his lip slightly, holding, taking down a couple of long, heartfelt drags and thinking something about the way old habits chose to die... before exhaling and handing it back to his grandson.

Above the prison, the clouds had begrudgingly begun to cough up flakes of snow; they fell solo, with neither the mind nor body to settle. Lewis and Francis stood there in their jackets, together, a cigarette between them, a man and boy simply smoking.

The title, *Move on Without Forgetting,* lay face down on Deborah's bedside table, the weight of an empty mug on its back. She was deep in thought, the telephone reaching its seventh ring by the time she answered, wholeheartedly believing that she'd made up her mind.

'No need for alarm,' James announced, skipping the preliminaries. 'My physician assures me; sudden and funny turns are surprisingly common in women of your age – especially after experiencing an acute emotional connection to a handsome stranger. What you're feeling is perfectly normal.'

Deborah gave him a gracious tut.

'Phew!' James mocked at the sound of her on the other end; his voice was brisk, she could hear him smiling. 'So you're still breathing, then…? My spies tell me that you're under the weather, are you okay?'

'I'm fine, just playing truant.'

'Oh…' He sounded surprised. 'You should have said; I could've joined you.'

'Really…? I would've thought you disapproved.'

James chuckled. 'Don't be so gullible,' he said. 'I'm a solicitor; they trained me to find loopholes.'

'In that case,' Deborah said, 'if you fancy a couple of hours out of the office, and you promise not to tell on me, you still can if you like…?'

'Sounds promising…' James pretended to think about it. 'I give you my dishonest word,' he said, 'your secret is safe, providing, that is, that you keep it to yourself if I order wine with lunch…? I'm feeling European.'

'Deal,' Deborah said. 'But I was thinking more of coffee, I haven't slept.'

There was an audible pause … and then James asked: 'Nothing to do with me, I hope?'

'No. I've just had a strange night. I'll tell you about it when I see you.'

'Okay…' James sounded unconvinced. He consulted his clock. 'Shall we say about midday? I can meet you around the corner from the station, at that little panini place that you like…'

'Perfect…' Deborah said, and then went back to trying to convince herself that what she was doing would be for the best.

Voices, trapped behind cell doors, sang farewell:

'…*Winston McDaniels is our friend, is our friend, is our friend …Wince McDaniels is our friend, 'cause he kills coppers…*'

Winston could no longer register his footfalls; they went ahead of him, creaking, constant and unreported like boards on a ship's hull. He had been altered, he was other than before – and that song they were singing belonged to another man; it belonged to Harry Roberts.

These steps, this route he was taking, in meditation had always seemed to be somehow spiritual. On so many nights he'd imagined the way out, keeping it as a mirage of light at the end of the tunnel. But now, in reality, his footing was as grounded and as human and as scared as on any other stroll. The prison wing was no springboard underfoot. It was no platform for reform. And it was un-poetic, just a line drawn in the dirt by a hypocritical hand, as solid and hopelessly eternal on the last walk as it had been on the first.

Winton's time had passed at a wicked, long-legged pace. It had been slow and hard, and it had offered him none of the privileges the moral pirates in the Home Office regularly afforded to the nation's rapists and sex cases. It seemed that to kill a man in uniform, as opposed to a naked child or its mother, was to deem your soul unreachable. Over the forty four years leading up to this day, Winston had seen little or nothing of the outside world adjustment schemes or the back to work programmes provided by the state. He had never even sniffed day release. Lady Justice had only ever bent so far as to ship him from an A to a B cat facility when he turned sixty five, retirement age. By then, he supposed that they considered him worthless – a worker bee that could no longer fly. He was a mere word, a piece of paperwork, a name on a small file inside a big drawer.

Beside him, Victor stopped and raised his keychain to open the gate at the end of the wing. Locks and bolts... he gave Winston a philosophical raise of the eyebrows and then guided him through. Eventually, the noise of the singing and the banging of doors subsided and became something more mournful.

Beyond yet another room – this one housing plastic chairs and a wooden door – Winston was finally allowed to sign for his belongings: a stack of court documents, a pair of leather shoes, and a three-piece Savile Row suit which would no longer fit. Receiving the bundle of folded cloth, he could feel it immediately: the pocket watch was still there, its spherical weight hidden inside the crumpled waistcoat. Winton's beard lifted into a thankful grin; he had doubted that he would ever see it again – it had always been Francis who'd held the greater faith.

'The retirement package,' said the prison officer behind the desk. He slid an envelope across the counter. 'There's a rail pass and forty pounds to get you started. You have to sign for it.'

Winston looked at him. 'Keep it,' he said politely. 'I've got someone picking me up.'

The officer left the envelope where it was. 'Good for you,' he remarked. 'By the looks of things, it's trying pretty hard to snow out there.'

Victor interjected: 'Would yer like me to have a poke about in the lost and found, Winston? Someone might well have left a coat behind.'

'Don't trouble yourself, Guv. I'll manage.' Leaving the waistcoat to one side, Winston stuffed the rest of his things into his sack. 'Have a drink on me,' he said, nodding towards the envelope on the table.

Victor smiled. 'I wouldn't like to bend anyone's nose out of shape, but cheers all the same.'

Winston leaned over the desk and signed the forms without reading them. 'Suit yourself.' He straightened up and unravelled the waistcoat to get the watch out of the pocket. 'I'm surprised this is still here,' he said humorously, pushing the envelope back towards the desk officer. 'The staff in these places are usually as light-fingered as everybody else.'

'Why, is it valuable?'

'Sentimental,' Winston said.

Victor and the other officer watched as Winston carefully opened the watch face, his fingertip brushing over the Hebrew inscription in the gold. The dagger tipped minute hand had ceased ticking at half past nine on some unknown day, an insurmountable time ago. The numerals were still recognisable, like Winston, four decades having disappeared around them and seemingly having only made a second's difference. The watch had done the time with him; it had been institutionalised, confined to a box, forced to eke out an existence in the dark untouched by human hands and unseen by angels. It had languished with him, ignorant of its self-worth and values; and now, like Winston, more than see the light of day, it was anxious to be reunited with its brother.

Winston unfastened the watch chain from the fabric and added the waistcoat to his plastic sack. 'So,' he said, keeping hold of the watch. 'Am I free to go?'

The scale of freedom was frightening; it reached, Goliath-like, far beyond the wilds of imagination.

As if intruding, Winston stepped from the prison gate and into the glorious cold. The sky was no longer just the lid of a rabbit-hole; unbound, it flaked away, big and blank above a wall-less world.

A tribute to valour, Francis was waiting right where Winston knew he would be. He went towards him, strong-faced and battle-weary. Lewis hung back and allowed them the privacy of the wide open; he looked on, unprepared for the swell of emotion in his chest.

Winston and Francis embraced; they clung on, arms shaking, holding fast as children and as men, as old friends who'd together had picked life's pocket of a little more time. They were their first love, their chosen blood. They were brothers – two lions – both killers and thieves.

They came apart, eyes stained, the pocket watch old and golden in Winston's palm. Together, they sparked into a hail of tearful laughter.

'I found out what the inscription means,' Francis told him, pulling his own watch out of his pocket and showing it to him. 'Avram told me. It says: *where you bleed, I will feel*.'

To that, Winston could only smile fresh tears.

Francis turned and waved to his grandson, 'Come on over and introduce yourself.'

Lewis stepped forward, hesitant, taking and shaking the

rough hand of a work of fiction in front of him.

Winston cleared his throat, eyes studying the young man's face. 'Well then,' he said. 'You must be, Charlie's boy...'

James rotated his tiny espresso cup on its saucer. 'I did warn you I was feeling European today.' Without using his teeth, he made a tear in his sugar sachet and lightly poured. The miniature silver spoon made a clink on the porcelain rim. 'So,' he said, smiling. 'Did you mention me to her – or rather, us?'

Deborah watched him, a thought passing behind her face. 'We talked about everything,' she said honestly. 'And I didn't realise how much I needed it, especially from her. I've been feeling like I was doing something sordid. That's not like me; I don't like keeping secrets.' She lifted her own coffee cup and sipped at the froth. 'It was nice just to say it out loud.'

'And what was her reaction?'

'She was lovely about it. I'm not sure how or when, but somehow I think I'd forgotten who she was; I'd been building it all up, imagining that she was going to hate me for, you know...? It wasn't like that; in a funny sort of way she made it feel natural. She said that she understood.' James's attention had been grabbed by his inside pocket – a vibrating mobile phone. 'It was heart-breaking,' Deborah was saying, 'she was so open. She told me things about her life and about the family, things which Charlie had never even said. We even spoke about Lewis; she said that, eventually, she thought

445

he'd come round.' She smiled. 'It really made me start to believe that, maybe –'

Apologetically, James had halted her with a hand. 'I'm so sorry,' he said, looking up and then back down at the flashing screen. 'It's always the way … do you mind? It'll be two minutes tops.'

'Its fine,' Deborah smiled. 'Honestly.'

'Are you sure?'

'Of course, answer it.'

'Hold that thought then,' James said, standing up and walking away from the table. 'I want to hear what you were about to say…'

Deborah's gaze pursued James until he got to the café door and stepped outside. Another man – a scaffolder – brushed past him on his way in. Deborah dawdled on him, and then on the girl behind the counter busying to his order. On the other side of the glass James was now talking into his phone, gesturing to no one. The café door bumped open again, allowing the sound of traffic and blues. Two more men entered, blowing out their cheeks after jogging across the road from the station. They were in their twenties, junkies to something, the pair of them underfed and scratchy-looking. The girl behind the counter slipped the scaffolder's note into the till and then handed him his change. He turned around and stared at the two men who were stood behind him with their hands out, not even having to open his mouth to refuse them his change –

James tapped on glass to get Deborah's attention: he held up a finger to buy himself another minute.

The junkies had got out of the scaffolder's way (no worries, no worries). They were now mooching about their begging, meandering between the tables and muttering something about needing to find train fares. They hovered longer around the soft touches; the grubbiest of the pair tilting his squalid face over the rusty buttons of his denim jacket until one of the business suits in the corner had swept a crop of change into his mitt.

James shrugged again.

Deborah sipped her coffee.

A few tables in front, the two beggars were now looming over an elderly couple. Forced to neglect his conversation, the old gentleman lifted his head to take them in. He waved them away.

'On your way,' he said, slowly turning back to his wife. 'There's nothing for you here.'

The young man in the denim jacket leaned closer, chancing his arm. He focused on the lady 'C'mon, please!' he said, arranging his face into a yellow grin, pointing at her handbag. 'Check your bag. We only need a couple of quid … It's just so we can get home.'

Before the junkie's dirty fingernail had closed back inside his fist, the old man was on his feet. 'What did I just say?' He snatched up the stainless steel teapot from the centre of the table and brandished it; the lid rattled, hot tea splashing their shoes. 'I told you once; I've got nothing for you. Now, get on your way.' Immediately, the two beggars backed away behind chafed palms of wary laughter. 'You should have some bloody respect,' the old man continued. 'That's my *Wife*...' He had said it simply, staring them down, as if that word, *Wife*, should still mean something.

A muted round of applause rose from some of the other tables...

The junkies lurched off, laughing, backing out of the door and onto the street.

The old man set the teapot down. His wife reached across the table and stroked his hand – then she set about mopping up the mess with her napkin. She glanced up at him, communicating in teenage tones, pushing out the spare chair on her side so he could avoid the spillage. He did as he was told, squeezing in and placing an arm around her shoulders. She smiled at him with supple eyes, the look of a woman whose heart has long been contented by its choices – a woman who not only still loves the man she keeps beside her, but one who, even after a lifetime, still believes in him.

Outside the window, his phone call over, James had been stopped in his tracks. The junkie in the denim jacket was dancing with him, two stepping back and forth on the pavement to block his path. With protestation – as if it had been pre-prepared and tucked there in anticipation of his being asked – James plucked a ready ten pound note from his trouser pocket and handed it over. It was done simply, without even looking, as if the money had no meaning whatsoever.

A moment later, the café door waved and a fresh-faced James came back inside, his lips parted in part apology. Deborah blinked ... and within the milliseconds recess she had changed her mind. As though through a long lens, she could suddenly see herself: a thirty-seven year old apparition, one half of couple which she didn't belong to, sitting there at the table and waiting for him to come back and talk to her. It wasn't actually her; it was a flicker of a life she might have, the opposite of the one she'd lived. He was not *him*, not hers. He was an understudy; the nice guy she'd allowed a self-help book and her best friend to chaperone her into bed with. He was basically a decent stranger, who, before she'd closed her eyes, she had been persuading herself to have feelings for. In the blink, glaucoma gone, it was impossible to even imagine them together; she couldn't witness herself with him, under or around him, her arms and legs splayed and him heaving and breathing in false time with her. She couldn't remember it, or how things had gone so far; how a long weekend had upped and downed to the point where she'd needed an intervention from a crack head for a moment of clarity. And he, James, had done nothing wrong; none of this was his fault. To use one of Mara's chick-lit euphemisms: it was *her* not him.

'Sorry about all that,' James said, sitting down and feeling his espresso cup to check it was still warm. He looked at her, a little standoffish. 'Are you okay?'

Deborah gave him a faint nod. She swallowed a mouthful of coffee to drown her tongue, deferring, wanting to be sure. It had happened so quickly; in the time it took to spend a tenner, before the telephone had interrupted, she had gone from being about to commit herself to seeing where this thing between them was going – to giving it a go – to probably sitting her son down and telling him about it – to now wanting it to suddenly stop. *Things will look different in the morning,* that's what her mother had told her when she was fourteen-and-a-half years old and she came home from school declaring that she had fallen in love with Carl Richards during detention. And they had; by the end of Saturday morning television the next day, she had fallen deeply in love with Boy George. Just like that, in the blink of an eye things had become crystal: it was a betrayal; but not of Charlie or Lewis or Connie, or anyone else, it was a betrayal of herself. She was doing what everybody did: finding someone just for the sake of having *something.*

'So,' James prompted. 'You were in the middle of telling me something about your mother-in-law, about how talking to her made you start to believe something...'

'That I'm not ready,' Deborah said. 'What I was going to say, was that spending time with her and speaking how we did, made me start to believe that I'm not ready. Not for this, anyway ... I mean *us*, or whatever we are.' The words come swiftly now. 'I thought I was, or that I would be by now. I thought that I was worried about what everybody else thought or felt about it, but now I think that I was probably just sticking on them because I was questioning myself. I mean, if I really wanted this, now, I think I'd be sure and I'm just not sure that I am.' She sighed. 'If this was to be *anything* – what with Lewis and everything – I'd have to be sure. There's just too much still there in my past; and if I'm honest, right now, I'm not sure that there ever won't be.'

Fifteen minutes later, Deborah was walking away, side-stepping the on-coming crowd and having to choose her patches of pavement carefully in order to keep seeing the road ahead. There was something written up there, far away and almost invisible, penned in a neon language. She passed beneath a tall, scaffolded building, the plastic wind breakers sailing from poles which could've been touching the sky. A high, workman's whistle hailed out in appreciation, catcalls and compliments singing from the heavens. Smiling, Deborah slowed but did not stop. She closed her eyes and imagined she was hearing a voice she recognised, one she knew and had known...a voice which she could still remember falling in love with.

Deborah carried on ahead, forward and towards ... moving on without forgetting.

At four o'clock that afternoon, Avram Abrahams raised his face from the book he was reading. There were knuckles rapping on the shop window. He stood up, expecting company, his oversized shoes billowing dust as he shuffled through the clutter.

He rubbed his hands together.

On the other side of the glass, tapping and holding up a pair of pocket watches, was a teenage boy. Standing behind him, were two old friends: one who Avram had last seen yesterday and another who he hadn't seen in a lifetime.

Barley Sugar

SAMMY

Tuesday morning was momentous.

A paisley scarf slithered off the mahogany coat stand in the hall and coiled cashmere around his throat. On his way out the door Alistair Cassels stopped, stooped, and touched Tolstoy's tortoise shell for luck. Two words came to mind: *carpe diem.*

He was a full half an hour earlier than usual, the large envelope tucked under his arm thick with significance. And he wasn't driving, not today; today he'd allotted time so he could stroll, allowing himself to pass by the post box on his way to the school. He wished to relish his achievement; a thing like this demanded it be done correctly. The envelope – which contained the first fifty pages of his manuscript, a brief synopsis of his story, as well as a handwritten cover letter – was addressed to a Mrs Marian Dyke, literary agent. Her online submission information had suggested email, but this time, the first time, he wanted to do things the old-fashioned way.

When he got to the post-box, he inhaled hard through his nose the envelope only half offered. It took almost a whole minute for him to let go, blowing out his cheeks like a child making a wish.

As he turned in the direction of the school, Alistair Cassels' thoughts turned to the Butler boy and his cocky friend. Unconsciously, his pace quickened and a grin began to furnish the blank spaces around his features.

The first trickle of students banged through the double-doors downstairs, excited voices trampling the halls. Upstairs in the thin, faculty corridor the hush was official, court soon in session. Pam Weatley, school receptionist, was clipping between the Headmaster's office and the far window, pinching her cardigan closed over her blouse and watching the police car parked outside the school gate.

'I can't stand that woman,' Deborah muttered.

Lewis surveyed the potted plants, wondering what time Sammy would turn up.

'Are you nervous?'

'Not for me,' Lewis said. 'I just don't want them to kick Sammy out.'

'Let other people take responsibility for their own actions,' Deborah returned in earnest. 'These policemen aren't here for the fun of it, Lewis. They've come to find out what happened. You need to tell them the truth.'

Lewis regarded her. 'I will.'

'Good. Honesty's the best policy–' Deborah's lips stopped, her voice suddenly sounding as flimsy as the cliché she'd just used. She studied her son, her boy. When she reached out to touch him, Lewis drew his head back. She furrowed, spraining the tiny muscles around her mouth to smile. Overnight he was becoming his father, and beyond that, his grandfather. It had been months since she'd been this close to him, longer since they'd really spoken – at some point she must've just given up to let him grow. And now he had.

Pam Weatley walked to wait at the top of the stairs, hands on hips. Within a minute, Sammy Butler's head came over the hill, the grown out sides of his cropped hair sprouting over his ears. He nodded in muted acknowledgment, mooching along at his own pace after having gone to the effort of wearing proper school shoes. Still some way behind him, his mother called out:

'Sorry we're late! I had to make sure my girls got off alright before I could leave. If I ain't there to shove 'em out the door they won't budge.' Sammy's mother's blotchy face finally breached the top step – she'd stuffed her nightdress into her jeans. She gave Deborah a squinty grin. 'I wound up forking out for a cab in the end,' she said, allowing herself a breath. 'Not that it did us any good, we're still bloody late.'

'It's probably best if we don't keep everybody waiting any longer,' Pam Weatley said, setting an example with her whisper. She halted outside the headmaster's office, poised to knock. She flitted between the two mothers, her expression magnified by her glasses. 'I believe the Head wishes to take a moment to brief both of you. Then each boy will be seen in turn.' She motioned for Deborah to stand up. 'If you'd like to follow me...'

'Are you going to tell them anything?' Sammy said.

Lewis shook his head, inclining himself towards his friend. 'Listen,' he said, 'when they ask you, I want you to say that you were outside –' The headmaster's door opened before he could finish. Weatley came out carrying a tray of cups and saucers. Lewis buttoned his lip, perusing her cautiously until he thought she'd travelled out of earshot. 'Tell them that you were outside the whole time; say that the first you knew about anything was when –'

'No conferring!' Weatley hissed, hurrying back along the corridor. 'There should be no talking at all.'

Mr Lynch's office was already crowded with opinion. The radiators were on, gurgling. Lewis walked inside. Only Cassels didn't look at him; an adult ignoring a child.

'Come on in and have a seat, Lewis,' Mr Lynch said, alluding to the only spare chair in the room.

Lewis sat down, avoiding his mother's gaze. Not hearing what Lynch was saying about the seriousness of the situation, he contemplated the two police officers. The WPC smiled at him as she was introduced; she was pretty. Lewis reciprocated, knowing by now Cassels would be scrutinising him, waiting for shakes. The male officer nodded and Lewis nodded back, thinking that the man would look substantially less without his stab vest. He didn't like his expression, or what it implied. Lewis knew full well why he'd been brought in first.

For Cassels, everything was academic, an experiment in behavioural science to see how long it would take for the boys to turn on one another. And why had he lied? Because the ignorant little shits had granted him the opportunity to raise the stakes, that's why. After all, it was his responsibility to teach. And not only because Sammy Butler had spat at him, no, not just that; but because the grubby little bastard reminded him of every single bully he'd ever had to hide from…

The WPC spoke now: 'Okay, Lewis…' She gave herself a starting point. 'Let me begin by informing you that – at this time – you're not actually under arrest for anything. It's entirely up to you what you tell us, but first and foremost what we'll be doing here this morning is taking a statement from you.' She smiled again, soft and clear. 'We're only interested in hearing your side of the story.' Her notepad rustled. 'Now, as you're aware, your teacher, Mr Cassels, has reported that some of his personal things went missing on Friday lunchtime. Do you know, or can you tell us anything about that?'

Lewis nodded, resolute in his decision. It hadn't occurred to him until yesterday outside of the prison, but standing there and waiting for Winston with his grandfather, he'd realised quickly that the best and only way out of this situation for Sammy, was *him*. As far as he could see, it was the only way. For him to sit there and deny all knowledge of Cassels' bullshit theft would be playing into his hands, besides, doing that would look like fear. And there should be no visible nerves; if his voice faltered, if he even hinted that he'd had absolutely nothing to do with the wallet or keys, by elimination that was basically as good as telling them that it was Sammy – who else could it have been otherwise? The whole thing was a stitch up, so why give Cassels the satisfaction? Why hand them an excuse to kick Sammy out of school and pack him off to a secure unit for something he hadn't even done? Doing it this way Cassels would be forced to see Sammy every day for at least another year. Plus, for Lewis it would be a first offence; he had no criminal record, so they were more likely to be lenient. Cassels would have to live with his lie; see it staring him in the face and laughing behind his back each time he turned to scribble on his whiteboard.

'I can tell you exactly what happened,' Lewis told the room. He could now feel the collar of his school shirt around his neck, feel the daggers in his back, Cassels was glaring at him. Lewis stood up, the rush of blood suddenly making him aware of his skin. He was proud, something Winston had said yesterday ringing in his ears and galvanising his spirit: It's what a person takes pride in which makes them different from others, not their birth. And that's how it was now; this was the difference, between him and the men in this room – from him and the other boys running in these halls. 'I stole the wallet,' he said. 'And the keys; I took everything from the cupboard. I thought I could show off to my friends. I did it by myself so I could surprise everyone by getting them their confiscated things back. Sammy didn't even know about it. He was in the playground the whole time. The first he knew of it was when I came outside and started handing stuff out to everyone. I gave him back his phone. That's the only reason he had it.'

'Lewis!' Deborah said, embarrassed. 'You told me you didn't take your teacher's things...'

Lewis didn't waver.

The WPC waited to regain his eyes. 'So,' she said. 'Where are they now? What did you do with them?'

'I dropped them in the rubbish bins behind the school canteen,' Lewis answered. 'There wasn't any money in the wallet, and the keys I only took for a laugh. I thought somebody would find them and hand them in.' He shrugged his shoulders. 'Like I said, I gave some cigarettes and sweets and stuff to people in the playground. That's how comes Mr Cassels found Sammy with some. But, honestly, Sammy didn't know where they'd come from.'

Incredulously, Deborah swivelled in her chair to offer Cassels an apology. Lynch was looking at him too, but Cassels was unrelenting; he satisfied neither of them with any eye contact. The boy had his attention, all of it. But Lewis wouldn't grant him an audience, not just yet; he wanted to wait a few more seconds and enjoy the heat on the back of his neck. He stood there, showing him a straight back. The WPC first conferred with her partner and then jotted down what Lewis had said, pages turning. And then, slowly, Lewis began to turn, fiercely defiant, eyes brave, giving away the colour of the cloth he was cut from.

Cassels refused to blink, understanding fully the power that the boy was wielding – the other voices in the office were all now secondary. Cassels measured him enviously; there was no fear or fraction in the young man's expression. His vanity was maddening. Lewis looked at him, no smile. Cassels was jealous of him, of his heart, of his eyes – like mirrors – giving him back everything which he'd forever hated within himself. He could sense the boy discovering him; that arrogant stare was seeing through him. Cassels could feel his own eyelids flickering, his pupils starting to betray him, widening and selling his secrets. The boy wouldn't look away; he was finding him out, copying down the insults of his younger years, spying on the private humiliations, even the ins and outs of the divorce. He was reading him, honing in instinctively on his weaknesses, smelling the cuts. He knew about his frustrations, about the name calling, about the tears which had dried into his pillow, dating all the way back to the indignity of the changing room. He could see that he'd been jealous his whole life, frightened and angry, but jealous...always fucking jealous...

'Alistair...?' Lynch's voice echoed around the office. Cassels withdrew from Lewis, stoned, his blurred gaze eventually settling on the headmaster. '...The officers would like to know whether you wish to take matters further...? Do you want to press charges?'

Cassels composed himself – Lewis still watching him. He knew now that he couldn't win, not here, not today. Not unless he wanted to purge himself by telling the truth. He paused, pretending to consider the alternatives... 'I fail to see how I cannot,' he muttered. 'After all, this is a school and we're here to teach. If this isn't a lesson for the young man then I don't know what will be...' He tipped his brow towards the boy's mother. 'We owe it to our students to prove that there are indeed harsh consequences for wrong doing. I for one would fear for the effect it might have on the other pupils if we were not to make an example of this kind of behaviour.' He transferred his concentration back to Lewis. 'So in answer to your question: I'm afraid, I feel I have no choice but to press charges and seek full prosecution.'

Lewis didn't flinch.

Summoned into action, the male constable rounded Lynch's desk and placed a hand on Lewis's shoulder. 'Stay in your seat please, madam.'

Deborah had started to get up…'Do you have to cuff him?'

'It's standard procedure,' the policeman replied, rationalising it before swiftly clipping a handcuff onto Lewis's wrist. Deborah was shaking her head. 'Lewis Coles,' he said. 'I'm arresting you for theft. You do not have to say anything, but it may harm your defence if you do not mention when questioned something which you later rely on in court.' Lewis held out his other wrist willingly. 'Anything you do say may be given in evidence. Do you understand?'

Lewis nodded and then turned towards the door…

'Coles…?' Cassels called, failing to restrain himself. 'Just so you know… the dole queue is first on the right.'

Tudor ran…large paws cutting up the narcotic frost which was christening the grass. It was primitive worship, a restless appreciation for life, a fleeting moment of beastly genius offered up to an overcast heaven. He was giving thanks for his freedom.

Francis stood up, one damp knee leaving the earth and the loose end of a dog-lead swinging from his glove.

Connie and Winston had gone on ahead. He watched them turn to wait for him, the dog drawing circles around their conversation. He waved them on, preferring to stay where he was, enjoying just seeing them there together, red-nosed and with diamonds in their eyes, Putney Common, their own December garden, wrapping all the way around them and back again. He admired them, their young and old faces, completely unable to conceive how the world could swallow forty years in a single night and yet still make dreams last forever. He wondered whether they could see themselves; whether they understood the violent sacrifices they each had made in order to love him. God knows, *he* could; and standing there, humbled, he was still afraid that he'd done nothing to earn either one of them.

He saw light, the colour of barley sugar, coming through the flap in the cell door.

Lewis sat up on the slap thin mattress, wondering how much the whitewashed bricks and rubbed floor could've changed in four decades. He was undaunted; he knew where he was and why. He was there because Winston, Micky and his grandfather had all been here before him. Wandsworth police station already knew his name; it recognised him, his description and blood type were supposed to be carved into the hardwood bunk. The place made it easy for him to identify himself. He understood now...not only who he was but who he wasn't, who he wanted to be.

Before the key turned in the lock, Lewis had made his promises – the kind of promises boys make when they're alone. They were more like prayers than wishes and they were spoken more in hope than oath.

ACKNOWLEDGEMENTS

I am eternally grateful to Sasza Bandiera for making the introduction which took this to print. I would like to thank Dan Whomes and Chris Jackson for believing in me and this story enough to make a dream come true. Northside House for the opportunity. All the friends and family who read paragraphs and chapters and shared their thoughts, even if just in conversation; it all helped. Leon Dawson for more than I can mention, I thought of you much during the writing of this book. My sister, Melissa, for absolutely everything... always. My father, Charlie, for a lifelong education. My mother, Jane, for knowing I would write this before I did. And finally, with love and admiration, I would like to thank my wife, Bib, for living every single day amongst these pages with me. Here's to forever learning...